"What are you doing?" She was dismayed to hear that her voice was an octave higher than it should be.

"I'm going to take a bath."

"You can't do that." She tried, and failed, not to look as he started to remove his drawers.

"Can't I?"

With eyes growing ever wider, she watched him discard his drawers. She had not expected him to look so good, all lean, supple muscle.

When he stepped into the water, she bolted, but one strong brown arm quickly wrapped around her waist. "Are you afraid of me, Leanne?" He slid his hands down her back and pressed her closer.

"No. Yes." She trembled, the heat of desire flooding her.

"I don't intend to hurt you," he murmured against her skin as he smoothed kisses over her throat. "I won't hurt you. You must know that by now." As he spoke, he moved her against his hard body and knew by her quickened breathing that she felt the proof of his desire. "Tell me you don't want me, Leanne. Tell me and I'll walk away right now." He placed his mouth against hers. "Tell me," he whispered.

Leanne wanted to. She tried desperately to find the strength of will to utter the words. But the way his hands felt on her, the way he moved her body against his in a pantomime of what they both craved, the way his mouth teased hers, robbed her of that strength. She wanted him, wanted him so badly that even the cold water they stood in did little to cool the heat in her body. Saying no was the last thing she could do . . .

Books by Hannah Howell

The Murrays

HIGHLAND DESTINY
HIGHLAND HONOR
HIGHLAND PROMISE
HIGHLAND VOW
HIGHLAND KNIGHT
HIGHLAND BRIDE
HIGHLAND ANGEL
HIGHLAND GROOM
HIGHLAND WARRIOR
HIGHLAND CONQUEROR
HIGHLAND CHAMPION
HIGHLAND LOVER
HIGHLAND BARBARIAN
HIGHLAND SAVAGE
HIGHLAND WOLF
HIGHLAND SINNER
HIGHLAND PROTECTOR
HIGHLAND AVENGER
HIGHLAND MASTER
HIGHLAND GUARD
HIGHLAND CHIEFTAIN
HIGHLAND DEVIL

The Wherlockes

IF HE'S WICKED
IF HE'S SINFUL
IF HE'S WILD
IF HE'S DANGEROUS
IF HE'S TEMPTED
IF HE'S DARING
IF HE'S NOBLE

Seven Brides for Seven Scotsmen

THE SCOTSMAN WHO
SAVED ME
WHEN YOU LOVE A
SCOTSMAN
THE SCOTSMAN WHO
SWEPT ME AWAY

Stand-Alone Novels

ONLY FOR YOU
MY VALIANT KNIGHT
UNCONQUERED
WILD ROSES
A TASTE OF FIRE
A STOCKINGFUL OF JOY
HIGHLAND HEARTS
RECKLESS
CONQUEROR'S KISS
BEAUTY AND THE BEAST
HIGHLAND WEDDING
SILVER FLAME
HIGHLAND FIRE
HIGHLAND CAPTIVE
MY LADY CAPTOR
WILD CONQUEST
KENTUCKY BRIDE
COMPROMISED HEARTS
STOLEN ECSTASY
HIGHLAND HERO
HIS BONNIE BRIDE

Vampire Romance

HIGHLAND VAMPIRE
THE ETERNAL
HIGHLANDER
MY IMMORTAL
HIGHLANDER
HIGHLAND THIRST
NATURE OF THE BEAST
YOURS FOR ETERNITY
HIGHLAND HUNGER
BORN TO BITE

Published by Kensington Publishing Corp.

HANNAH HOWELL

STOLEN ECSTASY

ZEBRA BOOKS
KENSINGTON PUBLISHING CORP.
www.kensingtonbooks.com

ZEBRA BOOKS are published by

Kensington Publishing Corp.
119 West 40th Street
New York, NY 10018

All Kensington titles, imprints, and distributed lines are available at special quantity discounts for bulk purchases for sales promotion, premiums, fund-raising, educational, or institutional use.

Special book excerpts or customized printings can also be created to fit specific needs. For details, write or phone the office of the Kensington Sales Manager: Attn.: Sales Department. Kensington Publishing Corp., 119 West 40th Street, New York, NY 10018. Phone: 1-800-221-2647.

Zebra and the Z logo Reg. U.S. Pat. & TM Off.

First Zebra Books Printing: May 2011
ISBN-13: 978-1-4201-4375-1
ISBN-10: 1-4201-4375-1

ISBN-13: 978-1-4201-2425-5 (eBook)
ISBN-10: 1-4201-2425-0 (eBook)

Previously published by Leisure Books.

10 9 8 7 6 5 4 3 2

Printed in the United States of America

Chapter One

Colorado, 1870

"I'M NOT YOUR MA."

Hardly aware that she still lay sprawled in the dirt where her mother had pushed her, Leanne stared at Charity. "Not my mother?"

"Not your mother," Charity said with every evidence of glee. "You little bitch." Charity spat out the words. "Since you've been home, I've had to put up with your fancy ways, and I won't any longer. I told Grant this wouldn't work, told him years ago when he forced me to take you on. Wouldn't even let me be your aunt, had to be your ma. Well, I'm not your ma. Never was. Not even your blood kin. Your ma was nothing but a cheap whore, and it's clear blood will tell. Not even a month back home and you're stealing my man."

Clovis, standing behind Charity in the doorway, whined, "She tempted me sorely, Charity. I'm only a man, darling. I couldn't help myself."

"Shut up, you fool," Charity snapped and Clovis disappeared into the house. She then went back to glaring at Leanne. "Well, that does it. I'm finished. He doesn't pay me enough for this. You're on your own, honey."

"But, Mama . . ." she began, her voice shaking.

"Don't call me that. I should've left you to rot at that school."

Leanne almost said, 'You did,' but now was not the time to be airing grievances and old hurts. Even though she was facing yet another rejection in a life painfully filled with them, there was a more immediate concern.

"But who . . . where can I go?"

"Go to your pa—Grant Summers. And tell that bastard he owes me three months upkeep."

"Grant Summers—who is he? And where is he?" Leanne demanded somewhat hysterically as Charity started to shut the door.

"Denver."

"But that's hundreds of miles away."

Staring at the shut door, Leanne told herself it was all a nightmare, that she would wake up any moment back in her own bed—a bed without a sweating Clovis crawling all over her and telling her how good he was going to make her feel. Something fell at her side and she stared at her cloak. She looked up in time to see Clovis shoved away from the window just before Charity slammed it. She wondered dazedly if Clovis was going to suffer any punishment at all for what he had done.

A cool breeze made her shiver and she reached for her

cloak. Standing up, she started to put it on, staring at the house she had thought was her home. A part of her waited for the woman she had always thought of as her mother to open the door and let her back in. It was not until the house grew dark that she finally gave up hope.

"I'm not your ma."

The words echoed through her mind, making her wince. She found it impossible to believe. She had no memory of anyone except Charity. The woman had been cold, sarcastic and sometimes cruel, but she had been all the family Leanne had ever known, the only real tie she had ever had anywhere. She had formed none at school, where she had been viewed as a kind of barbarian, an uncivilized Westerner, no matter how hard she had tried to fit in. She had formed none in Clayville, where she had been viewed as an outsider because of her schooling and the long absences it had entailed. There had only been Charity, and now even that thin bond was cut.

"And who the blazes is Grant Summers anyhow?" she muttered and kicked at a stone, only to be painfully reminded that she was barefoot. "That is what I call adding insult to injury," she groaned as she bent to rub her sore toes.

Suddenly, she was all too aware that she was standing in the streets of Clayville in her nightgown. The cloak was adequate cover, but knowing that a thin cotton nightgown, somewhat torn by Clovis's rough hands, was all she wore beneath it was enough to cause her acute embarrassment. Glancing around she was both relieved and frightened to find the streets deserted. She realized how very late it was. That meant that probably no one had witnessed her being thrown out, but it also meant she would have even more difficulty in finding someone to help her.

There was always the sheriff, she mused, but she did not see how Martin could help her. Hers was a family problem, not a legal one. Leanne did not think there was any law against a parent throwing a child out into the street.

"I'm not your ma."

Charity had certainly not acted much like any mother Leanne had ever heard of or met. Other mothers might be aloof, but none of them had had a succession of "gentlemen friends," as Charity called them. Or if they did, they were far more discreet about it. Probably had more taste too, Leanne thought nastily as her anger began to rise.

Everything she owned, little as it was, was inside that house. She decided that was reason enough to go to the sheriff. It was robbery plain and simple. If the woman was going to thrust her out into the streets she could at least thrust out what belonged to her as well. With a final glare at the house, Leanne marched off to the sheriff.

By the time she saw the sheriff, she had pushed aside her hurt and confusion, replacing it with anger. She did not stop to wonder why the sheriff was lurking outside the bank. He looked horrified when she marched up to him. Leanne decided he was probably just shocked. She doubted he had seen many young ladies wandering around in the middle of the night half-dressed.

"Sheriff, I require your assistance."

"Get out of here, Miss Summers," he croaked. "Go on, get out of here."

"I would," she snapped, "if I had someplace to get out of here to. Is there something wrong?" she asked when she noticed how he kept looking in the window of the bank. "Is there supposed to be a light on in there?"

She glanced at him curiously when he groaned. He was shaking, and his eyes were the most restless she had ever seen. The sheriff's gaze flickered nervously over the town, to her, to the inside of the bank and back to the town. She felt he ought to be concentrating on the bank, for Mr. Poitier never left a light on.

"I think you ought to look into this, Sheriff," she said as she sidled up to the window.

"Please, go home, Miss Summers," he said, a distinct tremor in his voice.

"I have no home to go to. That is what I came to speak to you about."

Standing on her tiptoes she was just able to peer in the bank window. What she saw made her heart skip a beat. There were five masked men in the bank, and they were in the last stages of picking it clean. She looked at the sheriff, sure he must be aware of what was going on, but he just stood there staring at her.

"The bank is being robbed," she hissed. "Aren't you going to do something?"

"Please go home, Miss Summers," he whined.

"I keep telling you, I have no home to go to. Well, if you are just going to stand there and cower, I shall do something."

She yanked his gun out of his holster, and stared as he hissed a curse and raced off down the street. There was a chance he was going to get some other men and she wondered if she should just wait. Then she shook her head. The man had been acting so strangely, there was no depending on him. Although she did not know what she could do against five men, she decided she had to do something. She could not simply stand there and let them steal everything, nor could she run for help. There was no time left. From what she had seen, they were very nearly done.

Straightening her slender shoulders, she decided that surprise would be her best weapon. Throwing open the bank door, she marched inside and pointed the gun at them, hoping that they would not guess that she had little idea of how to use the weapon.

"Put down your weapons—now." She was pleased with the iciness of her voice.

Even as they turned to gape at her, Leanne realized she had made a serious error in judgment. She had seen five men when she peered in the window, but now she saw only four. By the way the other men kept looking from her to some point beyond her, she had the sinking feeling that the fifth man was right behind her. Rushing in to stop the bank robbers could well be one of the rashest things she had done in all her eighteen years. She wondered when and how the fifth man would strike.

Tarrant Hunter Walsh stared dumbfounded at the tiny lady facing down his companions. She was so small, she had to hold the pistol in two hands, but she did not seem to waver in her militant stance. He found it hard to believe that something so unexpected could threaten to ruin months of work.

"If you do not come out where I can see you, I will shoot your friends." Leanne hoped she had made that dire threat sound believable. "I shall count to five. One . . ."

Hunter wondered where Sheriff Martin had gone.

"Two . . ."

He wondered how such a slim, delicate neck could support all that rich blond hair.

"Three . . ."

"Hell, Hunter, do something about the stupid bitch."

"Four . . ."

Hunter wondered what Luke thought he could possibly do that would not end up with someone shot.

"Five."

Leanne did not really think. She simply followed through. She had made her threat, she had finished counting, so she fired. The gunshot sounded very loud in her ears as she was sent careening backwards.

Cursing viciously, Hunter grabbed the young woman who stumbled into him. He cursed even more when he found himself in the midst of an undignified struggle for the pistol. When he finally wrestled her to the ground and took the pistol from her, he sat on her and wondered idly how such a delicate hand could have such a tenacious grip. He had not had so much trouble trying to snatch something from someone since he had tried to yank a sugar candy from his brother Owen when they were small boys. Ignoring her muffled cries, which sounded very much like curses, he looked at the other men, suddenly realizing that Jed was howling like a wounded bull.

"She done shot Jed in the foot," Luke growled.

"I hit someone?" Leanne asked in surprise as she turned her head in a fruitless attempt to see something.

"What the hell do you expect when you shoot a gun?" Hunter snapped, glaring at her.

"Certainly not to end up with some jackass sitting on me."

He ignored that. "We have to get out of here. That shot could have roused someone. Get the money on the horses."

"You cannot take that." Leanne found speech difficult in her current position. "The people here need that money."

"Ain't that a shame." Luke threw her a glare as he hurried by her.

She gave a squeak of surprise as the man on her stood up then yanked her to her feet. Although she listened closely, she could hear no outcry and feared that the town was going to sleep blissfully through its own ruin. Thinking of the people who needed that money for food and mortgages and livestock, she glared at the man who was keeping her from fleeing and rousing the townspeople herself.

"Why don't you go out and earn money like decent folks do? You're all strong and healthy."

"I used to be 'til some stupid bitch shot my foot clean off," growled Jed as Tom helped him out to the horses.

"We're smarter'n them sodbusters," Luke said as he came back in and collected the last of the money. "What do we do with her?"

Hunter knew only one answer and hated it. "We take her with us."

"What for?" demanded Leanne.

"You know too much."

"All I know is that five masked bits of refuse from the gutter are taking what doesn't belong to them."

After glaring at her, Luke said, "She's right. She doesn't know anything."

"She might not see it yet, but she knows and it'll only take a few smart questions to bring it out. She's coming."

Tom stuck his head back inside the door. "Someone's seen us."

Leanne tried to drag her feet as her captor towed her out the door. Her lack of weight made her delaying tactics futile. He was still dragging her along at a near trot.

Her eyes widened when they got outside. The whole town seemed to be spilling out into the streets. Leanne saw the sheriff, as well as Charity and Clovis. She also saw rescue.

"Help me," she called, trying to pull free of her captor's grip before he could get her onto a horse.

"There she is. She stole my gun," the sheriff cried as he pointed an accusing finger at Leanne. "She sidled up to me all sweet and helpless, then turned on me. I was lucky to get away with my life."

Something told her the man who held her was as surprised as she was by the sheriff's accusation, for his grip on her lessened enough for her to pull free. She took a few steps toward the suspicious, angry crowd. A part of her was aware that the thieves were not standing around waiting to see how this confrontation came out. They saw an angry, armed crowd and were running for their lives. She had a sudden urge to tell them they need not worry about those guns. There was no one in town who could hit the broad side of a barn, but it was a fact quickly revealed when a few people shot at the fleeing men. She had the unsettling feeling that she should have gone with them.

"That's a bald-faced lie," she snapped. "You were just standing there cowering, Sheriff. I took your gun to try to stop those bandits taking what little this town has." She did not like the way the crowd kept advancing on her.

"You expect us to believe a mite like you was thinking of taking on five outlaws?" growled one man in disbelief.

"Pull the other leg," mumbled another angry voice.

"You was helping them and they left you holding the bag."

"Ain't no honor amongst thieves."

"Wait a minute," she cried as she was grabbed by two men in nightshirts. "Mama!"

Charity held a fine lace handkerchief up to her face, tears glistening in her eyes as she followed the man dragging Leanne toward the jail. "I should have suspected something like this," she wailed. "I should have seen it. She's always been so wild. When I found she'd snuck out tonight . . ."

"Snuck out?" Leanne squawked in outrage and nearly tripped as she was yanked up onto the boarded walk before the jail.

"I thought she'd gone to see a man," Charity continued as if she had not been interrupted. "Young hearts can be foolish. Never did I suspect that she was meaning to rob us blind. I have clasped an adder to my bosom."

"How the hell would you know that?" Leanne snarled as she was thrust into a cell and the doors clanged shut. "You'd never notice a mere adder with all the rest of the snakes you've clasped to your bosom over the years."

There was a collective gasp of outrage from the gathered townspeople. Leanne glared at them all. They all knew that the men who boarded at Charity's house did not pay for an empty bed. She supposed it was simply shocking because she, a desperado, had given voice to the truth. Neither would they appreciate someone they had always considered an outsider slandering one of their own. Although she knew it would help her cause not at all, she looked at them with contempt.

"And while you hypocrites are standing here priding yourselves on catching one tiny, unarmed female, your money is disappearing into the hills."

She turned her back on them, went over to the cot, and sat down. A great deal of muttering was followed by the sound of people shuffling out of the jailhouse. Wrapping her cloak around herself, she lay down.

Disbelief warred with despair. She simply could not believe all that had happened to her. No one could possibly have so much go so completely wrong in so short a time. It had to be impossible. It had to be a nightmare.

She pinched herself then cursed at the very real pain that assailed her. For a moment she fought the crushing weight of deep despair. She was not sure there was any way to get out of the predicament she found herself in.

Why had Charity helped to put Leanne into jail? It seemed to be an excessively spiteful act. Clearly Charity still thought that Leanne had lured Clovis into her bed. There would be no convincing Charity that Leanne would never want anything to do with such a poor specimen of humanity.

Or perhaps Charity hoped to hide all that had really happened, Leanne mused. It must have occurred to Charity that some awkward questions would be raised when people noticed that her daughter was suddenly gone. After all, she was now a little too old to be exiled to school. Charity's accusation took care of the loose ends very neatly. People would now sympathize with Charity over a child gone bad. Since so few townspeople had taken the time to get to know Leanne, it was a story that would never be questioned.

Leanne suddenly realized that she was completely

alone. She had no one to turn to, no one to help or defend her. The woman she had always thought of as her mother was not her mother. Somewhere, previously unbeknownst to her, she had a father, but he had handed her to Charity and never looked back, simply paying Charity to keep her. Leanne doubted the man would be delighted to hear from her now. No, she thought as she gave up the fight to hold back her tears, he would consider her a burden well shed.

She wallowed in misery for a while, feeling extremely sorry for herself. Even reminding herself that she had one good friend who would come to her aid did not raise her spirits. There was no way to get in touch with him. O'Malley was either secluded in his hunting cabin in the San Juan Mountains or home at his ranch, wherever that was.

A soft sound brought her out of her misery a little. Her ears told her it was the cell door being unlocked. Slowly she turned towards the door, then tensed.

Sheriff Martin's thin frame was silhouetted by the light outside the cell. His pale hazel eyes were fixed steadily upon her and there was a look in them that caused her to shiver with distaste and fear. She knew she would soon be fighting him just as she had fought Clovis.

Sitting up slowly, she glared at him, putting all her sudden hatred of the male species into that look. He faltered briefly and she branded him a coward in her mind. Most any male would find such a tiny woman easy pickings. She had made the mistake of thinking that the low-life who would try to force her was a rare breed and easily avoided. It was now becoming clear that they were as common as cockroaches.

"Remove yourself," she commanded and a strange imp inside of her almost laughed when he started to obey.

"You haughty bitch," he snapped, angered by his reaction to her imperious manner.

"Swamp slime."

If he wanted to trade insults, he had picked the wrong partner, she mused. There was nothing he could say that she could not match or better. She knew it was not a skill to be particularly proud of, but, when one was barely five feet tall and only one hundred pounds, one's choice of weapons was severely limited. It was a talent that also aided her in hiding her fear, and her dear friend O'Malley had always told her that that was important.

"You nearly ruined everything." Glaring at her, he cautiously approached her.

Understanding dawned quickly and Leanne nearly gaped. The sheriff had not simply been too afraid to face the outlaws, he had been part of the robbery. He had obviously been standing watch for them when she had sauntered up to him.

You really stumbled into it this time, Leanne, she told herself. She could not even count on the law to help her now. The law was Sheriff Martin and he, more than anyone, needed a scapegoat. Even if she could find some evidence to clear herself, he would swiftly eradicate or suppress it.

"I see," she murmured and looked at him with contempt hardening her usually soft lavender eyes. "Such a brave man you are, letting a small, innocent female shoulder the blame for your abuse of the town's trust."

He flushed with anger. "I told you to go home. You were too stupid to listen. You got what you deserved."

She leapt off the cot and sprinted out of reach as he lunged for her. Her dash for the open cell door was halted when he tripped her up by the crude but effective tactic of grabbing her cloak and yanking. He lunged for her again, but she rolled out of the way. Scrambling to her feet, she readied herself for his next move.

"This will hardly enhance your reputation, Sheriff."

"And just who are you going to tell?" He smirked as he stalked her. "And who'd care? Or believe you?"

That struck home. The very fact that she was in jail showed that no one really cared. They certainly did not believe her.

"I would think that a crime as monstrous as the one you plan would be visible. I'll fight you every inch of the way. I suggest you leave me, Sheriff, before you do something you will sorely regret."

"Just listen to you," he hissed. "You think you're some kind of princess, don't you? Been off to a fine Eastern school and think you're better'n us. Well, you ain't, dar-lin', not for all your highfalutin ways. When I'm done with you, you won't be holding that little nose up so high."

Even as she searched for some kind of weapon to use against the man stalking her, Leanne wondered if his words explained why the whole town was against her. They thought she held herself above them, looked down on them. If they did, Leanne could think of nothing she had done to make them feel that way. She knew in her heart that she did not act like a snob. Though she could become aloof when she faced animosity, she knew she had tried very hard to be friendly.

He sprang at her again. And this time, her evasive

move was foiled by her long hair. She cried out when he grasped it and yanked her towards him. The pain in her scalp brought tears to her eyes. For a moment it was hard to see her assailant well enough to strike at him as he wrestled her to the floor of the cell.

She felt bile sting her throat as he mauled her, his hands inflicting pain and revulsion as he tried to get to her flesh. She cried out as the front of her nightgown tore. By sheer willpower, she stopped herself from being violently ill when his mouth roughly assaulted her bared breast.

"You're going to give me what you've been giving Clovis," he growled as he struggled to pin down her hands.

"I gave Clovis nothing."

"That ain't what he's been saying. Tight and hungry, he said," the sheriff panted. "Always wanting it. Said he was wearing himself out trying to service you and your ma both."

"Clovis is a filthy liar. He snuck into my bed tonight while I was sleeping."

She was frustrated in her attempts to use her long nails on his face. When he shifted position a little to push up her nightgown she found another tactic to use. She had tried to use it on Clovis, but he had guessed what she was up to. Now she knew she would have to be more subtle.

Forcing herself to ignore the man yanking up her nightgown, she concentrated on moving her leg into the right position to strike. O'Malley had told her it was a man's weak point, that if she was in trouble she should strike there and strike hard. As soon as her leg was properly placed, she did just that, ramming her knee into the sheriff's groin with all the power she could put behind the blow. The man above her screamed and she found herself released.

Scrambling to her feet, she stared at the writhing, swearing sheriff in some surprise. She cursed softly when she saw that his twisting body was between her and the open cell door. Cautiously she started by him but he lashed out with his hand and nearly grabbed hold of her ankle. She danced back out of his reach. To her dismay, he got to his feet, ready to renew the attack despite his pain.

A chill went down her spine as she faced the slightly crouched man. She was shocked to see that his pants were half undone. She also saw that, while lust still glinted in his eyes, so did fury. She knew he would do his best to make it hurt now.

"You filthy bitch. You've probably ruined me."

"Unfortunately, I doubt it, but I will if you come any nearer. Perhaps not before you rape me, but sooner or later. It will be my life's work to see that you lose what you abuse women with." She smiled coldly when he hesitated in his advance, checked by her icy threat.

The only thing in reach was the slops bucket. As she reached for it, never taking her gaze from the sheriff, she decided it would have to suffice as a weapon. Even as he charged her, she grabbed the bucket and hurled the contents over him. He screamed in horror as the last prisoner's waste landed all over him. It did not stop him, however, only enraging him so that Leanne had to swing the bucket itself at him. It made a satisfying clang as it struck him. She continued to beat him with the bucket until she had driven him into the corner of the cell. Once he was no longer between her and the open cell door she threw the bucket at him and ran.

She could hear him swearing and stumbling after her as she darted out of the jail. She glanced behind her to see how close he was and ran into what felt like a brick wall. Strong hands grasped her by the shoulders and she stared dazedly up into the masked face of the bank robber called Hunter.

Chapter Two

HUNTER STARED DOWN AT THE GIRL. HUGE LAVENDER EYES bright with fear stared back at him. His gaze flickered over her body and stopped at the sight of one bared breast. He felt as if someone had just hit him full in the stomach—hard. It was a small breast; its ivory fullness would probably snuggle just nicely in the palm of his hand. The pink tip hardened in the cool night air and he felt his mouth water. He even started to bend towards it when he heard Martin's stumbling approach. Immediately brought to his senses, he tugged the girl behind him and drew his pistol, even as Martin came out of the jail.

"What the hell are you doing here, Hunter? Give me that bitch."

"No. I'm taking her with me."

"Not until I'm done with her."

The sheriff took a step toward him. Hunter grimaced and took a step back. The girl, pressed to his back, matched his retreating step.

"You stink, Martin."

"That whore threw the shit bucket at me."

Although he never ceased to watch for any sign of danger, Hunter waited as the sheriff staggered to the horse trough and pumped water over himself. The small, unofficial posse that was stumbling around ineptly in the dark had been easy to elude, but there was always the chance that there was someone with skill and courage left in town. Looking at the dripping sheriff, Hunter decided it would take more than a rinse to clean the man off and lessen the stench clinging to him.

"Damnation, I'll never get clean," the sheriff grumbled.

"You never were," muttered Leanne from her safe position behind the tall, broad-shouldered outlaw. She pressed her lips together when the outlaw sent her a quick glance that clearly told her to be quiet.

"Let me at her, Hunter."

"She goes with me."

"What the hell for?"

"Try thinking, Martin," Hunter drawled. "She knows too much. Someone just might start listening to what she has to say."

"No one's going to listen to that haughty slut."

"I can't take that chance."

"Then just wait 'til I've had her and you can take her where you want."

Hunter felt the small woman pressed to his back shudder. "There's no time. I suggest you start thinking of a way to explain her absence." Still keeping an eye on Martin, Hunter tugged the girl forward and looked at her. "You're coming with me." When he tugged her towards his horse, he felt her fight his pull and looked at her.

Leanne stared up at him, seeing little of his face save narrowed obsidian eyes beneath dark, frowning brows. He was an outlaw. Whatever he intended to do with her, it would not be good. He had to be over six feet tall and was all lean, hard muscle. There would be no fighting him. She would be mad to ride off into the night with him.

Then again, she mused, if she stayed she had to deal with the sheriff. She had been thrown in jail, accused of robbery, and no one was interested in defending or listening to her. She could easily find herself transported to the territorial prison—or worse.

"I really have little choice," she murmured.

"None at all," Hunter replied.

He mounted, then held his hand out to her. She allowed herself to be pulled up behind him and struggled to hold her cloak closed over her torn gown. Once behind him she wrapped her arms around his trim waist and tried very hard not to think about what she was doing. When he started off at a gallop and showed little sign of lessening that pace, she pressed her face against his back and concentrated on simply holding on until they got wherever they were going. She prayed that she was not riding to her death.

Glancing down at the small, pale hands clutching his shirt, Hunter wondered how he was going to get out of this mess. Taking her along was dangerous not only for her but for him and all he was working for. Unfortunately, it was also dangerous to leave her behind. He was trapped and he hated that.

By taking her with him, he had saved himself the worry of her talking, but now he had taken on other worries. He would have to watch her and watch out for her. From what he had seen, she was a pretty little thing, so he would also have to watch his men.

Recalling his reaction to that brief sight of her breast, he grimaced, admitting he would have to watch himself too. It was just another complication he did not need. Complications could result in failure, and he had little taste for that. In this matter, success was vital.

His luck had been running bad for the last year and, just when he had let himself think it was taking a turn for the better, it went bad again. The tiny lady clinging to him could easily be the worst turn of luck yet. However, no matter how hard he thought about it, he could not think of any place to put her where she would be both safe and silent. His first robbery could not have gone more awry short of capture and an immediate lynching.

When they stopped, Leanne peered around him and grimaced. His four outlaw companions sat around a small campfire. It seemed very arrogant of them to camp so near to town, but she admitted that they were in little danger. The posse could stumble right over these men and not realize it. It was fortunate that no other outlaws had discovered just how vulnerable the town was.

Warily, she slid from the back of the horse, still trying to hold her cloak together.

"What the hell'd you get her for?" one of the men growled.

"I explained that, Luke." Hunter's voice was soft but chilly as he tugged Leanne closer to the fire. "Sit."

Leanne sat and studied the four outlaws crouched around the fire. The one she had shot glared at her. He was a short, burly man of average looks. The one named Luke was also burly, but he was just plain ugly. Tom was big, almost as tall as Hunter, and broad. He had a look in his dark eyes that made her shiver. The last man was ineptly bandaging Jed's foot. He was just average—average looks, average height, and average build. They were all unclean, unshaven, and unsmiling.

"If you're so worried about her talking, shoot her." Luke spoke with a cold, matter-of-fact voice.

"Here now," Jed said, his face revealing his shock, "you can't be shooting women."

That Jed was the one to speak out against shooting her surprised Leanne. That Luke suggested such a thing did not. What really bothered her was that Hunter seemed to be thinking over the suggestion.

Handing her a tin cup filled with strong coffee, Hunter drawled, "Simple, but not too smart."

"Why not?" Luke growled. "Surest way to shut her up."

"True. However, it's also the surest way to bring a hell of a lot of men after us."

"They think she's a thief."

"Doesn't matter. You don't kill women. So far we're only thieves. Let's keep it that way. 'Sides, the fact that she's accused of helping us is one reason she'll shut up. We're going to help settle her some place safe from the law. She's got a choice between us and jail. That's good enough."

"So you mean to drag her all the way to Mexico with us?" When Hunter nodded, Luke growled, "Well, if we're stuck with her, we might as well make good use of her." Luke was already reaching for her as he spoke.

Leanne was as startled as Luke when Hunter drew his gun. For one long, tense moment the two men just stared at each other. Then Luke retreated a step. Although the situation frightened her, Leanne was relieved at this sign that she was not going to become entertainment for the outlaws. She knew it did not mean her virtue was safe from assault, but it did seem to indicate that she would not be subjected to the horror of multiple rape.

"She's mine, Luke."

"You mean you ain't gonna share her at all?"

"That's exactly what I mean. I took the risk of going back for her. I claim her."

"Fine then," Luke snapped. "She's yours. Don't expect no help keeping the stupid bitch in hand."

"I won't." Hunter slowly put his gun away and then began to sip his coffee.

After that Leanne found herself virtually ignored. She took the time to covertly study the man who held her life in his hands. He was lean in face and body, almost too lean. His aristocratic nose gave him an air of breeding and haughtiness she thought totally out of character considering his chosen profession. As she noted how his dark, faintly arched brows tended to be mostly set in a frown, she realized that his dark eyes were circled with surprisingly long lashes for a man. It was an oddly soft feature on an otherwise hard face. That harshness was emphasized by the stubborn set of his jaw and the way his fine mouth was now drawn tight.

She wondered about the anger, even bitterness, she

sensed in him. She was not the real reason for his anger, she was sure of it. She was an annoyance, a momentary problem. His bitterness was caused by far more than that. She would not even try to imagine the reasons for it. One thing she had learned in her life was that it was not easy to understand another person's emotions or the reasons behind them.

Her thoughts were abruptly interrupted when Hunter took her empty cup from her hands and asked rather curtly, "What's your name?"

"Leanne. Leanne Summers."

"I'm Hunter. That's Luke, Tom, Charlie, and Jed."

Only Charlie and Jed nodded. Tom and Luke simply stared at her. The coldness of their looks chilled her and she surreptitiously sidled closer to Hunter.

"What were you doing roaming the streets in the middle of the night?"

Though it was not really any of his business, she replied, "My mother kicked me out of the house. Although, actually, she isn't my mother. She said she isn't even blood-related, just an aunt by marriage. Told me that while she was kicking me out of the house."

"Your mother kicked you out in the middle of the night?"

"I just said she wasn't my mother, although I always thought she was. She used to claim to be."

"Why would you think it and why would she claim it if she wasn't?"

"Because my father paid her to play the part, or so she claimed. She also said he hadn't paid her in three months."

"And that's why she kicked you out?"

"No. She has men friends, you see. Her latest is Clo-

vis. Well, Clovis decided to tiptoe out of her bed and try
to get into mine. She believed him when he claimed I had
tempted him." She scowled as she thought of the injustice
of it all. "That's ridiculous, because if I was going to do
any tempting I certainly wouldn't do it with ugly old Clovis."

"Ah, she thought you were stealing her man," Charlie
said.

Leanne realized she had a larger audience than Hunter.
Although Luke and Tom seemed bored, Charlie and Jed
were listening avidly. She felt herself blush then decided
it was too late to stop her tale. "Yes, she did. Or maybe
she just realized that she had to get one of us out of the
house, and she wasn't about to throw out Clovis."

"All that doesn't explain how you ended up at the
bank."

"Well, I got to thinking she had no right to throw me
out without throwing my things out as well. According to
her, my father had been paying her, so his money probably bought my clothes and all. I was after the sheriff so
that he'd get her to give me my clothes. He was outside the bank, standing there quaking and peering in the
windows or down the street."

"Told you he was spineless," Luke muttered.

"Spineless or not, he accomplished what Watkins said
he would. Watkins didn't claim his brother was any
hero." Hunter looked back at Leanne. "And?"

"He just kept telling me to go home. Then I decided to
see what he kept looking at in the bank and I saw you
robbing it. I told him to do his job and, when he wouldn't,
I took his gun. He raced on down the street and I did the

stupidest thing I've done in a long time. You know the rest."

"And the townsfolk didn't believe you?"

"No, and the one yelling the loudest about me being guilty was my mother or my aunt or whatever she is."

"Why'd she turn on you? Don't seem right, kin turning against kin," Jed muttered.

"I think she saw it as a good way to explain why I was out on the street at such an hour. It made a better story than her booting me out without a cent, without even any shoes. Now folk'll give her all sorts of sympathy. She'll like that."

"And the sheriff?" Hunter asked quietly.

"What about the sheriff?"

"What happened with him?"

"I think you know what happened with him." She shook her head. "Clovis has been telling tales and the sheriff was dumb enough to believe the cockroach. I dread to think how many others in town believe him."

"You expect me to believe all this?"

"Why not? Why would I make up such a ridiculous tale?"

He shrugged. "You might have been out with some man."

"I almost wish I had been. I doubt I could have gotten into any more trouble."

"Perhaps we should take you to your father," Hunter mused aloud.

"He'd have her singing to the law in a minute," Luke said.

"There's the chance he won't. He won't want the scandal. She'll have been with us for a while and that would have to come out."

"And there's always the chance he'll hurry to toss me into someone else's lap like before." Leanne spoke the distasteful truth in a flat voice. "Then we'll all be right back where we started. I'm tired," she said, changing the subject sharply.

"I laid your bedding out over there, Hunter," said Charlie.

Hunter pointed to it and looked at her. "Go to sleep then."

She looked at the bedroll, then at him. He simply stared back at her. With a sigh she stood up, went over to the bedroll, and crawled in. At the moment, she could not think of anything else to do.

Turning her back on the men, she closed her eyes. Sleep was a long way off and she knew it. Although she was exhausted, she had too much on her mind to sleep, too much to think about.

Her mother was not her mother. So who was? Her father was a man who dutifully paid for her upkeep but plainly wanted nothing to do with her. She did not even know who the man was, except for his name. Suddenly she felt like a total stranger to herself. Her whole life had been a lie.

Knowing there was little to be found by staring into a past she could not fathom, she turned her thoughts to the present, only to find as great a muddle. Since she had no gun, no horse and no shoes, and everyone in town thought her part of the outlaw gang, escape seemed impossible. Even if she found the means to escape, and the opportunity, there was no place to escape to.

For a brief moment she fought the urge to cry. It would accomplish nothing and she really did not want to reveal such a weakness before the outlaws. Then, as the first tear oozed out from beneath her eyelid, she decided that if anyone deserved a good cry, she did. Trying to be as quiet as possible, she gave in to her tears. She prayed Hunter would not come to bed too soon.

As he sipped his coffee, Hunter surreptitiously watched his reluctant and all too attractive guest. He was not sure he believed all she had told him, but, as she had said, why would she make up such a ridiculous tale? An accomplished liar would never use such a wild story. She was either telling the truth, or she was a very bad liar.

He shook his head. She had looked him straight in the eye when she told her tale. If she was a bad liar telling a poor lie, there would have been some sign. Implausible as the tale was, he was beginning to think it true, or mostly so.

There was one part of her tale he was not so sure of. From what the sheriff had said, she had a reputation in town. While it was highly possible the man Clovis had lied to puff himself up, it was also possible that she was lying about seducing the man. He had discovered early in life that women were very good at lying about that sort of thing. Well, if she was no virgin, he might enjoy her himself.

And that, fool, could land you in even more trouble, he scolded himself.

The last thing he needed now was any sort of entanglement, even one of the most basic sort. Some instinct warned him that with Leanne it would never be a simple matter of gratifying his lust. But in his mind's eye he could see that small perfect breast, that silken ivory skin, and he was not sure his lust would tolerate being ignored, especially not when he was forced to keep her close at hand.

Suddenly he realized the others were turning in. Cursing softly, he moved to do the same. He had claimed the girl as his and he had to act as if he meant to take her, or he would have more trouble than he needed. The minute he showed any reluctance or disinterest, Luke would step in.

Sitting down on the edge of his bedroll, he yanked his boots off. What really had him concerned was the reason he had pulled his gun on Luke. The sharing of a woman only led to trouble, for few men could do it fairly or calmly, and even fewer women would tolerate it. Neither could he tolerate rape, and he knew the girl would have fought Luke as hard as she had fought the sheriff. Neither was the reason he had pulled his gun, however. He had simply loathed the idea of Luke touching her. His statement that she was his had more truth to it than he liked.

It took only a moment after slipping beneath the blanket for Hunter to know his companion was not asleep. An instant later he knew she was weeping and he silently cursed. Women's tears never failed to move him. He could not ignore them, even when he knew they were simply a ploy. He turned on his side, noting that her slim back shook only faintly as she tried to hide her distress.

"Crying will help nothing."

"I am not crying." She cursed softly for her voice was shaking and hoarse, a sure sign that she lied.

"Of course not. Just sniveling." He had to clench his hand to keep from caressing her soft, thick golden hair.

"And what if I am? I have every right to be upset." She turned onto her back and glared at him.

"I got you out of jail."

"How kind. It might have been nicer if you had not dragged me into this den of thieves."

She could see his eyes narrow and wondered at the wisdom of her words. It was hardly clever to insult this man. He literally held her life in his hands. She was too tired and upset to be concerned about that, however.

"You're not the smartest little thing, are you."

"Clearly not or I wouldn't be in this twice-cursed muddle."

"Crying won't get you out of it either." He felt uncomfortably moved by the moonlit sight of her tearstained face.

"I know that," she snapped, "but I have a right to a moment's weakness." When he produced a handkerchief she took it, studied it a moment to assure herself it was clean, then put it to use in wiping her tears away.

"You put yourself in this mess."

"I did not ask that lump of dog spit—"

"Dog spit?"

"Clovis—to maul me. It's hardly my fault that the woman I thought was my mother is not. I certainly did not ask my father to drop me in her lap and pay her for her poor mothering. It never occurred to me that Charity would believe Clovis instead of me, or that she would throw me out with only my nightgown. And it is hardly surprising that when I came upon the sheriff who was duly elected to protect the town, I asked him for help. I never expected *him* to be part of a bank robbery. And then you just left me there to face that mob." She blew her nose.

"Since you were not one of this pack of thieves, I hardly thought you would wish to come along."

"Of course I didn't. I never in my wildest dreams thought everyone would accuse me. Then I get tossed into jail like some common criminal and that pile of horse droppings attacks me. And now look at me. I am out in the middle of nowhere with a bunch of bank robbers, the town thinking I am a thief, and I don't even have a pair of shoes. I have earned a good cry."

"Earned or not, it still won't get you anywhere."

"That is quite clear." She turned her back to him again. "Why did you come back for me?"

"Because you knew about the sheriff."

"As if that mob would have listened to me."

"Someone might have—eventually."

She frowned as she thought about what he had said. Perhaps she should try to get back to town, to make someone listen to her.

"Don't even think about it."

"How do you know what I'm thinking?"

"Because I know what I'd think in the same situation. It won't work. One—I have no intention of letting you slip free to start blubbering your side of the story to anyone. Two—even if you got to town the sheriff would hardly let you say how-do. Three—You are now on the run with this pack of thieves and that goes against you. I broke you out of jail, remember?"

"I broke myself out of jail. You just happened to be there when I started to run."

"That won't be the way the sheriff tells it."

The truth of that quiet statement hit her so hard she

gasped. Sheriff Martin had his own neck to worry about. He would paint her as black as possible. She doubted he had wasted any time in telling anyone who would listen that her desperado friends had returned to break her out of jail. If she went back to town, she would be lucky if she was not immediately hanged. It was enough to make her want to weep some more.

"Don't start bawling again."

"Oh, shut your big mouth."

"You know, some folk in your position would have the wisdom to keep the edge off their tongue."

The chill in his voice hardly troubled her at the moment. "Some folk in my position would put a bullet in their head."

Her voice was so flat he could not help but wonder if she was contemplating just such an act. It alarmed him, but what alarmed him more was the thrill of panic that shot through him.

"Don't be an idiot."

"It would certainly relieve you of a burden." The dark thought had only been a fleeting one, but she did not feel inclined to tell him that.

"And hand me another one. I'd find myself trying to explain how it was you ended up dead. Even if you're thought a thief, that wouldn't go well for me."

He spoke so callously that she was annoyed. "Your concern for my well-being humbles me."

"Go to sleep."

"What? No ravishment? Well, the world is full of wonders."

"I don't rape women," he ground out.

"No, just steal every last dime from hardworking people."

He glared at her back. "I see you've changed your mind about suicide. Now you're trying to get me to murder you."

Slowly she turned to look at him. A tiny alarm went off inside her. He looked furious. He also looked disturbingly handsome. She decided she would be wise to concentrate on his fury. Unfortunately, she was in no mood to soothe that anger.

"Are you going to tell me you're some sort of Robin Hood?"

"Yeah. I steal from the rich—them—and give to the poor—me."

"Such philanthropy. I am overwhelmed."

"You will be strangled in a minute if you don't shut your mouth and go to sleep. Or maybe there's another reason you're still awake."

She was not sure she liked the way he smiled at her. "I just want to be sure I'm wide-eyed and alert when the law catches up with you. That's one hanging I don't want to miss."

"Is that so? I thought maybe you were waiting for me to join you in that snug little bed."

Before she could deride the very bed he referred to, he was on top of her. She gave a soft cry of alarm as he pinned her beneath him. Although her heart beat so fast it was nearly painful, she fought to hide her fright. Frowning sternly, she glared at him. When she spoke she was pleased to hear that her voice sounded cool and calm.

"Just what do you think you're doing?"

Hunter had to admire her. He could feel the rapid pace

of her heart, could sense her fear. Nevertheless, she acted calm. Her bravery might be an act, but it was a good one.

"Giving you what you want."

"I did not realize I had expressed a desire to be squashed flat. Remove yourself."

"Damn if you don't sound like royalty ordering the serfs around. Did you learn that at some snooty Eastern school?"

As she opened her mouth to reply, he kissed her. Leanne was too stunned to move. At first it was the fact that he was kissing her that shocked her; then it was the way the kiss was making her feel. She should be frightened and revolted. Instead, she began to feel weak inside and rather warm. To her great dismay she realized that she liked being kissed by this bank robber.

When he nudged his tongue between her lips to stroke the inside of her mouth, she found no strength to resist. It felt too good to fight. She could only pray that he would not guess her response.

Slowly, and with a reluctance he was loath to admit to, Hunter drew away. He had never been so affected by a mere kiss. His insides were knotted with hunger. For the first time in his life he actually, if briefly, contemplated forcing himself on a woman. He moved away from her and heartily wished he could have left her in Martin's less than tender care.

Looking at her wide-eyed face did not really help him regain his calm. She had not once moved beneath him, but the heated response of her full lips had told him of her desire. It was clear it had surprised her as much as it had him.

"You didn't learn that at any finishing school."

That cool insult snapped her out of her shock and she glared at him. "Oh, shut up. Are you quite done?"

He wondered what she would say if he told her exactly how much more he felt inclined to do, then decided he had given her enough to think about. "Yup."

Hissing a curse, she turned on her side, her back to him. "Then perhaps I can get some rest now."

Lying on his back and crossing his arms beneath his head, he murmured, "Be my guest."

Chapter Three

"**W**HAT IS THIS?"

Leanne grimaced in disgust at the pile of clothes Hunter had just tossed at her feet. She knew they were clothes because of the buttons. Other than that, they looked like little more than a bundle of dirty rags.

"Your clothes."

"What did you do? Rob the town drunk?"

"They are cleaner than you think."

"They would have to be."

"Put them on."

"Not if I was stark naked."

"With only that thin, torn nightgown to wear, you probably will be in a day or two."

There was an uncomfortable amount of truth in that, she mused. Sighing in resignation, she gingerly picked up the clothes.

"Now, the question is, where can I dress in privacy?"
She frowned as he took her by the arm and strode towards
a few closely growing trees. "You needed only to point
the way."

"Behind those." He gave her a gentle push towards the
trees.

"Surely you don't intend to lurk so close?"

"Surely I do. Hurry up. I want to head out."

As she stepped behind the clump of trees, she realized
that they did not provide much cover. She could see his
broad back through the leaves. At least he had had the
courtesy to turn around, she thought crossly as she hurried to dress.

She had often wondered what it would be like to
wear men's clothing, but what she had envisioned had
been a fine coat and fashionable trousers, not worn
Levis and a faded flannel shirt. Shaking her head, she
yanked on the trousers and hoped she would not feel too
strange or immodest wearing them. About the only
thing she was sure of was how good the rawhide boots
felt on her feet.

Hunter turned to stare at her when she stepped out
from behind the trees. He swallowed hard as he looked
her up and down. The clothes fit her far too well. He had
gained some sense of her figure when she had been beneath him briefly last night, but his estimation had been
far short of reality. The worn, soft clothes hugged every
slim inch of her lithe frame, delineating with discomfort-
ing exactitude the shape of her breasts and the curve of
her hips. He was not sure that she was much better than
naked. Even her torn, thin nightgown had seemed more
modest.

"That'll do." He spoke curtly as he grasped her by the arm and tugged her toward the horses.

Leanne found his reaction a little strange. But then, nothing understandable had happened to her for what seemed like years.

"I don't know what your trouble is now. I did as you asked."

"Yeah, you did."

"Then why are you being such a sorehead? Does waking up on the wrong side of the law make you irritable?"

"I would love to stand here bickering, but we have a lot of miles to cover."

When he tossed her onto the back of his horse, she briefly thought about bolting. However, the thought had barely formed when he swung up behind her. It was obvious that, at least for now, he did not intend to give her the slightest chance to flee. She would bide her time, she decided as they started on their way. He would have to ease his guard sometime.

"And might I be so impertinent as to ask just where we are going?"

"Mexico."

"Ah, yes, the retreat of all good desperadoes. It's a long way. There's a lot of land between here and there."

"Sure is," he drawled as he nudged his mount into motion.

"What are you doing all the way up here in Colorado?"

"Emptied all the banks down that way."

Ignoring that sarcastic remark, she drawled, "You've got a long way to go before you reach home territory.

That means there's all the more chance of your being caught and hanged. There has to be at least one honest lawman between here and Mexico."

"I wouldn't place any wagers on it."

By the time they camped for the night, Leanne was unable to think clearly about anything, let alone plot any escape. Her only really coherent thought as she numbly ate the beans served her was that she would have to take over the cooking. She was certain that if the constant riding did not kill her, the men's cooking would. Promising herself she would begin in the morning, she staggered off to bed. When Hunter slid in beside her, she was too tired to do more than grunt crossly and sidle over to give him room.

Daylight brought a new surprise. Hunter was gone.

It was not until she had relieved herself—with Charlie lurking embarrassingly close—and washed up and begun making her breakfast that she noticed that Hunter was not the only one gone. Only Charlie and the wounded Jed were still with her. And Jed was still sleeping.

Later, as she sat by the fire sipping her first cup of decent coffee for days, she plotted and discarded several plans for escape. She sensed that Charlie and Jed were the weakest in the gang. There might not be a better chance for her to break free. Considering the direction they were headed, she was sure Pueblo could not be too far away. It surprised her that Hunter had left only those two to guard her.

Unfortunately, her planning was interrupted by a new problem: Jed. The wounded man looked decidedly unwell, and Charlie kept glancing worriedly at his friend. Cursing softly over what she considered a treacherously soft heart, she rose and walked over to Jed. Even as she reached the man's side, Charlie loomed up beside her.

"You just get away from him. You've done him enough harm."

"It was hardly a mortal wound."

She frowned at Jed, who was giving her a weak glare. He looked awful. His color was a sickly shade of green, and sweat beaded on his face. Though she found it hard to believe that a gunshot wound in the foot could make a man so ill, she knew improper care could make even the smallest scratch dangerous.

"You did take the bullet out, didn't you?" she addressed the question to Charlie, who was leaning against the tree Jed lay under.

"Yeah, with this." Charlie briefly stopped cleaning his filthy nails with his knife to show it to her.

"Cleaned off first, of course."

"Cleaning it couldn't make it no sharper."

Inwardly, Leanne cursed. She had a good idea of what ailed Jed. It was not something she was eager to deal with. Nevertheless, she could not turn her back on the problem. If the man's wound had become infected, leaving it untended could kill him. That was not something she wished to have on her conscience.

"Let me see his foot."

"What for? You've done it enough hurt, if you ask me."

"I did not ask you, Charles. Now let me see his foot."

When a wide-eyed Charlie scrambled to obey, Leanne decided she had sounded as imperious as she had meant to. It was astounding, she mused, what could be accomplished with the appropriate tone of voice.

Then Charlie bared Jed's foot. It took Leanne a moment to stifle the urge to be sick. She fought to gain some semblance of calm. She did not think she had ever seen a dirtier foot.

"Don't you ever bathe?"

"Sure I do. Nearly once a month. 'Bout that time now, ain't it, Charlie?"

"Reckon so, Jed. Can't rightly recall."

"I'm not surprised. Charles, get me some water."

"What for?"

"To clean this foot. It's infected, poisoned. If nothing is done, it could kill him. That filth is what's helping to make him look like death warmed over."

"I look that bad?"

Charlie stared at his friend for a moment, then nodded. "You do look poorly, Jed."

"Reckon you better get the water, then."

Once Charlie got her some water Leanne began to wash Jed's foot. She had Charlie heat up another pot of water as she did so. Everything went smoothly until she asked Charlie for his knife.

"No sirree, ma'am."

"I need the knife to lance this wound."

"Why?"

"It needs to be opened. Then I'll use the heated water to draw out the poisons."

"Yeah, and just maybe you'll use this knife to stick us and then run."

"Now, I might be able to—er, stick one of you, but I

would guess the other would act quickly. I couldn't possibly kill both of you. As far as Jed is concerned, if I wanted him dead, I only need to leave this foot to rot."

"Rot?" Jed looked at his friend with pleading in his eyes. "Give her the knife, Charlie."

After careful deliberation Charlie finally gave her the knife. Leanne cleaned it, then held it in the fire for a moment. Once it had cooled some, she had Charlie hold Jed still as she lanced the wound. Quickly she began to place cloths soaked in the hot water. on the wound. She idly wondered where Charlie had gotten the rags until she recognized the modest lace trim of her nightgown. Shaking her head, she continued until she felt she had drawn out as much infection as she could for the time being. After pouring Charlie's whiskey over the wound she sat back to view her handiwork.

The injury did look better. Jed, however, looked pale. She decided it was the pain she had had to inflict that had made him look so bad.

"The knife, ma'am."

Sighing, Leanne placed the knife in Charlie's outstretched hand. "Better scrub it off first."

"You just gonna leave it open like that?" Jed asked as Charlie washed off his knife.

"For now. I intend to treat it once more. Perhaps twice more."

"You ain't going to be hacking at it with Charlie's knife again, are you?"

"I did not hack at it. I lanced the wound. And, no, I won't. I'll just do the hot water again." She looked at Charlie. "You had best get some more water heated, Charles."

It was mildly amusing when Charlie scurried off to the nearby creek in meek obedience. He had clearly forgotten that he was supposed to be guarding her. Jed was useless as a guard. It was the perfect opportunity to escape, but she could not take it. Jed's wound still needed work and a half-finished treatment was almost as bad as none.

Twice more she treated Jed's wound. It was only then that she felt confident she had gotten out the poisons. She stitched the wound, then wrapped it in a clean bandage. When Charlie moved to put Jed's socks back on, she stopped him.

"Those are filthy. Doesn't he have a clean pair?"

"These're clean. Washed them when we had a bath."

"You'll wash them out, Charles, before you put them on his feet."

"You can wear things out washin' 'em too much, you know," Charlie grumbled even as he moved to wash Jed's socks.

Once the socks were scrubbed, Leanne draped them over a stick and held them over the fire to dry. She instructed Charlie to strip Jed and scrub him down. She ignored their grumbling, a grumbling that grew louder when Charlie was done washing Jed and she told him he now had to scrub out the man's clothes.

"I ain't been this clean in a dog's age."

Glancing at Jed and almost smiling at the way he clutched his blanket around him like some modest maiden, she drawled, "No doubt—and that's why your foot went bad so fast."

"You learn doctoring at that school back East that Hunter says you been to?" Charlie began to drape Jed's wet clothes on the tree.

"No, but I assisted a doctor back there for a while. When he came to tend one of the teachers, I helped, and he noticed I had some aptitude for the work. Since he was very short of help, he asked the headmistress if I might assist him from time to time. The headmistress always stressed the importance of good works so she was quick to agree."

Seeing that Charlie was finished with the washing, she mused aloud about how nice it would be to have some fresh meat to cook. It did not take many such hints before the man slipped away. The only thing that surprised her was the speed with which he returned with two gutted and skinned rabbits for her to cook.

Hunter frowned as he neared the camp. Something smelled suspiciously good. However it was not what was cooking that immediately grabbed his attention when the camp came into view. Dismounting, he wondered crossly where Tom and Luke had disappeared to. With only Jed and Charlie for guards, he was very surprised to see Leanne still in camp. He found it hard to believe that she had not seen what useless guards the pair were.

"Where the hell are Luke and Tom?" He strode up to the fire and tossed down the supplies he had brought.

"They went to town, Hunter," Charlie replied.

"Why? They knew I was getting supplies."

Recalling the crude remarks she had overheard Jed and Charlie making concerning what Luke and Tom had gone after, Leanne murmured, "I suspect they did not feel you would return with what they felt a need for."

Looking at her, he suddenly became fully aware of what she was cooking. "Where the hell did that come from?"

Glancing at Charlie, Leanne could see that the man now realized the error he had made in leaving her alone with Jed to go hunting. "It was the oddest thing, Mr.

Hunter." She began to look through the supplies he had brought to see what might go well with the rabbit. "They just hopped into camp."

"Skinned and ready for the spit, hmmm?"

"No, they had neglected to prepare themselves. Charles was forced to perform that service."

Hunter caught sight of Jed half-sitting up and clutching his blanket around him. "Why are you setting there buck-nekked, Jed?"

"Well, the lady there had to fix my foot."

"I see, but I don't think that required you to take all your clothes off."

Leanne had to bite her lip to keep from giggling. She concentrated on making biscuits to go with the rabbit. Hunter clearly wanted some explanations and she knew that he would have trouble getting complete and clear ones from Charlie and Jed.

"I know that. First she washed my foot, then my socks, then she made Charlie scrub me and my clothes. She's the washingest woman I've ever known. See, my foot had gone bad on me."

Moving to Jed's side, Hunter tugged up the blanket to look at Jed's foot. "Looks fine to me."

"Yeah, now. She had to do a lot of work to get it looking so good."

It was several more minutes before Hunter got the full story of what had happened while he had been gone. It still puzzled him. Moving back to the fire, he sat down and poured himself some coffee. For a moment he just sipped the brew and studied Leanne Summers. The coffee had never tasted so good.

"I'm surprised to find you still here."

"I was well guarded, Mr. Hunter." .

"Those two couldn't stop a baby from crawling away, and you know it." He scowled as he watched her prepare what he knew would be the best meal they had had in a very long time. "What game are you playing?"

"Game?"

"Yes, game. You shoot Jed, then tend his wound. Doesn't make sense."

"Why not? When I shot him he was helping to rob a bank. I wasn't trying to kill him. But ignoring the condition of that wound today *would* have been murder. I suppose that in certain circumstances I could kill someone. However, when my life is not being openly threatened I cannot, not even if it is killing through negligence."

"His wound had gotten that bad?"

"Bad enough to be life-threatening but, fortunately, not so bad it could not be mended."

"He does look better than he did this morning." He eyed her carefully. " 'Course, your feeling that way makes me think your constant remarks about being eager to see me hang might not be truthful."

"No? That would not be murder, Mr. Hunter, but justice. I have never had any difficulty seeing justice done."

Even as she said the words, she knew they were a lie. She was glad when he made no reply. Concentrating on making a meal that would compensate for the poor fare she had suffered since joining the outlaws, she forced herself not to think about the matter. Something told her she would not like the answers she might come up with.

Just as she was preparing to take a plate of food to Jed, Luke and Tom rode back into camp. The look on Hunter's face told her there would be a tense confrontation. She quickly filled a plate for herself, deciding she would sit by Jed and Charlie as she ate. As she hurried over to Jed's side she told herself that the gnawing feeling she had was not concern for Hunter, but for her own future if anything happened to him. Glancing at Luke and Tom as they squatted before the fire, Leanne felt sure there would be trouble. Luke was looking very antagonistic.

"Where the hell have you been?" The stench of heavy, cheap perfume that clung to the two men answered Hunter's question, but he was curious to hear what they had to say for themselves.

"To visit a whore. I had coin in my pocket and an itch." Tom grunted agreement to Luke's blunt reply.

"You were supposed to stay here and guard the woman."

"She's still here, ain't she?"

"Sheer luck. While you were out rutting, she could have been halfway to Kansas."

"And halfway to a noose. Martin's painted her guilty."

"There's other sheriffs." Hunter kept his voice low, not wishing to give Leanne any ideas she might not have come up with on her own. "One of them might be inclined to listen to her."

"Then shoot her like I first said."

"I'm not shooting a woman."

"Then I will."

Leanne nearly choked on her food when Luke suddenly drew his gun and aimed it at her. She was only vaguely aware of Charlie and Jed tensing, their hands on their own guns. All she could see was that gun aimed at her heart and the deadly purpose in Luke's small, hard eyes.

Hunter had his gun drawn and aimed at Luke's heart in an instant, before Tom could move to support his friend. "No, you won't. Another thing you won't do is leave camp when you've been told to stay here." He waited a moment after Luke reholstered his gun before slowly putting his own away.

"You want her watched, you watch her."

"It's not just her. There's a lot of law between here and Mexico. We'll be skirting towns like Pueblo, Albuquerque, and El Paso, but she could try to escape and reach them. There may be a posse out searching for us. We can't afford to get careless."

Tom nodded slowly, and Hunter felt relief surge through him. He could handle Luke. The man was dangerous, but mostly bluff. The tall, dark, and broadly built Tom was the one he was not sure of, and that made the man doubly dangerous.

No one really knew Tom. He had joined Watkins not long before Hunter had and now appeared to have paired himself with Luke. So far, Tom had stayed out of the confrontations Hunter had had with Luke, but that could change with deadly swiftness. It was impossible to know which way a quiet, secretive man like Tom would jump.

"Ain't right for you to deny others when you've got a warm piece right at hand," grumbled Luke, his too thin lips twisted into a scowl. "It ain't my fault you ain't got the sense to make use of her."

"What I do or don't do with the girl is not important. Getting the money to Watkins is. I doubt Mister Watkins would understand the loss of the money due to your whoring." He noticed Luke could not argue with that, did not even try to.

Leanne realized that she was not frightened anymore. She was angry. They talked about her as if she were baggage and she sorely resented it. If she had forced herself upon them, she might have understood their feelings. However, it had been their criminal activity that had started everything.

The vision of Luke pointing his gun at her kept her from spitting out her anger in caustic words. She did not trust herself to maintain such restraint, however. She decided that the smartest thing to do at the moment was retire for the night. As she walked by the fire where Luke, Tom, and Hunter still sat, she tossed her plate down, then kept on walking.

"Where're you going?"

A little surprised that Luke would speak to her, she glanced back at him. "I'm turning in for the night."

Tossing his now empty plate on top of hers, he said, "You got some cleaning up to do, woman."

"I cooked it. You clean up." She strode over to Hunter's bedding and sat down to tug off her boots.

Before Luke could say another word, Charlie hurried over to gather up the empty plates. "I'll clean up."

"It's woman's work."

"If it'll keep her cooking, Luke, I don't mind doing the cleaning up."

After Charlie hurried away, Luke glared at Hunter. "That woman's useless. You let her act the damn queen, Hunter."

"Leave it." Tom took out a pouch of tobacco and began to roll a cigarette, no expression on his dark face but a cool deadliness in his voice.

"What?"

"I said leave it, Luke. Coffee was good. Food was good. Charlie's cleaning up. We just have to fill our bellies. Leave it."

Hunter was a little surprised that Tom had spoken out. He was not, however, surprised at Luke's quick obedience. Tom seemed to be able to silence Luke's blustering with little effort. A quick glance at Leanne told him she was scrambling into the bedroll and turning her back on them all. Hunter hoped she did not think she had won an ally in Tom, for he would be a dangerous one to play games with.

When Tom finally left to stand watch, Hunter sought his bed. Although he was tired, the bed did not look welcoming. The hard ground was not what troubled his sleep. It was the soft Leanne. No matter how weary he felt, his body was suddenly reawakened when he crawled in beside her.

Sitting down, he began to tug off his boots. He wished he could put her in her own bed. While it would not cure him of the wanting she stirred in him, at least it would keep that longing from getting so acute it robbed him of much-needed sleep. Sighing, he slipped in beside her and wondered if it was humanly possible for a man to get accustomed to nestling so close to such a tempting bundle of femininity.

Murmuring with pleasure, Leanne snuggled closer to the warmth surrounding her. It took several moments for her sleep-clouded mind to realize that that warmth was a man. Slowly she opened her eyes and looked up into Hunter's moonlit face.

Looking into her wide eyes, Hunter told himself not to do what he was thinking of, but the admonition carried little strength. He had finally gone to sleep, only to wake to Leanne's moving against him in a way that had him instantly taut and alert. The soft noises she was making had his blood running hot. He put his hand on the back of her head to bring her lips closer to his.

"No." Leanne wondered why she could not make her body act out the denial she spoke.

"Sssh. You'll wake the others."

The moment his mouth touched hers, Leanne thought waking the others might have been a good idea. It would have been a little awkward, but she was sure it would have been safer. Lying there in the dark being passionately kissed might be exhilarating, but she knew it was dangerous. The danger was not that Hunter would force her to do something she did not want to do, but that he would be able to make her want to do it.

When his tongue slipped between her lips to stroke the inside of her mouth, she found herself clinging to him instead of pushing him away. It was delicious, intoxicating, and she realized that she lacked the strength to turn away from him. Ever since that first kiss, she had given herself a stern lecture on the liability of getting involved in any way with a man who robbed banks. She realized now that she had not listened to that lecture very well.

She felt him begin to undo her shirt and weakly placed her hand there to try to stop him. He quickly kissed her into ceding her grip on her shirt, and when his hand covered her breast, she gave up. She did not question what she was doing or care about the why. She simply felt.

Hunter felt the change in her. He sensed when the last shred of resistance melted and nearly cheered. The willingness he felt in her erased what little hesitation he had felt. Briefly he wondered if she would blame him after-

ward, if fury would replace her passion. Then he decided
he did not care if it did.

Giving in to the urge that had taken hold of him from
the moment he saw that one small, perfect breast outside Martin's office, Hunter kissed her hardened nipple. Slowly, he drew it into his mouth, sucking gently.
She was as sweet as he had thought she would be. She
arched toward him and her muffled sounds of pleasure in-
flamed him. He quickly undid his shirt and placed her
hand on his chest.

Leanne shivered when she felt his warm, taut skin.
Never in her wildest dreams had she imagined a man
could feel so good. Tentatively, she moved her hands
over his skin. When he trembled beneath her shy touch,
she grew bolder.

A small part of her mind was shocked when she realized she wanted to touch all of him. She ached to discover if the rest of his lean, muscular body felt as good as
his chest.

Just as Hunter reached to unbutton her pants, a deep
voice whispered, "Posse."

The man who had been so tender, so exciting, suddenly tensed in Leanne's arms. "How many, Charlie?"

"Near a dozen. Could be more."

"Those townspeople?"

"Some of them. Some of them aren't."

"It's the ones that aren't that bother me. Hell. It's just
as I feared—word of the robbery is racing us to the border. Rouse everyone. We're getting out of here."

Still reeling from the strong desires he had roused in
her, Leanne suddenly found herself cast aside. She had
no time to recover before she was ordered out of bed and

curtly told to get her boots on. Numbly, she straightened her clothing and did as she was told, only half watching the frantic activity going on around her.

There was no time for the shame nibbling at her to really take hold. She had barely stood up when Hunter was back at her side. He grabbed her hand and dragged her to his horse at a near run.

"Maybe you oughta gag her."

"She won't say anything, Luke."

"I won't?" Leanne suddenly came out of her stupor enough to realize that a chance for rescue could be at hand.

"No, you won't. I figure you're a smart girl."

"Such effusive flattery."

He ignored that interruption. "You'll figure that, if you alert the posse, they'll come in shooting. They'll shoot at all of us—you included, because the world and its mother thinks you're one of us. If you survive the shoot-out, they might feel inclined to listen to your tale and they might even believe it. But you've got enough wit to know the odds of your surviving such a fight are very small."

She met his cool gaze for a full minute while she hurriedly thought over what he had said. To her dismay, there was a lot of truth in his words. Until she could convince someone in authority, she would be viewed as an outlaw along with the rest of the group. She could not count on anyone in the posse having qualms about shooting a woman. Softly, she cursed.

Hunter, pleased that she had the wit to heed his warning, grasped her by the waist and tossed her into the saddle. He mounted behind her. Without a word to the others, he spurred his horse forward.

The fact that the posse was riding when dawn was still a good hour away meant they were hot on the trail and hoped to catch the outlaws by surprise. He intended the surprise to be that the quarry had successfully fled the net. He also intended to be as far away as possible before the posse could pick up the scent again, so he kept his mount at a quick but steady pace. The other men followed close behind.

Chapter Four

Biting Back All The Curses She Felt Inclined To spit out, Leanne cautiously sat down on the ground. They had lost the posse. In a way she was relieved. Unfortunately, that long hard ride had left her aching. She did not believe there was a part of her that did not twitch with pain.

After a few moments of watching the men lounge around, she eased herself along the ground until her back rested against a rock. With a sigh, she closed her eyes. Since the men clearly intended to rest, she would too.

As she began to slip off to sleep, she thought of Hunter—more exactly of what they had been doing before the posse interrupted them. She knew that succumbing to his lovemaking had been a serious error. It was wrong, terribly wrong. What puzzled her was that it felt so good. She did not understand how something she knew was wrong could feel so right.

Hunter stared down at the sleeping woman. He half smiled as he recalled Charlie's comment only moments ago. She did look like a cute little kid. Charlie was also right to wonder how someone who could look so sweet while sleeping could be so tart when awake. The girl was a bundle of contradictions.

He nudged her with his foot. His eyes widened slightly at the curse she sputtered as she kicked out at him. She didn't learn that at any fancy boarding school, he thought and chuckled softly.

"Come on. Wake up." He nudged her again and almost smiled at the cross look she gave him as she sat up rubbing her eyes.

Frowning as she looked around, Leanne asked, "Where is everyone?"

"East, west, north, and south. One each way. They're making sure we really lost that posse."

"Well then, what did you wake me up for?" Her eyes narrowed as she looked at him. "Are you thinking of bolting with the loot?"

"Nope." Taking her by the arm, he gently tugged her to her feet. "We're going to town."

"To town? There's one near?"

"Three miles to the southwest." He watched as she used water from a canteen to dampen his handkerchief, which she had obviously cleaned and usurped for her own use, then wiped her face and neck. "You can stop plotting. It'd be a waste of time to try anything."

That cool voice interrupted the plan for escape she had been formulating and she eyed him crossly. "Why? No law in this town?"

"Oh, there's law—of a sort."

"Martin's sort, huh?"

"Not quite that low. But this man intends to retire alive, so he—well, ignores a lot. Besides, he's a friend of mine."

"I begin to think it's past time someone in authority had a good look at what passes for law out here."

"It's no better or worse than what they have back East." Taking her by the hand, he tugged her along with him as he strode to his horse. "Fact is, I think our lot is far more honest in their dishonesty."

"There's an enlightened observation on human nature."

"Get on the horse."

"I don't suppose I can walk to town."

"Nope," he grasped her by the waist and hefted her up into the saddle, "I don't suppose you can."

"Just what are we going to town for?" she asked as he mounted behind her.

Collecting the reins, he started them on their way. "You need a few things before we go any further. You need a hat, some gloves, and another set of clothes."

"Ah, this place has a town drunk too?"

"And you need your lips sewn together."

Not able to tell by his tone of voice whether or not he was jesting or furious, she decided she would take the safer course and be silent. She had begun to see that she would gain very little by needling him.

As they rode into the small, somewhat ramshackle town she spotted a bathhouse. Only for a moment did she dismiss the idea of using such a place. A hot bath was a luxury she might have few chances of enjoying.

"You know what else I need?"

"What?"

"A bath."

Glancing towards the sign she was staring at, he murmured, "You are getting a little ripe."

"And you, of course, are a proper bouquet of roses."

"A bath would be appreciated."

It was not until they were inside the place that Leanne realized that a moment of private indulgence was not going to be hers. Hunter ignored her hissed complaints as he ordered two tubs of hot water. What privacy he demanded was only to separate the pair of them from whoever else might decide to use the facilities. It was not until they stood by two steaming tubs of water in a blanket-curtained alcove that she was really able to voice her complaint about the arrangement.

"I refuse to take a bath right where you can see me."

"Then I guess that nice hot water will go to waste." He hung his hat on a peg and sat on a rickety chair to tug off his boots.

"I should be allowed some privacy."

"I'll turn my back." He did so even as he started to undo his shirt. "That's all the privacy I can allow, Leanne."

She fumed for only a moment. Although she knew it was probably unwise to trust him, the lure of a hot bath was too strong to resist. She turned her back to him and began to undress.

What really troubled her as she shed her clothes and hastily stepped into the tub was the overwhelming urge she felt to look at him. It was shocking. It was also alarming.

A plump Mexican woman stepped into the alcove, disrupting Leanne's thoughts and causing her to sink down into the water.

"I will take your clothes to freshen them, *sí*?"

"Yeah, thanks, Rita," Hunter replied as he started to soap his foot. "They're in sore need of it."

"*Sí*. Then I come back and help the *niña* with her hair."

"*Niña?*" Leanne muttered as the woman left. "Doesn't that mean baby or something?"

"Child."

"That's not much better. I'm no child."

"Oh, I know that."

"Hunter," she squeaked, "you said you would keep your back turned and not look."

"I'm not looking. Just remembering."

Leanne was certain she was blushing from the roots of her hair to the tips of her toes. She decided not to talk to him. Sitting naked in a tub, with Hunter doing the same not far away, made it difficult to find her usual sharpness of tongue. He would have the advantage if she tried to exchange quips with him now.

When the woman returned to help her wash her hair, Leanne found she was glad of the assistance. Without the tools she was familiar with, washing her hair in the bath suddenly became difficult. The only thing she did not like was the way Rita and Hunter chatted so amiably, Rita often looking toward him. She was glad when the woman left.

Their clothes were fresher, but also a little damp when they finally left the tubs to get dressed. The dampness was not really uncomfortable, since the day was so warm, but it reminded Leanne of something else she needed. If Hunter was going to supply her with some extra clothes, he could also supply her with some underthings.

It was not until she stood patiently in the store while

Hunter plunked an assortment of hats on her head that she got up the courage to say, "There's something else I could use."

"Nothing frivolous. We can only take so much with us. I'm beginning to think your head shrunk in the wash," he muttered.

Ignoring that, she pressed on. "I do not consider this request frivolous."

"Well? What is it then?"

She felt herself blush and mumbled, "Some under-things." When he grinned, she nearly kicked him. "I saw some over there."

Glancing where she pointed, he saw, discreetly tucked away in a corner, all the frilly accoutrements women wore beneath their dresses. She was right. She needed some underclothes. But he was not sure they were the sort that would be useful or, more important, comfortable. As he adjusted the latest hat he had set on her head, deeming its fit as near to perfect as he would get, he mulled over the problem of underthings.

"All right, go find yourself two camisoles, as plain as possible, but no drawers."

"No drawers?" She was too surprised to be embarrassed by discussing intimate attire with the man. "I need those too."

"You do, but those bulky, frilly things women wear won't set right under the pants. I'll get you some boy's drawers." He glanced down at her feet. "And socks."

She sighed as he walked off. Her life had turned into one big scandal since she had seen him in that bank. She was riding over the countryside with five outlaws, sharing a bed with one, not to mention bathing in the same room with him, and traipsing about in male attire. Wearing boy's

drawers was just a minor addition to that name-blackening
list.

When she handed him her two camisoles, delicately
trimmed with lace and embroidery, he said nothing, just
looked at her once before taking them to pay for them.
She knew her desire for those less than sturdy clothes was
foolish. However, she wanted to have at least one dis-
tinctly feminine piece of clothing on. She decided it
would not be wise to look too closely at that desire.

As soon as Hunter had paid for their purchases, they
headed towards the sheriff's office. Evidently, Hunter had
not lied when he had called the man a friend. Leanne
began to wonder if there were any honest lawmen between St. Louis and the Rio Grande.

Hunter gently nudged the foot of the gangly man doz-
ing in a chair before the sheriff's office. "Sleeping again,
Josh?"

"Hunter." The man did not move except to flick his hat
back slightly so he could peer out from beneath the brim.
"Not sure you ought to linger here too long."

"I don't intend to. I just want a short word with Tuckman."

"He's inside."

"Good. Do me a favor, Josh. Watch the young lady."
He jerked a thumb towards Leanne. "Don't let her out of
your sight."

"Sure thing, Hunter."

It took only a minute after Hunter had disappeared into
the sheriff's office for Leanne to decide she did not like
the way the man Josh eyed her. He looked at her as if
he knew something she would prefer he did not. Seeing
the deputy's badge on his vest and recalling how friendly
he was with Hunter, she shook her head in disgust. Her

opinion of the law was reaching a new low. After giving the man a cross look, she began to stroll up and down the boardwalk, hoping Hunter would make his visit a very short one.

Hunter sprawled in the chair facing Sheriff Henry Tuckman and accepted the cigar the older man offered him. He knew this meeting was dangerous for more reasons than he cared to count. Being so close to Texas, and home, increased the temptation to go to his ranch and see his family. Although he felt an urge to linger, he would resist it.

"Things go well?"

"Well enough, Henry."

"You don't sound too sure." Henry scratched the gray stubble on his chin and frowned at the young man he had known for years.

"I'm not. Picked up some extra baggage."

"You said there'd be only one stop. You haven't gone home, have you? We agreed that would be a mistake. Hell, that's why I traveled to this godforsaken place instead of meeting with you in El Paso or even Little Creek itself."

"I know. There was only one stop. That's where I got the extra baggage." Hunter stood up and moved towards the window. "Right out there."

Moving to look, Henry frowned even more. "Where?"

Hunter swore softly. Leanne was nowhere in sight. With Henry close behind, he strode to the door to have a closer look.

Leanne paused to glance at the wanted posters tacked up outside the jail, then stopped short. An instant later, she forced her mouth closed. There was no mistaking the face on the poster, but she stared at it in total disbelief.

Watching her curiously, Hunter called, "Leanne, we'll be leaving in a minute."

Even though a mocking voice in her head told her not to be so silly, Leanne turned to face Hunter and pressed against the wall where the posters were nailed, trying to obscure one particular poster with her head and hat. "Fine. I'm ready."

He stared at her hard for a moment, then disappeared back into the sheriff's office. She wanted to tear the poster down, but Josh was still staring at her. She ached to flee town. If not for Josh she would have done so and let Hunter find his own way back to camp. Leanne prayed that Hunter's minute was more like a second.

"She was acting odd," Hunter murmured as he stubbed his cigar out in the tin plate on the desk.

"Reckon a person can look odd trying to hide her wanted poster, especially when it's probably hung higher than she stands."

"There's a wanted poster on her?"

"Yup. That's what she was standing by."

"Get it down, Henry."

"Can't do that."

"Why the hell not?"

"Did it the first time it was nailed up 'cause I could recognize the description of you, vague though it was. That fellow came back through, nailed up another one. It'd look suspicious if I kept removing them. The wrong person might ask why. Don't think it'd help anyways. The man was tacking those things up far and wide."

"Damn it, Henry, the girl's innocent."

"Then why ain't she at home?"

"The only thing that girl's guilty of is rushing in without thinking."

"That happens to a lot of folk." Henry looked meaningfully at Hunter. "I can't use that excuse for everyone with a price on his head."

"I know, but it's true this time. Who was this fellow nailing up posters?"

"The sheriff of that town—Martin."

"Well, he certainly has found a unique way to punish a woman for resisting rape." Starting towards the door, he added, "See what you can do about that poster. I've already got enough fools on my trail."

"So many you might not finish what you've started?"

"It doesn't look that way yet." He looked for Leanne, only to see her still lurking by her poster. "Leanne, we're leaving."

She hurried over to him and was glad that he did not indulge in any protracted good-byes, simply lifted her onto his horse and mounted behind her. All she wanted to do was get away from that black and white proof that she was branded a criminal. It made her feel sick. It certainly made her feel terrified. Now there really was no chance that anyone would stop to ask questions. They would simply grab her or shoot her. She was as good as hanged, she thought morosely as they started on their way.

Henry Tuckman watched Hunter ride off. The girl had looked very young, very pale, and very scared. Shaking his head and wondering if he was just an old fool, he walked to the poster and ripped it down. He really could not afford to have too many people tracking Hunter.

Hunter frowned at the top of Leanne's head. He was worried about her, he reluctantly admitted to himself. She looked pale and he was sure he felt her trembling slightly.

The most worrisome thing was how quiet she had gone. Though she was not an annoying chatterbox, she was not usually given to such long silences. He felt sure that that wanted poster was at the root of what troubled her and decided the best thing to do was to get the subject out in the open.

"I know about the wanted poster, Leanne."

Startled out of her brooding, she glanced at him. "But you didn't see it."

"The sheriff told me."

"I expected to see one for you or one of the other men, but not for myself."

"You're the one they could all recognize. Probably even had some photograph to aid the artist."

"And of course Sheriff Martin could never admit to knowing what you looked like."

"Nope."

"Who's offering five hundred dollars? Why put such a big price on me? I've never done a thing wrong."

"Feelings can run high when people think one of their own has turned against them."

She sighed and fell silent again. It hurt that the people she had known all her life could believe she would steal their money.

Later, as she sat watching Hunter make up a fire she began to think about the money, the five hundred dollars offered so boldly beneath her picture. It was a lot of money. A man could get a good start with money like that. She would be hunted now, perhaps hunted more avidly than any of the others.

In fact, she mused, it was no longer safe for Hunter to drag her along. As far as she could see, the tables had turned. It was now more to her benefit to stay with the outlaws. They not only knew the country and how to avoid the law, but they were five guns that she might well need to hide behind.

She sighed. It might be to her benefit to remain with the group, but she could not in good conscience endanger the others. Tom and Luke could go to hell in a handbasket as far as she was concerned. But she would hate to see Hunter shot. Or Charlie and Jed for that matter. They were sweet, if somewhat dull-witted—not true desperadoes. In truth, she desperately wished she could turn them onto the straight and narrow before they paid too dearly for tagging along on criminal ventures. But she would have to leave before she could help them.

Hearing yet another soft sigh, Hunter sat down by the fire and looked at Leanne. "If you're going to keep doing that, come sit closer to the fire. It could do with some stoking up."

"How droll." Leanne started to sigh again, then swallowed it. "I think it's time I rode out on my own."

"You do, do you." He proceeded to roll a cigarette.

"I may have gone to school back East, but I am hardly a stranger to this area."

"Which means?"

"Which means I fully understand what that wanted poster means. It's as good as a noose around my neck."

"Not everyone with a price on his head ends up dead."

"Of course not. I suspect five or six out of a hundred are kept alive long enough to die on the gallows."

He winced. There was some truth to her words. Even if the poster did not say dead or alive, it would be read that way. It was easier to bring in a corpse than a reluctant criminal. The men who collected bounty money always preferred the easier way. However, he wasn't about to agree with her. His intention was to soothe her, not upset her even more.

"I doubt the prospects are that dismal. You're not wanted for murder, just bank robbery."

"All that'll matter to anyone hunting me is that I'm worth five hundred dollars. The point is, there will be men hunting me."

"There are men hunting us now."

"Not paid killers. I think it'd be wise if I rode out on my own. Then at least you won't have to tangle with bounty hunters."

"Worried about my safety?"

"Not in the least." She wondered crossly why when she was offering to rid him of a problem he was being so stubborn. "Up until today it wasn't my fault that people were after you. Now it is."

"We're described on that poster too."

"Vaguely. But your being with me tells anyone who's seen that poster that you're one of the wanted men."

"And just where would you go?"

"I have a friend who would help me. O'Malley has known my family forever. I spent part of every summer with him and his boys at their hunting cabin."

"Where?"

"Up there." She pointed towards the San Juan Mountains which loomed against the horizon.

"And of course the bounty hunters won't follow you into the mountains."

Leanne felt her heart sink. Even the mountains would not be safe. In fact, bounty hunters were probably used to chasing criminals into the hills. She would arrive at O'Malley's door trailing a pack of trouble that could easily get her friend killed.

"He might be able to get me to someone who would listen to my story," she mused aloud.

"Which is just what I don't want."

She suppressed a sudden urge to scream in frustration. If she stayed, she put them all in danger, but if she left she would put O'Malley in danger.

Hunter noticed how the color had returned to her cheeks, how that frightened, cornered look had eased. She was looking more normal, as if she wanted to hit him with some very solid object. He might not have soothed her, but at least he had put the spirit back into her and he was satisfied.

"I'll just get us something to cook up for dinner," he murmured and abruptly walked away.

Leanne was only a little calmer when he returned with a brace of prairie chickens. She was tempted to tell him to cook his own meal, but then recalled the dismal culinary talents of the outlaws. By the time the others returned, she was finished with the preparations for what she confidently felt would be a fine meal. Her pride in her accomplishment was forgotten as she saw what an agitated Charlie held as he approached her and Hunter.

"Look, Hunter. They're asking five hundred for her." After thrusting the poster into Hunter's hands, Charlie squatted by the fire and helped himself to some coffee.

"Five hundred." Luke's rough voice rose in a near whoop of joy as he too helped himself to some coffee. "And we wouldn't have to hand that over to Watkins."

"You can't turn her in," Jed protested.

"Why the hell not?"

"Who are you going to turn her in to, Luke?" asked Hunter. "The sheriff? He'll grab you too."

"Yeah," Charlie agreed. "They describe you too."

"Ain't a very good description," Luke muttered. "Fine then. We'll just leave her behind."

"You can't just desert her." Charlie looked deeply shocked.

"And what's wrong with that idea? She's been nothing but trouble. Now she's going to bring the bounty hunters after us."

"And she can do that even better," Hunter pointed out, "if she's left behind to give a clearer description of us."

Luke caressed the handle of his Colt. "Then let's shoot her. That way she can't talk when we turn her in, and we can take the money and run."

Tom looked up from helping himself to some food, his dark gaze cool as he looked over the group. "I won't turn bounty hunter."

That silenced Luke, but not for long. He repeated his suggestion about leaving her behind. It took Hunter quite a while to end the dispute.

By the time Leanne sought her bed, she had a pounding headache. Fear knotted her insides. Luke was more of a danger to her than any bounty hunter. She began to wonder how long Hunter could keep the man in check, or even how long he would want to bother.

Curling up beneath the blanket, she wrapped her arms around herself, closed her eyes, and prayed for sleep. It was the only time she was free of her fears. It was also the only time she was free of the increasing temptation Hunter presented, although her dreams reminded her of it in a rather scandalous manner.

Sleep was still stubbornly eluding her when Hunter slipped in beside her. She tensed when he wrapped his arm around her waist and tugged her close to him. The way he nuzzled her hair sent shivers through her.

"I'm trying to go to sleep." A telltale huskiness entered her voice as he nibbled her earlobe, and she silently cursed it.

"Of course you are."

"I am."

"You seem to be having a little difficulty." He could sense her fighting to maintain her tense resistance to him.

She resisted the urge to snuggle against him as he smoothed his hand down her side. It was so easy for him to shake her resolve, she thought with self-disgust. He probably knew it too, she supposed. She had always been so good at hiding her feelings before.

"That could be because I have a few little things on my mind, such as a five hundred dollar price on my head, the knowledge that every bounty hunter in the area is probably oiling his gun this very minute, and the distressing feeling that I have presented Luke with a terrible quandary—should he turn me in for the reward or just shoot me."

Gently, he turned her onto her back. He found himself heartily wishing he could ease the fear she felt. She was too smart to swallow any lies, however, and it would require lies to make her believe she had nothing to fear.

"You're going to fret yourself into an early grave, Leanne Summers."

Before she could reply, he was kissing her. She succumbed helplessly to the heated intoxication of his lips. It was only when she reminded herself that this man was an outlaw that she found the strength to push him away. She noted a little groggily that he only allowed the distance between them to be a very small one.

"Stop that," she ordered.

"You don't really want me to stop, Leanne."

She wanted to deny his words, and to her dismay, she

heard herself speak with far more truthfulness than she wished. "That may be so, but it's far from wise. I intend to continue to struggle for some common sense."

"Do you now." He slid his hand along her side to her breast.

Leanne gasped softly as his hand covered her breast, his thumb moving back and forth over the tip. How could she fight him when he took unfair advantage like that? He undid her shirt and she couldn't stop him. When his warm, soft lips enclosed the nipple he had taunted to aching hardness, she moaned, burrowing her fingers in his thick hair.

For a while she sank beneath the surging tide of her own passions. The feel of his calloused hands and warm lips against her skin robbed her of all coherent thought. It was not until she felt him undo her trousers that she began to come out of her stupor. He eased his hand beneath her waistband and between her legs. The shock of such an intimate touch brought her back to reality. With an unsteady hand, she grabbed him by the wrist.

Hunter looked up at her as he let her tug his hand away from the sweet warmth he had been so thoroughly enjoying. "You are very slow to say no."

"Maybe, but no it is."

"Didn't feel like no to me."

She blushed. "My common sense has returned."

"Wonderful."

When he moved away, she quickly redid her loosened clothing. "Some day I might extricate myself from this mess and return to the lawful world, or what passes for it," she muttered. "Consorting with a bank robber will hardly redeem me to society."

"And, of course, people will never think that, after

weeks of riding with five outlaws, you never consorted with any of them—willingly or otherwise."

The truth of that struck home with such force that she nearly gasped. People generally did think the worst. It was one of the more appalling aspects of human nature that she had discovered. One thing they had stressed at her school was how dangerous it was to be alone with a man, how quickly and completely it could blacken a woman's name, whether she had erred or not.

Turning on her side with her back to him, she tried to deny the truth of his cool pronouncement. It was impossible. She had been condemned the moment she had ridden off with him.

"I'll simply tell them the truth," she said, thinking out loud.

He rolled his eyes and wondered if the girl was truly that naive. "The way you did when they accused you of being part of the robbery?"

"Oh, shut up." She closed her eyes and prayed she would fall asleep before she gave in to the urge to throttle him.

Chapter Five

IT WAS GETTING WORSE, LEANNE THOUGHT DISPIRITEDLY AS she aimlessly poked at the ashes of the campfire. Last night she had barely grasped sanity in time to halt Hunter's lovemaking. One more minute and it would have been too late to turn back.

She ached to say yes. Common sense, however, told her to say a resounding no. If she gave herself to a man, it should be out of love, not lust. There should also be at least the promise of some future together. Hunter could not offer any even if he wanted to.

There was no choice left. She had to get away from the man. Her no was too weak to last all the way to Mexico. She did not even feel confident it would last one more night.

Gazing at the mountains, she sighed. They looked very far away, very forbidding, but O'Malley was up there. If she could reach him, he would help her clear her name. And if any bounty hunters found her there before she was declared innocent, she could simply give herself up, thereby lessening the risk to O'Malley.

Glancing toward Jed and Charlie, she grimaced. She was going to feel bad about taking advantage of their trust and thickheadedness, but she would do it. Despite Hunter's orders that she not be left with only those two for guards, Tom and Luke had disappeared again. However, they could well return at any time, as could Hunter, so she had to move quickly.

Keeping a close watch on Jed and Charlie, she stuffed some supplies and a canteen into a clean blanket, then bundled it up. It was not much, but she did not dare take more. A large bundle would be noticeable even to her lackadaisical guards. Clutching the blanket, she started towards the creek.

"Where're you going?"

"To have a bath, Charles." She did not hesitate in her advance towards the creek.

"Now, I ain't sure you oughta be doing that. We're supposed to keep an eye on you."

She paused to give him a haughty look. "You are not watching me take a bath."

Charlie blushed, as did Jed, and mumbled, "No, course we ain't. But Hunter said . . ."

"Aw, let her go, Charlie. Hell, where can she run to?"

"I reckon. Just don't take too long or I might have to come looking for you."

The fact that Charlie's face was bright red with embarrassment beneath his brown, scraggly beard made her confident the threat was an empty one. Nevertheless, she moved quickly. As soon as she was out of their sight she put the blanket down and packed what little she had more securely and conveniently. She heartily wished she could have stolen one of the horses, but there was no way she could do that without Charlie and Jed seeing her. Hefting her makeshift pack over her shoulder she started towards the mountains at an easy jog, hoping to cover as much distance as possible before her absence was noted.

There was a reluctance within her that she tried hard to fight. Part of her did not really want to leave Hunter, not even to save herself from an obviously ill-fated love affair. She told herself not to be an idiot and kept on moving, but it was not advice she took very easily.

Another thing weighting her steps was the knowledge that the land she must traverse to get to O'Malley was not exactly hospitable. There were snakes—both the kind that walked and the kind that crawled. There were also Indians.

Hunter frowned as he dismounted and looked around the campsite. Charlie and Jed were idly playing cards. Luke and Tom were starting up a campfire. It all looked peaceful, but Leanne was nowhere to be seen. Not pausing to see to his mount, he strode towards Jed and Charlie.

"Where's Leanne?"

"She went to take a bath."

"When, Charlie?"

Charlie looked at Jed, his face revealing his growing consternation. "Do you recall, Jed?"

"Nope. Can't say I do."

Swearing viciously, Hunter raced to the creek. He was not surprised to find no one there. Just to be certain, he looked around very carefully, but there was no sign she had even gone near the creek. As he headed back to camp, he searched for signs of her trail. He found footprints in the soft earth just out of sight of camp. The trail led straight for the mountains. Cursing her foolishness as well as the dimwittedness of Charlie and Jed, he raced back to camp. It would be dark soon. That left him little time to find her.

"She gone?" Charlie asked as he and Jed hurried over to where Hunter was mounting his horse.

"Yeah, she's gone."

"Good riddance, I say."

"No one asked for your opinion, Luke."

"That girl's been trouble since she stumbled into the bank, Hunter, and you know it."

"Leaving her out there looking for someone to talk to won't make her any less trouble."

"The reason she prob'ly bolted is 'cause you keep threatening to shoot her," Charlie growled as he and Jed hurried to saddle their horses. "We'll help you look for the kid, Hunter. She shouldn't oughta be out there alone, on foot. Could get hurt."

For just a moment Hunter mused angrily that an injury or two might knock some sense into the girl. It was a thought that passed quickly. There were too many dangers she could run into, the sort that got a person killed. The mere thought of such a thing happening to Leanne tied his stomach into knots and he cursed her even as he started out to look for her.

He did not want to feel this way. Not about her. Not about anyone. And especially not now. He was already neck deep in trouble and in dangerous intrigue; to get emotionally entangled with a woman would be all he needed to submerge him.

There was also the fact that he did not like feeling as he did. He disliked worrying about where she was and what might be happening to her. Only once had he let a woman touch his emotions. He thought he'd learned his lesson but, clearly, he hadn't learned it well enough.

"Don't worry, Hunter. She ain't been gone all that long. Couldn't've gotten into that much trouble."

"I'm not worried, Charlie," Hunter lied, "just furious. I'm going to strangle her when we find her."

Leanne used Hunter's handkerchief to wipe the sweat from her face. She had to slow her pace or collapse. All she could do was hope she had covered enough ground to make a search for her more trouble than it was worth.

Stuffing the handkerchief back into her pants pocket, she continued on her way. She mentally argued the wisdom of finding a place to camp for the night. Afraid someone might be following, she wanted to keep moving as long as her body could endure. However, traveling at night was dangerous in and of itself.

A deep cry dragged her from her inner debate. She looked up from the rough ground she had been watching so carefully and cursed. So involved had she been in deciding whether to rest or not, she had come within yards of a small group of Indians. They looked as surprised to see her as she was to see them. She doubted, however, that they felt the depth of fear and dismay that she did:

A voice in her head screamed for her to run, but her feet seemed rooted to the ground. As she struggled to break shock's immobilizing grip, she noticed two things about the six nearly naked men before her. They were not moving too fast or too gracefully. And, judging by the bottle one held, they had been drinking. When one made a lewd gesture, she finally found the strength and wit to move.

Even as she urged her weary body into a run, she heard the Indians move to give chase. They seemed to be having some difficulty, but she did not slow her pace. They might be drunk, but they had horses and she did not.

She suddenly realized that she was running straight back to the outlaw camp and Hunter. Heading for the foothills of the mountains would have been wiser. There was cover in that direction, places to hide. Now all she could do was run and pray that the Indians were too drunk to get their horses under control. The sound of hoofbeats behind her told her it was already too late for that prayer to be answered.

For a moment the shouts and whoops of her pursuers added to her terror. Then she grew angry. They saw this chase as some sort of game. She was running for her very life, and they found it amusing. She began to pray that Hunter was out looking for her, that he would soon appear, and that he would shoot every one of the drunken lechers chasing her.

"Hey, hear that, Hunter?"

"I do, Charlie, and I have the feeling I know who's smack in the middle of that ruckus."

Even as he spoke, he spurred his horse to a gallop. He recognized Leanne the moment her slight, running figure came into view. Even though the sounds he heard had warned him, the sight of the half-dozen Indians chasing her caused his heart to skip a beat. Bending low over his horse's neck, he urged his mount to its greatest speed.

As he drew closer, his fear for her eased slightly. The Indians were not gaining on her as swiftly as they should have been. They seemed to be doing an extremely poor job of riding her down. He doubted he had ever seen Indians handle their mounts with such a lack of skill. The nearer he got, the surer he was that the Indians were not incompetent, they were just drunk.

"Fire a few shots over their heads, Charlie."

"Over their heads?"

"Yep. I want to try and chase them off if I can. They're drunk."

When Charlie and Jed obeyed his order, the results almost made Hunter laugh. Frightened by the sounds of gunfire, each horse went its own way. The six Indians went in six different directions as they struggled to gain control of their startled mounts. One fell off, staggered to his feet, and awkwardly ran after his horse.

Halting next to Leanne, who stood panting, watching her inept attackers try to regroup, Hunter grabbed her by the arm. Without a word, he yanked her up behind him. As soon as she had wrapped her arms around his waist, he headed back to camp at a gallop, Charlie and Jed quickly falling in behind him.

When they returned to camp, he decided they should move to a more defendable position. He could not be sure just how drunk the Indians had been, nor how quickly they would sober up. Sober and suffering from the effects of drinking too much, they might decide to put right their shameful routing and reclaim the prize they had lost.

"Don't see why we're running from a half-dozen Injuns," Luke complained, even as he joined the others in breaking camp.

"That half-dozen could become a lot more." Hunter kicked out the fire with more vigor than necessary.

"What the hell was she doing out there anyways?"

"She clearly has a desire to be rid of our charming company." Hunter barely glanced at Leanne as he tied his bedroll on the back of his mount.

"Well, if you'd let me shoot her—"

"Shut up, Luke."

"I—" Leanne began in her own defense but she fell silent when Hunter's furious gaze rested on her.

"It would be very wise if you kept that pretty mouth shut for a while," he said, his voice hard and cold.

Leanne sat still and quiet on Hunter's horse as the men finished packing up. When Hunter remounted, she cautiously put her arms around him and sighed. He was furious. She could feel it in every taut inch of his frame. He tensed his body away from hers as they rode, but when she finally let go, he grabbed her wrists and yanked her back.

"I don't know what you're so testy about," she snapped.

"Don't you?"

"I can only assume it's because I tried to escape."

"What a clever girl."

"I had every right to."

"Another vain attempt to clear your name?"

"It could work."

"And you could end up earning someone five hundred dollars."

She pressed her lips together, forcing herself to shut up. She didn't want to reveal what had really sent her running for the hills. She did not want him to know how close he was to succeeding in his seduction.

By the time they reached a suitable camping place, it was dark. Hunter was treating Leanne like an extra saddle-bag, and she was on the point of tears. She sat down by a large rock to stare blindly at the men as they saw to the horses and set up camp.

A soft noise finally broke into her dark, confused thoughts. It was the sound of water. She realized they had stayed close to the creek. Suddenly all she could think of was having a bath. She did not think there was an inch of her that was not sweat-streaked and dusty. She grabbed her spare clothes, still tied up in the blanket, and started towards the creek. A hand on her arm put an abrupt stop to her movements.

"Where do you think you're going?" Hunter was not sure she had gained the sense to know how dangerous it was to go off on her own.

"To have a bath."

"That's what you told Charlie and Jed before you crept off."

"I did not creep off. I ran."

"Fine. I'm not giving you the chance to run again."

"I don't intend to try it again."

"And I'm just supposed to take your word for that, am I?"

"Mr. Hunter, I may be prone to acting on impulse, but I am not totally lacking in wit. I can read the signs that tell me my impulse was an unwise one. Read them and learn from them. Six drunken Indians making lewd gestures and chasing me on horseback was a very clear sign which I had no trouble understanding."

He stared at her for one long moment, then nodded. It

might prove a mistake, but he honestly believed her. She was certainly not stupid. He was not sure, however, that a bath was such a good idea.

"It's not safe to swim in the dark."

"That fat, full moon provides enough light for my needs. I have done a lot of running over dry, dusty ground. I have to at least rinse that dust off."

"Don't take too long." He released her arm.

Hurrying away, she knew she would have a very quick bath. Hunter had not said he would come looking for her if she took too long. But the threat was there. She also knew that, unlike Charlie, Hunter would fulfill that threat.

Once she reached the water's edge, she hastily stripped off her clothes. She took only a moment to rinse the dust out of them before grabbing her soap and plunging into the water. The first shock of the cool water wore off quickly, leaving only the pleasure of getting clean. She was soon caught up in that chore, determined to remove every grain of dirt.

Hunter helped himself to a cup of the coffee Jed had brewed. His first thought was that he should have made Leanne brew it. Jed's was only barely drinkable.

He fought the urge to go after Leanne. Those feelings she could rouse in him would only be strengthened if he gave in to the desire he had for her. It would be best to avoid her completely.

It all made good sense, but he had very little sense when it came to the lithe, tempting Leanne. He stood up. Luke made a lewd remark as Hunter started towards the creek, but Tom hushed the man.

The moment he reached the water's edge and saw her,

he knew there was nothing that could turn him from her, from what he wanted of her. She stood waist deep in the slow-moving water, her wet blond hair snaking over her body. He tossed his hat on the ground and began to undo his gunbelt.

Leanne decided she had lingered long enough and turned to leave the water. When she saw Hunter standing there she felt her face heat with a blush, crossed her arms over her breasts, and sank down into the water. She then realized that he was wearing only his trousers, and he was unbuttoning those.

"What are you doing?" She was dismayed to hear that her voice was an octave higher than it should be.

"I'm going to take a bath."

"You can't do that." She tried, and failed, not to look as he started to remove his drawers.

"Can't I?"

With eyes growing ever wider, she watched him discard his drawers. She had not expected him to look so good, all lean, supple muscle. The sight of him, naked and aroused, did not stir fear or shock as she thought it ought to. It stirred lust, want, an aching desire for him that she knew would not be quelled by good sense—not this time.

When he stepped into the water, she bolted. One strong brown arm was quickly wrapped around her waist. She cried out as he turned her in his arms and yanked her body against his. The feel of their flesh touching pushed aside all coherent thought. It was all she could do to bite back a soft moan of enjoyment as he slowly pulled her up his body until they were face to face. Her feet were off the creek bed, so she put her arms around his neck.

"Just where did you think you were going all wet and buck nekked?" Hunter was not surprised to hear the thick huskiness of his voice. The feel of her lithe, naked frame against his body had him reeling with hunger for her.

"Away from you," she answered with an honesty born of desperation.

"Are you afraid of me, Leanne?" He slid his hands down her back to cup her slim, taut backside and press her closer.

"No. Yes." She trembled, the heat of desire flooding her.

"I don't intend to hurt you," he murmured against her skin as he smoothed kisses over her throat.

She gave a nervous laugh. He had no idea what he could do to her. Leanne supposed that was for the best, but a part of her wanted to tell him, wanted him to know he could tear her heart to pieces. The realization was too new, too startling, and too personal to share with a man whose only feeling for her seemed to be lust.

"I won't hurt you. You must know that by now."

Not physically, she thought but knew that answer would give too much away. "Dragging me to God knows where and making me your whore is hardly harmless."

"Why is it a woman always thinks a man's trying to make her a whore just because he wants to make love to her?" As he spoke, he moved her against his hard body and knew by her quickened breathing that she felt the proof of his desire. "Tell me you don't want me, Leanne. Tell me and I'll walk away right now." He placed his mouth against hers. "Tell me," he whispered.

Leanne wanted to. She tried desperately to find the strength of will to utter the words. But the way his hands felt on her backside and thighs, the way he moved her body against his in a pantomime of what they both craved, the way his mouth teased hers, robbed her of that strength. She wanted him, wanted him so badly that even the cold water they stood in did little to cool the heat in her body. Saying no was the last thing she could do.

"Damn you," she whispered.

He laughed softly, a mixture of triumph and amusement. "Just don't curse me afterwards. Remember, I gave you a chance."

"Some chance," she muttered, but his hungry kiss ended any further remarks she might make on the tactics he'd used to gain what he wanted.

Holding her close, he walked out of the water. Unwilling to release her, he kicked the blanket open and nudged her things out of the way with his feet. Kneeling, he then laid her down and slowly lowered his body onto hers. She accepted him in her arms with no sign of reluctance.

"So sweet," he murmured against her skin as he kissed the hollow in her throat. He cupped her breasts in his hands, his thumbs brushing over the hardened tips, and she arched towards him slightly. "That's it, honey. Let it free. Hold nothing back."

When he laved the tips of her breasts with his tongue, she thought dazedly that she could hold nothing back even if she wanted to. She moved her hands over his lean frame, at first shyly then, encouraged by his appreciative murmurs, more boldly. He felt so good to her. She remembered all too well how good it felt to touch him.

She cried out with hoarse delight when he drew the aching tip of one breast deep into his mouth, sucking gently. Each slow, hungry draw increased the cramping need centered low in her belly. She buried her fingers deep in his thick hair to hold him closer as she arched towards him, urging him to continue.

When he slid his hand up from caressing her inner thighs to the soft curls that lay between them, she tensed. But his soft, husky voice soothed her brief shock even as the intimate caress sent her hurtling back into the blind depths of passion. So enflamed was she by his stroking, she felt nothing but eagerness when he began to join their bodies, easing into her with a slow, rocking motion. Even the short, sharp pain that came when he finally ended her innocence did little to quench the fire of need raging through her.

At first he moved slowly, kissing her deeply, his tongue imitating the thrusts of his body. She clung tightly to him, soon matching his rhythm. When he grew fiercer in his movements, she was more than ready to meet his intensity. She felt driven. As her release seared through her, tumbling her into its blinding maelstrom of total feeling, she realized what she had been seeking. She called out his name as she clung to him, trying to pull him deeper inside her, and was rewarded by the sound of her name bursting from his mouth in a hoarse cry of joy.

Hunter eased himself free of her lax hold when he was finally able to catch his breath. He dampened his neckerchief in the creek, cleaned himself off, then rinsed it out. Returning to her side, he found Leanne blushing deeply and trying to cover her nakedness with the tangled blanket. He hoped recriminations would not follow. Gently but firmly, he tugged the blanket away and cleaned her off, ignoring her deepening blush.

Tossing aside his neckerchief, he quickly lay down beside her and took her tense body into his arms. Never before had he experienced such a rich passion. It was both exhilarating and frightening.

"You can't retreat now, Leanne," he murmured as he gently dragged his fingers through her thick, drying hair.

"I didn't realize I was." Held close to him, she felt her embarrassment begin to ease.

"It looked like you might be thinking of it."

"That look was embarrassment. I'm not accustomed to being naked in front of a man."

Pressing his face against her neck, he smiled briefly. Her total innocence had been a heady surprise. He had suspected that she was a virgin, but the strength of her passion had sometimes stirred doubts. Now he realized that desire had gripped her as strongly as it had gripped him. She had wanted him enough to give up her virginity. Just thinking of that stirred his hunger for her.

"Regrets?"

"Only an idiot would have none. I can never go back," she whispered, suddenly realizing the finality of the step she had just taken and a little frightened by it.

"Would you want to?"

"What do you think?"

"I don't know. A woman does her damnedest to cling to her virginity. A man does his damnedest to lose it—fast."

"Men arranged that, I am certain."

He laughed softly, glad to hear the bite in her words, for it meant she was back to her normal, tart self. "Could be. A man likes being the first." He trailed his hand down her spine, then idly caressed her backside. "If nothing else, it means he'll be remembered."

Leanne knew she would never forget Hunter. The fact that he was her first lover had little to do with it, but she had no intention of admitting that. "It does, does it? Do you remember your first?"

Frowning slightly, he tried to bring the familiar memory forward, but holding her, the memory was not as clear as usual. "More or less."

"Mostly less."

"No. It's pretty clear. It was a dozen years ago, when I was just sixteen. I remember the time and place and being scared."

"Scared? Of what?"

"Of doing it wrong or, worse, not being able to do it at all."

"Well, at least you had some knowledge to work with. Women are told nothing at all."

"Except how to say no in more ways than can be counted."

"And, clearly, that lesson isn't always remembered."

Cupping her chin in his hand, he tilted her face toward his and gave her a slow, gentle kiss. "I'm glad of that."

"You would be. It means you got what you wanted."

Nibbling on her earlobe, he murmured, "And I wanted it bad."

"I did notice that." She smiled as she smoothed her hand over his chest, finding that, although it was not what she desperately needed to hear him say, she was flattered and thrilled to know she could stir his passion so.

"Do you still notice it?" he drawled as he pressed her closer to him.

She was surprised to feel his arousal so soon after their lovemaking. Her own growing desire, despite the slight twinge caused by her introduction to passion, she attributed to her love for him. She had not expected him to feel the same greed.

"Again? So soon?"

Rolling onto his back and settling her on top of him, he kissed her nose, smiling at her surprise. He was surprised himself. His sexual appetite had always been a moderate one, only occasionally driving him to buy a little relief. She stirred a deep craving within him. It was exhilarating, making him feel almost lightheaded. There was something about what he felt for her that was joyous, smile-inducing. He thought wryly that laughter was not something he had ever associated with desire.

"Why are you grinning at me?" She smiled faintly as she brushed his tussled hair from his forehead.

"You, sweet Leanne, make me feel young again."

"At eight-and-twenty you are hardly ancient."

"I was referring to the heady greed of youth."

"Greed?"

"Greed for lovemaking. Insatiable. That's how I feel. Are you sore?" he asked in a soft voice.

"Well, not really. And"—she daringly brushed her mouth over his—"I will admit to a touch of greed myself."

"Only a touch, huh?"

"Well, maybe more than a touch."

"That's good."

"Why?"

"Because, little one," he growled as he tangled his fingers in her hair and pressed her mouth to his, "you will soon see that I am a very greedy man indeed."

Chapter Six

SHIFTING SLIGHTLY IN THE SADDLE, LEANNE TRIED TO ease the growing ache in her backside. Having her own mount was nice, despite her strong suspicion that it was stolen, but she wished she had Hunter to lean on now. They were spending long hours in the saddle. Mexico was near and all five men seemed anxious to reach the border.

Glancing at Hunter, she almost smiled as the sight of him caused a familiar ripple of delight low in her abdomen. He had not lied or exaggerated when he had said he was a greedy man. The fact that they were on the run and had four other men with them had not deterred him, although it had caused him to be very innovative at times to provide some privacy. She had no complaints. In truth, she was positively happy, and if that was not playing the fool she did not know what was.

There was one shadow on her horizon. She glanced towards Luke and shivered when he smiled at her. There was pure lust in his look. It was there all the time now. She quickly looked away, then felt her skin crawl when he rode so close to her that his leg brushed hers. He had found far too many excuses lately to brush against her.

"We'll be in Mexico soon," he said, his gaze fixed upon her breasts.

"How nice." She tried to ride ahead of him, but he kept pace with her.

"Now if old Hunter finds better things to do and you get to feeling a mite lonely, you just call on old Luke."

He smacked his lips in a lewd, suggestive manner and she cringed. She ought to tell Hunter about Luke's constant harassment but she was afraid of stirring up trouble. Unfortunately, ignoring the man did not work. She was at a loss as to what to do next.

The sound of a shot cracking the still, hot air startled her out of her thoughts. It also startled her mount. She barely got the mare under control in time to respond to Hunter's curt order to ride for the cover of some rocks. She reined in by the scattered boulders, and Hunter yanked her from the saddle and pushed her down behind them, his own body providing some of her cover.

"A posse?" she gasped.

"Bounty hunter, I reckon."

"Only one? What can he do against five of you?"

"Pick us off one by one or get us to hand you over."

"So why don't we hand her over?" Luke growled. "We can be in Mexico before she opens her big mouth."

Before Hunter could respond, Tom murmured, his voice as flat and chilly as ever, "Shut up, Luke, and try to spot this bastard."

"You'd rather lie here and get picked off one by one than hand the skinny bitch over? She ain't doing us no damn good."

"I'm not dealing with any bounty hunter," Tom said firmly.

"He's in that small ravine just to the left," Charlie whispered.

At that instant a shot came from their left. It skimmed over the rock Leanne and Hunter were hiding behind. Leanne winced as chips of rock stung her cheek. As she rubbed her cheek she noticed that Hunter and Tom glanced only briefly in that direction. The other three whirled, guns at the ready and mouths agape.

"We're surrounded." Luke glared at Leanne.

"Hearing shots from two sides doesn't mean we're surrounded," Hunter said.

"Maybe all of them just ain't showed themselves yet. They could even be behind us." Luke turned to peer intently in that direction.

"If there was anyone behind us, you wouldn't be alive now to worry on it."

"I reckon he's in that scrub over there," Charlie announced.

Straining to look that way, Leanne frowned. "How can he see that far?"

"Don't know," replied Hunter as he rechecked his guns. "Just has a knack."

"Send out the woman and the rest of you can ride off," bellowed the man in front of them.

"Good idea," muttered Luke.

"Shut up, Luke." Tom quickly checked his gun, then started to move away. "I'll get that one in the scrub."

"Can he get over there without being seen?" Leanne whispered.

Hunter, unsure of that himself, kept an eye on Tom only to see the man suddenly disappear from sight. "Reckon he can."

"Hand the woman over, cowboys, and we'll let you ride off."

"And then you'll shoot us in the back," Hunter answered. "No deal."

"I give you my word, I'll let you men go."

"Your word ain't worth spit, bounty hunter," Luke yelled, then fired, shooting somewhat blindly in the direction of the small ravine Charlie had pinpointed.

"Don't waste your bullets, Luke," Hunter advised. "You can't hit him."

"So let's ride for Mexico."

"With him at our backs? No thanks."

"Fine. Then just what're we going to do, smart boy? Wait him out? I've got no stomach for that."

"We wait to see if Tom accomplishes what he set out to do." Hunter wished there was some alternative, because he did not like the idea of killing a man, not even a bounty hunter.

"If anybody can do it, Tom can," murmured Charlie, and Jed nodded.

"And you think that'll be enough?"

"Yeah, I do, Luke. That man in front of us isn't going to take on all of us once he knows he's alone."

Luke apparently saw the sense of that, for Leanne saw him relax a little, although his gaze remained malevolent. She lay half beneath Hunter and heartily wished she were elsewhere. This was a part of outlawry she could not condone. Tom was going to kill a man, and all four outlaws accepted that calmly. No one had been killed yet, not even seriously wounded. Flight had been the main strategy of the outlaws. Now she was forcefully recalled to a fact she had blithely ignored. Outlawry was a violent business. Worse, the violence was often done, by necessity, against those working for the law.

This was how it would be if she tried to make a future with Hunter. This was the future that stretched out before him. The only way around it was if he turned himself in and served his time in jail. Leanne doubted she could stir the sort of emotion in him that would prompt him to make that sacrifice. For a moment her fear was pushed aside by sadness.

A burst of gunfire broke in on her thoughts. For a while, the man to their left shot at them as well. Then, abruptly, the firing from their left stopped. Amoment later the man in front of them halted his firing too. Leanne caught a brief glimpse of a hat just as Luke neatly shot it off, causing the bounty hunter to disappear into the shallow ravine again.

"Dooley?" the man in front bellowed. "Dooley!"

"Dooley ain't able to answer."

Leanne shivered as Tom's cool voice cut through the sudden stillness. She felt Hunter heave a sigh, but the soft sound held no relief. Hunter clearly regretted the need to kill anyone. She realized the tactic of retreat was his. She felt comforted by that thought.

"He did it," she whispered and, although she had no love of bounty hunters, felt sickened.

"Yeah, he did. The man has talents I didn't suspect." Hunter could not help wondering why a man with such skills was trailing along with them, working for another and not for himself.

"You sonuvabitch, what've you done to Dooley?" screamed the bounty hunter.

"I'd start worrying about myself if I was you," Tom drawled, his voice raised only enough to carry the distance.

The bounty hunter did not take long to heed that advice. It was less than a minute before Leanne caught a glimpse of the man as he scrambled out of his hiding place and ran. Luke tried to shoot him down despite Hunter's hissed order to hold his fire. A horse's rapidly retreating hoofbeats could be heard an instant later. Then Tom suddenly appeared, walking toward them with his usual unhurried stride.

"We'd better ride," Tom murmured as he strolled towards his mount.

"Why?" Luke stood up and brushed himself off. "They're gone. Ain't no need to hurry now."

"No? What if that fool stops running for a minute? He might just think he's got some chance of picking us off one by one. He could dog our heels every inch of the way, maybe even over the border into Mexico. I've got no liking for dodging bullets all across the Rio. Do you?"

"Nope," Hunter answered for Luke. "We're heading out."

Leanne had no chance to protest. She had barely finished brushing the dirt from her clothes, when Hunter grabbed her by the waist and swung her up into her saddle. It was not until she straightened up and glanced his way that he paused.

"You're hurt." His first thrill of fear faded as he saw

that the blood on her cheek, though well mixed with dirt, was neither plentiful nor flowing very freely.

Touching her cheek with her fingers, she winced, then frowned at the muddy bloodstains on her fingertips. "I think it happened when the bullet hit the rock. I recall the stinging now."

"It needs cleaning." Even as he spoke, Hunter fished a handkerchief from his pocket and dampened it with water from his canteen.

"Thought we was in a powerful hurry and all."

Hunter ignored Luke's sneered words as he gently bathed Leanne's cheek. He hated seeing her hurt, minor as the injury was. It brought home to him, all too starkly, the danger she had been dragged into.

Once cleaned, the abrasions looked unsightly but not in need of much care. He felt an urge to kiss her injured cheek but restrained himself. Revealing such softness was not the way to keep the men in line, especially not men like Luke who already thought him too soft.

As Hunter led the group toward the rapidly nearing Mexican border, he thought about how good it would be to be rid of Luke. In Mexico they would part, and Hunter decided he would do his best to be sure the parting was permanent. He did not trust the man, nor did he like him.

Glancing covertly at Luke, he caught the man staring at Leanne with an expression on his homely face that had Hunter aching to shoot him. The ferocity of his distaste surprised Hunter, but no amount of inner scolding could turn it aside. He forced his attention to the land they were crossing.

The scrub growing out of the hard, dry earth was slowly thickening, turning greener. It was a clear sign that there was a steady, large source of water nearby. Soon they would be at the river that formed the border between Texas and Mexico. Soon he would be one large step closer to achieving his goal. He still had to fight the urge, however, to turn around, to stay in Texas and go home.

When they finally halted at the edge of the Rio Grande, Leanne was so tired she swayed in the saddle. Hunter quickly reined up beside her. Even as Charlie took the reins of her horse, Hunter pulled her from the saddle and set her before him. She slumped against him as she stared at the water.

"It does not look all that grand to me," she murmured.

Looking over the wide but shallow river, Hunter smiled faintly. "It can be. Reckon it looked pretty grand to the Spaniards who found it after dragging themselves over a long, dry stretch of land."

"Be dark soon." Tom lounged in his saddle and slowly rolled a cigarette.

Hunter glanced idly at the sky. "Real soon. Still, we're so close it seems dumb to stop and camp now."

"How close?" All Leanne was interested in was how soon she would be able to dismount and rest.

"Across the Rio then six, seven miles to the southeast. Think you can make it?"

Even one mile was going to feel like fifty to her, but she nodded. "Is there a proper bed where we're going?"

"Soft and big." He covertly pressed a kiss to the top of her head, his mind filled with images of the use he intended to make of that bed.

"Sounds like heaven. What are we waiting for?"

"Not a damn thing, darling."

She managed to stay awake until they reached the

other side of the river. Luke gave a whoop as they rode onto Mexican soil. Tom reminded Luke that being in Mexico did not guarantee an end to all pursuit. Even as she prayed Tom was wrong about that, Leanne gave in to exhaustion.

"She all right, Hunter?"

Nodding briefly at Charlie, who had edged up alongside him, Hunter murmured, "She's just exhausted."

"Yeah. She ain't made for this," Jed said as he edged up on the other side. "A little lady. That's what she is."

"You think she'll ever get the law off her back, Hunter?"

"Don't know, Charlie."

"It just ain't right, a girl like her having to run from the law. She didn't do nothing."

Shrugging, Hunter murmured, "It could take a while to get people to see that."

"What're you going to do about Lucia?" Charlie asked after a moment of pensive silence.

Hunter took a quick look at Leanne, reassured to see that she was still sleeping. "Hell, I'm not too sure. I never promised the woman I would come back to her."

"Reckon she expects it, though. She won't like seeing company with you. She could cause some trouble, don't you think?"

"Very possibly. I'll try to get to her before she sees or hears about Leanne and make sure she understands how it is."

"Maybe you oughta keep Leanne outta sight."

"Because some woman is under the delusion she has a claim on me? No, that'd be asking for trouble."

"Well, best you keep her right outta sight anyways, when we get where we're going."

"Why?"

"Watkins. That's why."

"You think he'll be trouble?"

"Oh yeah, he could be. Damn right he could be. She's a right pretty little thing, with learning and fine ladylike ways when she feels like using them. Watkins'll want her. Ain't no question in my mind about it. Keep her real close, Hunter. Real close. And, watch your back. If Watkins wants her, he won't ask nicely or deal or nothing. He'll take. You ain't dealt much with him. Have to take my word on this."

"I think your word's good enough for me, Charlie."

Inwardly, Hunter cursed, long and viciously. He was not leaving trouble behind. From what Charlie said, he was riding straight into it. It might be trouble of a different sort, but he knew it could be just as dangerous.

So hand her over to Watkins, a small voice whispered, and Hunter felt ashamed of himself. He had been too long with outlaws. The fact that he would even think such a thing told him he had not fully succeeded in remaining above those he rode with. He would have to strive harder to cling to his principles.

The violence that stirred in him at the thought of any other man touching Leanne told him that, although that shameless thought had passed through his mind, it would never have taken root. He would do his best to keep Leanne well hidden while they lingered near Watkins. If worse came to worst, he would fight. Battling Watkins and his private army of outlaws might be fruitless, but at least he could make sure that stealing Leanne cost the man dearly.

Suddenly he ached to be home, to step back that year

or more before all the trouble started. He needed to see his family again. A grimace crossed his face as he admitted that he missed even his mother. All the machinations which had so infuriated and galled him seemed a petty grievance now. To be with his brothers and his father, to have his life back to what it had been, he could put up with his mother.

He shook away those thoughts. Thinking of home only served to depress his spirits. There was a long way to go yet before he could return. The best thing to do, the wisest, was to concentrate fully on what lay ahead.

When they reached the low, small adobe house that had once been a pleasant retreat and was now his only real home, he felt little relief or pleasure. Its whitewashed walls were a reminder of all that had gone wrong in his life. Carrying Leanne through the low, wood-framed door, he was pleased to see that Jesus and his wife had done as promised. It was clean, cleaner than he had hoped. Even the timeworn plank floors shined. He only needed to buy supplies. When Leanne stirred in his arms, he set her on her feet, holding her until she steadied herself.

Leanne blinked, rubbed the sleep from her eyes, and looked around. Her first feeling was relief. It was clean and roomy.

"This is our destination?" She glanced over her shoulder at Hunter.

He nodded and moved to open one of the shuttered windows. "Yup. We'll be here for a while."

"What's a while?"

"'Til we get our business done."

She decided she was simply too tired, her mind too dulled by exhaustion, to argue that evasive answer.

Sinking down into a chair by the well-scrubbed table, she watched the men settle in. She wanted to go to bed, but felt it would be best to ask Hunter about that quietly, privately. There was no opportunity at the moment.

Despite Tom's cautionary remark at the river's edge, the other men acted as if all their troubles were over, but it suddenly occurred to Leanne that there could well be threats on this side of the border as well. Shaking her head, she decided she was too tired to sort it all out now.

Hunter was about to ask Leanne to make some coffee when he noticed how much trouble she was having simply staying awake. "Come on. I'll take you to our room."

"We have our own?" she whispered as she took his hand and stood up.

Seeing how unsteady she still was, he slipped his arm around her waist to lend her some support. She made no complaint. He almost wished she would. If she would only whine or complain, he might find himself growing tired of her.

"We do. The men will be staying here, but this is my place."

"How nice. I wish I wasn't too tired to take a bath. I think I need one."

"Indulge yourself tomorrow. I'll show you where everything is then. For now I'll get you some water to wash up with," he said. Once in the room, she sat down heavily on the bed.

After he left, she removed her boots and looked around the room. It was of moderate size, with a few pieces of plain but sturdy furniture. She looked a little askance at the bed. It was also plain and sturdy, as well as very large. Before she could stop the thought she found herself wondering how many women Hunter had shared it with. The thought was followed by a pang of jealousy.

Hunter walked in carrying two large pitchers of steaming water. A quick glance at Leanne as he set the pitchers down on the wash table got him a cross look in return. He decided her weariness was finally shortening her temper.

"A good hot wash will make you feel better," he murmured as he filled the basin. "Save a little for me."

Sprawling in a chair, Hunter sipped the coffee Jed had made, hoping fervently that Leanne would recover quickly from the ordeal of their long, hard journey and start cooking again. He longed for a good cup of coffee. Glancing across the table, he caught Luke glaring at him. He sighed quietly. Luke was proving a constant source of irritation.

"Something eating at you, Luke?"

"Yeah, Hunter, and you damned well know what."

"Do I now? So there's no misunderstanding, perhaps you'd better spell it out."

"You mean to keep that bitch with you, don't you?"

A quick glance at Charlie and Jed told Hunter he was not the only one weary of the way Luke spoke of Leanne. "She stays. She's not as much trouble as you'd like to have us believe."

"Ain't she? She brought those bounty hunters after us."

"She was just sweetener for their pot. We're wanted too."

"We aren't worth five hundred dollars."

"Not each, but we make a tidy sum collectively."

"And I don't deal with bounty hunters," Tom murmured, a cold finality in his voice.

"Fine," Luke ground out. "However, we're in Mexico now. We can, just dump her somewheres."

"She stays, Luke."

"Lucia will be real pleased with that, Hunter."

"That's my problem."

Inwardly, Hunter cursed. He did not relish that confrontation. Lucia was hot-tempered and possessive despite all his attempts to make her see she had no claim on him. Very soon after he had become involved with her, he had realized the relationship was a mistake. He had the sinking feeling he would soon see just how big a mistake.

"It just better not end up being our problem too. I got no stomach for being caught between your jealous whores."

"Here now," Charlie rumbled, "you ain't got no call to speak on Leanne that way."

"I don't, huh? What do you think those two've been doing every time they tiptoe off, idiot?"

"Nothing that's any of your business, Luke," Hunter growled, his anger beginning to gain control of him.

Tom looked up from the cigarette he was rolling. "I think you're a word away from being shot, Luke."

Luke stared at Hunter, who met his gaze squarely. He knew the fury he felt over Luke's talk showed in his face, in his taut stance, but Hunter made no effort to hide it. After a long, tense staring match, Luke abruptly stood up and headed for the door, pausing only after he was almost out the house.

"Just keep your bits of calico outta my way."

"Gladly," Hunter murmured, his remark lost in the slamming of the door as Luke left.

No one said anything after that, but Hunter found it an uneasy silence. Though they might not have agreed with all Luke had said, the other men shared his crudely voiced concern. There was enough trouble dogging their heels without adding women problems. He moved toward the bedroom, hoping he could solve the problem in the morning.

He entered his room quietly, smiling faintly when he saw that Leanne had left a lamp burning low for him. A quick glance at her told him only that she was in bed. He was not able to tell for certain whether she slept or not.

Leanne kept her eyes shut as she listened to him wash up and prepare for bed. Her body ached with weariness, but sleep still eluded her. For a while jealousy-inspired images had taunted her. Then she had lain tense and afraid as she listened to Luke and Hunter argue. She had not been able to make out all the words, but the tone had been unmistakable. Fear that this time angry words would lead to a gun battle had kept her wide awake. When Hunter finally slid into bed beside her, she was unable to resist the urge to move into his arms. Feeling his warmth, hearing the steady beat of his heart as she rested her head on his chest, eased her fear.

"So you are awake." He wrapped his arms around her and kissed the top of her head.

"I heard you and Luke arguing again. At least, it sounded like an argument."

Her last words eased his fear that she had heard Luke's insulting words. "He backed down again. His kind always does."

"You sound so sure of that."

"His kind won't face a man square unless he's real sure he'll win."

"Perhaps he'll try to weigh the odds in his favor one day."

"I'm watching for that." He could feel her body growing lax, heavy with oncoming sleep.

"He hates you."

"He resents my being made leader over him. You watch out for him too," he added, recalling the way Luke had been looking at her.

"I do. All the time."

"Now that we're here, I'll be busy. Don't ever be alone with him."

"I don't intend to be."

"Good. Get some sleep. You need it and now you can get it in a proper bed."

"A big bed. Lots of room."

There was an odd note to her sleepy words and he frowned. "Had it made special. Been coming and going from this place for years. Decided I ought to make it comfortable if I was going to use it so often. This bed was one of the first things I got. Comfortable. Plenty of room to stretch out."

"Mmmm . . . and other things." She grimaced, afraid statements like that would reveal her jealous fears.

Hunter bit back the grin that threatened to curve his mouth. Now he understood what put the anger in her voice. She thought she had been brought to a lovenest. Cupping her chin in his hand, he tilted her face up to his and gave her a slow, gentle kiss.

"Yeah, stuff like that," she grumbled as she settled her cheek against his chest again once the kiss had ended.

Holding her comfortably close, but ignoring his stirring desire, he smiled faintly. "Indeed. Tomorrow we'll have to christen this bed."

"Christen it?" She did not dare hope he meant there had never been another woman in the bed, yet could not think of any other meaning for his statement. "Are you saying this is a . . . a virgin bed?"

He laughed softly. "As pure as the driven snow. I've been no monk . . ."

"What a surprise."

". . . but," he continued, "this is my place. When I wanted a woman I went where they were. I didn't bring them here." He grimaced. "Almost took this bed back to Texas once, though."

"Texas?"

"My home's there."

Something in the tone of his voice told her not to ask too much about that now. "Why lug a bed back there?"

"I like it, and I was thinking of getting married for a while."

"Only thinking of it, huh?" She tried not to sound too interested.

"It turned out to be a mistake. Patricia was a big mistake indeed," he murmured, half to himself.

He sounded as if he meant it, so she told herself not to worry, not to give in to the strong urge to press for a lot more information. Whoever this woman Patricia was, she was a ghost from his past. Jealousy over a ghost would get her nowhere.

"What happens tomorrow?" She yawned as, with an end to both the worries that had kept her awake, sleep crept over her.

"I have a lot of business to see to."

"You'll be gone a lot?"

"Afraid so. So will the others. Am I going to have to set a guard on you?"

"No. I won't go anywhere."

"Is that a promise?"

"I suppose I can make it one. I know the bounty hunters are out there. I learned there are other dangers for a lone traveler—like Indians. I don't know this country at all, not even the language. Three good reasons to stay put."

"Wondered if you'd learned that."

"I'm not stupid, even if I've done a few really stupid things." She smiled a sleepy, wry smile when he laughed.

"I don't suppose there might be one or two other reasons you'd stay around?"

"Well, maybe one. After all, it isn't every day a woman gets a chance to christen a bed." She yawned again.

It was not what he wanted to hear, but he pushed the strange disappointment he felt aside and kissed her on the forehead. "True. Better get some sleep. Bed christening requires you to be well rested." After a moment of just holding her and letting his own need for sleep take him over, he murmured, "Leanne?"

"Mmmm?"

"Stay close to the house. Real close. Better yet, stay inside."

There was a tense note to his voice, but she was too tired to question it very deeply, just mumbled, "Why?"

"We're not the only outlaws hiding out here."

"All right. Okay."

"Okay what?"

"I promise I will stay tucked up in this house. That better?"

"Much better. Now get to sleep."

"Yes, master," she drawled, but the sarcasm she had reached for eluded her, and her exhaustion quickly forced her to be as obedient as he could wish.

As Hunter adjusted her body more comfortably in his arms, he wondered if he should have been more exact in his warnings. He closed his eyes. She had said she would stay put. There was no need to tell her about Watkins. She had enough to fear. He would solve the problem by finishing his business quickly and getting out.

Chapter Seven

"Ah, now this is luxury," Leanne murmured as she slowly sank into the hot water.

She decided, as she lolled in the tub, that Hunter had probably had it made specially for him. It was far larger than any tub she had ever been in. This one let her really submerge herself. The man clearly liked his comforts. That aspect of his character did not quite fit the image of a hardened outlaw but, as she picked up the lilac-scented soap he had mysteriously produced, she decided she would be a fool to complain.

For the first time since she had joined the outlaws, she was alone. Charlie and Jed had filled her tub, then left. The others had left earlier than that. She was not sure Luke had ever returned after storming out last night. It felt strange to know there was no one around, that she could simply walk away if she wished to.

But, she thought with a grimace, she would stay put. There were dangers between Mexico and the mountains where O'Malley roosted, dangers it was reckless to face alone. She knew that was not all that held her back, though. Hunter did. She simply had no urge to leave him as long as he wanted her. It was foolish, even reckless, to stay hoping for what he might not be able to give her.

Shaking away such troubling thoughts, she hurried to finish bathing before the water lost its warmth. There was no sense in constantly mulling it over. Right or wrong, she would go where her heart led her.

When she finally stepped from the tub to dry herself off, she heard a faint noise. Someone had returned. Not confident it was Hunter, she hurried to put some clothes on. She was dressed only in her pantaloons and camisole when the door was flung open. Grabbing her shirt, she held it in front of her like a shield and glared at Luke.

"What are you doing here?" she snapped, hiding her fear behind anger.

"Well, well, well. So the boss has left his little slut all alone, has he?"

"Get out."

"Now, let's not be hasty." He slowly shut the door and stepped farther into the room.

Fear began to form a knot in Leanne's stomach. Suddenly it was not only strange to be left unguarded, it was dangerous. There was no mistaking the look in Luke's eyes. It was the same one that had been chilling her blood for days.

"I told you to get out of here." She started to edge her way back toward the window.

"Don't get so haughty with me, bitch. All your protectors are gone."

"They'll be back."

"Not before we're done."

"I'm Hunter's. That was made clear."

"Was it? Well, I'm thinking it's not so clear now."

"What do you mean?" she asked, then hated herself for giving in to his taunts.

"He's off with his hot Mexican honey right now."

"You lie. He's off doing business." She did not want to believe him, but cold, hurtful fingers of doubt touched her heart.

Luke laughed. "Yeah, business with Lucia. He trotted right over there like he does every time he comes here. Seems to me his running to that señorita says he's getting a mite tired of you."

Leanne knew Luke was saying these things to undermine her resistance. This was certainly not the time to weigh the truth of his words or let them touch her in any way.

"You're a fool. Hunter will kill you for this."

"It's past time me and him had it out anyways."

Knowing there was no talking him out of what he intended, she bolted. She was halfway out the window when he grabbed her, roughly yanking her back inside, then throwing her onto the bed. She was badly winded but she tried to scramble off the bed. He was on her too fast.

The minute he caught her, she knew she was lost. She lacked the strength and skill to fight him. This time she knew she would not escape the assault. Desperation strengthened her efforts. He might get what he wanted, but he would have to fight hard for it.

"Bite me again, you little whore, and I'll ram your teeth down your throat."

"Get off me, you stinking bastard!" She cursed with fury and pain when he slapped her twice, dazing her for a moment.

He ripped her camisole open and, with one hand wrapped around her wrists, pinning her hands over her head, he mauled her breasts with his other hand. She gagged but fought the nausea choking her. It would undoubtedly cause her more harm than him.

"Get off of her, Luke."

Tom's deadly cold voice cut through her panic. Luke only glanced up. He barely paused in his assault. She looked at Tom, all her fear and pleading in her eyes, and wondered if he really would use the gun he held. Although a part of her was chilled by the thought, she hoped he would.

"Get out of here, Tom. This ain't your concern."

"Get off of her. Now."

Suddenly her hands were free. Luke reached for his gun, but Tom fired before Luke's fingers even brushed the handle. Leanne was too horrified to move. Luke's body seemed to fly off her. She saw the red blossom on his chest, felt the warmth of his blood as it splattered her. Even as Luke's now limp body slid off the bed, she remained frozen in place. A small part of her shocked mind heard the rapid approach of booted feet.

"Oh, my sainted mother," Charlie gasped as he stumbled to a halt just inside the room. Jed was right behind him.

"You shot Luke," Jed said, his voice soft with confusion. "Is he dead?"

"He's dead. I don't hold with raping women." Tom holstered his gun and looked at Leanne. "You okay?"

"Yes. No. I can't seem to move," she whispered.

"Best see to her," he ordered Jed and Charlie. "I'll get him outta here."

For once Jed and Charlie did not get flustered by her semi-dressed state. As they moved to the bedside, she saw Tom heft Luke's body over his shoulder and walk out. She looked up at Charlie, who was fruitlessly trying to pull her tattered camisole together.

"I think I'm going to be sick, Charles."

Even as Charlie moved her so she could hang her head over the side of the bed, Jed stuck a pan in front of her. By the time her illness was over, she was too weak to help herself, too wrung out to feel any embarrassment as Jed and Charlie cleaned her up and put a new camisole on her. They tucked her into bed like a child. Although she continued to feel listless, she deeply appreciated their help and tried to say so.

"Now, no call to be thanking us so," Charlie murmured, flushing slightly. "Right for us to pay back some tending."

Tom reappeared at her bedside, a glass of whiskey in his hand. "Drink this."

She wrinkled her nose with distaste even as Charlie helped her sit up. "I do not like that stuff."

"No one asked you to like it. Just drink it." Ignoring her protests and coughs, Tom forced it all down her throat.

"God, that stuff is awful," she rasped as she lay back down.

"Maybe we oughta get Hunter," Jed murmured.

"You know where he is."

"Yeah, Tom, but—" Charlie ran a hand through his hair.

The way all three men stared at her—Tom with his

usual remoteness and the other two warily, almost guiltily—
told her more than she wanted to know. Luke had not
been lying. Hunter had a woman and he was with her.
Suddenly she wanted them to go away, to leave her alone.
She could feel the numbness of shock leaving her and did
not want an audience to witness the outpouring of emotion she could feel stirring within her.

"You don't have to get him. I'll be fine."

"You don't look too fine, Leanne," Charlie muttered,
frowning down at her.

"I just need some time to pull myself together. Just
some time to get over the shock."

"Okay. You rest up. We'll be right outside the door if
you need anything."

"Thank you." She smiled her gratitude as they all left
her, Charlie quietly shutting the door after them.

With a shaky sigh, she closed her eyes. At first all she
could feel was revulsion, the sickening memory of
Luke's hands mauling her, then his face as his own death
overtook him. She told herself firmly to forget all of that.
He had not raped her, and his death was not one to waste
any grief or regret on. Eventually, the horror of that violence would fade.

Forcing her mind away from Luke brought it squarely
on the matter of Hunter and his other woman. The pain
that thought brought her was stunning in its intensity. She
was unable to stop her tears. For a little while, she gave in
to that weakness, weeping bitterly for lost hopes. Then
she let anger dry her tears.

He had no right to treat her so shabbily. She had
nowhere to go, no one she could turn to. He had taken her
on as his responsibility. He had seduced her, sensed her
weakness for him and played upon it until she gave in.

As she lay there recovering her shattered spirit, she re-
viewed her grievances again and again. When Hunter finally returned, she fully intended to unleash her anger on
him. She intended to end their relationship and to back
her decision with good solid reasoning. There would be
no inkling of the jealousy or hurt she felt.

By the time she reached that decision, she felt she had
regained the composure needed to face the others. As she
started to get dressed, she also decided that some activity
would help, even if it was just cooking up a good meal for
the men. She had no intention of letting Hunter find her
languishing in bed.

Hunter grimaced as he dismounted and tended to his
mount. The meeting with Watkins had gone smoothly, but
little had been accomplished. Waiting seemed to be Watkins's favorite game. That and ponderous deliberations
well mixed with threats.

It was the confrontation with Lucia that left such a bitter taste in his mouth. He had suspected it would be difficult, but difficult didn't begin to describe their meeting.
Before he had climbed into her bed that first time, he had
seen a hint of her alarmingly volatile nature, but he'd ignored it, responding to the itch in his loins instead of the
voice of common sense. He had paid for that slip today.

He gingerly touched the slash across his ribs on the
left side as he walked to the house; it was a shallow
wound that still oozed blood. That she would attack him
with a knife had surprised him a little, but she had run out
of things to hurl at him. He just hoped her violence would
end there.

Opening the door, he took a deep breath, smiling with

pleasure. Leanne had taken over the cooking again. Despite all the problems she'd caused, he was glad to return to her. She did not scream at him or accuse him of breaking promises he had never made. She did not expect from him more than he offered.

The sense of contentment he felt wavered when he sat at the table, deciding his hunger was more important than seeing to his minor wound. Leanne greeted him with a glare. She placed his plate of food in front of him with a distinct touch of violence. Then he saw the bruises on her face. He grabbed her by the arm and forced her to look at him.

"What happened to your face?" He reached out to touch her cheek and frowned when she jerked her face away.

"Luke happened to my face. He happened to a few other parts of my body too. Not that you'd care." From the moment he had entered the house, her simmering anger had flared and the heavy perfume that clung to him added fuel to that fury.

"Where is Luke?" he snarled, looking at the other three men and keeping a firm grip on Leanne.

"Buried in the back of the house." Tom hardly paused in his leisurely enjoyment of his meal.

"You killed him?" Hunter felt both relieved and sadly disappointed over losing the chance to exact his own retribution.

"Yup. Don't hold with rape."

Hunter felt a chill enter his blood and looked at Leanne. "He raped you?"

"Almost."

"I told you not to be alone with him."

"I did not have much choice in the matter. No one else

was here when he came back. Obviously, *he* didn't have a woman nearby to run to." She finally yanked her arm free of his hold and flounced into the bedroom. An argument was inevitable, and she did not want the other men to witness it.

She knows about Lucia, Hunter thought in dismay. Then he got angry. He had not been bedding Lucia! He had nothing to feel guilty about.

"Leanne," he snapped. The minute she turned to glare at him, he yanked up his shirt to reveal the knife wound. "Does this look like I've been out pleasuring myself?"

Her first reaction to the sight of his wound was to move to tend it. That infuriated her. There were any number of explanations for that wound. It hardly proved him innocent of her suspicions.

"It looks like your hot Mexican honey ought to trim her nails." She waved her hand towards his plate of food. "Better eat up. Your sort of lover must require a great deal of stamina."

She went into the bedroom and shut the door, then went to sit on the bed to wait. He would come. She was sure of it. The only uncertain thing was whether he would eat first. She felt an urge to weep; her hurt rose up through her anger, but she fought it down. Her decision had been to hide those emotions and she would stick by it.

After briefly debating marching right after her, Hunter sat down to eat first. He ignored the amusement of the other men, although it was hard to hide his shock when he actually saw a grin on Tom's usually impassive face. Hunter felt some form of sustenance was needed before facing Leanne. He also needed to find out more about what had happened while he had been squabbling with Lucia.

"So Luke attacked her?" He aimed his question at all three men.

Leaning back in his chair and lighting the cigarette he had just rolled, Tom nodded. "Jumped her while she was alone. None of us saw him return. I heard what was going on when I got back. Told him to get off of her. He didn't. Tried to draw on me." Tom shrugged and took a long drag on his cigarette.

"Well, I thank you."

"No need. That's one thing I don't turn my back on."

"I thought he was settled with a whore at the cantina. I saw him there."

"Yeah, and he saw you go to Lucia. Figured you'd left Leanne free for the taking," Charlie growled.

"He figured wrong, didn't he."

"She shouldn't oughta be treated like that."

"Jed's right," Charlie said before Hunter could speak. "You don't want to be bothered with her no more, say so, and me and Jed will take care of her. Better that than you keeping her part of some stable. She ain't like Lucia. She ain't no whore."

"I know that." Hunter pushed away his now empty plate. "This really isn't any of your business."

"Me and Jed are making it our business."

It was hard, but Hunter hid his surprise. Charlie and Jed had never gone against him. In fact, they never went against anybody. Yet, there they sat looking identically belligerent, clearly intending to fight about this particular matter.

"Are you now. That still doesn't make it your concern. However, to placate your spinsterish curiosity, I'll tell you that I didn't go to Lucia for a rutting. I went to tell her adios, to make sure she didn't come here. Satisfied?"

He felt almost guilty over his harshness when both men flushed. "Luke told her about Lucia?"

"Reckon so," Jed replied. "We didn't say it direct, but we mighta hinted it enough for her to figure Luke was talking true."

Hunter swore. Innocent though he was, it was going to be awkward at best to convince Leanne. Maybe if he went in and bled on her a little he could at least win some sympathy, he thought wryly as he glanced down at his wound.

"Lucia do that?"

"Yeah, Tom. She ran out of things to throw and came at me with a knife."

"Lucky she didn't have a gun," muttered Charlie.

"She calm when you left?"

Hunter finished his coffee before answering Tom. "Disarmed but threatening."

"She bears watching."

"What can she do?" Hunter was not sure an infuriated whore was worth worrying about, but suddenly he wondered if he was being careless.

"You like surprises?"

"No, dammit. All right, we'd better keep an eye on her until we're sure she won't try to exact revenge for imagined slights." He stood up. "Well, I'm for getting this seen to and getting some rest."

"You sure she'll let you in there?" Charlie eyed the closed bedroom door warily as Hunter headed towards it.

"Oh, she'll let me in. The question is whether she lets me stay in there or throws me out on my ear." He smiled crookedly and opened the door.

As Hunter shut the door quietly behind him, Leanne barely paused in brushing out her hair. It was not until he

sat down on the bed that she deigned to take any real notice of him. He eyed her as if daring her to complain. She
decided she dared as she turned to look at him.

"I would not get too comfortable if I were you."

"No? When I left this morning this was still my bed."

"A bed you have graciously allowed me to use," she
ground out, "and I have decided that I would prefer to
sleep alone."

"Why?"

"You can ask that after what you have done?"

"I haven't done a thing today that you should get annoyed about."

"Really." Her voice was heavy with scornful disbelief.
"From where I sit it smells like you have had yourself a
fine old time."

"She threw perfume at me."

He sounded so calm and sincere that she felt inclined
to believe him. That only added to her anger. Lucretia
Borgia probably sounded sincere too as she told her vic-
tims it was a health tonic she served, a nasty voice whispered in her head. She refused to let herself be
hoodwinked by a few softly spoken words holding the
ring of truth.

"I'm getting blood on the bed."

Giving a small, exasperated sigh, she gathered up
strips of linen to tend to his wound. Hunter never took his
gaze from her as she helped him strip down to his trousers, then washed and bandaged his wound.

For a brief moment he wondered why he was even
bothering to explain himself. He was doing it simply because he wanted to, because he felt she deserved some
explanation. She was totally dependent upon him, a victim swept up in the mess he was in. She had given him

her innocence but pressed for no promises. She had her pride. He also admitted to himself that he did not like her thinking that he could treat her so callously.

"I was not rolling about in lustful abandon with Lucia," he finally said, his voice quiet but firm.

She glanced up at him, noting how directly he met her gaze. "Then why go to her at all?"

"A reasonable question." He thought about the best way to answer. "I knew that she'd come around the minute she heard I was here. I wanted to avoid that."

"So what if she did?"

"Are you telling me I was wrong to be worried about a former lover meeting a present. lover?"

She decided not to answer that, on the grounds that she might incriminate herself. "Former?"

"Very former. Unfortunately, she never seemed to accept that we were through. I went over there to be sure that she understood." He sat down beside her on the bed, noticing that she no longer looked quite so furious. "She is hot-tempered"—he touched his bandaged wound—"as you can see, and possessive. She claims promises were made. It's a lie. I bought her just like hundreds of men before me and made no promises whatsoever. I knew she was a mistake from the beginning, but she was handy, cheap, and I had an itch."

Although she knew those hard words were not directed at her, she felt their sting. They described her as well. She tried to turn away, but he grasped her firmly by the chin and forced her to face him.

"No, little one, it's not the same."

"I didn't say—"

"Didn't have to. You looked like I'd hit you. She's a whore. You're not."

"Some might disagree."

"And they'd be wrong. Hypocritical as well, I'd wager. I don't usually speak so harshly about women like Lucia. Who am I to judge? But she earned the words. She could be married to the richest don, a dozen kids at her feet and a member of the church choir, and she'd still be a whore. I didn't want her coming anywhere near you."

He brushed kisses over the bruises on her cheeks. "I should have been here."

His soft words brought back the horror of that moment with Luke. She shuddered, then shook the memory away. It was a lot nicer to hear what he was saying concerning herself. The words were not sweet or romantic, but they eased a lot of her pain.

"You can't watch me every minute of the day and night."

She was studying him, and he endured the examination patiently, meeting her searching gaze without wavering. It was not until she looked away, frowning in thought, that he allowed himself the pleasure of looking at her. Her hair was loose and freshly brushed, falling down her back in tempting waves. She wore only her camisole and drawers, the former lacy and feminine, the latter plain and masculine. It was an intriguing mix. He decided she was adorable. His patience began to wane.

"Going to let me stay?"

Hoping she was not letting her heart make a complete fool of her, she looked at him. "You didn't do anything with her?"

Cupping her face in his hands, he answered, "Not a thing save duck a lot."

"All right." She stood up. "Lie down and I'll help you with the rest of your clothes."

As she started to put out the candles he almost told her he did not need help, but the temptation to let Leanne undress him was too much to resist. When only one candle near the bed remained lit, she started to undress him. As she bent to undo his trousers her hair fell forward to shield her face but he still knew she was blushing. Her slim neck was colored by it. He made little effort to hide how her actions aroused him. He almost laughed at the way she flipped the sheet over his lower half before slipping into bed at his side.

Leanne tried to calm the feelings running rampant within her. Although she had seen him naked before, it had always been with the heat of passion dulling her sense of modesty. He was so beautiful in her eyes, so strong and gloriously male. She was startled from her admiration when his arm slipped around her waist and he gently yanked her closer to him.

"What are you doing?" She fought to keep her voice calm, even stern, but there was still a hint of breathlessness in it.

"I thought we were going to christen this bed tonight."

Despite the fact that he was kissing her ear, she struggled for common sense. "You're wounded."

"A scratch."

"More than a scratch and it needs to be pampered for a while. What you suggest requires a little more effort on your part than you should expend right now." She was disappointed but knew it would be better for him if he simply rested.

"I might not have to exert myself at all."

"Oh? How's that?"

"You could be clever."

"Clever? Hunter"—she blushed—"I'm still new at this. I don't think I've reached clever yet."

"You're probably right." He brushed a kiss over her mouth and closed his eyes. "Tomorrow night for certain."

Leanne glanced up at his face. He looked relaxed, ready to go to sleep. There had been no note of annoyance or disappointment in his voice. Intuition whispered that he felt it, however.

Using a light touch, one she hoped was sensually pleasing, she slid her hand over his chest and slowly down his side. Having made that first bold step, she began to get some ideas. A few were gleaned from the way Hunter made love to her and a few were straight out of some of the scandalous dreams she had been afflicted with since meeting the man. Her thoughts made her blush, but she did not allow that surge of modesty to deter her.

Hunter felt his drowsiness fade with each stroke of her hands. He came wide awake when her tongue swept over his nipple. Sliding his hands into her thick hair he gasped when she gently suckled him.

"Leanne . . ."

"Shush." Caressing his lean hips, she kissed her way towards his taut stomach.

"Shush?"

"Mmmm. Shush." She dipped her tongue into his navel and felt him shudder. "If you say too much I might chicken out."

"God forbid." His voice was already thick with desire, a desire that soared to dizzying heights as she drew idle designs on his inner thighs with her tongue.

He closed his eyes. Using every ounce of will he had, he struggled to keep a tight rein on the passion she was stirring in him. He wanted to enjoy her lovemaking for as long as possible. What meager restraint he was able to maintain completely shattered when first her hand, then her mouth, touched upon the source of the aching need gripping him so tightly. He cried out, his whole body jerking in reaction to the shaft of pleasure that tore through him.

Surprised and a little concerned about his strong reaction, Leanne backed off. He had kissed her in such an intimate way once and, although shock had forced her to push him away, she had felt pleasure. She had assumed he would too, but now she wondered. She hoped she had not done wrong, for making love to him had stirred her own desires to a feverish pitch. The last thing she wanted was for him to call a halt.

"Wrong?" she whispered.

"Hell, no. Right." His grip tightening in her hair, and he urged her mouth back. "So damned right I don't think I can take too much of it."

Moments later, he knew he had to stop her. He dragged her up his body, then eased her down upon him until they were joined. The warm welcome he found, proof that she had been fully aroused simply by making love to him, stole what little restraints he still had.

Although startled slightly by the new position, Leanne was soon caught up in Hunter's intense desire. She drove them quickly towards the gratification of their needs. Weak from the strength of the release they shared, she collapsed in his arms. It was comforting to find that he was trembling as much as she. Surprisingly, she did not feel embarrassed at her daring, or at the pleasure they had shared.

"I thought you said you weren't clever," he murmured when they finally found the energy to separate and she curled up by his side.

"Was I clever then?" She unsuccessfully tried to smother a yawn.

"If you were any cleverer, I'd be ready for burying right now."

"I suppose that's a compliment."

He laughed faintly, then sleepily pressed a kiss to the top of her head. Never had he felt so deliciously sated. Her instinctive skill had given him more pleasure than the art of the most practiced courtesan. He grudgingly admitted to himself that it was because he felt something for her. What she gave him was fuller than a simple easement of his body's lusts.

"It was the best I've ever known, Leanne," he murmured, compelled to let her know in some small way what she meant to him, despite his own confusion.

She smiled faintly and curled herself more snuggly around him. The best was just what she wanted to be. A man should find it hard to walk away from what he considered the best.

Chapter Eight

"Boss? Boss, you better wake up."

Hunter managed to open one eye and glare at Charlie. "Whatisit?"

"Watkins is here."

"Here?"

"Yes, Hunter. Right here."

That cool voice wiped the last remnants of sleep from Hunter's brain. Trying not to look as horrified as he felt, he sat up to look at the man standing just to Charlie's right.

"This is a rare event."

"I had a report this morning from a mutual acquaintance. You do recall Lucia, do you not?"

"Vaguely." Hunter inwardly cursed his arrogance in assuming that Lucia was not really worth worrying about.

Watkins smiled thinly. "She informed me that you have

a guest. Strange that you failed to tell me about this added member of your little group."

"She's not part of the group, merely a tag-a-long." Hunter felt Leanne sit up behind him, shielding herself behind his body, and wished he had had time to talk to her before confronting Watkins, time to warn her that a lot of what he was about to say would be lies.

"Lucia also told me that you seem to have—er, misplaced one of your number. She felt certain he was beneath the freshly turned earth in the garden area of this hovel. I regret to say she proved correct."

Even as he wondered how they had missed what sounded like a prodigious amount of activity around the place, Hunter remained outwardly calm. "Just how did Lucia come by all this information?"

"Ah, it seems jealousy and offended vanity compelled her to indulge in a little spying. What happened to Luke?"

Although Watkins's mild tone of voice changed very little, Hunter heard the sharp demand for an answer. "He grew uncontrollable."

"I suspected as much. I would have preferred it if you'd turned the matter over to me, however."

"He drew on Tom. There wasn't any choice about killing him."

"And you intended to inform me of all this today, of course."

"Of course."

"And now you are going to introduce me to your charming companion."

That was the very last thing Hunter wanted to do. Despite the fact that Watkins had been talking to him, most of the man's attention had been centered on Leanne. Matters were getting uncomfortably complicated. He was not sure he had the agility of wit needed to keep Watkins from growing suspicious and Leanne from getting all the wrong ideas. He would have to walk a very fine line. Turning slightly so Leanne was more visible, he slipped his hand beneath the covers to rest it on the small of her back.

"This is Miss Leanne Summers. She joined us in Clayville. Leanne, this is Mr. Watkins."

When the man took her hand in his to kiss it, Leanne barely repressed a shudder. His lips and hand were cool and very dry. Although he was not unattractive, there was something nearly reptillian about his looks, especially his heavy-lidded, flat gray eyes.

"You must call me Henry, my dear."

She felt no wish to do so, but something in Hunter's expression made her believe extreme caution was best. "Of course, Henry."

"I hate to tug you away from such loveliness, Hunter, but we must talk. My man, Joseph, is preparing breakfast. I'm sure Leanne will want to join us."

Leanne had no wish at all to join him, but said nothing. It was clearly an order, not an invitation.

Hunter waited but, when Watkins made no move to leave, he finally rose to get dressed. He had hoped to speak privately with Leanne, but it was clear he was not going to be allowed that. As he buttoned his shirt, he bent to kiss her, praying she would understand the brief message he whispered against her lips. Then he strode out of the room with Charlie and Watkins.

Touching her mouth, Leanne frowned at the door. She could still feel the words he had pressed to her lips. *Trust me*. Two questions came immediately to mind. Why would he say that, and should she heed his admonition?

Shaking her head, she got out of bed to consider her options as she dressed.

Something was going on. She had sensed all sorts of undercurrents in the conversation. Unfortunately, she had few real clues. Edging closer to the door, she eavesdropped as she finished dressing.

"A very pretty companion you've gained, Hunter." Watkins sipped at the coffee Joseph served them.

Surreptitiously glancing from Tom to Jed to Charlie, Hunter found little help. All three men seemed fascinated by their coffee. He hoped they continued to stay out of the conversation, for he was about to talk a lot of nonsense. He wanted no one to gainsay him now.

"Pretty enough, I reckon."

"How did you acquire her?"

Hunter relayed a very condensed version of Leanne's involvement in the robbery. "So, you can see she's no threat. She's as wanted as we are. If we fall, she falls."

"So it seems."

"So it is."

"And she's yours."

"She's keeping me entertained for the moment."

Leanne had to bite her lip to keep from crying out. That cool statement was like a slap in the face.

"So entertained that you cast off the very adept Lucia," Watkins drawled.

"The costly Lucia. Why pay when I can be satisfied for free?"

"Then perhaps your Miss Summers would be amenable to a more—er, profitable arrangement."

It was hard, especially when he literally ached to plant his fist in Watkins's face, but Hunter just shrugged. "She's a free woman."

"Good. Ah, Joseph has prepared another fine meal. Where is our lovely guest?" Watkins asked as his man set out the food. "Do you think she fell back asleep?"

"Nope. She's just taking her sweet time like women do."

Hurrying away from the door Leanne quickly checked her appearance. She could not dawdle any longer. Something told her that Watkins would not hesitate to send someone to get her if she did not appear soon.

Hurt had given way to confusion. She could not fully believe Hunter was as callous as he sounded. Though it was true he had made no promises, never spoken of love, there were other things that contradicted his harsh words. There was the way he treated her, the way he spoke to her at certain times, and even their lovemaking. All those things said he was not as heartless as he now seemed.

Shaking her head she hurried out the door. She would have to study the situation more closely. Instinct told her something was going on, something she did not yet understand. It also told her that Hunter's cruel words were all part of it. She prayed she was right.

The breakfast progressed smoothly, but Leanne was not sure she learned much except to dislike Watkins even more than she had at first sight. He was all that was well mannered and elegant. She could fault nothing he said or did. Yet, beneath that veneer she sensed all that could be bad in a man.

Hunter continued to act callous and indifferent. It now puzzled her more than hurt her. Hunter no longer seemed the man she had come to know. Not even in the first few hours of their meeting had he seemed so insensitive, so cold, as he did now. He certainly did not act like the man who had cast off another lover for her sake and told her so softly that she was the best.

She smiled faintly at the man called Joseph as he collected her plate, her action one of absentminded courtesy as she wondered how or if she could find out what was afoot. Apparently, Watkins was the boss, the one who arranged, directed, and benefited from the robberies, yet none of her companions were at all friendly with the man. Jed and Charlie acted with a wariness that bordered on fear. Tom said almost nothing, even when spoken to directly. Hunter was coldly polite, at times nearly insolent, yet ever careful in his answers.

It was all very unsettling, very confusing. She hated not knowing what was going on, hated the way even Charlie and Jed seemed unreadable. Trying to figure it all out was giving her a headache.

Another thing that bothered her was Watkins's interest in her, an interest Hunter did nothing to stem. She did not want the man's interest but knew it would be stupid to boldly reject it. She tried to keep him at a distance by using her most coolly correct manners, but her strategy was failing miserably.

"I can see by your empty plate that you enjoyed the meal, Leanne."

"It was delicious, Henry." She started to form a polite leave-taking in her mind, only to freeze at Watkins's next words.

"Joseph's abilities are best judged over dinner. You must join me this evening. All of you, of course."

"As you can see, Henry, I did not bring along an adequate wardrobe. I would feel most uncomfortable dining out in these clothes."

"A problem easily solved. Hunter and I shall see to it immediately."

"How nice." She suspected her smile was weak.

To her dismay, Watkins truly meant immediately. He had Hunter out the door before she could think of anything that would delay them so that she could drag Hunter off for a moment's conversation. Worse, Jed, Charlie, and Tom were whisked away as well. In moments she found herself alone; there was no one to watch her and no one for her to question. She still had no answers, only questions. Shaking her head, she wondered if she would get any time alone with Hunter before they had to go to Watkins's to dine.

Although the men darted in and out all day, the sun was setting before she saw Hunter again. He had sent Tom to give her the new dress. It was a beautiful gown of the finest silk in a rich blue color that flattered her eyes. However, she felt little joy in it. It meant she had to see Henry Watkins again. She was struggling to pin her hair up when Hunter strode into their room, kicked the door shut, and tossed his hat on the bed.

"Watkins said he'd prefer your hair loose."

"Did he." She stuck another hairpin in to secure her hair. "Life's road is littered with disappointments."

"Leanne . . ." he began.

She whirled to glare at him. "What? Alone? No guard? Perhaps there's an ear pressed to the door."

"No. Not for the moment, at least."

"Managed to slip the leash, did you?"

"Yeah." He started to take off his shirt so that he could wash up. "Leanne, there's a lot you don't know, can't know, just yet. You'll just have to trust me. I reckon things don't look too good . . ."

"You reckon right. Things look as if the very last thing

I should do is trust you. Things look as if you mean to toss me to the wolves, hand me to Watkins on a silver platter. It's not only his slaveys that can press an ear to the door."

He swore softly as he splashed water from the basin over his torso. It was not hard to know what she meant. She had heard every word he said before she joined them for breakfast. He was lucky he was still breathing. Leanne should have been spitting fire, but she was not as furious as he'd expected. Evidently she was going to give him a chance to explain. He hoped she would accept the weak explanation he planned to give her. Though he hated using her, she was now vital to his plan.

Drying off, he admired her gown. It made him even more reluctant to use her. She looked beautiful. The dress revealed her lithe shape to perfection and flattered her coloring. She was temptation on two dainty feet and Watkins was a man who ruthlessly took what he wanted. The plan Hunter had formulated could well prove more dangerous than he had anticipated. Unfortunately, he had no alternative.

"You shouldn't believe everything you hear." He donned a clean shirt.

"I don't want to, but I haven't been given any good reason not to."

"You've got to trust me."

"That only goes so far, Hunter, especially when your words and actions tell me it's the last thing I should do."

"I haven't got the time now to explain everything. It wouldn't be smart either." Moving to stand before her, he lowered his voice to a near whisper. "There's only enough time to ask you to do something for me."

"What?" Following his lead, she also spoke softly.

Grasping her gently by the shoulders, he replied, "Play up to Watkins."

"Exactly what do you mean by that?"

"He's made no secret of the fact that he wants you. It would serve my purpose real well if you let him think that interest is returned."

"It isn't."

"I know that, but he doesn't. All I want is for you to draw him away from his guards."

"Why?"

"It's a long story. I promise I'll tell you all of it, but not now. Please, just trust me. I need your help."

"Just how much help do you expect me to give?"

Suddenly realizing what she suspected, he gave her a brief kiss. "Not too much. Just get him alone."

She felt the knots in her stomach slowly ease. "Only promise, not deliver?"

"Exactly."

"And you can make sure I won't be forced to give him the prize I use as a lure?"

"I swear to you, Leanne, you won't have to give him anything. Trust me."

Sighing, she shook her head, very inclined to do as he wished yet still uncertain. "You keep saying that, yet you give me so little reason to trust you."

"I know. I promise it'll all be clear after tonight."

"And this game you wish me to play is really necessary?"

"I need to get the man alone, away from his loyal hounds. Until today, when I saw his interest in you, I hadn't come up with a way to do that. You won't have to be alone with him for long."

"I'd better not be, Hunter, or you'll sorely regret it."

He smiled faintly, understanding her cross words for the agreement they were. Drawing her into his arms he gave her a slow, deep kiss. By the time the kiss ended, he was very reluctant to let her go, but she stepped free of his hold. He frowned when she walked to the mirror and tugged the pins from her hair.

"What're you doing?"

Watching him in the mirror as she quickly brushed out her hair, Leanne replied, "You said he liked it down."

"Yeah, so I did."

The grumpy tone to his voice nearly made her smile as she hastily braided the two front sections of her hair then looped them towards the back and pinned them there. It was the first indication that he did not like Watkins's interest in her. The last of her qualms eased. She would trust him.

"There. How does that look?" She turned around, allowing him a good look at her total appearance.

"I'm beginning to think twice about this plan of mine."

"You said you needed to get the man alone, away from his guards."

"I do."

"You also feel I can accomplish that."

"I don't feel it—I know it."

"And—this is guessing on my part—I think you are pressed for time to accomplish whatever it is you intend to accomplish."

"You guess right."

"Well, then, it seems you're stuck with the plan you've got."

"It seems so, but I'm liking it less and less. You're really not going to press for reasons, are you?" He was both pleased and slightly astonished at this sign of trust in him.

"You said you couldn't explain now but will later. I'll accept that. However, you can bet your life that I'll hold you to that promise once you've gotten whatever it is you seek."

"You'll get your explanations." He gave her a long look.

"Leanne, don't underestimate Watkins. He's dangerous. Play the game, but be on your guard."

"I intend to be." She frowned. "Just how dangerous is he?"

"He has no morals, obeys no laws. I know that sounds strange coming from me, but even outlaws have certain laws they stick to. Tom showed you that when he stopped Luke. Watkins seems to lack even the smallest sense of right or wrong. He cares for nothing and nobody. What he wants, he grabs. If something is in his way, he disposes of it. He's the worst sort of man to bait, but I can't think of any other way to get him alone," he muttered, running his hand through his hair in a gesture of agitation.

"I will only be alone with him for a moment."

"I don't plan on it being any longer than that." He shrugged. "But the best laid plans . . ."

"Oft go awry. I will keep all you've said in mind. I assume you will as well."

"I have since the first day I joined up with him." He cursed softly when there was a loud rap at the door.

"Time to go, Hunter," bellowed one of Watkins's men. "The boss don't like people being late."

"Can't have the boss displeased, can we," Leanne muttered as Hunter took her by the arm and started towards the door.

"His men would drag you there dripping from your bath rather than let that happen."

Outside the bedroom door lurked two burly, heavily armed men. Both of them looked her over in a way that chilled her. That they would not dare touch her because of Watkins's interest did not really ease her nervous reaction.

"Come on. He had a carriage sent for her."

"Well, I suppose it would be a little difficult to ride a horse in this finery," she murmured as she and Hunter followed the two men to where the carriage waited.

"Just wish I hadn't picked out one so fine," Hunter grumbled as he helped her into the carriage.

It pleased her to know Hunter had chosen the dress. She liked it far better knowing he had been the one to pick the flattering color and style.

To her annoyance, one of Watkins's men joined them in the carriage. It was evident that Henry Watkins did not trust anyone. For all his stolen riches and criminal genius he was, she realized, little more than a prisoner in a jail of his own making. It was justice of a sort, she mused, but something told her Henry Watkins was a man long overdue for a hanging.

And you're riding off to play flirtatious games with him, she reminded herself with a grimace. For all she knew Hunter planned to rob Watkins as he had robbed the bank in Clayville. But he had asked her to trust him, so she would. It was as simple as that. As the carriage halted, she prayed she was not making a terrible mistake.

Watkins's hacienda was breathtaking. The man was lavish with his ill-gotten gains, she mused as Hunter escorted her into the foyer. She could not help but wonder how many innocent people had gone hungry or lost everything because Watkins had robbed them to have chandeliers and fine Oriental carpets in his hideout. It was hard to hide the distaste she felt for the man when he took her hand in his.

"Leanne," Watkins murmured, kissing her hand, "you look lovely."

"You are most kind, Henry."

"Not kind. Merely truthful." He took her by the arm. "Come, Joseph is serving drinks in the front parlor."

She spared a brief glance for Hunter, who fell back with Jed, Charlie, and Tom. To play the game right, she would have to pay him little attention. She would have to fight her inclination to keep looking at him, to watch him move, to catch his faint rare smiles. For a little while she must fully suppress her fascination with Hunter.

Soon she was glad for all the lessons in manners and etiquette she had suffered through in school. She adequately feigned interest in all Watkins said, acting as if his conversation was the height of wit and wisdom instead of the conceited tripe or empty flattery it really was.

"An excellent meal, Henry," she said with the first honesty she had employed all evening.

"I can see you are a woman of breeding."

She smiled sweetly. "How kind." When he reached out to pat her hand, she fought the urge to pull away.

"Living in this cultural wasteland must be difficult for such a refined woman."

Lowering her lashes in what she hoped was an appropriately coy gesture, she murmured, "It *has* been difficult at times."

"Well, I believe I might have just the thing to alleviate the boredom."

"Really?"

"Some very fine paintings. True masterpieces."

"You're a collector?"

"In a manner of speaking."

"Oh, I should love to see them."

"And I will be proud to show them to you." Still holding her hand, he helped her to her feet.

"They are in your library?"

"No, my bedroom."

She hesitated. "Oh, Henry, I'm not sure . . ."

"Come, my dear, you can trust me."

Heartily doubting that, she let Watkins lead her away. She fought the urge to look at Hunter, to beseech him with a glance not to forget his promise. A moment alone with Watkins would be all she could abide. She chanced one glance behind her. Her questions about how Hunter could reach her in such a short time were answered. The guards Watkins waved away interpreted his gesture as complete dismissal and slipped out of the house.

"What the hell are you doing?" Charlie snapped the minute Watkins and his men were gone.

"Rolling a cigarette," Hunter drawled even as he tucked the makings back into his pocket.

"You've just let Watkins slip up them fancy steps of his with Leanne. They ain't headed up there to play checkers, y'know."

"I know." He lit his cigarette, fighting the urge to race right after the pair.

"You're up to something, ain't you? Planning something."

Jed's sudden insight was ill-timed, Hunter thought. "Sometimes a person's smartest when he doesn't know much and doesn't try too hard to find out anything."

That silenced Jed and Charlie. It was not for his own benefit that he wanted them ignorant, but for theirs. Ignorance of his plans could save their lives. He had come to see that they were outlaws mostly by accident. Though he had no time to save them from their ill-chosen path, as he increasingly wished to do, he wanted to be sure they were not dragged into the danger he was courting.

Grinding out the stub of his cigarette in the ornate ashtray by his seat, Hunter decided it was time to make his move. The guards had had time to wander far enough away and Watkins would be thoroughly occupied in cornering Leanne. He wanted to be sure to get to Leanne before Watkins frightened her.

"Where you going?" Charlie demanded when Hunter stood and started to leave the room.

"Best you don't ask."

After the door shut behind Hunter, Charlie and Jed frowned at each other. Their puzzlement grew when, a moment after Hunter left, Tom silently slipped from the room. For a minute they both scowled at the door.

"What d'you think, Jed?"

"Don't like it, Charlie. Something's going on."

"And Leanne's smack dab in the middle of it, poor kid. Reckon we oughta do something to be sure she ain't hurt."

"Reckon—but what? Who's doing what and who're they doing it to? Do we watch Hunter, Tom, or Watkins's men?"

Charlie shook his head. "Watkins's men. I got me a feeling that's where the real trouble'll come."

Leanne barely suppressed a shudder of revulsion when Watkins slipped his arm around her waist as they stood before his prized painting. It was obvious the man felt she should be awed by his ill-gotten gain, awed by him. What distressed her was the realization that Hunter had aided this man. How many other men like Watkins did Hunter deal with? She hated seeing this aspect of Hunter's life, hated thinking she might have to see more like Watkins if she stayed with Hunter.

"I can see you are an educated woman, one who appreciates the finer things in life," Watkins murmured after she expressed her delight in the painting. "You need a man who can give you those things."

"Hunter . . ." she began, sure it would not be too risky to defend her lover.

"Will never be more than a common thief."

And you are so much better, she thought. "I did notice he seems to have gained little from his efforts."

"He hasn't the intelligence or the experience to plan these little excursions. He is a follower, not a leader."

"I had begun to realize that he was little more than a lackey."

"And you deserve so much more, Leanne." He turned her towards him, tugging her into his arms.

She shaded her eyes with half-closed lids, feigning demureness while hiding her nearly violent distaste as he touched his cold, dry lips to her cheek. "You flatter me, Henry."

"Not at all. Your sweetness, your refinement, is wasted on that ill-bred drifter." He cupped her chin in his hand and turned her face up to his. "But say the word and I will make sure that he never draws near you again."

God help me, he's going to kiss me, she thought as he

lowered his mouth to hers. She knew she was going to have to endure it. Oh, where in the world was Hunter?

Watkins suddenly tensed and broke off the kiss. Leanne slowly opened her eyes, then sighed with intense relief. Hunter stood behind Watkins, his Colt pressed steadily against the base of the other man's skull. She quickly stepped out of Watkins's hold, unthinkingly but vigorously wiping the touch of his lips from her mouth.

"That was the longest moment I have ever had to suffer through. I began to think you weren't coming."

"I told you I would. Don't you have any faith in me, darlin'?" Hunter mistrusted the ease of his success but, smiling at Leanne, he was determined to hide his qualms from her.

"It was wavering."

"Glad I was in time to shore it back up. Get the curtain ties. We'll truss this bastard up."

"You won't get ten feet from this place," Watkins hissed.

"I feel lucky today. Tie his wrists together, Leanne," Hunter ordered when she returned to his side, the ornate but strong curtain ties in her hands. "Hands behind your back, Watkins."

Slipping in between Hunter and Watkins, she wrapped one length of rope around Watkins's wrists. "I'm not sure I can tie a very good knot, Hunter."

"Just tie it easy then. I'll finish it off."

"One word from me and twenty men will be up here to fill you full of holes—if I decide to let you die so easily."

"Say that word, Watkins," Hunter drawled, his voice low and cold, "and they'll find the first hole's been made before they set foot inside the door—right through your head."

"I'll hunt you down. You won't be able to crawl into a hole I can't find."

"True enough, because you'll be right there with me. You're coming back with me, Watkins. Back to the States to face the law."

Leanne felt as shocked as Watkins acted. "Taking him? I thought you were taking his money or something. Him? Why him?"

"This bastard's going to clear my name. He's going to a little town on the Texas–New Mexico border and talk to the law. Remember about a year ago, Watkins? A certain payroll job?"

"What about it?"

"I was responsible for the payroll your henchman took."

"You're that fool?"

Hunter's laugh was soft and bitter. "Fool is right. I left myself open to take the blame, failed my responsibility and a lot of people too. I've spent every day since then running from the trouble you put me in."

"And now you're going to buy your way out of it by turning me in."

"Damn right."

"There's a lot of territory between here and that sad excuse for a town. My men'll be at your heels every step of the way."

"I've just come nearly five hundred miles with the law on my tail. Think I can manage a hundred or so with your scum doing the chasing—if they even bother." He looked at Leanne, who still stared at him wide-eyed. "Knot done?"

"Almost finished."

"Hurry up. Time's wasting."

Suddenly there was the unmistakable sound of a gun being cocked. Leanne froze, as did Hunter, and stared horrified at Tom, who stood before them, his gun pointed their way. Watkins's soft laugh chilled her as much as his words.

"Time's just run out, Walsh."

Chapter Nine

"Better finish tying the scum up, Walsh," Tom in-structed. "Miss Summers seems to be having trouble."

"You're not going to shoot us?" Leanne whispered as Hunter holstered his gun and nudged her out of the way.

"Just what the hell game are you playing, Tom?" Watkins snarled. "You throw your lot in with this fool and you're a dead man."

"I've been trying to help Walsh ever since I found out your man set him up to look like a thief."

Hunter glanced at Tom. "Tuckman?"

"Yup. I've been after Watkins for longer than a year, but Tuckman managed to get word to me about you. The only one of Watkins's men who could recognize you was dead but"—he shrugged—"he figured you might need help sometime."

Leanne felt a strong urge to scream. Everything had suddenly changed. She had understood enough to know that Hunter did not work for Watkins; he had been working against the man. Apparently, so had Tom. Hunter must be working for the law, because she recalled that the man called Tuckman was a sheriff. Those facts brought waves of confusion instead of answers, however. Hunter was not the outlaw she had thought. Everything had been a lie, she realized, and she stared at Hunter as that conclusion transformed shock and confusion to fury.

Hunter looked at Leanne, saw the anger hardening her eyes, and sighed. Just as he had feared, she'd quickly grasped the implications of everything that had been said.

"Just who the hell are you?" she demanded.

"Tarrant Hunter Walsh of Little Creek, Texas."

"Well at least the name you gave yourself wasn't a complete lie."

He winced. "Leanne, let me explain. . . ."

"This talk'll have to wait," Tom said. "Watkins's men don't completely relax their guard when he shoos them away. They apt to check on him now and again."

"Your explanations had better be damned good," Leanne nearly snarled as Hunter grabbed hold of Watkins and the four of them cautiously left the room.

Hunter found himself praying they would be. Leanne was in a cold-eyed fury. She knew he had lied about his name and about what he was doing. Now she undoubtedly saw everything that had passed between them as lies. That, he realized, was the very last thing he wanted.

At the bottom of the stairs there was a brief, tense confrontation with Jed and Charlie, who had moved into the hall to keep a better watch on Watkins's men. Leanne looked at the four men she had spent so much time with and found herself praying vigorously that no one would fire the guns they were all aiming at each other. Watkins certainly was not worth it.

"What're you doing with him?" Charlie nodded towards Watkins.

"Taking him out of here," Hunter answered.

"What about Leanne? She going too?"

"Yes. She stays with me." Hunter inwardly breathed a sigh of relief when she made no immediate protest.

"You wanna go with him, Leanne?"

She stared at Charlie and Jed, a little stunned by the realization that this confrontation was over her, not Watkins. Then she saw that she had a choice. She could turn and walk away from Hunter and his lies right now. Charlie and Jed would take care of her. It both annoyed and surprised her when she realized that she did not want to take that way out, that she could not walk away from Hunter—not yet.

"Yes, Charles. I'll stay with Hunter. He has a little explaining to do."

"Gonna be some trouble getting Watkins outta here," Charlie remarked as he holstered his gun, Jed following suit. "Reckon you could use some help."

"Better get some horses, and quick. I readied only enough for us," Tom said.

"Out back?"

"Yeah, Charlie. As close to the back gate as I could, just beyond the wall and hidden in his damned fruit trees."

"We'll meet you there." Charlie left, Jed at his heels.

"You won't get past my men," Watkins snarled.

Leanne gasped, mostly with surprise, when Tom hit Watkins, knocking the man out. "Wouldn't it have been easier to gag him?"

"But not as enjoyable." With a little assistance from Hunter, Tom hefted the unconscious Watkins over his shoulder.

"Don't you think someone will notice us slipping out with him?" she asked as they hurried towards the back exit.

Placing his pistol against Watkins's temple, Hunter kept in perfect step with Tom. "They'll notice this too."

It surprised her that they got as far as they did. They were halfway across the courtyard before a cry went up. Hunter's assumption proved correct. None of Watkins's men dared shoot once they realized their boss's life was threatened. Nonetheless, Leanne was nearly dizzy with relief when they finally reached the horses.

"Three pack horses? Why so many?" Hunter asked as he helped Tom secure Watkins on the back of one of the horses. Neither of them relaxed their guard on the few men who still watched them.

"There's the money we stole, supplies for the trip, and every damn bit of money or valuables I could get my hands on. Just maybe we can help some of those who couldn't recoup the losses this piece of scum made them swallow. Ready?"

Barely mounted herself, Leanne had no time to respond before Hunter and Tom were mounted and spurring their horses on. Tom kept Watkins close, his gun still aimed at the man, until they were out of range of the hacienda's guards. Leanne listened for the sounds of pursuit, frowning when she heard none. The only men following them were Charlie and Jed who caught up just as the hacienda faded from view.

"Wondered if you'd changed your mind." Hunter hid his pleasure at their joining him.

"Takes time to cut so many saddle cinches," Charlie drawled.

To Leanne's amazement, all four men started to laugh. Men, she decided crossly, had the world's strangest sense of humor.

Leanne began to think Hunter and Tom meant to race all the way to Little Creek before they finally stopped. When they finally called a halt, she slid off her horse, wincing slightly as she steadied herself on her feet. It seemed she was never going to get used to such long stints in the saddle. She felt bone weary.

In an attempt to keep herself from thinking about the way Hunter had lied to her, she began to prepare coffee. The fire was small and sheltered so as not to draw much notice. It was a test of her skills to work over such a fire, and she felt her spirits rise when she succeeded. The men were too tense, too watchful, to be very appreciative. The now conscious Watkins glared at them and made such awful threats that Leanne began to tremble.

"You just ignore him, Leanne," Charlie mumbled when he noticed. "Shut your fat mouth, Watkins, before I shut it for you." He looked at Hunter. "You sure you need him alive?"

" 'Fraid so, Charlie." Hunter glanced at Watkins. Charlie's threat had caused the man to retreat into a sullen silence. "He has to talk to the law in Little Creek."

"Little Creek? Didn't we pass through there?"

"Yup. Watkins sent one of his men there about a year back, stole a payroll, killed a man, and left me to take the blame. He's going to clean up that little bit of confusion, then face justice for his crimes."

"You mean you ain't supposed to be an outlaw?" Jed scowled with confusion as he collected the empty mugs.

"Nope, and to be honest—"

"That makes a nice change," Leanne muttered.

Hunter decided to ignore that for now. "I never have been. I wheedled my way in with Watkins, then went on that job to get even closer to him. The money taken will be returned. I hope you can agree to that."

"Don't bother us none," Charlie said. Jed nodded. "We never saw much of the money anyways."

"Don't think we oughta be dealing with the law though," Jed added. "We are outlaws." His eyes widened and he hesitantly reached for his gun. "You ain't gonna turn us in, are you? And what about Leanne?" He stared at Tom with a look of astonishment. "Hell, ain't he wanted too?"

"I don't intend to turn anyone but Watkins over to the law." Hunter looked at Leanne. "When Watkins falls, he'll take Sheriff Martin with him and that should clear up your trouble." Looking back at Charlie and Jed, he spoke sternly. "I offer you two the chance to get out of this life."

"Without going to jail?" Jed pressed.

"Without going to jail."

"You think you can do that?"

"I don't think it'll be hard," Tom answered.

"And how can you be so sure? Who the hell are you anyways?" Charlie demanded.

"I was feeling a little curious about that myself," Leanne murmured, looking at Tom.

"The name's Sebastian Lucas Crane the third," he answered with a faint smile, "Deputy Federal Marshal."

Leanne felt as stunned as the others looked. "But . . . that bounty hunter. You killed him, didn't you?"

"Nope. Got up behind the fool, put my Colt to his head, and politely informed him that he was interfering in government business and I'd appreciate it if he'd get the hell out of there. Told him to play dead 'til we left, then hightail it after his compadre. Also gave him a bit of advice on the risks of bounty hunting."

"And Luke? You were after Luke as well?"

"Yes. I'd been after Luke Meede for a long time."

"Oh. Well, I'm not sorry you stopped him, but I am sorry you had to kill him to do it."

"I'm not." He grimaced upon seeing everyone's shock. "The lawman in me said to take him alive, but the man in me wanted him dead. He killed a good friend of mine."

"I'm sorry," was all Leanne could think to say. "All this time"—she shook her head—"and I never guessed. You seem to have become more talkative as well as legal."

"Talking too much gets more people in trouble than I dare count. Keep quiet and you're less apt to give anything away. I learned a long time ago that the steel-eyed, closed-mouth pose works best. When you do talk, folk listen real close. Puts more weight behind a threat. Makes you look more dangerous. If people don't know you and can't read you, they are wary of you."

She sighed, then glared at Hunter. Tom had his reasons for being secretive, as did Hunter. However, she could see no good reason for Hunter to be so secretive with her, not after all that had passed between them. His lack of trust cut her deeply, but she fought to hide that hurt behind anger.

"Seems I've been surrounded by liars ever since Charity threw me out."

"Now, wait a minute—" Hunter began to protest, deciding it was time to start defending himself.

"We didn't tell you no lies," Charlie said. Jed nodded.

"I know, and I thank both of you. You have been true friends."

Hunter scowled, knowing those last words were aimed directly at him.

She looked at Tom. "Are all our things in that collection of packs?"

"They are. Yours are tied in that blue blanket. Thought you might want them quick at hand."

"That was very thoughtful. Thank you. Now, if no one has any objection, I intend to change before this dress is destroyed beyond any hope of repair." When no objection was voiced, she moved to collect her things and find a niche that offered some sort of privacy.

Frowning after her until she was out of sight, Hunter asked Tom, "Think it's safe?"

"We're as safe now as we'll be for the rest of this trip. It'll take hours for Watkins's men to get saddles or mend what they have. It's also too dark now to find our trail. If they did start out before dark, they'd have been forced to stop by now."

"Do you really think any of those hired guns has the loyalty to care about getting him back?"

"Loyalty won't have much to do with it, although I suspect some of his men value the set-up he has enough to try and keep it going. Didn't Watkins tell you about what happens if he gets taken? The reward for the one who gets him back?"

"Oh, hell. Forgot about that."

"Two thousand dollars can buy a lot of loyalty."

"We'd better set up a watch then."

"Yeah. No telling if some maverick broke from the rest and is close on our heels."

After arranging the watch schedule, Hunter sighed and looked in the direction where Leanne had disappeared. "I suppose it wouldn't be wise to try to make my explanations now."

"If you wait, you won't be making them until we reach Tuckman. Reckon that mad she's nursing will have set real hard by then. Why didn't you tell her?" Tom asked.

"At first, I wasn't sure I could trust her. Her tale was a bit far-fetched."

"But true. Best move or she'll be back here, and I have a feeling she's in no mood to stroll off alone with you by choice."

Hunter nodded, rose, and set out after Leanne. When he found her, she was sitting on the ground holding her new gown and softly weeping. He felt something inside of him twist painfully at the sight. He crouched at her side, but she jerked away from his touch, rejecting his meager attempt to soothe her.

Leanne wiped frantically at her tears, keeping her face averted. She had not intended to cry, had not wanted to. Once alone, however, all the hurt she had felt upon discovering Hunter's lies swept over her. She heartily wished Hunter had not been the one to find her giving in to her tears.

"Leanne," he began as he sat next to her, "I know it looks bad."

"Nice to see you have the wit to reach that remarkable conclusion."

Although it was hard not to return her anger, he found it easier to handle than her tears. "My life was at stake. Any hint that I wasn't who I said I was, and I was a dead man."

She turned to glare at him. "Did you really think I'd risk your life? I was in the same position as you." Her eyes widened as she caught his fleeting look of guilt. "You thought I was lying. You never trusted me."

"That's not true, Leanne. In the beginning I did doubt you. Can you blame me? Your tale was rather wild. The reason I got into this mess was because I trusted too quickly. I trusted Watkins's man, didn't question his claim that he was a bank official. I practically gave him the pay-roll I was responsible for. I also trusted the woman he used as a lure to put me in the wrong place at the wrong time, so I would have no alibi. It all left me looking guilty as hell. I didn't dare trust you. I nearly lost my life before. I couldn't risk it again."

His explanation made sense. However, it only excused his initial distrust. She knew she had done nothing to justify his suspicions, nothing to warrant his lingering wariness. The hurt he had inflicted was not so easily banished.

"And even after we made love, you were afraid I was going to stab you in the back?"

He took her hands in his. "Not at all. By then I knew you were exactly what you claimed to be."

"Did you. Strange, but I don't recall your telling me who you were. You still didn't trust me."

"It wasn't lack of trust that kept me quiet, but lack of courage. I knew I should tell you, but I didn't want to face what I'm facing now. I put off the confrontation until there was no avoiding it. The only lie between us, Leanne, is that I am not really the outlaw you thought me."

Yanking her hands from his, she spat out, "Oh, and such a little one it is, too. Nothing to bother about, right? Shouldn't bother me at all to think I'm lying down with some outlaw. Shouldn't trouble me at all that I'm taking up with a man who's only future is jail, a bullet, or a rope. Why should I worry that I'm sinking myself deeper into the mire of outlawry by joining him instead of running from him? Why should I care that my first lover doesn't consider me worth enough to even let me know who he really is?"

Hunter felt wracked with guilt. He realized that he had given little thought to what she might be feeling. It was not just the lie he had to make amends for. He had cost her a great deal of peace of mind. He doubted that she had voiced all of the conflict she had been suffering.

"I'm sorry."

"How nice." She hated the sneering tone of her voice but was unable to soften it.

"It was blind of me, but I never thought of how it would affect you to keep thinking I was an outlaw. I should have. The moment I accepted the truth of who you were, it should have occurred to me. A woman like you doesn't usually take up with the kind of man you thought I was."

"Especially not when she could be throwing away her chances of proving her own innocence."

"My only excuse, and it's a weak one, is that I really didn't see myself as the man I was pretending to be." He took her hands back into his. "Especially not when I was with you. With you I had to constantly remind myself of the role I was playing and act it."

He seemed so honestly sorry that her hurt and anger began to lessen. "And all that business about keeping me close so I wouldn't talk and endanger you? Was that all a lie too?"

"No, just the results I left you to imagine. I couldn't risk anyone looking too closely at me or anything I was involved in. If I had gotten pulled in by the law, Tuckman probably would've gotten me out of it. He's not a sheriff, but a federal marshal. It would've ruined months of work, however. It might've even lost me my place in Watkins's gang."

"Of course. Your getting free would have been suspicious in itself." She took a moment to think over everything that had been said, then frowned. "Wait a minute. You keep talking about Little Creek, Texas, and this Tuckman. Didn't we meet him at the start of our journey way the other end of New Mexico?"

"That meeting was arranged as soon as I knew what job Watkins was sending me on. It was the one place we could meet without raising suspicion. It would require little deviation from the route we needed to take, and the chances of any of Watkins's men being there were pretty slim."

"And you didn't know about Tom? I mean, Sebastian?"

"Nope. I didn't know about him until exactly when you did. I guess Tuckman decided it was safer for both of us, less chance of giving ourselves away."

He watched her closely as she bent her head to stare at their joined hands, hiding her eyes from him. Her anger had faded, but not all her wariness and hurt. He wanted to take that pain and suspicion away, but he was not sure how to go about it. She had trusted him and he had rewarded her trust with a lie. It was not surprising that she now wondered if she had been a fool. He knew he would have felt the same.

Leanne was uncertain of what to do next. She felt lost, confused. Every step she had taken, every decision she had made, had been based on a lie. She felt unsure about Hunter himself; was he the same man she had fallen in love with? Perhaps, like Tom, he had kept more than his name a secret—perhaps he had hidden his real nature as well.

"Leanne, I know it was wrong," Hunter said softly. "Unfair as well. I was constantly asking you to trust me, yet I never told you the whole truth. All I can say is I'm sorry. I swear this—nothing else that happened between us was an act or a lie."

"It's just—" She took a deep breath to steady herself, then looked at him. "I'm not sure I know who you are now."

Cautiously, he pulled her into his arms. "I'm Hunter."

"No, you're Tarrant Hunter Walsh of Little Creek."

"I'm Hunter."

"Tom seems changed. He's Sebastian now—talkative and not so cold. What'll change about you?"

"Very little. I can hold your hand now or kiss your

bruises without thinking I'll look too soft to the men. What changes happened in me happened before I met you. I'm a little harder, a little more wary. Other than that, I'm the same man they know in Little Creek. I swear it. I'm not as skilled as Sebastian at playing a role." He felt some of the tension leave her and inwardly sighed with relief.

"What does your family call you?" In his arms, the last of her hurt began to fade.

"Tarrant. But if you like it better, there's no reason for you to call me that. You can keep calling me Hunter. I'll admit I've grown sort of used to it."

"And after our names are cleared? Will you help me find my father? Once you're back with your family, I'll need a place to go. Grant Summers might not want me around, but at least he can help me get settled somewhere."

"You'll be settled somewhere—with me."

She leaned away from him to look directly into his face. "Hunter, what's acceptable when you're an outlaw on the run is not something you can carry on with back in the bosom of your family. Our names will be cleared, and we'll be upright citizens again. More or less. I know that I couldn't bear the consequences of being your mistress."

"Then be my wife."

Briefly he felt as surprised as she looked, then decided it was the perfect solution. Now that his troubles were almost over, he knew it was the right step—the only step—to take. He did not want to lose her, and the surest way to keep her at his side was to marry her.

Brushing a kiss over her mouth, he murmured, "Well? Nothing to say?"

"You don't have to do that. I became your lover think-

ing you were an outlaw. There were no promises made
then. You don't have to make them now."

It was hard to say those words. Her first impulse had
been to grab his offer with both hands and hang on tightly.
It was what she wanted. Second thoughts had come
quickly. She did not want him marrying her simply because he felt it was what he should do, because he felt he
had to. That was not the way to establish and build a good
marriage.

"I know I don't." He sighed. "Leanne, I haven't got a
lot of pretty words for you. The only thing I've given
much thought to in over a year is clearing my name and
getting home. Since we stumbled into each other in that
little town, I haven't taken much time to think about us,
but I know how badly I want you. That I've always been
sure of.

"When you spoke about our parting ways," he went
on, "I knew there was one more thing I was sure of. I
don't want you leaving. I want you to stay at my side just
as you have since Clayville. I can't think of a better way
to keep you there than marrying you."

Cupping her face in his hands, he smiled crookedly.
"Not real romantic, I know. But I'm not just offering what
I think I ought to because you were a virgin." He smiled
briefly over her deep blush. "I do want to marry you. The
reasons may not be the kind to put stars in your eyes, but
they're good, solid ones. I don't intend to tuck you away
as a duty done. I mean this marriage to be a real one in all
the ways it should be."

He was right. It was not romantic. However, he expressed the desire to keep her near him and did not want
her to leave him. That, she knew, was not something to

scoff at. It was a start. She could build on that need, would be a fool not to try.

"All right." She laughed softly when he hugged her tightly, but her laughter was stopped by his heated kiss. "Shouldn't we get back to camp?" She gasped when he pushed her down onto the ground.

"Tonight's about the safest time we'll have until we reach Little Creek. I intend to take advantage of that."

"I can see that," she murmured as he undid her shirt.

"I promise you, Leanne, you won't regret saying yes. I might not be the best husband you could get, but I don't think I'll be the worst."

"No." She sighed her pleasure when he began to brush heated kisses over her breasts. "I don't think you will be either."

Their lovemaking was rough, fierce, and heated. Leanne savored every moment of it. Reeling from the strength of the release they shared, she held him close and thought about the future. There was hope that one day he would love her as deeply as she loved him. He needed to keep her at his side. That had to stem from some deeper feeling for her. She would simply strengthen it and bring it forward.

Nuzzling her neck, Hunter murmured, "I have a confession to make."

"Another one?"

"'Fraid so."

"Well, since you asked me to marry you, I must assume you are not about to tell me of a wife and a dozen children tucked away somewhere."

"You assume right. This is going to sound crazy. There was another, smaller reason I didn't tell you the truth about myself, a totally selfish reason. I reckon the others could be called selfish too."

"Protecting your life could be called selfish but it's something anyone and everyone would do. You do believe I never would have . . ." She met his gaze when he placed a finger against her lips to halt her words.

"I trust you, Leanne. You've been the one person I have trusted in all this. When you gave up a perfect chance to escape to tend to Jed's wound, I began to trust you."

Rolling onto his back, he settled her on top of him. "This selfish reason was—well, wanting you to want me even though I was an outlaw." He laughed ruefully when she frowned. "Whatever was happening between us was happening despite your thinking I was nothing but a bank robber with no future. I wanted that. Hell, I needed it.

"When everything went wrong, people turned against me. Even my father and two of my brothers. Theirs was a short desertion but it cut deep. Only my brother Owen stuck with me from the start, asking if I was guilty, but prepared to stay with me whether I was or not. There are still those, including my own mother, who'll need Watkins's confession before they believe in me again. When you came to me, you did so thinking I was a bank robber on the run. There was a part of me that needed your trust. I'm not explaining this very well."

"Well enough." She brushed a kiss over his mouth. "You're talking to someone who's been through the same. I know all about those crazy needs that spring up when you've been accused unfairly or tossed out."

"Of course." He kissed her, slowly but with a growing hunger as he smoothed his hands down her slim back.

A little breathless, she smiled at him when he finally released her mouth. "Then, too, there was my big plan to reform you."

"Oh?"

"Um—hmmmm."

"Into a farmer?"

"Maybe a storekeeper. After all, I wouldn't want you too tired when you came home at night."

"Heaven forbid."

"Hunter, just what do you do? What'll you—we—be going back to when your name is cleared?"

"A ranch. I'm the eldest son. Most of it'll be mine some day. I've been raised to it since I was born. Think you can stand to be the wife of a rancher?"

"Just so long as you don't mind being the husband of someone who's got nothing." She sighed. "I don't even know what my true parentage is, Hunter. All I know is Charity, and all that was a lie."

"And then you meet up with me and just get more lies." He felt a renewed sense of disgust with himself.

"Yours had some good reasons behind them, reasons I could understand. I don't understand the why of Charity's play-acting or the why of my father's desertion."

"Then we'll find out. We'll find your father if you want to do that."

"I think I do, if only to ask a few questions so that I can understand the past, who I really am."

"You're Leanne Summers soon to be Mrs. Walsh. I know what you mean, though. It's as if you just popped up out of nowhere. We'll find those answers for you, little one. As soon as we get our names cleared and join your name to mine."

She smiled and gave herself over to his lovemaking. It would be good to get those answers, but the need was not as strong as it had been. Knowing she would soon be Hunter's wife, that he wanted her at his side, dispelled a lot of the loneliness which had plagued her since Charity had thrown her out. Leanne prayed that she would find all she craved with Hunter in the years to come. If not, she feared the desertion of her father and Charity's rejection would seem small wounds compared to the blows Hunter could inflict.

Chapter Ten

"THAT ROUTE WILL ADD A WEEK TO OUR JOURNEY. WHY go up into New Mexico Territory and back down into Texas when we can just ride straight west?" Hunter frowned down at the crude map Sebastian had scratched in the dirt.

"It could add years to our lives."

"You think Watkins's men are that close?"

"I know they are."

Hunter glanced at Leanne. She sat a few feet from them, fanning herself with her hat and looking as tired and dirty as he felt. They had been riding hard for three days, and now Sebastian was suggesting a detour that could make the remaining journey take ten days instead of four. He did not know if she could do it. But Sebastian was right; there was a very good chance that the roundabout route would be far safer than the one that Watkins's men expected them to follow.

"She'll be worn to the bone, but she'll be alive," Sebastian said, speaking quietly so that Leanne would not overhear.

"That's true enough."

"I hoped the time Charlie and Jed bought us would be enough to keep us a step ahead all the way to Little Creek. Unfortunately, it wasn't. If we keep going straight, following the expected route, they'll catch us for sure."

"We'll be riding through some dangerous country if we turn from this route."

"True, but a lot of people do it and come through without an incident. We've got a hell of an incident sniffing at our heels. By my count, there's twenty of the bastards bearing down on us. Even if we ride as fast as we can, they'll be riding right over us by noon tomorrow. You want to risk her in that, or do you want to gamble we'll be one of the groups that travels over this other route without trouble?"

"Don't have much choice, do I? We'll go the longer but safer way."

For nine long days, Hunter wondered if he had chosen the right way. Leanne looked pale and drawn but made no complaint. They moved steadily, forever on the watch for Apaches or outlaws. The only good thing he could say about the arduous trip was that it worked to shut Watkins's mouth. As exhausted as the rest of them, his insults and threats had finally ended.

On the morning of the tenth day, when dawn's light barely touched the dark sky, Hunter crouched by Leanne where she sat by the low fire finishing a cup of coffee. She did not look as if she had the strength left to mount, let alone ride another full day through the scrub and the dust. He was not sure what he could say to give her that needed strength.

"How are you faring, little one?"

It was the honest concern in his voice that kept her from flinging some sharp answer at him. For a moment she continued to sip at the strong coffee, feeling the warmth of it begin to soothe her troubled stomach. She was so exhausted. It was undoubtedly that which had caused her to feel so nauseated for days. She almost wished she could be sick, but on the trail from dawn to dusk, always watchful for Indians, outlaws, or Watkins's hired guns, it was hard to give in to that. So she fought it and suffered in silence.

"We'll get there today, right?" she finally said.

"Yeh, darlin', by nightfall if not sooner. Texas and home is just over the horizon. Anything you need?"

"A bed and a hot bath."

He smiled and kissed her cheek. "As soon as we reach Little Creek."

"That a promise?"

"It's a promise." He winked. "Won't be hard to keep either, as I'll be looking for the same things."

She managed a weak smile. "I would prefer to be clean and well rested before I meet your family, but I'll understand if you want to go there first."

"They can wait a day or two. The marshal will want us close at hand for a while."

"Of course." She took a deep breath and finally gave voice to a fear she had been unable to fully conquer. "Are you sure the marshal won't want to put me in jail, too? Or Charlie and Jed? I've been in jail once. Short as my stay was, it was long enough. I'd really hate to see Charlie and Jed arrested either, especially after the help they've given us."

"I feel the same. Don't worry about it. You won't go to jail. Your name won't be cleared immediately, but I know Tuckman will leave all three of you in my custody if nothing else. Sebastian won't let it happen either, and he's got the last word. They don't stick so close to the letter of the law out here."

"That's a relief. It did worry me a little."

"Put your worries aside, darlin'. We're almost home free."

That "almost" was what troubled her, but she kept her concern to herself. Hunter and the others had more than enough to worry about without having to take time to soothe her. They certainly did not need to listen to a doomsayer. She would keep her mouth shut and her fears hidden and let herself be pleasantly proven wrong when they rode into Little Creek without trouble.

It was her lingering doubt that kept her from being surprised when, five miles from their destination, a shot rang out. The next few moments were bedlam as they scrambled for shelter, ending up behind a barely adequate wall of scattered rocks, saddles, and packs. Even as they settled down to fight back, Charlie, who had been sent ahead to scout out the approaches to town, came galloping toward them crouched low in the saddle to make a smaller target for the hail of bullets fired in his direction by the men hot on his heels. She watched in admiration as his horse sailed over their haphazard wall, and Charlie flung himself from the saddle and rolled into their midst.

"That was an astounding bit of derring-do, Charles,"

she said as he eased up to the barrier on the left side of her.

"Painful though."

"Are you wounded?" Although he was dusty and battered, she could see no sign of any serious wound.

"Nope. They missed." He winced as he shifted position.

"Think you have a broken bone?"

"Nope, but I think I've dented near every one I have." He grinned when she giggled softly.

The men who had sprung the trap and those who had been chasing Charlie found what cover they could, neatly encircling them. It looked to be a long, perhaps deadly, siege. Leanne saw no way out of it, not even in giving back Watkins. Freed, he would certainly do his utmost to see them all dead.

"I told you you'd never live to see me hang, Hunter," Watkins jeered.

"I wouldn't look so happy if I were you. Those bullets your men are so free with could hit you as easily as us."

"Just so long as I see you and your little whore die first."

Sebastian stopped Hunter when he whirled to aim his gun at the goading Watkins. "Don't do it, Hunter. Don't let him push you into becoming a killer when we're so close."

Although he eased his stance, Hunter snapped, "Close? We might as well be a hundred miles away. How in hell are we going to get through this ring of killers?" He regretted his hasty words when he saw how pale Leanne had grown.

"Not very easily. Think there's anyone left between town and this scum, Charlie?"

"No, they all came hightailing it after me."

"Then they were set there to be sure no one reached town before they could trap us all here."

"Seems that they've done that real well." Hunter decided there was no sense in hiding the full danger from Leanne. She was smart enough to see it for herself.

"Charlie got in. Someone could get out," Sebastian muttered, trying to locate each of their foes with narrowed eyes.

"And someone could find themselves shot full of holes."

"Hunter's right. I was just damn lucky."

"Is there any benefit to risking it?" Leanne asked.

"There certainly is, Miss Summers. I don't mean to alarm you . . ."

"Don't worry about it. I'm quite thoroughly alarmed already."

"If we just set here, we're dead. It's as simple as that. We don't have the ammunition to last longer than they can. They've also got the ability to go for more. In town is Marshal Tuckman and whatever men he can get. If I can get to him, I can bring him back here and catch at least half of this swine in a crossfire."

"But Hunter's right. There seems little chance of your surviving a run through a rain of bullets. Isn't there a chance someone could become aware of what's happening here and come to help?"

"Not much of one. Any poor fool who wanders into this is a dead man."

"And if you go out there, you're a dead man."

"Maybe. I can wait to die here, or I can chance dying out there—maybe get through and maybe get help."

"There really isn't much choice, is there?"

"Don't see that there is. Marshal Tuckman's got no idea of when we're coming in." When Leanne fell silent Sebastian pressed, "Nothing else? I was sort of hoping you'd come up with something that sounded good."

"I'm afraid I've run out of possibilities."

She winced when Jed muttered, "Got one of the bastards."

"Let me go, Sebastian," Hunter said. "I'm the reason we're in this mess. I ought to be the one to get us out of it."

"No, Hunter. You'll stay put. Can't say I'll do any better than you but I'm trained in all this. You're not. Anyway, it's Watkins who's put us in this spot, not you. I was sent out after him months before you arrived. Solving your troubles was just a little side business."

"I just don't see how you can do it."

"If I keep low and move fast, it'll make me hard to hit."

Leanne watched with a sense of hopelessness as Jed crept about to bring Sebastian's horse to him. Using the meager cover of the boulders that formed the sturdiest part of their makeshift fortress, Sebastian mounted. She ducked down with the rest of them as, after creeping back a short distance, Sebastian dug in his spurs to prod his nervous mount into a gallop and, a moment later, sailed over them and the low barrier they hid behind.

The moment Sebastian's mount touched the ground outside their precarious fortress, Leanne was deafened by a storm of gunfire. She held her hands over her ears as Jed, Charlie, and Hunter tried to provide some cover for Sebastian, even as Watkins's men did their best to hit the man speeding through their trap. Tensely, she waited for someone to tell her that Sebastian had fallen or that his mount had. When no word came and the surge of shooting ebbed, she dared a look. In the distance, outside the deadly circle of Watkins's men, she saw the dust of several riders.

"He made it?" She spoke softly, eager for yet fearing the answer to her question.

"Looks like he did." Hunter decided she did not need to share his conviction that Sebastian was riding with several bullets in him. "Unfortunately, a couple of Watkins's men are hard on his heels. We couldn't stop all of them."

"They won't chase him all the way to the marshal and town."

"Probably not. It'll be a damn long five miles, though."

"I kept thinking they'd shoot his horse."

They may yet, Hunter thought, but kept it to himself.

Time edged by, punctuated by savage attacks and swift retreats by Watkins's men interspersed with quiet moments when only a few potshots were exchanged. As sunset reddened the sky, she almost wished for some swift ending to the whole matter—or any change at all in the growing monotony of the siege, deadly as it might yet become.

Inching up so that she could take yet another look toward town, she was suddenly sent tumbling backwards by the impact of a bullet. It tore through her left shoulder, but for a moment she felt no real pain, simply astonishment. It seemed grossly unfair to her that she, the only one besides Watkins who was not shooting at anyone, should be the first of their number to be wounded.

"Leanne!" Hunter scrambled to her side.

"I don't think I'm too badly hurt."

"I'll be the judge of that. Wriggle over here where there's a little more cover."

By the time she was settled in the somewhat restrictive shelter of the taller rocks, her shock had faded and pain was sweeping over her. She grit her teeth against a scream as a strangely wan-looking Hunter ripped open her shirt, bathed her wound, and bandaged it. She wondered how anyone could live through the pain of a more serious wound. She knew hers was not a bad one, yet the pain was almost past bearing.

"It'll need stitching, darlin', but it's not a serious wound. What the hell were you doing?" Sprawling at her side Hunter took out a flask and, after offering her some whiskey, had a hearty drink to ease the fear that had twisted his insides when he saw her shot.

"Trying to see if Tom—I mean Sebastian—was returning." She took another sip of whiskey, hoping it would dull the hurt, then returned the flask to him. "Think he made it?"

"Jed and I were just wondering that ourselves."

"Reach any concensus?" After a third, larger drink of whiskey, she began to feel less hurt, less frightened, by her wound.

"Sort of. None of Watkins's men have returned to report whether Sebastian did or did not make it."

"And that means something, does it?"

"The only thing it means for certain is that we have four less men to contend with ourselves. We like to think it also means he made it. He either took down the men following him or the fools got caught up in the chase, following him into town, and Tuckman took care of them. Of course, that's looking on the favorable side."

She nodded and watched as he sent Charlie to take over his place at the front while he, near enough to where Charlie had been stationed, took over watching their backs. He did not have to tell her the unfavorable outcome. She could see it clearly for herself. Either Sebastian had been killed or he was pinned down like they were. Either they would be rescued, or night would fall. In the dark they would never be able to stop Watkins's men from eventually overrunning them.

After sitting for a few minutes watching the twilight enclose them and feeling the effects of the whiskey she had drunk cloud her thoughts, she began to think about dying. It seemed inordinately cruel for Hunter to be denied what he had worked so hard for when he was so close. So too was it cruel for her to be denied the future with him she had only just been promised. Facing her own mortality, she suddenly decided it was foolish to let pride keep her from telling Hunter all that was in her heart. Taking his hand in hers, she smiled a little weakly when he looked at her.

"Hot damn, boss—lookee there," Charlie shouted before Leanne could say anything.

It was a minute before Hunter could see what Charlie's sharp eyes had. A large force of men were riding from the direction of the town. When Hunter recognized Tuckman in the lead, he gave a shout of joyous relief. He gave Leanne a brief but hearty kiss, forced her to huddle down, then turned all of his attention to helping Tuckman and his posse take care of Watkins's men.

Watkins swore maniacally as he watched his men either shot as they tried to flee or surrender. He made it very clear that he would prefer them dead rather than captured to be used as witnesses against him. Hunter was

forced to keep the man from putting himself into the line
of fire by clipping him on the jaw, knocking him out.
Shortly after, a grinning Marshal Tuckman strolled over
to him.

"You did better than you know, Tarrant. Don't think
there's a face here that isn't decorating some poster." He
looked down at the unconscious Watkins. "What happened to him?"

"He got to thinking he'd rather be shot than hanged."

"Glad you changed his mind."

After looking over the men the marshal had brought
with him, Leanne was only interested in one thing.
"Where is Sebastian?"

Hunter frowned, looking around as he helped Leanne
to her feet. "He did make it, didn't he, Henry?"

"Yup. Kinda battered from having two horses shot out
from under him, but he'll recover fine enough."

"Where'd he get the other horses? He left here with
only one."

"Well, now, seems Watkins's men were kind enough to
let him take theirs."

"Must've been one hell of a ride. I really didn't think
he'd make it." Hunter shook his head, then looked at
Leanne who was leaning against him rather heavily. "Old
Doc Frazer still around?"

"Yup. Anyone else hurt?"

"A nick here and there, that's all."

"Seems you brought the whole lot with you. I got me a
feeling we'll be doing a lot of talking." He smiled faintly
when Hunter cast him a brief, guilt-tinged look. "Well,
let's get this little lady to a doctor."

Leanne gave herself over to being coddled. She felt
too groggy from pain, exhaustion, and whiskey to stand

on her own. As Hunter set her up on his horse, she managed a brief glance at Jed and Charlie. They looked as reluctant as she felt to follow the marshal. Hunter had said he would clear her name and get Charlie and Jed out of trouble, and while she trusted Hunter and knew he meant what he said, she could not feel as sure as he did that it could be accomplished.

Slumping against him as they started on their way, she decided not to worry about it for now. Until her wound had been properly treated and she had recovered her strength she could do nothing.

The moment they got into town, Hunter left the marshal with promises to return as soon as Leanne had been seen by the doctor and settled into a room at the hotel. Looking at the wounded men, posse and Watkins's crew alike, Hunter was anxious to get to the doctor first. Leanne was looking too pale and acting too weak for his peace of mind. He barely noticed Charlie and Jed dogging his steps.

"Another one?" Doctor Jamie Frazer grumbled as he helped Hunter lead Leanne to the table.

"It's not very bad," Leanne mumbled when the graying, plump doctor cut away Hunter's bandaging and part of her shirt.

"Now, who's the doctor here, lass? You two"—he scowled at Charlie and Jed—"can go set yourselves outside."

"The marshal will be looking for you soon," Hunter said after Jed and Charlie had gone, "for some of his men and a few of the prisoners."

"Damn fools," Frazer muttered as he thoroughly checked Leanne's wound. "Did you have to drag this lass into the middle of it?"

"There was no choice, sir," Leanne rasped, the doctor's probing of her wound making her dizzy with pain.

"Can't you give her anything?" Hunter felt as if he shared every pain that caused Leanne to grow so white, to moan softly in her throat as she struggled not to cry out.

Looking at Hunter, the doctor murmured, "P'raps you ought to join your companions outside."

"No. I'm staying right here with her."

At first Leanne was grateful for Hunter's presence. Shortly after the doctor started to stitch her wound, however, his presence became unnecessary. Despite her efforts to be brave and strong, she fainted from the pain.

The first word on Leanne's lips when conciousness returned was one of the many new and very colorful curses she had learned while traveling with Hunter and the rest. Soft male laughter forced her to open her eyes. She found Sebastian sprawled on a cot at her side and Hunter sitting on the edge of her cot holding her hand.

"Sorry. It hurts," she mumbled, glancing around and realizing that she was in a small room off of the doctor's main office.

"I know. I'm stitched up like some damn quilt," Sebastian grumbled.

"But you'll recover."

"Yeh, Hunter. Slowly but surely. A number of wounds, all painful but none really serious."

"It is truly amazing that you reached the marshal." With Hunter lending her support, Leanne slowly sat up. "The marshal told us you had horses shot out from under you." She could almost smile at the way her praise so obviously pleased him.

"They finally lowered themselves to that in an attempt to stop me. Fortunately the horses whose saddles I'd emptied had the courtesy to run my way. Also fortunate was the fact that none of those men was very successful at hitting a moving target." He grimaced and touched his bandaged shoulder. "Better than I wanted, though."

"Just how many times were you hit?" Hunter asked.

"Five. Don't look so horrified, Miss Summers. None of them was even as serious as yours. They cut open both my upper arms, nicked my left side and took a small chunk out of my right leg. The fifth one's the worst—the bullet actually went in and had to be dug out. It ain't a wound I'll be boasting on though."

She frowned, then her eyes widened as understanding came to her. He was lying on his stomach, something she had thought a little curious. There was one part of his body that would have been an almost continuous target for the men chasing him. She fought a giggle, not very successfully. Hunter's shoulders were shaking with silent laughter.

"Reckon I'll be standing at your wedding."

Hunter grinned, glancing quickly at Leanne to see her put her hand over her mouth to muffle her giggles. Then he grew serious. "And I reckon you'll be well enough to sit. I don't like it much, but there'll be no wedding for a while. I'm going to be too busy clearing away this Watkins mess to do more than make a brief stop before a preacher."

"I don't mind." Leanne did not want to press him, but could not fully suppress a deep fear over the delay.

"I do. You'll have a proper wedding, not some quick 'I do' then I'm off again. Tuckman warned me that I'll be needed each step of the way in this, right up to the hanging. I don't think that'll take too long, however. They've been waiting too long for him to dawdle now."

"Far too long," Sebastian agreed.

"Well, I better get Leanne over to the hotel."

"I suppose I can't have my nice long, hot bath now." She sighed as he helped her stand up.

"Not the long indulgent soak I know you were contemplating, but we'll think of something."

"Can you send Charlie and Jed in here?" Sebastian asked. "I'd like to get out of here."

"Sure. I'll tell them at the hotel that you're on your way and wanting a room. They'll be filling up fast once news gets out that Henry Watkins has been brought in."

As they made their way to the hotel, Leanne tried to ignore all the curious and sometimes shocked looks cast her way. She suspected they were caused as much by her male attire as by her wounded, dusty state. Even the man at the hotel desk gawked at her, and she was heartily relieved to get to their rooms and away from prying eyes.

After setting her on the bed Hunter tugged off her boots. "I'll have our things sent over here."

"Can you have some hot water sent up as well?" Seeing his frown, she assured him, "Not for a bath, but I must at least sponge some of this dust off. I'm sure your family will show up soon, and I'd like to at least be tidy."

"All right, although it'll be a day or so before anyone from the ranch shows up. In the message I'll be sending, I'll be telling them I won't be able to leave here for a few days. Since it's a good part of a day's journey here they might wait a little bit before sending someone out. It's a busy time of the year for them, and I'm not on my death bed or in trouble."

He gave her a brief kiss. "You sure you'll be all right here alone?"

"I'll be fine. You go take care of what you need to do. Marshal Tuckman's probably wondering what has happened to you. I'll just go to sleep anyway. I certainly need some rest after all we've been through."

After kissing her again, Hunter left her to order some hot water for her and arrange for their things to be sent to their rooms. By the time he reached the sheriff's office, it was to find Marshal Tuckman getting ready to send someone to find him. The deputy quickly served them some coffee and Hunter accepted the cigar Tuckman offered as they sat down at his desk.

"Began to think that little girl was hurt worse than I thought."

"No, she'll be fine. I just wanted to get her settled comfortably. Can you get her clear of this mess?"

"Already started on it, m'boy. Sent word to the federal marshal in Colorado to bring in that sheriff, Martin, and to get those damned posters down."

"Sounds too easy. I expected more trouble."

"Taking the posters down doesn't mean she's cleared, that any of you are. It's to keep bounty hunters off your tails until the matter of innocence or guilt is determined."

"Of course. Be honest, Henry. Do you think there'll be any real problem in clearing Leanne?"

"It'll just take time. Same with you. Now, what about those other two? You can't tell me they're poor, falsely accused innocents."

"Nope. But they're not real outlaws either. Fools maybe, but if we jailed folk for that there'd be no one left to lock the door."

Tuckman laughed. "Sebastian said they weren't crimi-

nals really, just got dragged into something and didn't
know how to get out of it. Seems they were asked to hold
the horses while Watkins's men robbed a bank. They
obliged and found themselves on the run. Then, too, they
helped bring Watkins in."

"That'll help them?"

"A lot. So will Sebastian talking on their behalf."
Henry took a deep puff on his cigar, then watched Hunter
closely as he asked, "About Luke Meede's death. Was that
killing necessary, unavoidable?"

"Yeah. Didn't Sebastian tell you what happened?"

"He did, but I want your side. Not to put too fine a
point on it, Sebastian had some cause to want Luke
Meede dead." After listening closely to Hunter's version
of the incident, Tuckman nodded. "The only one I haven't
asked is Miss Summers, but I won't trouble her with it.
The rest of you all give the same tale. Glad of it. Sebastian's a damn good lawman. I'd hate to see a black mark
on his record."

For a while they exchanged facts, and Hunter gave as
detailed an account as he could of Watkins's activities.
Hunter was pleased to hear that a number of Watkins's
men were ready to testify against the man in hopes of
lessening their own sentences. He was not pleased, however, to have clarified just how much of his time was
going to be taken up with the business. Feeling somewhat
dispirited, he finally rose to go back to the hotel to get
some much needed rest.

"I hear you're getting married," Tuckman murmured
as he walked outside with Hunter.

"Yeah, as soon as this business is done. I haven't got
the time to do it right until then, and I don't want it looking like some rushed hole-in-the-corner affair. Also, I

can't help but feel it'd be better to wait until both of us get our names cleared."

"No doubt about it. Well, we'll see what we can do about clearing this up as fast as possible."

"I'd appreciate that. If it takes too long, she'll start wondering if I'm backing out."

Chapter Eleven

LEANNE MURMURED WITH PLEASURE AS SHE SANK INTO THE hot, scented bathwater. It was the perfect cure for such a trying day. Even having her stitches out was easy after her confrontation with Sheriff Martin. The memory of that bitter meeting made her shiver. She wished they had taken the man straight to the territorial court. Their meeting had produced only a stream of filthy abuse and lies. She had feared someone might believe those lies, jeopardizing the clearing of her name.

Fortunately, that had proven an empty concern. A few of the bitter insults he had snarled at her had inadvertantly confirmed her story. A grim-faced Hunter had then hurried her out of the jail straight to the doctor's, where, still reeling from Martin's verbal assault, she had barely noticed Dr. Frazer tugging out her stitches.

Shaking away those memories, she concentrated on a good thorough bath. When, somewhat awkwardly, she poured the pitcher of rinse water over her soapy hair, it ran down her face. Her eyes squeezed shut to ward off any of the soap. She leaned over the edge of the tub slightly and groped for the towel she had left there. She touched the toe of a boot even as a leather-gloved hand took hold of hers and the towel was pressed into it. Hurriedly she wiped her face, eager to greet Hunter and find out what had happened concerning Sheriff Martin.

"You're back earlier than I thought you would be, Hunter."

"Hunter's not back yet."

It was hard to open her eyes. She had the brief foolish thought that if she kept her eyes closed, she could avoid embarrassment. Holding the towel against her breasts, she finally looked at the owner of that deep voice and her fear eased slightly. Anyone who looked so much like Hunter had to be a relative of his. She met his grin with a stern frown.

"And just who are you?"

"Owen Walsh. Tarrant's—Hunter's brother." He stuck out his hand.

"I am afraid the amenities must wait until I am more presentable. Could you please wait in the other room?"

As soon as he was gone, she got out of the tub, quickly dried off, and then threw on the robe Hunter had bought for her. While she did not appreciate being caught in her bath, she was pleased that one of Hunter's family had finally shown up. Hunter had not said anything, but she had sensed that the continued absence of his family was troubling him deeply. It had been over a week since he sent them word. She just hoped Owen Walsh was not here to deliver news that would only hurt Hunter.

Straightening her shoulders and quickly brushing a semblence of order into her towel-dried hair she stepped into the other room. Hunter had booked two rooms in a thin attempt to maintain an air of propriety. The connecting door between the two, however, had never been shut, and she suspected a lot of people knew that, including this younger, softer version of Hunter who again extended his hand.

"You must be Leanne Summers," Owen said as they shook hands.

Frowning a little as she waved him to a seat, she asked, "You know me?"

"Know of you. Tuckman told me a while back, shortly after you started riding with Hunter, I reckon."

"Oh. Would you like a drink? Hunter has some fine brandy. Oh, and some cigars."

"Sounds real fine. I'll have both, please. It was a long dusty ride here."

After serving him the brandy and lighting his cigar, she briefly thought about returning to dress more modestly. But, he had already seen her in far less and the robe was very modest.

"Hunter should be back before long. We're to dine downstairs this evening. Will you be joining us?"

"Reckon so. Is he still tied up with this Watkins business?"

"Yes, and he probably will be until the man is tried in the territorial court."

As they waited for Hunter, they quietly conversed. Although he was subtle about it, Leanne recognized that Owen was after as much information as he could wheedle out of her with his soft, polite ways and winning smile. She did her best not to give him much. While she did not feel she had anything to hide, she was not sure of what Hunter would or would not want his family to know. She felt relieved when Hunter finally strode into the room because it was not as easy as she would have liked to be politely evasive with Owen Walsh.

While the brothers greeted each other, she got Hunter some brandy and a cigar. After topping up Owen's drink, she excused herself to dress for dinner. She felt it best if they had some time alone.

"Very pretty," Owen murmured as Hunter sprawled in the chair across from him.

"And mine."

With a meaningful glance around the connected rooms, Owen grinned. "That did occur to me."

"I'm going to marry her." Hunter watched his brother closely but discovered that Owen was as hard to read as ever. "As soon as I've cleared our names and finished with Watkins."

"Congratulations. Don't look so stern. My hesitation was simply for a brief thought on our mother." He laughed softly at Hunter's exaggerated grimace. "Tuckman told me about the girl weeks ago. It sounded as if she got as raw a deal as you did."

"Maybe worse." He gave Owen a succinct version of how Leanne had ended up with him.

"Poor kid. Tuckman sees no real trouble in clearing her name though, does he?"

"No, not really. Fact is, it's mostly a formality now. A lot of law was standing around listening close when Sheriff Martin was brought in. The fool ranted loud and long when he saw Leanne and said more than enough to verify her tale and hang himself."

"And the tale's probably spread from pillar to post already, which can only help her."

"Has any of it spread out to the ranch? Just how much had you been told?"

"Not much more than periodic assurances that you were alive. Pa's itching to hear it all and to be sure that your name's cleared. I know it doesn't look that way with us taking so long to get here, but we were knee-deep in the roundup when you sent word. What we wanted to do had to be set aside until we'd done what we had to do."

"Of course. I've lost touch of the ranch's schedule. Tell me honestly, Owen, how warm do you think my homecoming will be?"

"Better than you're thinking, I'd wager. Pa, Justin, and Thayer are feeling pinched with guilt over hesitating in believing you. Craig was furious that he wasn't sent word immediately. Ma and Laurie"—he shrugged—"they're two sides of a double-headed coin. You know how Ma is."

"Yeh. I caused a scandal. Innocence or guilt doesn't much matter. And Laurie still follows her?"

"Like a stallion after a mare in season. Y'know, this business with you has drawn the line between our parents like nothing else before. Things haven't been good for a long time, but they don't even pretend they are now."

"I'm sorry for that."

"No call for you to feel sorry or guilty. Fact is, I find it easier. More honest. We're all old enough to handle the truth. I don't think our mother can ever forgive Pa for taking her away from New Orleans, and that's slowly turned it all sour. Her too really. I think Pa wishes it were different, but there's not much move for change on her part."

"Funny, isn't it? Pa was what he is when they met and wed, yet for as long as I can remember she's always tried to change him. Reckon that just wore thin after a while."

"Well, she still plays her games and Pa still just shrugs them off. Don't expect things to have changed that much."

Hunter cursed softly. "It might be best if I warn Leanne about her then."

"Just might be. She's still got some set ideas on the right mate for you. She's not going to appreciate you choosing your own."

Before Hunter could express his opinion on that, Leanne returned. She wore a simple blue gingham dress, but he thought her lovely. As he and Owen escorted her down to the hotel's small dining room, Hunter noted the subtle admiration in his brother's glances toward Leanne. He trusted Owen but recognized that he could face some real competition for Leanne now.

Pretty young women were scarce in the area, and marriage was the only claim a lot of men recognized. He briefly considered changing his plans and marrying her as soon as possible, then shook his head. Marriage was a new start, and until their names were cleared, their troubled past set firmly behind them, that start was not possible. Neither would it hurt for her to know what his life was really like with the ranch and his family before they took that serious step. Thoughts of his parents' troubled marriage strengthened that opinion.

When Owen expressed his delight over her and Hunter's impending marriage, he was so sincere that Leanne felt a lot of her nervousness melt away. As the meal progressed, however, and she listened to Hunter and his brother talk of the ranch, their family, and their acquaintances she began to feel uncertain. She had accepted that Hunter was no outlaw, but she now began to suspect he was a lot more than a simple rancher. It began to look as if he might be wealthy, his family one with some power and prestige.

And what was she? She had been educated and raised as a lady, more or less, but that was about all she had in her favor. She had no real family. The woman who had raised her was, not to put too fine a point on it, no better than a whore. For weeks she had been running around with five men, branded an outlaw and with a price on her head. That was not the kind of girl a wealthy, prominent rancher's son brought home to mama and papa, she thought bitterly.

The doubts and fears she had begun to talk herself out of began to creep up on her again. They were hard to fight. A treacherous little voice in her head insisted upon reminding her that her father had deserted her, Charity had tossed her out, and the town she had grown up in had turned its back on her. Why should a man like Hunter be more loyal?

"Everything all right, darlin'?"

Startled out of her darkening thoughts by Hunter's soft question, she realized that she had been toying with her food. The apple pie she had found so delicious a few moments ago sat half-eaten. Setting down her fork, she forced a smile for Hunter.

"Simply too full to finish." Her smile became more real when there was a brief tug of war between the two men over her plate, one which Owen won.

Narrowly eyeing his brother as Owen quickly finished the pie, Hunter drawled, "Pretty soon you'll be as wide as you are tall."

"I'm a growing boy." Flashing a quick grin, Owen leaned back in his chair and sipped at his wine.

"You're twenty. You're done growing. Only place you've got left to go is out."

"You'll be softening before me, brother of mine."

The mildly insulting yet playful banter continued for several minutes before, to Leanne's relief, Hunter spoke of turning in for the night. She enjoyed Owen's company and was pleased, especially for Hunter's sake, that the man had come. Nevertheless, she was failing in all her attempts to improve her sinking spirits and preferred to end the evening early rather than dampen the mood of their reunion.

Suspecting that Hunter had sensed her troubled state, that it prompted him to leave Owen sooner than he might have, she protested, "I can go up alone, Hunter. Visit with your brother a while if you want."

"We can visit tomorrow. I'm tired and, I think, so are you. It hasn't been the easiest of days."

She smiled at Owen as Hunter gently tugged her to her feet. "Good night, Owen. We'll see you at breakfast?"

"That you will, and probably more than you'd like in the days to come."

Even as she responded politely, Hunter started to tug her along to their rooms. She noted that he looked a little grim but said nothing. Selfish though she knew it was, she was too caught up in her own troubled thoughts to think much on what might be bothering him.

Hunter frowned as he watched Leanne disappear into the connecting room to get ready for bed. After stripping down to his trousers and washing up, he poured himself a brandy and sipped it as he sprawled on the bed.

Something was clearly troubling Leanne. He wondered if Owen had somehow relayed anything but acceptance but quickly dismissed the thought. Of all his family, he knew Owen the best. Owen's welcome of Leanne had been sincere.

Next he considered the confrontation with Sheriff Martin as the source of her moodiness. That scene had been appalling. He had had to be held back from attacking the man as Martin had spewed his lies, slander, and hatred. Leanne had gone quite ashen, clearly cut deeply by that hatred flung at her. He shook his head. She had recovered from that. He was sure of it.

That left him with little to blame her mood on. Living in the hotel was not the best of situations, but they had just spent week upon week in far worse conditions. He considered and cast aside several other possibilities, growing more and more frustrated at his inability to understand her mood. When she stepped into the room he was still without a solution.

Seeing the dark scowl Hunter wore, Leanne briefly contemplated retiring to the other room for the night. She was feeling uncertain and sad and in no state of mind to deal with Hunter's moodiness. Sighing, she made her way to the bed, shed her robe, and slid beneath the covers.

Setting his now empty glass on the bedside table, he lay down, turning on his side to look at her. "What's troubling you, Leanne?"

Briefly she was tempted to tell him the whole truth— but only briefly. They were not facing death crouched behind some pathetic barrier now. Her pride reasserted itself. She would not bare her heart and soul to him, not when he told her virtually nothing of his own feelings.

"Nothing really. I'm just tired." She was not surprised when he cursed softly but viciously, for she knew she sounded far less reassuring than she had intended to.

Standing up, Hunter yanked off the rest of his clothes. He could hear the polite, evasive lie in her voice. It infuriated him. He wanted to banish that quiet, sad-eyed mood, but unless he knew what fed it, he was helpless. Slipping into bed at her side after dousing all the lamps save the one by the bed, he took her into his arms. Although she felt soft and pliant, he sensed a holding back in her, a hiding. He hated it.

"I never thought you a secretive person, Leanne."

"Everyone is a little secretive at times. But what makes you think I am now?"

"Maybe your saying nothing's wrong when I can clearly see that something's troubling you."

"Well, I guess I'm just suffering a mood. Women are prone to such things." She hated spouting such nonsense but hoped Hunter would accept it.

"Don't take me for an idiot. We've been as close as two people can be for weeks. You're not given to moods."

She sat up and eyed him crossly. "Will you stop telling me what I am or am not."

"What you are now is difficult. In this I know what

I'm talking about. You're not secretive and you're not given to moods. I want to help, Leanne, but I can't do that unless you tell me what's bothering you."

Sighing, she lay down, staring morosely at the flickering patterns of lamplight on the ceiling. "Owen was most pleasant. He is also only one of your large family."

Beginning to see what might be nagging at her, he slipped his arm around her waist and tugged her closer, kissing her cheek. "The others will be just as easy to know and just as accepting." Deciding that now was the best opportunity to warn her of his mother, he added quietly, reluctance weighting his voice, "There is only one who might prove—well, difficult. My mother had, and according to Owen still has, some set ideas of what a suitable marriage for her son would be."

"A suitable marriage for the son of a prominent, maybe a little powerful and perhaps not too poor, rancher?"

"Why did that just sound like an accusation?"

"Well, when you told me who you really were, spoke of the ranch and all, you didn't really weight the revelation down with many details. There are many different sorts of ranchers. You are clearly not some simple cowboy grazing a few hundred head of cows." She frowned up at him, debating just how annoyed she should be over his reticence.

He brushed a kiss over her frowning mouth. "I hope you're not thinking I've been lying to you."

"No. Simply not very forthcoming. I am not quite sure what I pictured about your home and family, but I was obviously off the mark or the half-facts I picked up while you and Owen nattered away would not have bothered me so much."

"Why should those things bother you? It should simply be a comforting reassurance of my ability to care for you."

"Are you being purposely obtuse? You are from a wealthy, or near to, family and they obviously carry some weight in this area. I was tossed out on my ear wearing only a nightgown and cloak. The nightgown ended up wrapped around Jed's foot, and the cloak is in sad shape. I have no money. I have no real family. The only one I can refer anyone to is Charity, and she does not qualify as a glowing recommendation. I was hardly aristocracy before, but now I am little more than white trash."

"Don't be ridiculous." He had the uncomfortable feeling that she knew all too well how his mother would view her.

She ignored that. "I don't even have a good name now. I've spent far too long running over hill and dale with five men and no chaperone. I've been marching about in men's clothing. And we are not fooling anybody by having these two rooms side by side. That tidbit of gossip has certainly been added to by the news that you have had to buy me every little thing I wear."

"All of which is nobody's business."

"That won't stop anyone from discussing it—or your mother from hearing about it."

"The talk will die out." He saw no point in denying that there would be talk, that the whispers had already begun.

"Oh, most certainly, if your mother does not collapse from apoplexy when you appear on her doorstep with me in tow."

"Leanne, I'm marrying you, not my mother. I'd like to say she'll be gracious and accept you, but that would be a lie. My mother has some set ideas, ones she's been trying to ram down our throats all our lives. Those ideas have finally set her and my father as far apart as a man and wife can be.

"Yes, we have money, enough to carry us through the inevitable lean years, and we are not without some power and influence. Mother has always tried to make more of that than there is. Except for my sister, none of us pays her any heed. We are what we are and we'll never be society like she knew in New Orleans. We don't want to be."

"I understand all you're saying," she sighed, "but I do not relish being a bone of contention between you and her."

"It'll just be another in a long line of them. We've never seen eye to eye and probably never will. The final break came when she turned her back on me the moment scandal touched me. She didn't seem to care that I was unjustly accused or concerned about the trouble I faced. All she worried about was the scandal."

"And now you're bringing home another load of scandal—me."

"I'm bringing home the woman I plan to marry. If worse comes to worst, you can do what the rest of us do."

"What's that?"

"Step around her. Truth is, I don't think she'll be a problem for too long. She and Pa have grown so far apart, they don't even try to hide it from us anymore. I really think she'll take herself back to the New Orleans she so reveres."

"I'm sorry, Hunter."

He shrugged. "It may sound heartless, but I think it would be for the best. She's not happy. Pa's not happy. She has little to do with her sons and we try hard to keep it that way. Don't get me wrong. I love her, I just don't like her much. Our housekeeper, Molly Pitts, has been more a mother to us boys than our real mother ever was."

"And you don't think it can ever get better?"

"Don't see how. I think my sister was the result of a last gasp in a dying union. I wasn't very old before I saw that matters just weren't right between my parents. My mother married Pa with the intention of molding him into what she really wanted. It didn't work. All she has managed to do is push him away."

Suddenly she more fully understood his hiding the truth about himself. It was not just because so many had turned against him when he had been accused of the crimes Watkins had committed. He might not see it, but she felt certain that the state of his parents' marriage had also prompted him. After all, if she accepted him as an outlaw on the run, the chances were slim that she would play the sort of games his mother obviously indulged in.

"You've gone very quiet." He smoothed his hands over her back, slowly pressing her body closer to his.

"Just thinking on all you've said."

"If it's any comfort, until I get my name cleared, my mother will be seeing me as a scandal on two legs."

"So we can be united in diversity?"

"Something like that."

"No, it's not much comfort." His caresses grew a little bolder and she found it difficult to keep her mind on their discussion. "I hate to be the cause of strife in a family."

"The strife is already there. Look, I'll make a deal. If it grows to be too much, we'll move out. There's a small cabin just south of the main house. It was Pa's first shelter. It's been kept together to be used for extra hands or guests. My mother usually knows when to give up, but if she doesn't leave you alone after a while, I promise we'll move into the cabin. A little distance can solve a lot of problems. Just tell me when you can't stand it any longer."

"It's a deal then." She murmured her pleasure when he gave her a hearty kiss. "I put up with Charity. Your mother should be no real problem." She did not believe it any more than he appeared to, but he was kind enough not to question her boast.

After unbuttoning several of the buttons on the front of her frilly but modest nightgown, he brushed a kiss over the fresh scar on her shoulder. "It healed well." He gently pushed her onto her back. "So, no more undemanding, solicitous gentleman."

"Is that what you were trying to be? You were acting curiously." She made no protest as he tugged off her night-gown.

"Restrained, you mean." He crouched over her, admiring the slim lines of her body in the lamplight.

"It builds character, you know." Sighing with pleasure, she wrapped her arms around him when he lowered his body onto hers and tilted her head back slightly to give him better access to her throat. Her desire for him flared quick and hot. She doubted he could have found the restraint required while her wound healed any more frustrating than she had. That time had been added to the time of deprivation enforced upon them by the race from Mex-

ico to Little Creek. She felt starved for a taste of the passion they could share.

It quickly became clear to her, however, that Hunter
planned to dawdle. He ignored all her subtle urgings to
hurry toward the gratification she craved. If it were not
for the strong passion revealed in his face and body, a
passion he was rigidly controlling, she would have
thought he did not feel the same fierce desire she did.

Hoping to keep her passion in pace with his, she tried
to think of all the things she did not like or found distasteful. Even that trick failed when he teased her inner
thighs with warm kisses and strokes of his tongue. When
he touched his mouth to the very heart of her desire for
him, she cried out in a mixture of protest and pleasure. He
caught her by the wrists, holding her hands to the bed
when she tried to reach for him to tug him away.

She grew very still, caught up in shock and wonder. It
felt as if every fiber of her being was centered there. His
intimate kisses, the strokes of his tongue, worked to pull
at her every thought and feeling. Pleasure flooded her.
She gave a soft, low moan as she opened to him, arching
with mindless greed toward his mouth. He growled his
approval and released her hands to slide his beneath her
backside, to knead and stroke and hold her in place. Past
all thought of modesty, she burrowed her hands in his
thick hair, caressing the shape of his head, neck, and
shoulders. She was but faintly aware of his questions, of
the half-coherent answers she gave and of his soft, erotic
flattery as he drove her towards completion.

When her passion crested, she tried to pull him into her
arms but he eluded her. She then clutched at him blindly
as her release tore through her. Rationality was but a

flicker on the horizon when he began to restir her needs. This time he answered her plea to join her, his possession of her fierce. She cried out her delight and responded with a ferocity of her own. They found satisfaction together, clinging tightly to each other as it shook them.

With her body sated and her mind clear of desire's haze, Leanne felt embarrassed. She could not look at Hunter as he eased away from her to straighten the covers they had tangled in their lovemaking. The way she had carried on, with no sense of modesty or restraint, troubled her. Somehow, it did not seem right to be so controlled by her physical desires.

After tugging the covers over them, Hunter pulled her into his arms. He felt the tension in her and half-smiled. If she thought to withdraw with some mistaken idea of decorum, he would soon disabuse her of that notion. When her passion ran hot, she was glorious, free, and abandoned. He would not allow her to even try to shut that part of her away.

"Ah, Leanne, you're glorious."

Pressing her face against his chest, she muttered, "Shameless perhaps."

"Passionate."

"Lewd."

"You're trying to talk yourself into feeling ashamed of what we just enjoyed."

"Wrong. I didn't have to try."

"Darlin', you're hot and fine in bed. There's nothing wrong in that. We'll be spending a hell of a lot of our married life in bed. We've got something special between us here. Don't try to make it something to be ashamed of. Thinking like that could kill what we can share."

Slowly her discomfort eased. He was right. If she kept thinking like she was, she would soon believe it gospel and would turn from what flared between them.

"You didn't see me acting this way after you pleasured me like that."

Lifting her head, she eyed him with mock disgust and amusement. "I always knew you had no shame."

Knowing she had listened and accepted the truth of his words, he grinned at her. "Honey, you'll soon see just how shameless I can get."

"I can hardly wait." Even though her tone of voice was sarcastic, she smiled slowly, realizing that she meant every word.

Chapter Twelve

As the walsh ranch came into view, Leanne felt the knots in her stomach tighten. Owen and Hunter, beside her on the wagon seat, kept up a constant stream of conversation, often drawing Jed and Charlie, riding alongside them, into the talk. It was meant to keep her from getting nervous. She felt almost guilty when it failed.

"Well, I've damn well run out of things to say."

Leanne looked at Hunter and almost laughed despite the case of nerves that made her feel almost sick. "No? Truly?"

He gave her a mock scowl. "You weren't even listening."

"Nonsense. Every pearl of wisdom, every jewel of wit is emblazoned on my mind."

After a brief glare at a chuckling Owen, he gave Leanne

a quick kiss, laughing softly when she blushed. "Sassy. That's what I want to hear." He spoke quietly, trying to keep his words as private as possible. "That sharp-tongued temper of yours will be the best weapon you have against whatever nonsense my mother tries. If she scents a weakness, or thinks she does, she will push all the harder." He sighed and draped his arm around her shoulders. "I wish I was taking you to a happier home. I also wish I could say I'd be right there for you every minute, but for a while I can't be."

"What you'll be going after is far more important than trying to spare me some discomfort."

She meant what she said. The words, however, did not calm her nerves or instill the strength she would need. Only to herself would she admit that one of her strongest concerns was that Hunter would start to listen to his mother if the woman decided against her. She knew she should have more faith in Hunter, but she had already been cast aside by her father, Charity, and the whole town of Clayville.

The wagon was just pulling to a halt after running a gauntlet of welcoming greetings from the ranch hands, when the door of the large house burst open. Out strode a man she knew had to be Hunter's father. Sloane Walsh was an older, more weathered, and slightly grayed version of Hunter. When three younger men followed close on his heels, she decided the man had left his stamp on all his sons. Behind them strolled a lovely older woman—fair, straight, and elegant. At her side was a young girl who not only held the woman's looks but mimicked her way of moving. They remained on the veranda, hands clasped, as the men strode to the wagon.

"Damn, Tarrant, you're looking good." Sloane embraced his eldest son as soon as Hunter hopped down off of the wagon seat.

Since Hunter was occupied in a round of hearty greetings, Owen helped Leanne down and murmured, "See, little Leanne? It's all going well. You can stop worrying about Hunter now."

Startled, she looked at him. She had the sinking feeling that he could see straight into her heart to all she kept hidden from Hunter. Then Hunter was tugging her by the hand to meet his father and brothers. She was a little puzzled when he did not immediately introduce her.

"I'd like you to meet a few people." He signaled Jed and Charlie forward and introduced them. "These two helped me bring in Watkins. Sebastian feels certain whatever charges may be against them will be dropped. I was hoping we could find them some work."

"We can always use more hands, especially at this time of the year," Sloane said. He pointed toward a tall, thin Mexican lounging against the corral fence. "Just saunter over there to Ramón and tell him I've hired you on. He'll see to you." As soon as the pair left, he looked at Hunter. "Where are your manners, son? You should've introduced the lady first."

"I was saving the best for last. This is Leanne Summers. I've asked her to be my wife."

After an initial start of surprise, the Walsh men offered congratulations that she felt were honest ones. They greeted her with all the charm any Southern gentleman could aspire to and she felt a little of her nervousness ease. Nevertheless, when Hunter draped his arm around her shoulders, she could not fully resist the urge to edge closer to him.

As Sloane Walsh gallantly kissed her hand, she saw
him quickly glance towards the veranda. Despite a voice
that warned her not to, she too glanced that way. For a
brief moment there was a look of genteel horror on the
older woman's face, before her features grew calm but
cold. The girl at her side looked curious, then, catching
the look on her mother's face, quickly imitated it.

"Glad to meet you, Leanne," Hunter's father said. "We
did hear a few things about you from Marshal Tuckman.
Your troubles have been all sorted out then?"

"It's just a formality now, Pa," Hunter told him. "I want
it in writing from a territorial judge."

"Not a Texas judge?"

"Most of Watkins's crimes were committed in New
Mexico. It's been decided there's the best chance to get
him hanged there."

"Well, let's stop lagging about out here. We'll introduce Leanne to the missus and Laurie, then set ourselves
down in the parlor to chew all this over. Reckon you
wouldn't mind a cool drink to wash the dust down."

Leanne could feel the tension in Hunter's arm as they
walked toward his mother. She could see it in the faces of
the Walsh men as well. She found it sad that this woman's
intractability, her need to change people into what they
were not or did not want to be, had drawn such a clear
line through the center of a family. Leanne wondered if
the woman knew what she had lost. Worse, as she looked
into Lorraine Walsh's chilly green eyes, she had to wonder if the woman knew but simply did not care.

The look the woman gave Leanne told her more than
she really cared to know. There would be no welcome
from Lorraine Walsh. What Leanne read in that one look

was contemptuous dismissal. It stung her pride. Unfortunately, it also plucked at the feelings of inadequacy she
was trying so hard to shed. Lorraine gave no greeting,
simply stared a moment, then looked at Hunter.

"Did I hear you say you are not yet cleared of charges,
Tarrant?"

"You heard me say it is just a formality now, Mother. A
signature on a piece of paper."

"And you have had the audacity to bring three of your
outlaw friends into my home."

"Two friends, one fiancée. And none of them outlaws."

"And I suppose their pardons are but a formality as
well."

"Pardon implies I've done something wrong that
needs forgiving. Neither Leanne nor I has committed any
crime."

"I believe it's my home as well, Lorraine," Sloane
growled as he nudged past her and strode into the house,
everyone quickly falling into step behind him. "I believe
it's time you played the hostess. We would like something cool to drink in the parlor, a meal started, and a
room readied for Miss Summers."

"The room next to mine," Hunter said, glimpsing but
ignoring Leanne's blush.

Deciding that Mrs. Walsh's lack of protest was no
compliment, Leanne inwardly sighed. She did want to be
close to Hunter, especially since she would see little of
him for a while. It would have been better, however, if
Hunter had made his wants known with a little more dis-
cretion.

Conversation remained light until drinks were served and Lorraine left. Hunter's young sister followed her mother at first, but slipped back into the room a moment later. Laurie Walsh was not tied as firmly to her mother as the men seemed to think, Leanne mused as the girl found a seat in the corner of the room.

"Are you sure about getting your name cleared, Tarrant?" Sloane sprawled in a chair, his long legs splayed in front of him.

"Very sure." Hunter smiled faintly. "And I've been called Hunter for over a year. I find I like it."

"Y'know, that doesn't surprise me much. You favored it when you were younger too. I'll see if I can remember that."

"Do you think it'll take long to get this Watkins business really finished?"

Hunter looked at his brother Craig, just two years younger, where he lounged against the mantelpiece, a carved marble monstrosity their mother had insisted upon. "Depends on how long it'll take to get the man tried and sentenced. I have to follow it through to the end. I'm an important witness. Leanne"—he picked her hand up from where it rested next to him on the settee they shared and held it in both of his—"is not needed. She was only a victim, a kind of hostage. Enough of Watkins's men have sworn to testify against him that Charlie and Jed aren't needed either. It was felt it would be better for their chances of reprieve if they just stayed out of it. Sebastian will be vouching for them."

"They are good men, Mr. Walsh," Leanne felt compelled to add. "They are easily dragged into things. Once with Watkins, I fear they lacked the wit to think of a way to extract themselves from that man's web. They aren't his hired killers."

"I'll be honest with you, Pa. They didn't really come with us to help bring Watkins to justice, although they did that well enough. They tagged along because I had Leanne and they weren't sure what I was up to. They were watching out for her. However, once they saw I wasn't off my head, wasn't going to hurt her, they stayed anyway."

Hunter explained how Jed and Charlie had been drawn into an outlaw life. "Mostly now, they're just after a place to stay, regular meals, and a few coins in their pockets," he concluded.

"I know the kind of men you're talking about. Good-hearted bumblers. They'll be just fine here. Ramón will set them straight."

"I wish to hell someone had wired me when all the trouble started," Justin Walsh growled, his green eyes narrowed as he surveyed his kin from his chair. "I would've come straight home. Wasn't doing much in New Orleans anyway except tolerating Mother's kin. I might've been able to help."

"I appreciate the thought, Justin, but there wasn't much that could've been done except get Watkins. I had to be the one to do that, if only because he thought he'd made me one of his. Or so I thought. Truth is, the man didn't really remember me until I told him I was there to take him back to answer for his crimes."

Molly Pitts quietly entered to say Leanne's room was ready. Leanne, eager to wash off the dust from the journey, excused herself and left with the plump, pretty

housekeeper. It might be just as well if she left the Walsh
men alone for a while, although until Laurie slipped into
the room after Molly left, Leanne did not realize the girl
was following her. After murmuring a greeting, Leanne
turned her attention to washing up.

"Did you really ride with those outlaws?"

"I'm afraid so. I did not have a great deal of choice."

"Mother says you should have stayed in jail and
straightened out the confusion if you were really innocent."

"That would have been a little difficult, as the sheriff
who put me in jail was one of those outlaws." Watching
the girl in the mirror, she saw young Laurie mull that over
for a while.

"Mother says you won't be marrying Tarrant. She
won't allow it."

"I believe Hunter is a grown man, more than old
enough to do as he pleases. I'm sorry your mother does
not approve."

"Mother says you're nothing but a cheap little whore
who thinks to better herself."

It was an effort, but Leanne forced back her first reaction—a surge of anger that had her wanting to slap that
pretty face. The girl was about fifteen and knew very well
how those words could hurt, yet Leanne did not think that
was really why Laurie said them. There was a look on the
girl's face that gave Leanne the feeling Laurie wanted to
hear a rebuttal of her mother's slander, one she could believe. Leanne wondered if Mrs. Walsh was aware of how
precarious her hold was on her daughter.

"Considering the fact that I—er, took up with your
brother when I thought he was an outlaw, my intention

could scarcely have been to better myself." Drying off, she moved to find a clean dress.

"Tarrant *is* an outlaw. And why do you call him Hunter?"

"That's the name I came to know him by. And he's not and never was an outlaw. He was falsely accused, made to look guilty by the real criminal. If he was an outlaw, do you really think Marshal Tuckman and all the lawmen congregating in Little Creek right now would let him just ride off?"

Laurie shrugged. "My mother has already picked out a woman for Tar— Hunter to marry."

"Has she now. I would have thought that, at twenty-eight years of age, Hunter was quite old enough to choose his own bride. I'm sorry, however, that his choice has displeased your mother."

"No, you're not."

"Oh, but I am. Strife within a family is something worth feeling sorry about."

"You could fix it by going away."

Buttoning her dress, Leanne looked at the girl. "No, I couldn't, and I think you know that. The trouble here was well rooted before I set foot in this house. I think my leaving just might make it worse."

"The judge's daughter—"

"What judge's daughter?" Hunter growled as he stepped into the room and eyed his sister with suspicion. "Good God, not Patricia Spotford? Don't tell me Mother is still harping on that? She's married anyway."

"She's a widow now *and* Patricia Spotford has breeding."

"Sounds like a horse. Go on, get out of here." He shut the door after Laurie hurried out, then moved to help

Leanne, who was struggling to finish doing the buttons on the back of her red gingham dress. "What was she up to?"

"I do believe she was trying to balance the scales," Leanne murmured as, her dress done, she moved to tidy her hair. "Isn't your room next door?"

He ignored that last question as he sat on the bed. "What do you mean 'balance the scales'?"

"I don't think your sister is quite as much her mother's daughter as you may think. She's at an age where she feels a little rebellious. I think that is coming out in questioning what her mother says and does."

Hunter frowned. "Think so? She's always been Mother's little shadow. Mother made certain of that. Whenever we tried to play with the kid, Mother whisked her away, claiming that was no way to raise a lady. Laurie was always this little perfect doll."

"Laurie also has eyes and a brain. I think she sees the rift in your family and is determined to understand why it exists. It might not hurt to take a little notice of her. If I'm right and she's seeking answers, she must be having the devil of a time turning them up when six members of her own family don't have anything to do with her."

"Well, part of that is the result of Mother standing square between us and her. Also, just before I left, Laurie was starting to get very hard to tolerate. She can't seem to say anything that doesn't start with 'Mother says'."

"I noticed, but I think she does it on purpose."

"What'd she say to you?"

Seeing the way he was already glowering and tense, she murmured, "Nothing worth repeating."

"Let me be the judge of that."

"You'll just get angry."

"No doubt. What'd she say?" After listening to Leanne's recital, he swore colorfully for a moment. "Damn the woman."

"You can't tell me you're surprised. It's just as you warned me it would be. It's best to just ignore it."

"And it'll go away?"

"Well, maybe not, but it might just shut her up." She was glad to see his fleeting smile.

"And you think Laurie has a reason to repeat that poison other than spreading Mother's lies? What could it be?"

Moving to sit beside him, she answered, "She says it, then watches you like a hawk. She listens intently to every word you say. My first reaction was to get angry, slap her face, and shove her out the door."

"But you didn't. Why not? She deserves it for spouting that trash."

"What I think she deserves, what she wants, is someone to respond to charges like that with reason, with something she can think over and weigh against what her mother tells her. She might not be fishing for answers with the best of bait, but I feel certain fishing for answers is exactly what she's doing. Maybe, just maybe, if you give her some answers, a little of the division in this family could be healed. It wouldn't hurt to try, would it?"

His arm around her shoulders, he tugged her close and kissed her. "Couldn't hurt. Might be impossible when she opens her mouth and out pops 'Mother says' but, no, it couldn't hurt to try."

When they gathered for the evening meal, Leanne was a little dismayed. Lorraine Walsh claimed a headache and was not present. It was an insult, a slap in the face which she knew stung Hunter badly. She felt the sting herself but had rather expected it. Also, she mused sadly as she glanced at Hunter's brooding face, the woman was not *her* mother.

Laurie was late but marched in and took her seat as if all the men in her family were not staring at her, eyeing her with wary suspicion. Leanne suspected the lateness of the girl's arrival was due to the need to elude Lorraine. She could not fully suppress a touch of amusement. Laurie was but fifteen, yet she had six grown men on tenterhooks simply by entering the room.

"I'm sorry your mother is unwell," Leanne said after the food was served. She met Laurie's direct, intense gaze with calm.

"Mother says—" Laurie paused only briefly when a muttered round of curses came from the Walsh men. "She says she will have a headache until the house is cleaned of all trash."

Before any of the bristling men could speak, Leanne replied, "Then maybe you should rise early in the morning to take mop in hand and set to work. Perpetual headaches can be wearying."

A quick glance at the men showed Leanne they were all eating but watching her and Laurie very closely. She saw a smile twitch at the corners of Laurie's mouth before the girl controlled it. It helped to make her feel more certain in her judgment of the girl. There was a good chance that young Laurie was outgrowing her mother's tiny world.

"Mother says it's all the scandal she has to endure that makes her head ache."

"Laurie—" Sloane began, but Hunter quietly shushed him.

"Well, I'm sure Mother will survive," Leanne murmured.

"Ladies are expected to endure all—"

"'The slings and arrows of outrageous fortune,'" Owen drawled, and Leanne concentrated on her food to smother a laugh.

"'—all the trials their menfolk put them through,'" Laurie finished.

"Really?" Hunter watched his young sister closely. "Women don't put men through any trials, of course."

"No. Mother says a lady is at all times demure and obedient, catering to her husband's wishes."

"I hope you're listening closely to this, Leanne." Hunter grinned at her.

"As if it were gospel."

Laurie looked at Leanne. "Mother says there are some who will never be ladies."

Seeing the Walsh men bristle, Leanne smiled at Laurie. "The world is a richer place when there are differences between people."

The "Mother says" game continued for the rest of the meal. By the time Laurie left, the men were looking very puzzled. Leanne decided it might be best to leave them alone.

Hunter slouched in his chair after Leanne excused herself and sipped his wine. "Mother's not going to make this easy, is she?"

Sloane shook his head and sighed. "'Fraid not. I can talk to her 'til I'm blue in the face. It won't stop her doing what she's doing. The only thing we can do is wait her out. She'll turn her attentions elsewhere after a while."

"I know but, damn it, Leanne doesn't deserve such treatment."

"No, she doesn't, son. She seems a sweet kid."

"Well, I wouldn't go so far as saying sweet." Hunter grinned. "She can be as tart as green apples when her dander's up."

"Then maybe there's no need to worry. She'll handle your mother, and she'll know we're behind her and welcome her."

"Maybe. Sometimes she seems so strong, then . . ." He shrugged. "Remember what I told you about her? Her father deserted her, leaving her with that woman. That woman tossed her out without a by-your-leave and the town she grew up in turned on her. I think it's badly shaken her confidence. She might need more reassuring than we think. I wish I didn't have to be away as much as I will."

"We'll keep an eye on her, son. Least I can do is get Laurie to shut her mouth. I don't know what's gotten into that girl. She seems to be out from behind Lorraine a lot lately, tagging at our heels and goading us with that nonsense your mother has filled her head with."

"Yeah," agreed Owen, "and when you finally answer, she stands there staring at you like you're something very curious."

"Leanne has a theory about that." Seeing that he had everyone's attention, he related Leanne's opinions on the way Laurie was acting. "She thinks we ought to try just answering—reasonably."

"Can't hurt, can it," Sloane murmured. "Hell, if nothing else, at least the kid will have both sides of the story. Since she's started this 'Mother says' business, I've come to see just how much nonsense Lorraine has been feeding the girl over the years. Truth to tell, it's revealed a few things about the way Lorraine thinks that I never really knew before, and I don't like any of it."

After a murmured agreement, conversation turned to the business of the ranch. After a few more glasses of wine, Hunter's brothers rose almost as one to turn in for the night. Hunter, intending to do the same, started to rise only to have his father grasp his arm and urge him back into his seat.

"Something wrong?" he asked as soon as his brothers had left.

"No, not really. Tell me, are you certain about this marriage you're planning? Don't bristle. I'm not saying anything against that little girl. I'm only interested in what you feel. Are you real sure about this step?"

"Yes, I'm real certain. It's what I want."

"You love her then."

Hunter shrugged. "To be honest, I haven't given much thought to that. When I had Watkins in my hands and could see the end, see myself and her getting our names cleared, I saw us going our separate ways—only I didn't want her going anywhere, not without me. I wanted her right where she's been since Clayville—at my side. Marriage will settle that."

"I'm not revealing any big secret when I say my marriage is as sour as one can get. Hell, if I didn't feel so responsible for her after nearly thirty years of marriage and six kids, I'd toss the woman out. She only makes our lives miserable. Because of that, I'm anxious that you're sure, real sure, before you take that step. Are you sure you even know the girl?"

"After all we've been through together, Pa, if I don't know her now, I never will. I know I won't surprise you by saying we're lovers. She was a virgin, educated in the East, and has most of those well-bred morals despite what Charity—her foster mother—was. Yet she came to me when she thought I was nothing but an outlaw on the run. Oh, she had a plan or two to set me on the straight and narrow, but even those weren't grand or devious. She wanted me to be a storekeeper, if you can believe it. The fact that she accepted me for what I was, which wasn't much, meant a lot to me. She trusted me when I was apparently not one to be trusted. That means a lot too. I want her with me."

"I think you've said that clear enough. I wish you luck."

"Thanks. Pa? There's been talk. You might not have heard it yet . . ."

"Gossip travels faster than a dog with its tail on fire. I've heard it. Some anyways."

"Damn. Think it'll die down?"

"Most of it, soon as you marry the girl. Hell, that'll probably have some of those gossiping biddies turning it all romantic." He laughed at the disgusted face Hunter pulled. "Well, I'm easier in my mind about it now. Go on to bed, son."

By the time Hunter reached the top of the stairs, he was feeling almost lighthearted. In that short talk his father had made it clear that he accepted Leanne and he cared—cared enough to expose his own hurt and failure in marriage in hopes of helping his son.

He stopped in his room to strip to his trousers and wash up. As at the hotel, the two rooms were simply for appearance's sake, to placate his mother. Once ready for bed, he walked into Leanne's room. Smiling faintly at how tiny she looked in the large bed, he shed the rest of his clothes and slipped into bed beside her. He would play the game of separate rooms, but he would not sleep alone.

Feeling herself tugged up against a familiar hard body, Leanne murmured, "Hunter."

"Nope. George Lansing at your service, ma'am."

"Is that so. Well, I hope you reward a girl better than that pinchpenny Hunter Walsh." She laughed softly when Hunter gave her hair a gentle punitive tug, then yawned.

"You were supposed to respond with maidenly horror and leap from the bed."

"And provide you with untold amusement? Sorry, I'm too tired."

"I'm not surprised, after all the demands you've made on me the last few nights."

"My, we are feeling chipper this evening. Got some good news or something?"

"Not really. Just a comfortable talk with my father. To be honest, he wanted to be certain that I was confident of the step I was taking in getting married. Now before you start fretting, it had nothing to do with you. He was thinking on how wrong his own marriage had gone and wanted to be sure I knew what I was doing."

"Yes, he would worry, wouldn't he? Poor man. Your poor mother too."

"My poor mother? She's the reason this has all gone sour. She should have stayed in New Orleans and married some society dandy."

"Now, Hunter, if she had done that, you wouldn't be

here. Besides, there must have been something good between your parents in the beginning or there wouldn't be
six of you. I said 'your poor mother' because she has lost
so much, even if she did it to herself. If I'm right about
Laurie, your mother could soon find herself very much
alone. Some day, unfortunately, probably when it's too
late, she will wake up to what she's done and I pity her
that revelation."

He thought about that for a moment and nodded. "I
think it is already too late. Pa actually spoke aloud the
wish that he could just send her away. He's barely fifty
and still in good health. He could, perhaps, find someone
else, someone to add a little happiness to the years he has
left. He sure as hell won't find it with my mother."

Shaking away those sad thoughts, he kissed the top of
Leanne's head. "Anyway, I assured my father I did indeed
know what I was doing. We'll do fine, you and me,
Leanne."

Before she could respond, the door to the room was
flung wide open, and light from a hand-held lamp bathed
the room. Leanne took one look at the robed figure loom-
ing in the doorway, groaned, and hid her face against
Hunter's chest.

"Evening, Mother," Hunter drawled. "Come to say
good night?"

"It's just as I suspected. Did you think to fool me?"

"Wouldn't dream of it."

"I'll not have this in my house. It's immoral. Did you
lose all sense of right while with those thieves and
killers?"

"Lorraine!" snapped Sloane as he stepped up behind
his wife.

"Are you going to allow this—this shameful arrangement?"

"I don't see anything shameful. And they're getting married. Get out of here and let them sleep."

After a brief staring match, Lorraine strode off and Sloane gave his son a wry smile. "Sleep well, you two."

"Good night, Pa. Say good night to my father, Leanne."

He grinned when she gave a soft groan of embarrassment. His father laughed softly, then shut the door. Hunter slowly rubbed Leanne's back and waited for her to calm down. It was not going to be easy to convince her she had nothing to be embarrassed about.

"Why on earth did she do that?" Leanne muttered when she was finally able to speak.

"Damned if I know."

"How am I ever going to face your father in the morning?"

"Leanne, did you really think he didn't know about us? Even before I flat out told him we were lovers?"

"Why did you tell him that?"

"I told him you were a virgin. There was only one way I could know that for sure. I told him, just in case he had even the tiniest thought along the lines of my mother's about your morals."

"And, of course, seeing us here like this reassures him that my morals are exemplary."

"What he sees is that we're not hypocrites. This is my home, Leanne. I shouldn't have to play those games here. Not with my own damn family."

She thought about that for a moment. "No, I suppose you shouldn't have to."

"That was a quick capitulation."

"Well, on occasion you can be right."

"Thank you so much."

"You're very welcome."

He lightly hugged her. "Besides, until Watkins is tried and convicted, I'll be away a lot, sleeping alone too much as it is."

She returned his hug. "Then let's pray Watkins gets a very speedy trial."

Chapter Thirteen

"TOMORROW?" LEANNE STARED AT HUNTER AND SEBAS-
tian in dismay.

"To tell the truth," Sebastian said, "I'm surprised we
haven't left before now, but that fellow from New Mexico was being real careful about getting all the evidence
he could and Tuckman was being real careful about arranging secure transport."

"I can't really disagree with those two reasons, Sebastian."

"Nope, reckon you can't at that, Mr. Walsh."

Hunter sat down next to Leanne on the settee, put his
arm around her, and lightly hugged her. "You knew I'd
have to go sometime."

"Oh, I knew. I knew that's why Sebastian came. I was
just startled that it was such quick notice."

"Well, Miss Summers . . ."

"Don't you think you could start calling me Leanne now, Sebastian?" When he smiled at her, she decided he was a remarkably handsome man.

"My pleasure. As I was going to say, I left it this late on purpose. It's a long ride out here. I didn't really feel inclined to come out here to tell him we're leaving, then have to return to escort him back."

"There's no need for you to escort me," Hunter said.

"Don't get your back up, Walsh. I'm not talking about marching you in like a prisoner. You're an important witness, and we didn't get every last man that worked for Watkins. There might be a couple out there still thinking on cutting him loose."

After a moment's silence as that dark warning sank in, Sloane Walsh said, "Well, I'll get Molly to fix you up a bed in the guest house. She'll set you out a nice hot bath if you're wanting one."

"I won't say no, sir, but as for the bed, I can bunk down with the hands," Sebastian said.

"You deserve something a little more grand. You want to be well rested when you set out tomorrow."

Tomorrow. The word drummed in Leanne's head for the rest of the afternoon and all through the evening meal. So too did Sebastian's warning about some of Watkins's men still running free. She was surprised that the worry consuming her did not spoil her appetite, but ruefully admitted that nothing seemed to do that lately.

It was an hour after supper before she wrangled a moment alone with Sebastian. As they stood out on the veranda enjoying the cool evening air, Hunter left them to make a final check on what he would be taking with him. Leanne sat on the porch swing and watched Sebastian roll a cigarette.

"You're healed enough to make this journey?" she asked at last.

"I'd go on a stretcher if I had to. I've waited a long time to see Watkins pay for his crimes. But, yeah, I'm as good as new."

Glancing up at the sky, she murmured, "I noticed you had no trouble sitting down." She flashed him a grin when he choked on a laugh.

"Wretch. Not many people know about that particular injury."

"My lips are sealed." She sighed, her moment of levity quickly dampened by her worry. "Sebastian, is there really a danger from whatever men Watkins had who might still be free?"

"I honestly don't know. He had a few who were real loyal and we didn't get all of those. There's also that money he offers for anyone getting him loose. I prefer to be cautious."

"Yes, I prefer that too."

"And when we get back, you and Hunter are still getting married?"

She looked at him with a touch of surprise. "Yes. Why do you ask?"

"It's just that I've heard a thing or two. About his mother."

"Oh. Well, she has been less than welcoming, but that is more than made up for by Hunter's father and brothers. And at Hunter's age, surely his mother no longer has final say over how he spends his life."

"That's as it should be, but men can be funny when it comes to their mothers. I also wondered if, once things here are a little less hectic, you might find marriage wasn't what you wanted."

"I will admit that Hunter's different here, with his family. He's more at ease, more open. He doesn't worry at every turn that he might let slip something that'll get him killed. Also, I think it weighed heavily on his mind that he was branded an outlaw."

"It did. No doubt of that." He watched Leanne as she rose and moved to stand by the railing. "Sure you ought to wait 'til he gets back to get married?"

Frowning at him and wondering why he was studying her so intently, she replied, "It's what Hunter wants. It'll all be behind us then. We can start fresh. And there's no reason to hurry."

"Isn't there? What you two have been indulging in for so long"—he half-smiled when she blushed deeply and was unable to meet his gaze for a moment—"has been known to make babies." He raised his eyebrows slightly in silent question when she suddenly stared at him.

"Babies?" she croaked, her mind suddenly filled with stray bits of information that collected up into an alarming whole. "Good God! No. It can't be. And why are you looking at me like that? There's no brand on my forehead proclaiming it."

He ignored her testiness. "Leanne, I'm the oldest of a dozen kids. My sisters are busily building large families. I've been seeing pregnant women for as long as I can remember. There is a look. Don't ask me to explain what I see. Damned if I know. I just see it. Now, if you can say for certain you aren't, I'll accept that I'm talking through my hat."

"I can't," she whispered. "Damn, damn, damn. How long do you think you'll be away settling Watkins?"

"Can't think it'll be more than a month."

"That's not too bad. The child will still be arriving too

soon, even if we marry right this minute. Another month won't make much difference. Don't you say a word about this, Sebastian. Not a word."

"Why the hell not? He could marry you before we set out."

"Just drag the preacher out of his bed, mutter the right words, then wave Hunter good-bye? And what a lovely time to hit him over the head with this kind of news. He'll worry the whole way there and back." She ignored his muttered curse as he acknowledged the truth of her words. "I'll fret about him the whole time he's gone—but not as much as I would if he was taking this news with him."

"All right, but the minute we get back—the minute, mind you—you tell him. No more stalling."

"Yes, Papa."

"Hunter's right. You are a sassy little thing."

Later that night, as she watched Hunter get ready for bed, she wondered if she was right, if she should wait until he came back. Ever since Sebastian had mentioned the possibility, she knew without a doubt that she was pregnant. She wondered how she could have been so stupid not to have seen it before. She supposed she had simply had too much else on her mind. But it was news she ached to share.

She told herself firmly that her first decision was the best one. While she might not know much about how Hunter did or did not feel about her, she did know that he worried about her well-being. To tell him she was carrying his child before he had to leave on what could be a dangerous journey would be unnecessarily cruel. She would wait until he was safely home again.

Pushing away her troubled thoughts, she welcomed

him into her arms when he slipped into bed at her side. It was their last night together for a while. She was determined to make it one he would remember the whole time he was gone.

Rolling onto his back, he dragged her on top of him. "It's real hard to leave this to go back to sleeping on the ground—alone."

"I'll be much more comfortable than you, but I won't like it much either." She brushed a kiss over his mouth. "Just keep reminding yourself that this will end it at last. All our trouble will finally be firmly behind us."

Trying to hold her close for a fuller kiss, he frowned a little when she eluded him. "It's the only thing that'll get me to do it."

Sitting up, she smiled down at him as she unbuttoned her nightgown. She felt exceedingly bold. Some of it, she supposed, was because he would be leaving and she would be over whatever embarrassment her wantoness might stir in her by the time he returned. Her daring would also help make some memories that would stay with him, so she did not fight it. Still smiling faintly, she grasped the bottom of her nightgown and ever so slowly pulled it off over her head.

Hunter caught his breath at the slow exposure of her slim body. He was almost afraid to move. Leanne rarely acted so boldly. He did not want to do anything that might make her stop. Another thing that worried him was that, if she kept on, he would not be able to control himself for very long. Just watching her sensual removal of her nightgown had him breathing hard.

As she bent to kiss him, she grasped his wrists to hold his hands to the bed. He could break her hold with no effort at all but, as she had suspected, he did not even try. It was a heady feeling to have him so pliant beneath her. Slowly, taking her time and thoroughly enjoying herself, she kissed and licked her way down his body.

When her tantalizing little mouth reached the juncture of his thighs, Hunter groaned with the effort of controlling the tremors of need tearing through him. She released his wrists and he had to clench his hands into tight fists to keep from grabbing her. Finally, with a harsh cry as his control broke, he grabbed her beneath her arms, dragged her up his body and set her down upon him. For a moment he held her still there, enjoying the feel of their joining, savoring the warm, moist welcome of her body.

"God, woman, you feel so good. So damn fine."

"You don't feel so bad yourself."

"I wish I could hold us here, at this point of needing it so bad it hurts yet feels so damned good."

"I'm not sure that would be healthy."

He laughed softly. "You're probably right."

At first, they moved slowly. Then their need gained control of their bodies. Hunter encouraged her fierceness as she took them swiftly toward release. When her movements grew a little frantic as the culmination of her desire robbed her of all control, he held her tightly against him. He lifted his hips off of the bed slightly in response to the force of his release. He held her close when she sagged into his arms, sharing the trembling that afflicted her. If her intention had been to remind him of the beauty of what they could share, she could not have done a better job. As soon as he recouped his strength he would turn the tables on her. It would not hurt to do a little reminding of his own.

Easing out of Hunter's lax hold, Leanne rose and went to wash herself. Her own daring had surprised her but, she thought with a little grin, she had also had a very good time. Casually tossing aside the cloth she had freshened herself with, she walked back to the bed—only to discover the man she had thought half-asleep was very much awake.

He slid over to her side of the bed and gripped her hips in his hands before she could climb into bed. His soft kisses over her stomach and thighs soon had her desire stirring again. When his lips touched the heated softness between her thighs, she sighed and closed her eyes. It was obviously going to be one, long scandalous night, she mused as she opened to his kiss. She was beginning to like this sensual abandon—and how could that be such a bad thing?

Leanne slowly opened her eyes, then sat up with a soft cry. She was alone. Noticing a slip of paper on the bedside table, she grabbed it, reading: "It's better this way. Take care of yourself. When I get back, this'll all be over. Hunter." Tossing the note back onto the table, she lay back down, thinking idly that his handwriting was appalling. She waited for the feeling of loss to hit her, but all her body was interested in was sleep. Closing her eyes, she decided the worry and loneliness could wait.

Hunter started to yawn, caught Owen grinning at him, and smothered it. "You find something amusing?"

"Nope. Not a thing. Didn't get much sleep, huh?"

"Just why do I have the dubious pleasure of your company?"

"Pa didn't want you riding off alone this time."

After glancing around at the dozen well-armed men they rode with, Hunter looked back at Owen. "You call this alone?"

"Without family along."

"I would've thought you'd be needed more at the ranch."

"Charlie and Jed more than make up for my loss." Glancing toward the prison wagon that held a coldly glaring Watkins, Owen murmured, "Seeing the kind of hate you've stirred up makes me glad I came."

Looking towards Watkins, Hunter felt a chill snake down his spine. The man had gone beyond hate and fury. He felt certain Watkins's mind had gone, that the man had become insane with a need for revenge. It would be hard to relax his guard until Watkins was securely jailed and waiting only to be hanged.

By the end of the first day of travel, Hunter was aching with exhaustion. Even the hard ground that was his bed would not stop him from sleeping. It might have been wiser to get some sleep the night before he left, but he knew he would pass the night the same way if given a second chance. Just thinking about it stirred a wanting even in his exhausted body. When Leanne let her sensual nature run free, she was beyond compare. If her intention had been to plant herself firmly in his mind, she had done a superb job. He decided he would be a complete idiot if he told her the truth, that she did not have to go to such efforts to make him remember her. She never really left his thoughts.

He frowned as he acknowledged that fact. She had been firmly set in his mind from the first. No other woman had accomplished that feat—he had forgotten most of them as soon as he stepped out of their beds. He could bring Leanne to mind with no effort at all, and so clearly he could smell the sweet, clean scent of her.

And that, he thought with an inner groan, should tell him something. She was in his head. She just had to smile and he was hot and ready. He himself had nearly died of fear when she was shot. He had proposed because the thought of her leaving had chilled him. She made him laugh. She had, in fact, the ability to touch and twist every emotion he possessed. He had never felt as possessive about anything in his life as he did about her. He loved her. He swore.

Owen, stretched out at his brother's side, looked at Hunter. "Something wrong?"

"I was thinking about Leanne," Hunter snapped, fear of revealing his true feelings making him testy.

"The last thing I'd have thought that'd do is make you mad."

"Why do you say that?"

"Because there's only one thing that can make a man look like you did today—dead tired yet as happy as a pig in mud. Looking at you today was enough to make a fellow jealous." When Hunter said nothing, he pressed, "So what's got you cussing her?"

For a moment Hunter still made no reply. He was not sure he wanted to expose such a newly discovered vulnerability. Then he sighed. He felt a real need to discuss it with someone, and he trusted few people as much as Owen to keep his mouth shut.

"I just had a revelation that set me back a pace."

"Ah, you finally realized you're in love with little Leanne."

Scowling at Owen, Hunter muttered, "Just what makes you think that?"

"I'm neither as blind nor as stupid as some people I could mention. What made you finally see it? It didn't just pop into your head."

"No, but she did and I got to thinking on how often and how easily she does. She's there all the time. Hell, I swear I can sometimes smell her, the memory's so clear. That started me to thinking on a lot of other things."

"And they all added up to love. Things like how possessive you are, glaring at any guy who smiles at her. I saw that right off. It's why I didn't tell you that when I first saw her, she was in her bath."

"What?" Hunter snapped, half sitting up, then grimaced and lay back down when Owen laughed. "Maybe that's why she didn't tell me either."

"Reckon she just didn't think on it or wanted to forget it. It sore embarrassed her, though she recovered herself well. It was that pretty, bright red face of hers and that brief look of horror that made me realize she wasn't some girl from Jennie's Palace or the saloon."

"Hell, there's something else I should've seen. I haven't touched another woman since I set eyes on Leanne. I had a mistress in Mexico who knew every trick in the book and then some—but I told her adios because of some purple-eyed girl with a smart mouth."

"Why do you sound so annoyed about it—like you'd just discovered you'd caught something nasty at Jennie's?"

"I should be happy, should I? Look what being in love got Pa. I don't need that sort of trouble."

"You won't get it from Leanne and you know it. She's nothing like our mother. Pa's being in love didn't hurt or help that situation. It made him blind to her faults maybe, but the best of us can suffer that. Somehow I don't think you do."

"No, I don't think I do."

He thought on that for a while. Leanne did have faults, such as a quick temper, but her good qualities softened them. Why, he had more faults than she did. She was far more pliable, more compromising, than he was, for a start. He sighed.

"I know what it is that's really eating at me," he admitted despite some reluctance to do so. "I don't like being the one bitten while she doesn't suffer the same affliction."

"Damn, but it's hard on the youngest son to realize the oldest son can be such an idiot."

"Thank you."

"My pleasure."

"She hasn't said she loves me."

"Maybe she's as thick as you, or maybe she doesn't want to say it when you haven't. Look, I can't say for certain she loves you, but I'd be damned surprised if she didn't. She accepted you, trusted you, when she thought you were nothing but an outlaw trying to outrun a posse. She's become your lover, yet I know she's what we all call a good woman. Someone like that doesn't take that step lightly. Hell, she's been putting up with our mother so she can stay with you. If you'd think for a while, you'd probably come up with a lot of things that show how she feels."

"She loves him all right."

Owen and Hunter looked behind them and found Sebastian standing there smoking a cigarette. "Damn it, this was a private conversation," Hunter snapped.

"I made sure it stayed that way too."

Owen laughed and Hunter glared at him, then at Sebastian. "And what makes you so sure she does? What do you know about it?"

"I've got me a few sisters. I watched them as they fell in love. Listened to them. Saw how they looked, how they acted. Leanne does all the same things. She's also waiting, like you wanted, to get married."

"She agreed with my reasoning."

"Yup, she did. Probably really does. She's deep-down scared, though—scared that while you wait, you'll change your mind. But she sits and waits and tries not to be scared. Well, don't you worry on it. Even if you do change your mind, you don't need to worry on her. She'll be taken good care of." Sebastian quietly walked away.

"He means by him, doesn't he?" Owen murmured after a few moments of stunned silence.

"That's exactly what he means. Damn, I should've seen it. Well, he can just whistle into the wind."

After a few moments of quiet as they tried to get as comfortable as possible in their rough beds, Owen called, "Hunter?"

"Um?"

"I'm glad you found Leanne. She's taken the bitterness away."

Hunter looked inside of himself and realized that Owen was right. The bitterness and disillusionment had gone. A touch of cynicism remained, a little wariness, but he knew that was not a bad thing. It would keep him cautious. Without his even seeing it, Leanne had healed his wounds.

"Yeh, she has—but damn, Owen," he whispered, "I fear she could put it back tenfold with little effort."

*   *   *

By the time they reached their destination, Hunter knew he was not the only one who felt inclined to forget the trial and hang Watkins outright, Martin at his side. Neither man missed a chance to threaten, jeer, or goad anyone within hearing distance. Marshal Tuckman had taken to gagging them at first, but it had helped little. They seemed to save up their vitriol for the few times they had to be ungagged. One dismal attempt by Watkins's men to free him had ended in utter defeat, added two more prisoners, and increased Watkins's vengeful fury. Hunter watched in cold-eyed satisfaction as both men were dragged off to their cells to await their trial.

"Soon it'll be all over." Marshal Tuckman gave Hunter a sympathetic slap on the back.

"I'm inclined to toss aside my original intention of leaving as soon as he's sentenced and stay to see the bastard hang."

"Ever see a hanging?"

"Yes." Hunter sighed and shook his head. "I swore to God I'd never watch another one, no matter who it was."

"Might be an idea to stick to that promise. They're apt to hang more than one at a time here."

"God. I think I need a drink, a bath, and a bed."

"That's where Sebastian's headed. Follow him. I'll send word when you're needed."

More than glad to leave, Hunter strode off after Sebastian, Owen falling into step at his side. He hoped he would not have to wait long for the trial. All he wanted to do was go home—home to Leanne.

*   *   *

Leanne slowly rocked in the porch swing, staring some-what blindly into the distance. Out there were the Walsh men. She wished she could be with them. In that general direction, too, were New Mexico and Hunter. She dearly wished she was with him. She laughed wryly. In truth, she wished she was anywhere but where she was.

When the Walsh men were home, things were fine. The moment they left in the morning, Lorraine swept into control and life was miserable. Lorraine made her dislike, even her distaste, very clear, and about the only diversion Leanne had from persecution was when Lorraine turned on Molly Pitts, who stoically endured being treated like some galley slave. Leanne was beginning to suspect that Molly put up with that nonsense for one reason only—Sloane Walsh. It was, all in all, an appalling situation. Unfortunately, she was failing miserably in bettering it in any way.

And today, she thought with a deep sense of weariness, started the worst campaign of all. At the moment, Lorraine had all her friends in the parlor sipping tea and, Leanne was certain, having their ears filled with gossip about her, gossip they would undoubtedly spread. She would soon be an outcast just as she had been in Colorado. It made her want to weep when she thought of how it would hurt Hunter. While he was so busy clearing her name, his mother was blackening it, perhaps beyond repair. She had no idea of how to keep it from happening either.

"May I sit with you, Leanne?"

Startled a little, for she had not seen Laurie approach, Leanne sighed. "I think if I hear one 'Mother says' right now, Laurie, I will toss you to the ground and jump up and down on you while I scream like a stuck pig."

"I won't say it." Laurie sat down. "They are all talking about you, y'know."

"Well, I did think they were. They are very busy spreading lies about me."

"Are they all lies?"

"Probably not. There's enough that's happened to me, and to Hunter and me, to fulfill a gossip's wildest dreams. It's none of their business, however. They will also make it all sound so bad, so sordid, and it isn't."

"Did she really see you in Hunter's bed?"

A little surprised that Lorraine would have told the girl about that, Leanne decided to be fully honest. "I'm afraid so. We are going to be married. Not that that makes it right, really. But when you're running from posses and bounty hunters, and you've been marked as a criminal and have a price on your head, what a bunch of women over tea are going to say about you just doesn't seem very important. Silly I may have been, but I've only ever been one man's woman. I have no intention of changing that, and they have no right to go passing judgment on me."

"No, they don't. But they will anyway. Leanne, can you love someone but not like them very much?" Laurie asked in a small voice.

"Yes, that's entirely possible." She gave Laurie a terse explanation about Charity. "Even now, it's hard not to think of her as my mother. That's what she was to me up until a few months ago, when she spat the truth in my face. I never really liked her. She could be mean, cold, and sarcastic. She cheated her boarders and had no interest in me. For a while I felt guilty, but then I met others who had families they could not really like or get along with. I would do anything expected of a daughter—give the loyalty, defense, support and care required—but I realized I didn't have to like her."

Laurie sighed. "I don't think Pa or my brothers like me very much."

"They don't know you enough to like or dislike you. They've never been allowed to know you very much."

"No they haven't really, have they? I can grasp at enough memories to know you're right about that."

"That doesn't mean you can't get to know them now. They wouldn't push you away."

"True, and they don't. Not even when I say 'Mother says' now, and that's because of you. I know it is. Until you came, they'd never try to talk to me once I said that. They'd just yell and walk away."

"I only made a suggestion. If they're behaving differently, it's because they want to."

"I suppose that's true. Maybe I'll stop playing the game of 'Mother says'."

"You might find things go a lot more smoothly. You'd probably see fewer gritted teeth and retreating backs." She smiled when Laurie giggled, then realized sadly that was the first time she had heard the girl laugh.

"Can I ask what made you start that game? You don't have to answer if you don't want to." She feared pushing the girl too hard.

"I want to. I saw how my father and brothers would laugh and talk together. Then one day, I realized Mother never laughed with me and only talked at me. Then I caught her in two lies. It doesn't really matter what they were. It just started me thinking there might be others, and I was mad enough about her telling me those two to start looking for answers—Even though they were usually short and loud." She smiled when Leanne laughed softly. "I did get some answers and I overheard a lot. She's done a lot of lying. I got really mad at first, then decided there was no point in that when she didn't even notice I was mad at her. So I decided to start thinking and doing for myself. Now it's time to step out from behind Mother and look around with my own eyes."

"I think, Laurie, that you are very grown up indeed."

"Well, maybe. I don't know. I do know it hasn't been easy and it certainly hasn't been much fun."

"It never is."

"I better get back in the house. The ladies will be leaving soon, and Mother will be looking for me."

"Leaving soon, you say?" Leanne murmured as Laurie stood up.

"Yes. Even Patricia Spotford."

Leanne muttered "Thank God" and rolled her eyes, which caused Laurie to giggle a little before slipping back into the house. Leanne then rose to take a walk so that she did not have to meet Lorraine's visitors after they had had an earful about her. Besides, she conceded, she did not want to see the pretty widow, Patricia, again. This morning she had had her fill of the insinuations concerning Patricia and Hunter—vague references to thwarted love and chances for reconciliation. She had tried not to listen, but Patricia did seem to know a great deal about Hunter. It was hard to fully shake a flicker of doubt. Worse, she had a sinking feeling that Lorraine had scented blood, and Patricia would soon be very hard to avoid.

Shaking away that concern, she told herself she would worry about it if and when the need arose. There was something good she could think on, and that was Laurie.

Laurie had broken free of Lorraine's grip of her own accord, which could only be for the good of everyone concerned. She was sorry for the inner conflicts the girl had to struggle with, but she was pleased beyond measure that Laurie would not become just another Lorraine. She would not be doomed to the sort of bitter, lonely life her mother had made for herself.

Despite her efforts not to, for it only made her sad, she found herself thinking of Hunter. She wanted him back, needed him. This was the first time they had been apart since the bank robbery and it made her afraid. She feared the effects of his mother's constant poison feeding on her doubts. Most of all, she feared how the time apart could affect Hunter, how it might make him begin to think again about marrying her. Telling herself it was foolish to think like that did not help. She needed Hunter, needed him home to prove all her fears were baseless.

Chapter Fourteen

A *COMMITMENT I NEED TO EXTRACT MYSELF* FROM.

The words seared through Leanne's heart as she crushed the letter in her hand. He called her "a commitment", "a difficulty," and "a stumbling block." That was almost as painful as reading his declaration of love to another woman would have been. It reduced her to little more than a nuisance.

Smoothing out the letter, she compared it to the brief note Hunter had left her when he rode off that morning, a time that seemed years ago instead of barely a month. The handwriting still matched. She had not imagined it did, nor was this some new trick by Lorraine to get her to leave. When Patricia had brought this letter to Lorraine, Lorraine must have seen it as manna from heaven. Hunter was not coming home to marry her. He was coming home to "extract" himself from a "commitment" and then marry Patricia Spotford.

She sprawled on the bed and stared blindly at the ceiling. She needed to plan her next step, but her mind refused to function. She wanted to weep and, despite firmly telling herself it would solve nothing, she turned on her stomach, buried her face in her pillow, and burst into tears.

It was a long time before she pulled herself free of the emotional maelstrom afflicting her. She felt drained, dead inside. Staggering to the washbowl, she bathed her face. She was just feeling able to cope when a soft rap sounded at her door. Before she could say a word, Lorraine strode into the room. Leanne cursed her weakness of a moment ago, knowing her bout of tears was easy to detect upon her face. But she squared her shoulders and faced Lorraine with cold-eyed calm.

"Your impeccable manners are slipping, Mrs. Walsh. I don't recall telling you to enter."

"Have you finished with the letter?"

"Quite finished. It's on the bed. Help yourself."

Moving to pick up the letter, Lorraine said, "If you wish to depart now and avoid a distasteful scene with my son, I will be sure to give Tarrant any message you wish to leave."

I doubt your prim little mouth could form the message I feel like leaving that bastard, Leanne thought, but smiled instead. "How kind. However, I am not sure leaving would be the wisest course for me." Although, when Lorraine turned to face her, the woman's expression was as remote as ever, there was a flicker of surprise and uncertainty in her cold green eyes.

"This letter makes it rather clear that there is no reason for you to linger here."

"Isn't there? One quickly comes to mind. A breach of promise suit." The look of pure horror Lorraine could not fully hide gave Leanne some fleeting satisfaction.

"You can't do that."

"Can't I? I have plenty of witnesses to Hunter's declaration of his intention to marry me."

"You don't expect his family to be witnesses against him, do you? Those two saddletramps are not acceptable witnesses either."

"You may be right on both counts, although I should like to think the Walsh men would not stoop to perjuring themselves in court. However, I don't really need to involve them. I have other witnesses—ones who would not be questioned. I have Federal Marshal Tuckman and a deputy federal marshal."

"Surely you don't want a husband you've had to force to the altar."

"No? According to you, I've already tried to trick him into marriage. A little public embarrassment and legal coercion should not bother me now."

"How much will it cost to make you reconsider?"

Leanne wondered, almost idly, if she had ever been quite so insulted. Lorraine Walsh clearly had a lower opinion of her than even she had imagined, but it did not really matter now. It was time to end the conversation. Grasping the somewhat shaken woman by the arm, she pushed her out of the room, said "I will have to give that some serious consideration," and shut the door in Lorraine's face.

Sagging against the door, she listened to her footsteps hurrying down the stairs. Leanne was sure Patricia and Lorraine would be deep in consultation for quite a while. Now was the time to decide exactly what was the best thing to do.

For one brief moment, she considered playing out her threat to bring a breach of promise suit against Hunter. It had some delicious possibilities for revenge. She shook away the thought. It would be too painful. The anger she held now would not really sustain her. Nor did she really want a husband who would undoubtedly hate her. She certainly did not want monetary compensation.

There was, of course, the option of staying put and fighting for Hunter. All that brought to mind was his written declaration of love for Patricia. He had never made one to her. There really was nothing to fight for. She had already lost and she had neither the heart nor, she thought as she covered her faintly rounded abdomen with her hands, the time.

That left her with only one choice—to leave. But where could she go? All connection with Charity was severed. Now was not the time to go looking for her father. That would have to wait until after the baby was born. It left her with only one place to go—O'Malley's. If she left immediately, she could get there before the really severe winter weather set in.

"But I can't go alone," she admitted and hurriedly went in search of Charlie and Jed.

Laurie frowned and edged the connecting door to the parlor open a crack so that she could hear better. Her mother and Patricia Spotford were very friendly lately. She found that extremely suspicious.

"Are you sure she didn't see that a piece had been torn off the top?" Patricia asked as she watched Lorraine pace the room.

"Very sure. She accepted it as completely genuine."

"Then why are you acting this way? Everything has worked to your satisfaction, hasn't it?"

Sinking into a chair, Lorraine helped herself to a large glass of wine from the crystal decanter on the table in front of her. "Has it? How does a breach of promise suit sound to you?"

Laurie frowned, wondering what that was.

"She wouldn't," gasped Patricia.

"I can't be sure of that. I think I underestimated her. She would have two lawmen as witnesses too. Think of the scandal." Lorraine nearly drained her glass of wine in one swallow "God, I should never live it down."

"You're not thinking. If she plans that, it means she plans to stay around, you fool. Eventually she'll see Tarrant again and a suit is the last thing you'll need to worry about then. She'll find out there's no breach of promise, and he'll find out about your little game."

"*My* little game? You were very eager to jump in. Damn little bitch, she got me so upset by doing something I had never expected of her that I got confused for a moment. Well, I offered her money."

"Did she take it?"

"She said she would have to give it some serious consideration."

"Well, that's something."

"What if she doesn't take it?"

"I wouldn't worry until it happens. If you have a reasonable sum to wave under her nose, it might help."

"I would have to go to the bank."

"If you leave with me now, you can get to the bank today. Stay at my place, then come back here tomorrow."

"Is there a need to rush around so?"

"He said he'd be gone about a month. It has been nearly that now."

"Get your carriage ready. I'll get Laurie, throw a few things in a bag, and we will be right with you."

Laurie did not even bother to shut the door. She dashed into the hall, up two steps of the hall stairs and acted as if she was just coming downstairs when her mother stepped into the hall. Her mother snapped out a few orders as she hurried up the stairs, and Laurie reluctantly followed her upstairs. She did not want to make the trip. Something told her that being away for a night just now was not a good idea. Unfortunately, she could see no way to get out of it without raising suspicions.

"She's gone now," Charlie hissed.

Leanne stepped from her hiding place in the corner of an empty stall and moved to the stable door to peek out. She frowned as a moment later she saw Lorraine hurry out of the house, a foot-dragging Laurie in tow. They both carried small bags. After they got into Patricia's carriage, the woman urged her team into a smart trot and headed off toward town.

"Now where are they racing off to? That doesn't make much sense," Leanne muttered.

"You ain't making much sense neither," Charlie growled. Jed nodded. "You come racing in here saying you gotta talk to us then babble something about Colorado. Then that woman calls out and you scurry to hide. What's going on?"

Sighing, Leanne leaned against the inside frame of the stable door. "I want to go to my friend's cabin in the San Juan Mountains—well, in the foothills really, not far from a pass through the mountains. It's only a day or so from where we all started out together."

"But Hunter will be back soon."

"I know, Jed. That's why I have to leave as soon as possible. I have no intention of being here when he comes back." She almost smiled at their identical looks of total confusion. "There isn't going to be a marriage between Hunter and me." She was a little surprised at how much it hurt simply to say the words. "He has just written to that pretty little widow who just left to tell her he loves her and is going to break his promise to me to marry her." The words tasted bitter in her mouth.

"Naw, I don't believe it. Don't make sense to me. You real sure, Leanne?"

"Please, Charles, please don't make me keep repeating it."

"Well, maybe you oughta wait a bit. Me and Charlie could beat some sense into him."

"No, that really won't work. No one likes to be dragged into something they don't want. Look, you don't have to come. I just didn't want to go so far alone." She almost mentioned her pregnancy, then decided that would not really be fair.

"You ain't going anywheres alone. Me and Jed'll take you."

She hugged them both, smiling at their blushes. "Oh, thank you. You don't have to stay there. You can come back here."

"Don't reckon we'll do that. It's been good here, good men, but"—Charlie shook his head—"Hunter's done disappointed me."

Jed nodded. "That he has. There is one problem. Not a big one. We'll have to steal us what we need. Horses and everything."

"Wait—Mrs. Walsh offered to pay me off. I threatened to take Hunter to court on a breach of promise. I didn't mean it, but she made me mad and I knew she'd be horrified over the threat of scandal. I'll just write a note saying I took the supplies I needed instead and, in writing, release Hunter from his promise. That'll clear us. Just don't take any of their best horses."

She shook her head. "My wits must have gone begging. I completely forgot that the marshal took everyone's horse except Hunter's and Sebastian's."

"Well, they was stolen horses anyways. Lucky we didn't get hanged for takin' 'em."

Seeing the way Charlie frowned, then Jed, Leanne realized that they felt they owed Hunter a lot. "You don't have to stay up there with me," she assured them.

"We'll see about that when we get there. No matter what, you ain't trotting off to the mountains all on your lonesome." He nudged her out the door. "Get your things. Best we get going right now. It's several hours before dark, and we can get a good start. Me and Jed'll get the supplies and the horses ready."

Without another word, she raced for the house. She knew as well as Charlie did that there was an even better reason for getting out of there as soon as possible. By some stroke of luck, they were the only ones on the ranch now that Lorraine and Laurie had left. The sort of all-round handyman, Jake, would have been there, but he had driven the buggy to take Molly visiting a sick neighbor. It was too good an opportunity to miss.

After packing only what was necessary, she paused to write two notes, one for Lorraine and one for Laurie. She only briefly thought of leaving a word or two for Hunter. There really was nothing to say. The note to Lorraine was easily written. The one to Laurie was harder. She felt bad about leaving the girl when she had such a need of someone to talk to, someone to listen to her. After placing each note on the proper dressing table, she grabbed her carpetbag and hurried out to the stables.

"We're going to ride as hard as we dare without ruining the horses," Charlie said as he swung her up onto her mount. "Get as much ground covered as we can before dark."

"I don't really think anyone will be following us, Charles," she murmured as he and Jed mounted.

"Don't want to take any chances. To be frank, Leanne, I don't trust that Mrs. Walsh as far as I can spit."

Neither did Leanne, so she just gritted her teeth and kept up with her companions. There was very little respite until dusk settled over the land, and she was impressed with the distance they managed to cover. She was also exhausted. When Jed lifted her out of the saddle and set her on her feet, she crumbled. She bent over slightly, rubbing her back where a mild but nonetheless uncomfortable ache had lodged. Suddenly she feared for the child she carried.

"You all right, Leanne?" Charlie asked as he and Jed crouched in front of her.

She looked at her two friends and sighed, knowing they were not going to like what she had to say. "I'm afraid I can't ride like that again. Covering distance quickly is something I will have to forgo."

"It's probably just that you're not used to riding hard no more."

"No, Jed. It's a little more than that. I am going to have a baby." For a moment, they only stared at her as if she had suddenly sprouted another head. Tentatively she asked, "Could you please lay me out my bed?" Then Jed scrambled to do that, and she added, "With something to rest my head on and something to put my feet up on."

Within minutes she was settled on her bedding, feet up. Slowly she began to feel better, her fear easing. Charlie and Jed set up camp but kept a very close eye on her. When a nervous-looking Charlie brought her a plate of beans and a cup of coffee, she sat up.

"You're all right? Haven't hurt yourself or nothing?"

"No, Charles. I'll be fine. I think it was just a warning. The doctor I worked with when I was at school told me that a body does give a warning, and a lot of problems are caused because people simply don't heed it. That was what this was—a little warning. I'm already feeling better. If you don't mind, I think I'll leave everything to you two, however, and stay right here with my feet up to be sure."

"That's fine, Leanne. You rest all you need."

She concentrated on eating. There was one positive thing about her condition at the moment, and that was that her body was so desperate for sustenance it could even tolerate Charlie's coffee. When she set her plate and cup aside and started to undo her shoes, Charlie was immediately back at her side. He gently pushed her back onto her bedding and took off her shoes for her.

"You don't have to do that. I'm fine. Really. I don't need this much pampering, nice as it is."

"Me and Jed have been talking," Charlie said, setting her shoes aside.

"I saw you two whispering." She prepared herself for the argument she was sure was coming.

"We think you ought to go back."

"Well, I don't."

"It's Hunter's baby."

"And mine. I told you he doesn't wish to marry me now."

"But he doesn't know about the baby." Jed moved to crouch at her other side. "It'd be different if he knew."

"I don't want him to marry me just because I'm carrying his child."

"Yeh, but if you don't get married, it'll be a bastard."

"Did you two happen to notice what Sloane Walsh's marriage was like?"

"What's that got to do with this?"

"Just answer the question, Charles."

"Yeh, it was bad. Ain't seen many that poor, 'though they're real civilized about it. I woulda tossed her out. She don't even do any work."

"Well, I don't want to end up like that. Don't argue,"

she said when they both opened their mouths to speak. "Marriage between me and Hunter could turn just as sour. Sure he would want the baby, but he doesn't want me. He wants to marry Patricia Spotford. He loves her. He's going to be angry and resentful if he has to turn his back on her. That'll sour our marriage. Better the child be a bastard than suffer in an unhappy home."

"A child oughta have a pa." Jed frowned then brightened. "One of us could marry you."

"That's very sweet, but friends don't necessarily make good marriage partners. I know a child should have two parents. That is the best way. I can't have that now, so I'll make do with what I've got. As for a father—well a lot of friends who just happen to be men can almost be as good. I've got you two, O'Malley, and his sons. Plenty of good examples for the child to look up to."

"Well, I don't think me and Jed can be called good examples."

"Of course you can. You aren't perfect, to be sure, but I think that's better. Perfection can be very trying to have around."

"Aren't you ever going to tell Hunter?"

"I can't answer that just now, Jed. It depends on so much—what happens in Hunter's life and what happens in mine. There's plenty of time to make a decision. Considering how I feel about Hunter just now, I don't think it'd be a good idea for me to make any decision that concerns him." She could not fully stifle a yawn, her body's need for rest blessedly stronger than her inner turmoil.

"Here now, Jed, we better let her rest. We'll go easy from now on, Leanne. Any old time you want to stop, you just call out."

"Thank you. You are being very good to me," she murmured as she closed her eyes.

In the morning she felt as good as new, although it took a little while to convince Charles and Jed of that. They proceeded at a pace she thought a little too slow, but it was not until after their noon rest that she was able to convince them to go just a little faster, that it was only the hard riding for several hours that had caused the problem.

As they continued on, she looked back in the direction they had come from. Crumbled dreams were all she left behind, except for a budding friendship with a lonely young girl. She hoped Laurie would not return to her mother's shadow.

Even as the buggy drew to a halt before the house, Laurie knew something was wrong. Her father's immediate appearance on the veranda to demand if they knew where Leanne was made it very hard for her to act calm as she got out of the buggy, but she struggled to do so. By the time she was in the house, talk of supplies and horses gone—as well as Charles and Jed—told her Leanne was gone. Still fighting to act as if she did not care, she meandered up to her room. Dropping her pose only after she was inside of her room, she looked around frantically, then snatched up the note left by Leanne.

"I'm sorry to leave without saying good-bye," she read. "In fact, I'm sorry to be leaving at all, as I think we were near to being very good friends. In case 'Mother' doesn't 'says' this time, I'm leaving because Hunter loves and intends to marry Patricia Spotford. Your mother showed me a letter he wrote the woman saying just that.

As soon as I calm down, I promise I will write to you. Please, do not stop looking for answers, looking at the world through your own eyes. Much love, Leanne."

Laurie slowly sat down on her bed. She read the letter over and over again. Each word made her recall the overheard conversations between Patricia Spotford and her mother. They were behind this. She was sure of it.

Looking at the letter she held, she muttered, "I'll keep looking for answers all right—and by the time Hunter gets home, I'll have them!"

"Damn it, why is this dragging out for so long?" Hunter growled as he strode toward the saloon with Sebastian and Owen.

"That's what you pay a good lawyer for," Sebastian drawled.

Hunter silently cursed all lawyers as they found a seat in the crowded saloon and Sebastian ordered them some whiskey. He was accomplishing so little and using so much time to do it in, Hunter reflected. After downing a shot of whiskey, he felt a little calmer.

"I figure a day, maybe two more, then it has to go to the jury."

"Sebastian's right, Hunter. That lawyer's dragged it out as long as he can."

"I told Leanne I'd be home in a month. That's come and gone."

"You'd better send her word telling her why you're not." Sebastian laid out his cigarette makings on the table.

"It'd cost me a fortune to tell her everything that's

gone wrong. You'd never know they wanted this man so bad."

"They've got him. No rush now. Of course, if you weren't so determined, the lawyer could have succeeded just by delaying long enough for you to up and leave. The fewer witnesses, the better. That's also why he's called on you more than once and tried to discredit you. That little game has sent witnesses storming off before. It seems longer than it's been, too, 'cause it started so much later than we thought it would—the judge being sick, the backlog of trials. He'll still hang."

"Sure about that? Watkins's lawyer's one good talker."

"Not that good, Hunter. He can't talk down the truth or make that trail of robberies, murders, and rapes less offensive than it is."

"Well, at least we managed one thing—Leanne's name and mine are clear, and Charlie and Jed are pardoned. They'll be glad of that. You can talk a damn good show, too, Sebastian. And that reminds me—something that lawyer asked, but I didn't catch the answer. Just what was a federal law officer doing crossing into the sovereign territory of Mexico?"

"I was relieved of duty when I set out after Watkins and reinstated the minute we arrived in Little Creek with him. I was not acting with the government's knowledge or approval, but as a private citizen."

"Hell, maybe you oughta be a lawyer too."

Sebastian half-smiled as he lit his cigarette. "Trying to make Watkins's capture and all that look illegal didn't work anyway. You could see it in the jury's faces. They saw that tactic as a waste of time. Just like everyone else in the area close enough to Mexico to make it a problem, they're sick to death of having outlaws commit their crimes here, then dart across the border into the safety of Mexico."

Finishing off his whiskey, Hunter stood up. "I'm headed back to the hotel now." Looking around the saloon he grimaced. "This isn't really where I want to be. See you later."

As he walked to the hotel, Hunter yet again talked himself into just a day or so more of patience. The way the matter dragged on was frustrating beyond words, but he had to see it through. He had to finish what he had set out to do—to see that Watkins paid and to hear the sentence passed, to know the man was finished.

He missed Leanne, missed her more than he would have thought possible. All he wanted to do was get back to the ranch, marry her, and get started on their life together. It was small comfort knowing that she would understand all the delays, that she too wanted to be sure Watkins got what he deserved. That did not make his bed any less empty.

Hunter struggled through another three days before it was over at last. Watkins's lawyer finally finished pleading his case. The jury, for all the man's cleverness and eloquence, took barely three hours to reach their verdict of guilty on all counts. When handing down the sentence, the judge expressed the regret that it was impossible to hang a man more than once, for Watlcins had been convicted of more hanging crimes than any other man ever set before him.

Feeling a weight lifted from his shoulders, Hunter started out of the courtroom only to be confronted by a wild-eyed Watkins struggling in the hold of his guards.

"You'll pay for this, Hunter! You'll pay dearly."

"In three days' time, you'll be past making anyone pay for anything. You're for hanging, Watkins."

"I'm not dead yet, you son of a bitch."

"Get him outta here," growled Sebastian as he stepped up beside Hunter.

The guards dragging him off, Watkins screamed, "There is no place you can hide, Walsh! No place. And you won't be dying easy. Neither will that little bitch of yours. You and that whore are as good as dead."

For a long moment after Watkins was gone, Hunter stared after the man. Then he looked at Sebastian. "There isn't a chance he can get out, is there? That he can fulfill any of those threats?"

"I'm not going to tell you it's impossible—nothing's impossible. But the chances of it happening are damn slim."

"Hell, I don't like hangings but maybe I . . ."

"Go home. Tuckman's staying for the hanging. He'll let you know. Go home."

"Will Martin's trial take long?"

"It starts in less than an hour. I have a feeling it won't even go until suppertime."

"Then I'll stay." Hunter returned to a seat in the courtroom.

There were several surprises in Martin's trial. Hunter was relieved to see that the revelations startled Sebastian as well. Before hiding behind a badge in Leanne's hometown, Martin had cut a lurid trail of crimes through the territory. There was more than enough to hang him.

For a brief moment, Hunter was dismayed to see that Martin was using Watkins's slick lawyer, but either the lawyer realized he was wasting his skills before this jury or he was dispirited, for he did his job efficiently but quickly. In less than four hours, Martin was tried, convicted, and sentenced. He would hang right alongside Watkins.

Martin said nothing as he was led out. Hunter felt compelled to meet the man's fixed glare. In Martin's look was an echo of all of Watkins's hissed threats. It robbed Hunter of the feeling that the matter was finally finished.

It was not until he, Hunter, and Sebastian were seated in the saloon, each of them sipping at a beer, that Owen broke the silence between them. "There's not much reason to stay around here, Hunter. It's done."

"I know." He shook his head. "Yet I don't have that feeling of something being finished. Y'know the feeling I mean?"

"Yeah, like you want to kick up your heels or something."

"It was there for a minute when the judge pronounced sentence on Watkins, but it didn't stay long."

"You shouldn't let that man's poison rob you of peace of mind."

"I know, Sebastian. I keep telling myself that, but it just plain doesn't work. Ghoulish as it is, I think my peace of mind will only come when that bastard is cold in the clay."

"You're not still thinking of staying for the hanging?"

"Not to watch it. Maybe just to be here to be sure."

"Look, Hunter, the chances are slim that he can slip the noose this late in the game."

"But, as you said, not impossible."

"Nope, but where do you want to be if he does perform that miracle?"

"What do you mean?"

"I mean, do you want to be behind him, trying to catch him before he reaches Leanne, or do you want to be in front of him, standing between him and her?" The grim look on Hunter's face was all the answer he needed. "Well—leaving at dawn, are we?" He stood up, picked his hat off the table, and set it on his head.

"Yeah, dawn." Hunter frowned. "We? Are you riding with us?"

"Wasn't I invited to a wedding?"

"You were—are. I just thought you had to be back on the job. You said you were reinstated."

"I was. I'm on leave."

"On leave? You've been relieved of duty for over a year. How can they put you on leave now?"

"Well, hell, I worked real hard that year as a private citizen. They figured I needed a rest before I started work." He grinned when Owen and Hunter laughed. "My posting's down your part of the country anyway. That was one reason I said I'd be at your wedding."

"Fine with me." Recalling the conversation about Leanne on their first night on the trail, Hunter asked, "Sure you want to be?"

Sebastian smiled faintly. "I'm not such a fool that I don't look first to see how high a fence is before I try to jump it. That one was pretty damned high, so I reined in. Just couldn't resist a peek now and again to see if it had been lowered some. 'Night, boys."

"A good man," Owen murmured after Sebastian had gone.

"I can't help but be glad he'll be riding with us."

"Aw, Hunter, do you really think Watkins can get away? This is no small-town jail he's sitting in."

"I know it. The odds are real small, but I'm of a mind

with Sebastian. I don't believe in marking anything as impossible. Until that man's six feet under I'll see him as a threat."

Martin shifted position, and the shackles on his ankles clinked. "Some damn lawyer you found. Did us a lot of good."

"Stop whining, Chester." Watkins leaned his back against the stone wall and rested his manacled wrists on his upraised knees.

"Well, I'm real sorry if I can't be pleased about hanging. You said he was the best damned lawyer money could buy."

"He is, and he's done what he was paid for."

"Getting us hanged?" Chester squawked.

"No, idiot. He tried every trick he could to stop that but—face up to it, Chester—no one could stop that sentencing. Not with our glorious past." He lowered his voice, forcing his half-brother to lean closer to hear. "He played the game and he lost it. Now he's playing out the rest of it. Neither of us will be dancing in the air for these bastards."

Looking around the fortress-like cell, Chester Martin frowned. "Can't get outta here."

"If one uses one's brains, no place is impenetrable."

"If we do get outta here, think we can get safely back into Mexico?"

"We won't be going there right away, not until I take care of a few things."

"Hunter and that little bitch of his?"

"Nobody betrays me and gets away with it. When I'm done with them, they'll welcome dying."

"Well, before you kill that little bitch, I want her. Nearly had her back in Clayville, but Hunter snatched her up."

"You'll get your turn. So will I. She'll give me what she used for bait to get me alone."

"Might need some men, some extra guns. Hunter won't fall easy."

"It'll all be waiting for us. We'll see to Hunter Walsh and Miss Leanne Summers, then go to my place in Mexico. From there I intend to make this whole damn area bleed."

Chapter Fifteen

AFTER STARING DOWN AT THE RANCH FOR A LONG TIME. Hunter grinned at the two men with him. "Surprising how good it looks."

Sebastian shifted in his saddle. "It's a fine place, but to be honest, any place with a roof'd look good to me now. And a soft bed."

"And a bath," added Owen, his companions mumbling agreement as they simultaneously spurred their horses forward.

Hunter sensed something was wrong before he even reined in at the main house. There were too many men lingering around the main house. They should have been out on the range. They were also well armed. His father's face was grim as he greeted them and tersely ordered them into the parlor. No one said anything until all three new arrivals had a brandy. Hunter did not like the implication that he was going to need it.

"You've had trouble," Hunter said abruptly.

"Not yet, but we might." Sloane sighed. "Watkins and Martin have escaped. Tuckman sent a wire to warn us. There's a chance they'll head our way."

Sebastian swore. "So much for slim odds."

"Where's Leanne?" Hunter demanded, suddenly alarmed that she had not already greeted him.

"She's not here, son." Seeing the horrified look on Hunter's face, Sloane hastened to add, "Watkins had nothing to do with her being gone. She left—hell, over three weeks ago. Her and those two men, Charlie and Jed. They took horses and supplies."

"I don't understand. Why would she just up and leave?" Suspicion slipped through his shock and he looked at his mother, who sat slightly apart from the group of men. "Did you have something to do with it?"

"I will admit I was not pleased with your choice, but I did not send the girl packing. She obviously had a change of heart."

"No. You changed it for her, Mother." Laurie stepped into the middle of the gathering, half-smiling at the surprise her appearance caused everyone.

"You've got to stop sneaking around like that, child," Sloane grumbled. "Startle the wrong person and you could get shot."

"Sorry, Pa. It's become a habit."

"What are you saying—Mother changed it for her?" Hunter pressed her.

"The child refers to the fact that I was less than welcoming—but really Laurie, that would not have made the girl run off. Everyone made it very clear that my opinion was of little importance."

"The *child* refers to far more than that," Laurie replied and tugged three pieces of paper from a pocket in her skirts, handing Hunter the largest of the three. "Mother gave this to Leanne." She idly watched her mother's face as Hunter read the letter. A brief flare of panic in Lorraine's eyes was quickly hidden, the still lovely features swiftly composed.

"What is this?" Hunter frowned at his sister. "This has to be—what, six years old? How is this important?"

"What is it?" Sloane asked.

"A letter I wrote Patricia before she married Colin Spotford, Pa. Remember? Fool that I was, I thought I was in love with the woman and I was asking her to wait for me until I solved that problem with the Cutter girl."

"Oh yes, I remember—the one who tried to say her baby was yours. Turned out it was Simon Taylor's. He'd scared that poor girl into pointing the finger at you because he had arranged himself a better marriage. Monied girl. Cutters didn't have a penny to spare."

"That's old history, Pa. So's this letter. What does it have to do with Leanne? She could see it was old."

"How, Hunter?" Laurie tapped the top of the letter with one finger. "You wrote the date on the inch or so that is missing, didn't you?"

Lorraine met the furious gazes the men of her family turned on her with outward calm. "I have no idea what the girl is talking about."

"Then how'd this letter get here?" Hunter crumbled it in his hand and angrily tossed it toward her.

"Perhaps Patricia was playing some devious game.

Being a widow now, she needs a husband, poor girl."
Lorraine turned a sad, hurt look upon Laurie. "What have
I done, child, that you wish to hurt me with such lies?"

"I'm telling no lies. You are, Mother. It took me a long
time to see how often and how easily you do. I'm sorry,
but I can't let you hurt Hunter and Leanne with them."
She handed Hunter the two notes Leanne had left. "One
is to Mother and one is to me. Just read what she says and
you'll know who is telling the truth. Mother and Patricia
plotted together. If I had not been dragged off to town that
day, I might have stopped her."

After reading the notes, Hunter stared at his mother
with a mixture of fury and confusion. "Why did you do
this?" he demanded.

"I was doing what any mother would if she saw her
child making a terrible mistake. That girl was not good
enough for you. She would have held you back, cut you
off from decent society. I was looking out for your future."

"You were putting your damned nose in where it didn't
belong. Leanne wasn't any damned mistake."

Sloane grasped a rising Hunter by the shoulder and
held him in his seat. "Don't waste your breath, son."

"When I have Leanne back, we'll not be coming here
to live, Pa. I won't have Leanne suffering Mother's scorn
and insults."

"But you have to bring her back here. That's why I
worked so hard to find out why she left." Laurie blushed
when everyone looked at her in mild surprise. "Well, you
won't be too far away, will you?"

Hunter smiled faintly. "No. Not too far away."

"You will be right here." Sloane strode into the library,
leaving everyone staring after him in confusion.

"Pa," Hunter began as soon as his father stepped back into the room, "I really think it'd be best if I leave, live elsewhere."

"You're not leaving," Sloane repeated. He looked at Lorraine. "Your mother is."

"Sloane!" It took Lorraine a moment to recover her composure. "You can't be serious."

"Oh, I am very serious. To be honest, I don't know why I have tolerated your scheming and snobbishness and lies for as long as I have. That you were my wife in name and the mother of my children wasn't really enough. We haven't been man and wife for years. You were no mother to the boys, only to Laurie, and I'm beginning to think you weren't too good a one." He looked at the paper he held in his hand. "We are getting a divorce."

"A divorce?" she croaked.

"Yes. I looked into it when the trouble with Hunter started. I'm ashamed to admit it, but I did hesitate in believing his story over all the evidence to the contrary. However, while I hesitated, you completely turned your back on him. The scandal was all that worried you. I suddenly saw what I'd been trying to ignore for years. You don't give a damn about any of us. So I decided to have John Cooper look into the possibility of divorce on the grounds that you deserted my bed fourteen years ago and have never returned."

"Don't speak of such things. Not in front of everyone," she hissed.

"You're a fool if you think our children don't know. They're concerned in this, and they have a right to know the why of it."

"Well, you can forget this idiocy right now. I will never agree to a divorce. Never."

"Oh, but you will. You have two choices. You refuse to sign the papers agreeing to the divorce, and I simply throw you out to make your own way. Or you. sign them and I will see you reasonably supported wherever you decide to live for the rest of your life or until you marry again."

"You can't throw me out with nothing."

"I can and I will unless you agree to sign these papers."

"You realize you will probably never see your daughter again."

"Yes he will, Mother." Laurie spoke softly and the look she gave her mother was a mixture of sadness and determination. "I will stay here with Pa. If he doesn't mind, that is," she added.

"I don't mind at all, child."

"Thank you, Pa. Mother, I will visit you anytime you wish me to. I'll write to you. However, I don't want to leave here."

"You ungrateful child. How can you treat me so after all I have done for you?"

"What you have done is treat me like some little toy doll, a clay one for you to shape as you see fit. I woke up one day and realized there were seven other people in my family besides myself, but I only knew you. I had no friends. I have never even been allowed to play. All I know is etiquette and how to be a society matron. I believe I will stay here and maybe not be such a lady all the time."

"All right, Sloane. You win." Lorraine got up, snatched

the papers from his hand, and marched off to the library, Sloane following her.

No one spoke. Laurie moved to sit in the chair her mother had occupied. Hunter suspected that everyone felt as uncomfortable as he did when Sloane returned alone. Who would have suspected Sloane Walsh would even contemplate divorce? It was something deeply frowned upon and rarely done. But, Hunter admitted to himself, it was the only real solution to the problem.

"Let's put that aside for now, shall we?" Sloane murmured. "I let my anger get the best of me. That could have waited. This business with Leanne gone and those two killers loose can't."

"Hell, I don't even know where to look for her," Hunter said despairingly. While some of his sharp fear had been eased by the knowledge that Watkins had not taken her, he was deeply worried about her being out there somewhere with no warning of the danger she could be in.

"I know she has a father but not where he is. She didn't know either. Somewhere near Denver was all she knew. She spoke of a friend called O'Malley in the mountains, but I don't know where. I only know where Charity is, and I don't believe Leanne would ever go there. Not after what that woman did."

"Just how did Watkins and Martin get out of that place?" Sebastian asked Sloane.

"It was quite well thought-out, Tuckman feels. There was a switch of the guards, which got them the keys to the cell door and manacles. Good men were replaced by Watkins's loyal dogs. After that, it was fairly easy. They got out of the compound concealed in a wagon. The lawyer had horses waiting for them. It's pretty sure the pair hasn't gone back to Mexico."

"No, they haven't." Hunter ran a hand through his hair. "Both of them swore to come after us—me and Leanne. Damn it. If only I knew where to look."

"I was about to say I could help you some on that, son, but Sebastian diverted me for a moment. I know where that father of hers is," Sloane said.

"How did you find out? Did he finally get in touch with her?"

"Nope. She told me about him, said you two thought you'd try to find him when this mess was straightened out. Well, I took it upon myself to look into it a little. I do know a few people who know a few people and so on. I didn't get any word until after she left though, and it might not help. He's about fifty miles south of where Leanne lived with that woman in Colorado."

"Are you sure? That'd put him just inside New Mexico Territory, nowhere near Denver."

"He has a business in Denver. A partner who lives there and his eldest son handle most of it. I reckon he used that address for privacy."

"Or to be sure the daughter he deserted couldn't find him."

"Don't be too quick to judge, son. Most of what I was told points to him being a good man, honest and hard working. 'Course that doesn't mean he's a good father. Still, it could also mean he had a damned good reason for what he did."

"Fine. Judging him's not my biggest worry now. Finding Leanne is." Hunter started to rise, only to have his father urge him back down again. "This is getting to be a habit with you, Pa. I have to find her before those two madmen do."

"I know. Just remember those madmen don't have any idea of where she'd go either. There's only a few hours of daylight left. You won't get far before nightfall stops you. Wait until morning. Eat, wash, get some rest."

"Pa's right," Craig said. "You've got three days' start on the men anyway."

His other brothers quickly joined in with even more reasons for Hunter to wait at least until morning. Hunter finally conceded that he could do with a rest, although he wondered if he would get much sleep with worry over Leanne gnawing at him. For such a long and possibly dangerous journey, there would also be preparations to make. By the time he finished mentally reviewing all he needed to do, he strongly suspected he would need most of tomorrow as well before he could leave.

When that assumption proved right, he was far from pleased. Craig and Thayer had had to make a mad dash to town, leaving when dawn's light was barely visible to get some of the supplies required as well as cash for the journey. It would take them the whole day to make the round trip. Time was needed simply to map out as best they could the fastest route to Leanne's father.

The delay also meant he was home to see his mother's departure, something he had torn feelings about. He could feel no real regret over her leaving, yet he was sorry it had come to that. While he usually cared little about what others thought, he found himself wincing slightly over the word 'divorce'. In the hope of pushing aside his own confused emotions, he turned his attention to Laurie, who looked somewhat lost as she stood on the veranda watching her mother leave. He moved to stand by her.

"You sure about this, punkin?"

"Yes." Laurie sighed as she watched her mother, seated as erect as ever on the buggy seat, disappear down the road. "I just feel a little lost because she is all I've ever known."

He tentatively put his arm around her shoulders. "Well, then, you'll have to come to know us, won't you?" He was a little surprised to see that she was very pretty indeed when she smiled, faint though the smile was. "You might find you'll want to hightail it after Mother."

"I don't think so. I've met all those relatives in New Orleans. They are all as unhappy as Mother is. I don't want to be such an unhappy person. I'm sorry I couldn't stop Leanne."

Although a little startled by the sudden turn in the conversation, Hunter replied, "You did the best you could. You made sure she won't stay away long. I just wish to hell it hadn't happened now," he muttered.

"She has Jed and Charlie with her. They won't leave her alone. They rather love her, I think. I think I know why too."

"Well? Enlighten me."

"She treats them the same as she does everyone else. She treats them like they're gentlemen." She patted Hunter's hand where it rested on her shoulder. "Don't worry. You'll find her."

Hunter wished he could share in her optimism. There was a lot of country out there. Leanne did not have to go to either her father, O'Malley, or even Charity. For all he knew, Jed and Charlie might take her someplace they knew about. He really had little idea of where to look.

There was only one good thing about it and that was that Watkins would know even less. She was, in fact, lost and it could easily be a matter of who found her first. He wondered if his mother was even aware of what she had done in driving Leanne away.

Lorraine stared straight ahead, ignoring her driver and the well-armed man who rode at her side. Sloane had to be mad to think she would stay in that house one more minute than she had to. Him and his choices. There were no choices. She was an object of scandal either way. It was simply that one way gave her the funds to keep body and soul together. Well, he would pay for doing this to her—and pay dearly. So would Hunter and that little slut he was so enamored of.

She was ripped from her vengeful thoughts by the sound of shots. Her driver was flung from the seat as if by some invisible hand, his body jerking backwards, then slumping to the side and tumbling out of the buggy. Clinging to her seat as the startled team leapt into a gallop, she saw her guard fall. A man suddenly appeared racing his horse alongside her team until he drew them to a halt. Another rider reined in on her side of the buggy. Both men looked at her and smiled in a way that chilled her.

"Greetings, Mrs. Walsh. Allow me to introduce myself." The rider bowed slightly in the saddle. "I am Henry Watkins and that is my brother Chester Martin. You may have heard of us."

Shaking free of her frozen state, Lorraine looked at them, then at the other men slowly encircling her. She screamed.

*   *   *

Watkins watched as Martin threw Lorraine Walsh's body into the buggy with those of the driver and the guard. "Hurry up. It'll take a couple of hours before they're found, but we need every minute of it. Don't waste time."

"This was a waste of time." Martin slapped the buggy team into motion, watching as they trotted along for a few yards then slowed to an amble along the familiar road. "We didn't find out much."

"Enough. That little bitch has run out on Hunter. She's with those traitors Charlie and Jed."

"So we go after Hunter now, then trail her?" Martin swung himself up into his saddle.

"You saw that ranch. It's like a fortress. Fact is, dear Mrs. Walsh did us a kindness when she sent Leanne packing. We can get them one at a time. Hunter will also be going after the girl, so he'll be drawn away from that ranch and easier to get."

"We don't know where the hell the girl is."

"So? Neither does Hunter, from what his mother said. We'll start by talking to Charity. She ought to be back from her honeymoon by the time we reach Clayville."

"Don't seem right to be so close to that bastard and not at least trying to strike at him."

"Chester, we just killed his mother. Her body will be found before he leaves to find Leanne, and anyone who finds the bodies will know just what dear Mrs. Walsh endured before she died. Unlike you, dear brother, some people carry a soft spot for their mothers. We have just struck at him. Now, ride. He just might head for Clayville, and I want to reach Charity first."

*   *   *

Despite cursing the delay, Hunter watched the day draw to a close feeling rested. He knew that was important. There would be little rest for him until he found Leanne and defeated Watkins and Martin. It would be him, Sebastian, and Owen again. He felt good about that. They had learned to work together and did it well. It was hard to convince his father that the three of them would be enough, though. There were obvious advantages to having more men and more guns, but three would be able to move more swiftly and, if necessary, more stealthily than a larger group.

A call from one of the men that someone was approaching the ranch drew him from his musings. His wary stance eased only slightly when he saw that it was Craig and Thayer. They had a buggy with them. When he recognized it as the one his mother had ridden off in only hours earlier, he hurried to meet them.

"Mother?" He saw the answer to his soft, urgent query in their pale faces as they stopped before the house.

Craig stopped Hunter from pulling the blanket off of the smaller of the three shrouded bodies. "Don't look, Hunter. It's not pretty."

"What happened?" He had the numbing feeling that he already knew the answer.

"This note was pinned to poor old Sam's chest with a knife."

Taking the bloodied missive Craig held out to him, Hunter read, "This is only the beginning. No one betrays me. Watkins."

"Oh my God. He's here." Hunter heard the sound of someone approaching and turned to meet his father. "It was Watkins."

Ignoring his sons' attempts to stop him, Sloane lifted

the blanket covering his wife's body, paled, then quickly covered her over again. "Sam and Ted too?"

"Yeh, Pa," Thayer answered. "We found the buggy headed toward town."

"Did anyone else see the bodies?" Sloane laid one hand on Craig's shoulder, the other on Thayer's, gripping them briefly in sympathetic understanding of what it cost to find their mother that way.

"No, Pa. No one. Oh, damn, here comes Laurie and the others."

Sloane caught Laurie before she could reach her mother's body and lift the blanket. "Don't look, child. Better for you to remember her as she was." He held her close when she burst into tears. "No sign of the ones who did it?" he rasped.

"We saw where it happened. The trail from there headed north," Craig answered. "They've had hours to get away."

"To find Leanne," Sloane murmured, looking at Hunter. "This was Watkins's way of letting you know he means business."

"I know. God, I'm sorry, Pa. I'm sorry."

"You have nothing to be sorry for. I'm the one who sent her away." He urged Laurie into Hunter's arms. "Take your sister into the house. Have Molly come to your mother's room. I'll need help readying her for burial."

A pall hung over the house. Hunter found consolation for his own feelings of guilt in easing those Laurie suffered. His father, however, was unreachable, staying closed up in the library, speaking to no one. In desperation, Hunter sought out Molly, who had pulled their father out of black moods in the past. The guilt that had his father so locked up in himself had to be broken. He located Molly sitting at the heavy kitchen table staring into a cup of cooling tea. She looked up and grasped his hand in hers as he sat down.

"I'm sorry, boy. All trouble aside, she was your mother." She tightened her grip on his hand for a moment. "It wasn't your fault."

"Thank you, Molly. I'd sorted that out already. Poor Laurie was feeling guilty, and in easing her guilt, I eased my own."

"Good. Good. No one can plan for a thing like this."

"Molly, Pa's not managing very well. He's in the library, black-browed and silent. He's thinking on how he was the one who sent her away. He can't seem to remember anything else—like how she insisted, against stern warnings, on leaving today."

"I know. Fool man. I could see it coming when we tended your ma's body. Seeing what they'd done to her didn't help."

He nodded, wincing from the images a fuller account from Thayer and Craig had left him with. "This is going to sound damn hard of me, but I have to leave in the morning as planned. I have to. I just don't like leaving things this way."

"Of course you have to go. Of course you do. Your ma's dead, boy. There's no changing that. That little girl of yours is alive, with her whole life ahead of her. You have to get to her before that madman does. You can't dither here no matter how strong you feel you ought to." She pointed to one of the cupboards lining the wall of her kitchen. "There's a bottle of good whiskey and two glasses in there. Get them down for me."

He did as she asked, setting the things on the table. "You need a drink?" he asked, a little confused.

"Not here. In with your pa." She stood up, picking up the bottle and glasses. "Me and him have straightened out many a problem over a bottle of whiskey in the past. I'll pull him outta this. The man just needs some sense talked into him. He's got to spit that guilt out too."

"I think we all suffer it some."

"Well, you shouldn't. I don't like speaking ill of the dead but that woman was no mother to you lot and no wife to him. Yeah, she gave birth to you, and no one should be killed so viciously, but if you don't feel a deep grief, it ain't a fault in you. A person's gotta earn feelings like that, even mothers. And I'll tell your moping pa the same."

By the time dinner was served, Molly had worked her magic. The mood was somber, but it was clear that everyone, their father included, had overcome their guilt and shock. Hunter had to fend off another attempt by his family to send him off with what amounted to a small army. Sebastian finally convinced Sloane of the good, sound reasons for only the three of them going, three who had worked together already and two of whom knew the territory to be traveled fairly well.

Therefore Hunter was curious when, after he had retired to his room, his father arrived. "I thought we'd settled everything."

"We have. I just wanted to be sure you're not feeling bad about leaving at a time like this."

"I do in some ways. The need to help Leanne . . ." he faltered, unsure of how to explain himself.

"The need to keep someone alive has to take precedence over the mourning of the dead."

"I have to get to Leanne before he does."

"God, yes. I've seen what the man can do and Lorraine

was not even one he sought." He shook his head. "Three innocent people. That damn practical Molly and her whiskey may have stopped me from blaming myself, from feeling so godawful guilty, but even she won't stop me from wanting that bastard dead."

"I won't make the mistake of not making sure he's dead and buried this time."

Sloane clapped Hunter on the arm. "Get that girl of yours back here where she belongs. And those two faithful puppies of hers as well," he added as he walked out the door.

"I pray to God they're still with her," Hunter whispered.

Leanne sat down at the well-scrubbed table and looked around. "Now this looks much better."

Glancing around as he and Jed sprawled in chairs at the same table, Charlie muttered, "Didn't look so bad to me before."

"Charles, it was filthy." She frowned. "O'Malley couldn't possibly have come here this past summer. It never would've gotten so dirty in just a few months. O'Malley and his sons were very particular. I hope nothing's happened to them."

"Could be a lotta reasons he didn't get here this year. Don't have to be real bad ones."

"Charlie's right, Leanne. Why, didn't you tell us he and that woman Charity knew each other? Maybe she told him you'd gone off with Hunter and he didn't see no reason to come up here, having other things to do and all. Maybe he's waiting to hear from you—y'know, through her."

"Of course. I worry too much. He always collected me at Charity's. She would have told him what happened." She smiled faintly. "And he always called coming here playing truant because he slipped away from work that needed doing. If you are still here come spring or summer, you'll meet them. I think you'll like each other."

"We'll still be here."

"Now, Charles, you don't have to stay because of me."

"As good a reason as any."

"Right." Jed poured them all a cup of coffee from the pot Leanne had set in the middle of the table. "Good place this."

"Yup," Charlie agreed. "Not too far up into the hills. Easy to move about. Not too many people, but a good sized town only a few hours away. 'Sides, you can't stay here alone."

"I am not incapable of taking care of myself, Charles."

"Nope. But," he pointed at her rounding stomach, "ain't only going to be you to care for soon. Now, don't argue," he said when she opened her mouth to speak. "Me and Jed talked it all over and it's decided. This place has all we need—beds, a roof, food on hand. Good a place as any to set down in. And if this fellow O'Malley decides he don't want us squatting here, you'll be glad to have us around. We'll be able to help settle you someplace else."

Resting her elbow on the table, she cupped her chin in her hand and smiled at them. "Oh, I'm glad to have you here now. It's always much better to have friends near." She smiled even more at their identical looks of embarrassment.

"Me and Jed'll do some hunting before winter sets in firm. Thought we'd sell one of the horses and use the money to get more supplies." He flushed faintly. "Thought we'd also see if there's a midwife or a doctor about." He glanced at her stomach. "We don't know nothing 'bout babes or women having them. Thought you oughta know that."

Standing up, she moved to start their supper. "I had rather guessed that. Don't worry. There's months left."

"How many? You've gotten rounder in just the time it took to get here."

"I have, haven't I? Unfortunately, I can't give you a definite answer. Three, four months. Probably three."

"That'll put us right in the middle of winter. That ain't too good."

"Don't worry about it, Charles. I'm not."

That was a lie and she knew it. A quick, covert glance at the men told her they knew it too, but were too nice to say so. When she had assisted Doctor Chelmsford while at school she had unfortunately seen what could go wrong, horribly wrong, in childbirth. There had also been no shortage of horror stories whispered by her classmates. She told herself to be sensible, not to think the worst, but it did little good at times.

It was after supper, as they sat comfortably before a small fire, that Charlie touched upon another subject she had tried, and failed, not to think about. She had sensed that he wanted to talk. His hesitation had warned her that she might not like his choice of topic.

"Now, I know you don't like talking on Hunter and I've been real careful not to."

She sighed, then braced herself to discuss what he wished with calm and maturity. "And I thank you for that. But?"

"I think we gotta come up with a way to have a word

or two with him and most likely before you wanna tell him about the kid."

"Why?"

"We still don't know if he got your name cleared."

"Or our pardons," Jed added.

She stared at them for a moment, then shook her head, muttering, "I can't believe I forgot all about that."

"You had something else to weigh on your mind."

"Perhaps, Charles, but you're right. We need to know about that, need to know if we still have to watch out for the law."

"Me and Jed could be the ones to do it. By wire maybe."

"Perhaps you could wire Marshal Tuckman instead. Or Charity. Someone must have told her something. Because of this baby, I'd just as soon try to keep from letting Hunter know where I am." She shrugged. "Heaven alone knows why he would try to find me, but he could even just come this way for another reason and decide to look in on me. I don't know. I just wish to avoid any possibility of a confrontation, at least until I am good and ready to have one."

"Yeh, Tuckman would know," Jed agreed. "Ain't no reason for him to tell Hunter he'd heard from us neither."

"That's settled then. We'll slip into town in a few days and send a telegraph message to the sheriff," Charles said.

"You'll feel better for the knowing, Leanne."

"I know I will, Jed. So will you. I would have recalled it before much longer, I'm sure."

"Well, since we're talking on going to town soon, it's best we set to thinking on what supplies we'll want."

She was more than willing to follow Charlie's suggestion. It would keep her mind from settling on Hunter. Brief though the mention of him was, it had stirred up all she sought to bury, all the hurt and memories.

As she lay in her bed later that night in the room O'Malley had made especially for her, she was not surprised when Hunter was all she could think about. Exhaustion from scrubbing the cabin clean had kept those thoughts at bay. She should have found more work to do, she thought sadly.

What hurt most was that she had trusted him, had begun to believe that he would stay with her. Instead, she had to face yet another rejection. Covering her rounded abdomen with her hands, she felt her child move. They could have been such a lovely family together. She swore that her child would not know the bitterness of rejection. If that meant that Tarrant Hunter Walsh never knew of the child he had created, then so be it.

Chapter Sixteen

Hunter urged his horse down the small rise, Sebastian and Owen silently following. He was torn between hoping Leanne was safe with her father and dreading the confrontation with her. It was his mother's fault that Leanne had fled, yet Hunter knew he had to shoulder some of the blame. He had known what his mother was like, known she had not really accepted Leanne, yet he had left the poor girl to his mother's mercy. Neither had he given Leanne the words or promises she needed to hold out against his mother's insinuations, to believe that he really would return and marry her.

It did not surprise him when three men appeared on the veranda, rifles held with deceptive carelessness. He and his companions had made no attempt to hide their presence. Any stranger was worthy of caution, and Hunter knew the way they had lingered on the hillside had added to that. As he reined in before them he idly noted that the rifles were Henrys. Hunter sat relaxed in his saddle, studying the oldest of the three men and trying not to let the man's excellent taste in weaponry or his apparent readiness to use it sway his opinion. Grant Summers had deserted his child.

"I'm looking for your daughter." He spoke coldly, remembering Grant's treatment of Leanne.

"Who the hell are you?" the older man snapped, closely studying the three young men before him.

"Are you Grant Summers?"

"I am, and you better tell me quick who's asking."

"Tarrant Hunter Walsh."

"And how'd you come to know Leanne?"

"That's a long story, Mr. Summers."

"I got time."

"Is Leanne here?"

"No." The brief yet sharp look of disappointment that passed over the younger man's face worked to ease Grant's suspicions. "My daughter hasn't seen fit to confide her whereabouts for quite a while," he said as he lowered his rifle. His sons following suit. "You meet her in that time?"

"I not only met her, I was with her for most of that time." He was not surprised to see the rifles pointed at him again.

"You're one of those damn outlaws that dragged her off."

"Dragged her off? She was facing jail under false charges."

Grant frowned, studied Hunter closely for a while,

then lowered his rifle again. "I think we'd better talk. Joe," he called to a man loitering at the far end of the veranda. "See to our visitors' horses."

"Since Leanne is not here, I don't see any need to linger."

"You just might be surprised. You also don't have much choice. It ain't a polite invite I'm handing out."

Hunter cursed, but he dismounted, Sebastian and Owen slowly following suit. Joe led their horses away, and one of the younger men flanking Grant took their guns. It was clear they were not to be trusted until Grant had heard their story and decided on its worth. Grant Summers was acting like any other father, and Hunter found that puzzling.

He, Owen, and Sebastian had barely stepped inside, Grant and the other two right behind them, when Grant nudged the three of them towards a door to their left. "We'll just set ourselves in here."

Once everyone was seated, Grant facing them, one son behind the settee they were crowded onto and the other guarding the door. Hunter snapped, "I don't have the time for this. It's very important that I find Leanne."

"I know how important it is, boy, but I'm still waiting to hear about you and my daughter."

"You're very concerned for someone who hasn't had squat to do with her since dumping her on that whore's doorstep."

Holding up a hand to stop his sons' angry move towards Hunter, Grant drawled, "I'd set aside those thoughts, seeing as they're formed on only part of the facts. Now, I'll give you a minute to pull in your horns and introduce my boys. Brandon and Matthew." Sebastian and Owen introduced themselves, then Grant looked at Hunter again. "Now, about you and Leanne?"

Forcing himself to remain calm, Hunter related the basic story. He could tell by the slow narrowing of Grant Summers' eyes—eyes exactly like Leanne's—that the man knew exactly what was left out of the tale. It annoyed him to see that look of fatherly outrage on the man's face. Grant Summers had not earned the right. He met the man's glare with a look of silent challenge.

"You're a cocksure young bastard," Grant murmured. "You drag the poor girl . . ."

"I had no choice. If I'd left her with Martin she would've been raped and undoubtedly murdered before long. She certainly wouldn't have gotten any help from that bitch who threw her out in the middle of the night. You could have chosen a little better before you handed her over to that woman."

"Will you two sit down?" Grant snapped at his sons who were again moving toward Hunter.

"But, Pa," protested Brandon even as he and Matthew did as they were told, "he's got no right to talk to you like that."

"He thinks he does." He turned a piercing gaze on Hunter. "I'll be asking why he feels that way soon enough. First I'm telling you a few facts, young man. We'll get nowhere trying to work around that chip on your shoulder."

"Perhaps when I finish what I need to do . . ." Hunter began to stand up.

"Sit down!" bellowed Grant and nodded with satisfaction when Hunter, after a brief glaring match with him, obeyed.

Grant Summers was a damned autocrat, Hunter thought. He was not sure which annoyed him more—that or the way the man's sons smirked when he obeyed their father.

Suddenly he took a closer look at Grant's two sons. One had dark eyes, the other blue—that soft lavender blue he so admired in Leanne's eyes. The dark-eyed son, Brandon, had the same long, thick lashes Leanne did. Grant Summers had short ones. Matthew had neat arched brows like Leanne's. Grant Summers had straight brows. Hunter began to think he was looking at Leanne's brothers—yet, if that was so, it made Grant's desertion of Leanne even more confusing. Why keep some children and not all?

"Now, you'll listen. I know it's important to find Leanne, but you won't be going far this late in the day. You'll just about get off my land when you'll have to stop to make camp. You're done in and so are your horses. So set here and listen. Then you can decide whether we ride together come the morning or separately."

Crossing his arms over his chest, Hunter arched one brow. "It better be good."

"Hard-nosed too, I see. Leanne's mother and I were married for ten years, ten good years. Then everything started to go wrong. We were up Colorado way then, not too far from Charity.

"I saw you looking at my boys, so I reckon you won't be all that surprised when I tell you they're Leanne's brothers. My Delia gave me three fine sons and little Leanne. Then the trouble started. Small losses, a hint of some financial trouble in my business. I probably could've fixed it, but then Delia fell ill. Nothing helped. The doctors gave up. She just wasted away slowly and painfully.

I neglected everything to be with her, was there when she breathed her last."

He fell silent for a moment as he remembered that sad period of his life. "I was a broken man. No other way to say it. I did what I had to do to keep a roof over our heads and food in our bellies, but I let myself sink into despair. That's the only explanation I have for being such a fool.

"I was a prosperous man, but prosperity needs working at. I let it all slip and started taking on larger losses. By the time I came to my senses, my troubles were past fixing. I had more creditors than I could count. It was then that I understood Delia's dying wish."

"Which was?" Hunter pressed when Grant again grew silent.

"To make a long story short, she saw what was happening but couldn't get me to listen. As she lay dying, she asked me to give our baby girl to Charity. She wanted Leanne to be in a stable home and knew I wouldn't be able to provide one while I was running from creditors and trying to straighten out my life."

Shaking his head, he laughed bitterly. "I finally had to give in. What choice did I have? Suddenly, I had no home, nothing. I faced years of rough, hard living. Now, I'd never met Charity myself—she was my wife's cousin—so I posed as a family friend entrusted with the care of Leanne . . . said I was Grant Summers' emissary. By that time I couldn't even afford to show my face in the area, things had gotten so bad.

"Then began years of moving from place to place, hiding from creditors even as I sweated to pay each one off. Somehow I managed to keep scraping money together to send Charity to house Leanne, then even enough to send her to a good school. It slowed up my own recovery, however. Delia was right. It would've been a hell of a life for a tiny girl. It was nearly too much for my boys. Even when I started to see Charity's faults, she was still better than anything I could offer."

"Doesn't look like you're suffering now," Hunter drawled.

"No, not now. But this is all new. I was working towards bringing my little girl home. I even hired a woman to help look after her. Binnie's still here—waiting for my little girl to join us. I told Binnie so much about Leanne, the woman acts as if she's always known the girl."

"So why didn't you go get her?"

"She didn't even know about me. It takes time to sort out that sort of tangle. Then all this happened."

He sighed and shook his head. "I'll admit I seemed to go wrong each way I turned. I tried to give my baby girl a good home and a fine upbringing, but as the years slipped by and my circumstances improved, it got harder to straighten it all out."

"Are you sure you were ever planning to tell her the truth?"

"Oh, I was, but it ain't an easy truth to tell, is it? Then Charity—and there's a misnamed woman if ever there was one—went and told her the whole story, twisting it badly—not that there's any good way to tell it, but it could've been done softer."

"But did you have to keep yourself hidden from her? Why so damn secretive?"

"I didn't want my creditors or my enemies finding the girl. I didn't want them trying to use her in any way. If they discovered I sent money to her, they could've taken that away. It was best if I just disappeared from her life. So I did, and I did my best to keep it that way.

"The sad thing is, it was coming to an end. Now it's Leanne in trouble—and she's in a lot of trouble, isn't she? Charity wrote and told me some of it."

"Yes, she is in a great deal of trouble." Hunter told him all about Watkins, Martin, and their threats. "It's Leanne and me he's after, but he'll kill anyone connected to either of us if he has half a chance. He killed my mother just before I left home."

"I'm sorry to hear that, son."

"Thank you," Hunter murmured, and there was a moment's silence while both men composed themselves. "Think we could move now, Mr. Summers?" Hunter said.

Grant took the "we" as the peace offering it was. No apology was offered, nor did he expect one. He knew what he had done appeared the basest of desertions, that only a thorough explanation could alter that. A quick glance at the other two with Hunter showed they understood that the earlier animosity was now set aside.

"Well now, I reckon I can muster up some baths. Your personal things will have been set in the hall. A bath and a good hot meal will see us in much better shape to set out in the morning."

"It just might at that." When Grant stood and strode to the door, Hunter quickly moved to follow, Owen and Sebastian right behind him.

"Binnie!" Grant bellowed as he stepped into the hall.

"What d'you want, old man?"

"Got me three young fellows here who could do with a bath."

"Water's just about ready. I set it to heating when

you'd been settin' in that room a while and there was no shooting."

Hunter smiled faintly as he was introduced to Binnie. She was a tiny, sprightly lady with red hair, freckles, and big blue eyes, probably in her mid-thirties. Catching a certain warmth in the smile Grant gave the woman, one returned in Binnie's fine eyes, he decided that Grant Summers would not be a free man for very long.

By the time they were washed and changed into fresh clothes, Hunter found Owen and Sebastian as eager for the meal they could smell as he was. Binnie served with the help of one of the ranch hands' wives, then sat down at the table. She was clearly already considered family.

"So, you're going to find that poor little girl?" Binnie asked as the potatoes were passed around, the meal officially begun.

"I told you we were, Binnie. We're all headed out crack of dawn tomorrow."

"I just wish I knew where to go," Hunter said. "I feel sure she wouldn't search out Charity, but that's the only other person I can find. Charity might be able to tell me how to find this O'Malley fellow Leanne was always talking about."

"Ain't you told him anything?" Binnie gasped, staring at Grant.

"I've told him a lot. I had to clear the air about why Leanne wasn't where she belonged, didn't I? Things weren't too friendly to start. Just giving him the bare bones of it talked me out. Figured we could discuss the rest over a fine meal." He looked at Hunter, frowning slightly. "Just how did you find me? Charity didn't know, and Leanne couldn't have found out."

"My father looked you up. He started on it the day I came home with Leanne and we told him about you."

"How could he find out about me?" .

"Leanne and I were planning to find you once all this trouble was behind us. As you can imagine, she had a few questions. Pa used his various friends to track you down. When my father sets his mind on something, he usually gets it."

"I'd say. I know I covered my tracks well. My son Kane is handling the business in Denver. He would've warned me fast if he'd known your father had sniffed out the truth. Your father and his friends were clever in their digging."

"He can be. If I'd had the time, I'd have had him find this O'Malley fellow."

"Grant, will you tell the boy?" Binnie snapped. "Don't just leave him fretting."

"You know about this O'Malley?" Hunter felt his hopes rise, for he was sure Leanne had sought out her friend.

"You could say that." Grant ignored Binnie's muttering from the far end of the table as he leaned back from his empty plate. "You could say me and O'Malley are as close as brothers. Maybe even closer."

"You've been keeping an eye on Leanne through him?"

"I am him."

Hunter stared at the man in disbelief. Sebastian laughed softly. Owen shook his head and helped himself to some more of the roast beef before it was cleared from the table. Hunter was only partly aware of all that as he studied Grant.

"You're her friend O'Malley? The guy in the hills she trooped off to visit when she wasn't at school?"

"One and the same. O'Malley was the 'old family friend.' These are the O'Malley boys," he nodded at his sons. "Leanne's only met my eldest, Kane, once."

The woman who helped Binnie with the chores entered the room and Hunter fell silent again as Binnie and she cleared the table and set out dessert. It was going to take a while, he thought as he was served a large piece of apple pie, to figure out the why of it all. He hoped Grant would offer an explanation that eased the confusion he felt. It seemed a lot of unnecessary subterfuge to his way of thinking.

"Just what the hell was the purpose of that game?" he snapped as soon as Binnie's helper left.

"Temper," murmured Owen, pouring thick cream over his pie.

"Shut up and eat your pie. I've been sure from the start that she'd go to O'Malley and I've been worrying myself sick over how to find the damn man." He glared at Grant. "And now I hear O'Malley's you. What was the sense behind that charade?"

"I wanted to see my little girl. It was as simple as that. It was also another way to keep Leanne out of Charity's less than loving care for a while. Being the O'Malleys was for the same reasons I hid where Leanne was." He filled his cup with coffee and passed the pot on. "And it blew more smoke in my creditors' eyes until I could get them off my back. Smoke in this Watkins's eyes now, ain't it? Charity won't tell him about O'Malley if he goes looking there to find Leanne."

"Seems to me you might be putting a lot of faith in a woman like Charity to keep quiet."

"I put a lot of money in her pockets. Put a roof over

her head too. I bought that boarding house before I lost everything. Charity had nothing I didn't give her. What I can give I can take back. She knows it."

"I'm surprised you haven't already, after what she did to Leanne."

"I intend to, now that I've got the whole truth. Don't worry, Charity won't be sitting so pretty soon. Her new husband just might have to turn his hand to some work."

"Charity got married?"

"Yeh, some fellow named Clovis." Grant's eyes narrowed as he saw the look on Hunter's face at the mention of the man's name.

"He was the one in the house that night, the one who attacked Leanne," Hunter told him. "Leanne usually referred to him as 'that lump of dog spit.' Clovis not only tried to rape her, but it seems he had a lot of people in town believing she was—shall we say—free with her favors?"

"I'll kill the son of a bitch."

"You ain't killing nobody," Binnie said.

"Didn't you hear what he did to Leanne?"

"Clear as day, I ain't deaf. So beat the scum within an inch of his life, then toss him and that cow Charity into the street. Give him a good dose of misery. That'll soothe your anger, but it won't get you hanged." She ignored Grant's cross look as she offered more pie to anyone who wished it. "Now, Hunter, you feel very certain Leanne is at the cabin? That she went to the O'Malley place?"

"As sure as I can be. She didn't know her father or where he was. Charity had already shown that she wouldn't help if help was needed. That left O'Malley. She tried to go to him once, but I sort of stopped her."

"Sort of?" snapped Grant.

"Well, she ran into a group of drunken Indians. I'd set out after her and met her running back."

"I think there's a lot you ain't told me, boy."

"Without a doubt, Mr. Summers."

"Yeah, well, there's something else you can tell me now. Just why'd she run from you this time?"

Hunter sighed. He had skimmed over that part of his tale. The way his mother had acted was something he would have preferred to keep private. Even with Grant asking him outright, he found it hard to say the words. He glanced at Owen, but found only the same reluctance and discomfort there.

Sebastian murmured, "Allow me, boys." When neither of the Walshes protested, he tersely related the story. "For all those reasons she gave, sir," he finished up, "I believe she acted mostly because she had chosen a bride for Hunter herself."

It took Grant a moment to overcome a sense of outrage and insult. There was the bitter pinch of old memories too. His Delia's family had acted much the same toward him, but they had failed. The Walshes' mother had, to all intents and purposes, failed as well. He could only hope her action did not put his daughter into Watkins's hands.

"So you think to marry my girl, do you?"

Relieved to have his mother's part in Leanne's departure so smoothly put behind them, Hunter drawled, "Yeh, reckon I do."

"Don't suppose you thought to ask permission of her old man, did you?"

"Can't say that I did, seeing as neither of us knew where you were."

"I'm glad you decided it on your own. That means I don't have to persuade you."

"Persuade me?"

Seeing the way his brother's eyes narrowed, Owen stood up. "I think, if you don't mind"—he grabbed Hunter by the arm and tugged, relieved when after a brief hesitation, Hunter stood—"it's time we sought our beds. It was a very good meal, ma'am." He smiled at Binnie.

Sebastian and Hunter added their compliments and good nights. As soon as the door shut behind the three, Grant laughed softly. Shaking her head, Binnie began to collect the dishes.

"Now, what'd you have to goad him for?"

"Testing his mettle."

"That why you threatened you'd make him marry our girl if he hadn't decided it already?"

"I would have."

"Why?"

"Binnie, they were riding around unchaperoned for months. I look at that fine young stallion of a man, and I know damn well he didn't just hold Leanne's hand now and again."

"And don't you think our girl knows right from wrong? Don't you think she's got morals?"

"I know she does. That's why I was having a doubt or two. Then they told me why she left him this time. She couldn't stay around when she thought he'd picked another. Shows she's got feelings for the boy. Then I knew. She and him have been lovers. First chance I get, I'm seeing them wed. Now, do you need some help?"

"No. Millie's waiting in the kitchen. She's all the help I need."

"Fine then. C'mon, boys, I think we'll follow our guests and get to bed. I want us up before dawn and setting out at the first ray of light. You get to bed soon too, Binnie. I know you'll be up to see us off no matter what I say."

As he checked his saddle, Hunter glanced down the road that led to the Summers ranch. His eyes narrowed, then widened. It looked to him as if someone was approaching. Since the sun was barely cresting the horizon, he found it hard to believe.

"I think someone's coming, Mr. Summers."

"Coming? Now?" Grant turned from saying good-bye to Binnie and squinted down the road. "Damn. It's Lucas from the telegraph office."

Hunter tensed. The man had to have started out in the middle of the night. A wire delivered at that time could only be bad news. It took a lot of effort not to snatch the message from Grant's hand, to wait as the two men talked and Lucas went into the house for coffee and a nap. Binnie, he vaguely noted, made no move to leave and attend the man, merely muttered instructions and waved the man into the house. As Grant moved back towards the veranda, Hunter joined the others in gathering around him.

"Even if we were of a mind to, there's no need to go see Charity anymore," a pale Grant reported. "This is from your father. Tuckman wired him. Seems Tuckman's been setting in Clayville hoping to catch Watkins when the man tried to get to Charity, as we felt sure he would."

"And he did." Hunter felt an icy fear for Leanne curl around his insides.

"God damn it all to hell, yes he did. Charity and Clovis are dead. First night they got back. He must've been waiting for them."

"Do you think she told him how to get to the cabin?" Sebastian asked.

"I don't doubt it. As well as she could anyway, never having been to the place. Your Pa says she didn't die easy. He feels sure they did her a lot of hurt until she talked. Checking the place as was his habit, Tuckman caught the bastards slipping out. He took a bullet in the arm and one in the leg. Not bad, I reckon, but he's not going anywhere for a while."

"So he won't be helping us," Hunter said.

"Nope. But your pa says to send him the directions. Seems Martin said something about a cabin just before the shooting started. Your pa'll try to send some men if I tell him where to send them. Binnie, you can tell Lucas and pay the fellow real well. He's done us a fine thing staying by that machine day and night like he has since we heard Leanne was missing." She nodded.

"How long will it take us to get there?" Hunter already sensed it would be far longer than he liked.

"If we ride hard and fast, we can do it in little under a day. It's just up in the foothills of the San Juan Mountains, halfway between me and Charity. I know places where we can change horses so we have fresh ones as needed. It's not fast enough, but it's all there is."

"Faster than I'd hoped for."

"At least she's not alone."

"You sure about that? Figuring her safe and settled, Jed and Charlie may have moved on."

"Nope. Tuckman told your pa they're with her. Got

hold of a wire from them to Charity. Tuckman answered instead. Told them about Watkins and Martin. They said they were going back to her."

"Thank God. She's not only not alone, she's been warned." He started for his horse. "Let's get going."

"How good are those two boys?" Grant asked as he hurried to mount.

"Now that they're warned," Sebastian answered, "good enough. They'll set up some defenses, keep a close watch. Neither is very fast on the draw, but they're damn good shots. If anything comes within a mile of that place, Charlie will see it."

"Maybe they'll just run," Owen suggested.

Thinking of how far along in her pregnancy Leanne would be, Sebastian knew that would not be an option. Glancing at Hunter, he also knew he would not say anything about it. The man was already sick with worry.

"I doubt it. They'd choose a defensive position over being caught on the run every time."

Seeing that everyone was mounted, Hunter spurred his horse into a gallop. He could hear the others follow suit. Fear for Leanne was a cold, heavy stone in his belly. He knew he could never get to her before Watkins and Martin did. All he could do was try to get to her before Watkins and Martin won the fight he was certain Charlie and Jed would put up.

Grant proved as good as his word. They rode hard, never slackening their pace. He obviously knew every farmer and rancher along the route. There was no difficulty in switching their exhausted mounts for fresh ones when the need arose. Hunter admired the efficiency but resented every delay no matter how necessary.

"This is the last stop," Grant announced as their tired horses were led away and fresh ones brought out one more time.

Using the brief respite to roll a cigarette, Sebastian muttered, "Wish I could change this exhausted body for a fresh one."

"How much longer do we ride?" Hunter asked Grant.

"Two hours as I reckon it."

"So we'll be there before dark."

"Next best thing to getting there before them," Sebastian said, then lit his cigarette.

Hunter nodded, but that assurance did not do much to ease his fear. He alternately ached to reach the cabin and feared what he might find there. All he could think of was what Watkins had done to his mother, a woman for whom he had had no real feeling of vengeance. How much worse would it be for Leanne if the man got his hands on her? Cruelly, his mind proved all too willing to provide some possible answers to that.

"Stop thinking about it, Hunter." Owen briefly clasped his brother's shoulder in sympathy.

"I've tried to stop."

"It doesn't do you a damn bit of good."

"I know that too. Trouble is, I can hear his threats. I can see our mother," he added in a whisper. "I keep wondering, if we'd moved a little faster . . ."

"We've moved as fast as humanly possible. Oh, sure, you can pick out a few slow hours here and there, but maybe they would have been lost anyway because of exhausted horses or exhausted men. You can ride like this for a day here and there, but no one can keep that pace up for long. We couldn't do it now, except Grant knows where to get fresh horses. Hell, we didn't even wait to see our own mother buried. Don't try to find some way to blame yourself. There's none to find."

Hunter was not sure he agreed with that, but he nodded. "Nevertheless, he's been ahead of us all the way."

"Driven by his madness, probably leaving a trail of dead horses. Try to remember that she's not alone and that she's been warned. Watkins will have to climb over Charlie and Jed to get to her. We're only a few hours behind him. I feel sure Charlie and Jed can hold him back for that long."

That was his only source of hope. Hunter tried to cling to it, use it to push aside his morbid thoughts as they started on their way again. He also prayed, prayed as he never had before. Knowing how her life hung in the balance made him all too aware of how important Leanne was to him. In that cabin they raced for was his future.

Chapter Seventeen

Swearing, Leanne bent to pick up the bullet she had dropped. She was exhausted and increasingly uncomfortable. Since Charlie and Jed had burst into the cabin late last night to tell her Watkins and Martin were free, she had had little sleep. For all she knew, the two men were miles away, but fear had a grip on her that no amount of reasoning could loosen.

Looking at the weaponry she had been assigned to clean, load, and organize, she frowned. Charlie and Jed did not act as if Watkins and Martin were distant threats. The way they had worked all night to fortify the cabin left her feeling those two killers could appear at any moment. It suddenly occurred to her that these elaborate preparations were not simply to make her feel less afraid—Charlie and Jed truly felt a need for it all. There was something that they had not told her.

"I have let exhaustion and fear make me stupid," she muttered and looked at Charlie, who was stacking the firewood Jed had just brought in. "Charles."

He looked up from his work. "Something wrong?"

"Perhaps. There is something you're not telling me, isn't there? Tuckman's wire told you more than the fact that Martin and Watkins had escaped hanging." Jed entered as she spoke and the look on his face told her she had guessed right. "Tuckman said something that's made you expect trouble, not at some indefinite time in the future but soon."

Glancing at Jed, Charlie nodded. "The man's already been down Hunter's way." Both he and Jed rushed to her side when she went white and he hurried to add, "He didn't get Hunter, Leanne. Hunter's all right."

"You're not lying to spare me, are you?" She clutched Charlie's arm as she looked from him to Jed and back again.

"Well, we probably would, but we ain't lying now." Feeling she was not going to collapse, Charlie sat down and Jed did the same. "Hunter's still alive. Mr. Walsh said so when he sent word to Tuckman."

"It doesn't make sense. Watkins swore revenge, yet did nothing when he was so close to Hunter?"

"Oh, he left his mark. He must've seen how hard it'd be to get at Hunter there. I know Tuckman woulda warned Walsh, so everyone at the ranch was probably waiting for Watkins. Funny that the missus was out," Charlie muttered, frowning over that oddity.

"Lorraine left the safety of the ranch? Watkins got her, didn't he? I can see it in your faces."

"Yeh, he got her," Jed answered. "Killed her, but not before he got some information."

Charlie nodded. "He knows you left. He's coming after you first. He knows Hunter is coming after you, too, so he'll be out of that fortress of a ranch, easier to get to."

She massaged her temples as she struggled to understand all they told her. "Why would Hunter come after me?"

Jed shrugged. "'Cause he knows Watkins is hunting you. Hunter might not be wanting to wed you, but he ain't a man to set back and leave you to face that without as much help as he can give."

"No, he isn't," she murmured. "He'll feel obligated, since he was the one after Watkins from the start."

Worse and worse, she thought. Knowing Watkins and Martin were out there looking for her was chilling. She could all too easily recall those threats Watkins had thrown at their heads on the journey from Mexico to Little Creek. The man was sick in his mind. Her pregnancy would not save her. Watkins would probably savor the thought of sacrificing such an innocent to sate his twisted need for revenge.

And then there was Hunter, she thought with an inner groan. She wished he had stayed at his ranch where he would have been relatively safe. Instead he was riding around trying to find her, making himself an easier target for Watkins. So, too, was he coming out of obligation, riding to help her while filled with the very last thing she wanted him to feel towards her. She could almost hope he was already married to Patricia, but that would only add more complications. It seemed she had solved nothing by leaving that day.

"No wonder you didn't tell me everything," she muttered. "What a mess. I don't suppose running is an option."

"Nope. It ain't only you being—well, like you are. If we gotta face Watkins, I'd rather do it here, behind thick walls, than out in the open," Charles said as he rose and moved to look out the window. "Sun's rising. We better start keeping a steady watch."

"You said Tuckman was in Clayville to watch Charity. You didn't hear from her?"

Leanne almost wished they had not gone there, yet it had seemed a good idea at the time. Sending a message to Charity from St. Anne would have been added insurance against Hunter locating her. Charity had to have been told something about all that had happened, and she would have known how to get in touch with Tuckman. There was also the chance of getting some news about O'Malley. Instead they had heard from Tuckman himself and spent a harried time exchanging telegraph messages.

Discovering Watkins and Martin had cheated justice, Charlie and Jed had nearly killed their horses racing the long miles back to warn her. Shaking her head, she told herself not to be so silly. Ignorance could be bliss at times, but in this matter it was far better to have some warning.

"Nope. Seems she got married," Jed answered. "Was off on a honeymoon or something like that."

"Charity got married? Good God, to Clovis?" She found herself wondering if Charity had blackmailed him into it.

"Yeh, that was the name. Hey, wasn't he the one that grabbed you that night? The reason she tossed you out?"

"He was, that lump of dog spit. Well, if two people ever deserved each other, it's those two." She sighed, her spate of animosity slipping away. "It's good she was away. Watkins must know about her since Martin does. They'd try to find me through her and she knows, sort of, where this place is. And if they'd kill Lorraine Walsh, they'd kill Charity."

"No question about it. Fact is, I got the feeling that man Watkins purely enjoys killing." Jed's eyes widened as he realized the tactlessness of such an observation at that moment. "Well, mebbe I was wrong 'bout that."

"And maybe you weren't." Leanne shivered. "Just think of the things he said when we were taking him to the law in Little Creek. The man is not right in the head. I hope to God no one got in his way, but I suppose that would be too much of a miracle to hope for."

"Naw, couldn't do that. Then you and Hunter'd still be outlaws. Me and Charlie too."

"Of course." She gave a start and looked at Jed with a smile. "We're not any longer?"

Jed lightly slapped his forehead with the palm of his hand. "Clean forgot about that. Tuckman says you're cleared, and me and Charlie got our pardons. I expect Hunter's got the papers. It feels good knowing the law don't want us anymore. Just wish Watkins didn't."

"Amen." She reached across the table and patted his hand. "He'll need an army to get us out of here. O'Malley said everything he built he made strong enough to resist the fiercest Indian or bandit attack. He'd lost a number of friends to Indians, you see. Then too, Tuckman might stop Watkins and Martin in Clayville. That's why he's there. And we have Hunter racing to find us. Probably Sebastian too. They'd be sure to keep in touch with Tuckman and he with them."

"Yeah, you're right. He ain't even here yet, anyways."

"He is."

They both stared at Charlie in horror and Leanne croaked, "You're sure?"

"Someone's tiptoeing around in them rocks. Slipping up closer to take a peek, I reckon."

"They couldn't have found us by sheer chance. They got to poor Charity. She must have arrived shortly after you left town, so Tuckman couldn't reach you. And Tuckman! He wouldn't let them slip by if he was able to stop it."

"Now you don't know anything for certain, Leanne," Jed said as he collected his rifle and moved to take up a position by a window. "You're just guessing. 'Sides, even if you've guessed right, nothing to do about it now. We have our own selves to watch out for."

"And you have that babe. So"—Charlie pointed to a three-sided barricade of bales of hay and stuffed bags they had erected in a sheltered corner of the large main room—"get yourself in there. There'll be a lot of stray lead soon. We don't want you catching any."

"I could help," she protested even as she hurried to put the guns and ammunition in the little shelter.

"Yeah, and you could get shot too. You'll help by keeping the guns loaded and keeping low so we ain't worrying on you."

"Hey, that looks like Pete, don't it?" Jed pointed out to the man Charlie had seen edging up to the cabin.

Staring out the window, Charlie grunted, then fired a shot that kicked up the dirt around the foot Pete had just set in the clearing as he slowly edged out from behind the last bit of covering before the cabin. "One more step and you're dead, Pete."

"That you, Charlie?" Pete yelled after diving back behind cover.

"Ain't your ma, you pissant. Best you run home to her. You stay here and you're dead, sure as I can spit."

"Now, you listen to me, Charlie. I'm here to give you a chance—we being old friends and all."

"We ain't friends, Pete. Never have been. I'm a mite choosier about who I call friend. Say your piece, then skedaddle before I shoot you just for practice." Charlie glanced towards Leanne, who was poking her head out of the shelter. "Get in there, girl." As soon as she disappeared inside, he looked back out the window. "I'm getting impatient." He shot at the rock Pete hid behind.

"All right, stop shooting. Watkins wants the girl."

"What girl?"

"C'mon Charlie, you know what girl. That damn little bitch that tricked Watkins so Hunter could get him alone. He wants her. Now, you hand her over all pleasant-like and we'll let you and your friend Jed walk outta here. Watkins will forget you had anything to do with his getting caught."

"Hell's bells, Pete. Me and Jed ain't the smartest fellows around, but we ain't that dumb."

"You calling me a liar?"

"Yeah," bellowed Jed, "we're calling you a liar. Wanna step out from behind that rock and deny it?"

"You ain't got a chance, y'know. No woman's worth dying for." Pete started to scramble away from the cabin. "You're dead, you stupid sons o' bitches. We're gonna cut you to pieces and get that little bitch anyways."

Charlie took aim at Pete's retreating backside and fired, smiling when the man's insults turned into howls of pain. "Think they really thought we'd just hand her over? They've forgot we know what Watkins is like."

Venturing slightly outside of her shelter, Leanne asked, "Are you really sure the deal was just a hoax?"

"Real sure, Leanne," Jed answered. "He's offered deals

like that before and the poor fools ended up dead. He was just hoping that we were dumb enough to think it'd be different with us or we'd not remember how his word don't mean squat."

"Oh." She suspected they were telling the truth, for such ruthlessness seemed wholly in character for Watkins. "What do you think they'll do now?"

"Reckon they'll set there a while and consider how to come at us," answered Charlie as he stared up into the hills.

Watkins stared down at the cabin. "It seems our old friends are not as stupid as we thought." He whirled to glare at Pete, who was loudly bemoaning his injury and the treating of it. "If you do not shut up, I will put you out of your misery." Pete quieted and Watkins returned to staring at the cabin. "That place was built for defense."

"Yeh." Martin scowled down at the cabin. "It'll cost us."

"Well, we have a fairly large force."

"Won't if we throw them away. I remember Charlie. He can see for miles and shoots as good as anyone I know."

"Then we lay siege. They can have only so many supplies. We wait them out. Draw out their fire now and again to deplete their store of ammunition." He rubbed his chin as he thought it out.

"How long do you think that'll take?"

"I have no idea. It appears as if they have been warned. That could mean they are well supplied. It could take a while."

"We wait too long and we could have someone come after us. You said Hunter'd be after her."

"I have a watch set for him. That woman Charity said

no one knew about this place. You shot Tuckman. All of that considered, it leaves us with few to worry about. Hunter will come, but it'll take time for him to find this place. Clever building the place flush against the rock like that. We can't encircle it and they don't have to watch their backs.

"Send the men down, spread around as far as they can be but staying well covered. Make sure they understand that we want to draw their fire, get them to use up their bullets, but not lose men."

Martin started to obey, then hesitated. "How about burning them out?"

"Even if anyone could get near enough to set it alight, there's not much there that'll burn well. Also, I want that bitch alive. There's too much chance of her dying if we set the place ablaze. No, no fire." He waved Martin away, his gaze fixed on the cabin. "Let's get started."

Charlie swore as he caught sight of Watkins's men closing in. "Now it starts."

"They ain't thinking of rushing us, are they? Hell, it'd be like a turkey shoot. Watkins can't be that stupid."

"Don't think he is, Jed. Not one of them's trying to come into that clearing. I think he's going to play with us. Don't shoot too freely. Just keep the bastards pinned there, maybe pick a few careless fools off."

Leanne shivered, then jumped when the first shot was fired. This was a side of her friends she wished she did not have to see. Charlie and Jed knew the ways of violence, knew the world of guns and killing. It was hard to recognize this hard side of the gentle, shy men who had befriended her. She was not sure she liked it.

Then she shook herself, scolding herself for ill-placed delicacy of feeling. She should be glad of their skill in such matters. They were risking their lives to protect her. The man they faced had every intention of killing them. Including, she thought as her child stirred in her womb, an innocent. Such men had to be faced with a hard heart, with a violence equal to theirs.

As she grew almost accustomed to the sporadic gunfire, handing out loaded guns and reloading the emptied ones, she thought about Hunter. He might be riding to help, but she was not sure how he could find her. She had told him about O'Malley but not exactly where the cabin was, only that it was in the San Juan foothills. Since she felt certain Watkins had killed Charity and possibly Marshal Tuckman as well, there was no one to tell Hunter exactly where the cabin was. Of course, she thought wryly, as another of what few panes of glass remained was shattered by a bullet, if Hunter passed within a few miles of them he would easily hear where they were. Sound carried a long way in the hills and Watkins was making no effort at all to be quiet. She hoped that was not because he was confident no one would be coming to help.

When Grant signaled a halt, Hunter reined in beside him. "Why are we stopping?"

"We go any farther and we can be spotted. If Watkins is there, he might set out a watch. After all, he's expecting you to come galloping after Leanne. We ought to come up to the cabin as much on the sly as we can."

Looking around, Hunter saw little cover for six men on horseback. "The best way to do that would be on foot."

"'Fraid so. That copse of trees would be a good place to leave the horses, but it'll be a good hike up there."

"There is no alternative though, is there?"

"Not if we want to get there unseen."

At the copse, they dismounted and secured their horses. They took a few moments to select what they would need if they faced a fight. While Hunter did not enjoy the thought of the added time it would take to walk to the cabin, he admitted to himself that he would do just about anything to deprive Watkins of any warning.

Even as they started out, Hunter saw Sebastian's skill at tracking. The man made no sound at all as he walked along. To his surprise he saw some of the same skill in Grant. It occurred to him that Leanne's father had probably picked up a few tricks while ducking his creditors all those years. Falling back a little, he did his best to follow their example. Owen and Leanne's brothers did the same.

As Grant waved for them to stop, Hunter heard the sound of gunfire. It was both alarming and reassuring. While it meant that Watkins and Martin had found Leanne, it also meant she, Charlie, and Jed were still holding on. Then he saw the man Watkins had put on watch. He had an excellent view from where he sat high on the rocks.

"We try to go by and he's bound to see at least one of us," Grant said as all six men crouched together to plan their next step.

"I can see why we had to leave the horses behind," muttered Owen. "How the hell do we get around him?"

Grant sighed. "That, m'boy, is a puzzle. He sees just one of us before we get him, and he'll have plenty of time to warn Watkins. It's a shame Watkins had the wit to see that there's no better place to set a pair of eyes. I was hoping he'd be so bent on his revenge, he'd do little thinking on protecting his own back. Can't shoot the bastard either. Might get lost in the sound of shooting already about, but it might not."

"Then it seems to me we have to shut those eyes—quietly," Sebastian murmured.

Along with the others, Hunter looked at Sebastian. The man tossed aside most of what he had taken from his horse, keeping only his Colt and a knife. Then he sat down and took off his boots and socks.

"What're you doing that for?" asked Owen.

Standing up, Sebastian stared towards Watkins's rearguard. "It's nigh on impossible to move quietly over rock with boots on. I'm also going to have to do a little climbing to get to him. I climb better in bare feet."

"Can you manage if you take my Henry?" Grant asked.

Sebastian frowned slightly at the rifle Grant held out to him. "Why take it?"

"If you get up there, you'll see that you have a real good view of the cabin and what's around it. 'Course, there ain't much cover up there. Hell, ain't any. Made sure of that. Still, if you're willing, it'd be a good place for us to have a gun. Just make sure you don't get your fool self killed."

"Yes, sir." Sebastian took the rifle and, an instant later, disappeared.

"Think he can do it?" Grant looked at Hunter.

"If it can be done—yeah. Wonder why Charlie and Jed haven't shot that man? Isn't he in range of the cabin?"

"He is. I made sure of that before I started building. I reckon Charlie and Jed are too busy watching what's closer to the ground. It wouldn't help us much if they did pick him off. Watkins can stick another fellow up there quick. It'd take a while, more time than we want to wait, to make Watkins feel the cost of keeping a watch is too dear or his men flat refuse to go."

They fell silent as they waited. Hunter knew they were watching the guard as closely as he was. They scarcely saw the first fleeting hint that Sebastian was there before suddenly the man crumbled to the ground. Within the blink of an eye, it looked as if he was back up. Then an easily read signal aimed directly at them proved it was Sebastian. He had obviously slipped on the man's coat and hat in hopes of keeping Watkins from seeing there was any trouble.

"Hot damn, he's good," muttered Grant, then turned to look at his small army. "Brandon and I are going to the cabin. There's a way to slip in around the back that's really well hidden. The rest of you see what you can do about getting behind those bastards. The better a crossfire we can catch them in, the quicker we can end this."

Leanne was wishing for the hundredth time that the fighting would end when she heard Charlie cry out. She hurriedly looked out to see him clutching his arm. Keeping low to the ground, she scurried over to his side.

"I told you to stay in that shelter," Charlie rasped as he sank down to sit beside her.

"I'll go right back as soon as I stop this bleeding." She ripped away the cloth to check his injury and breathed a sigh of relief. "The bullet went right through. I don't think it hit anything important."

"Hit me."

She smiled as she ripped two strips of cloth from her petticoat, dampened one in the jug of water they kept at hand to ease their thirst and began to bathe his wound. "I meant muscle or bone. This arm will still be more or less usable."

"Don't matter if it's a little stiff. Not my shooting arm. Reckon one of us was bound to get stung."

"Yes, considering the swarms of bullets that fly through at regular intervals. Is there any progress out there?"

"We've trimmed the numbers a little," Jed answered because Charlie was gritting his teeth against the pain she had to inflict. "I figure Watkins is just waiting us out. He hopes we'll run out of supplies, especially ammunition. Then they can just walk in. Either that or they'll get in some lucky shots and we won't be able to muster enough fire to hold them back."

"That is rather what I thought. It seems he's not too worried about anyone coming to our aid." She finished bandaging Charlie's arm and sat back on her heels, absently rubbing at the ache in the small of her back.

"Yeah, and maybe he's just plumb loco," grumbled Charlie as he briefly tested his arm. "Now, you get back over there."

Looking at her shelter, she grimaced. "Just what's in those bags scattered amongst the bales?"

"Ran outta clean hay, so I stuffed them with not-so-clean hay."

"That's what I feared. The aroma is growing a little stronger than I like."

"Better a little stink than a bullet in you. Now get back there."

"You are becoming quite autocratic, Charles."

"That mean something about how I'm telling you what to do?"

"It does."

"Too bad."

"Leanne!"

All three of them froze. As one, they stared at the door at the rear of the house. When Jed and Charlie aimed their guns at the door, she signaled them to hold their fire. There was something familiar about that bellow, but she did not dare to hope.

"Leanne? Answer me, girl. It's O'Malley."

Charlie grabbed her by the arm when she started to move towards the door. "You sure it's him?"

"It certainly sounds like him, and he'd know about the hidden back entrance."

"One of Watkins's men could have slipped by us," Jed murmured. "They know about O'Malley too."

"Leanne," the voice called, "I've got anise drops."

She smiled at Jed and Charlie's looks of confusion. Jed muttered, "What the hell?"

"It's O'Malley. Even Charity didn't know about how he always brought me anise drops, so Watkins wouldn't either."

Charlie released her, hissing, "Keep real low." She noticed, as she half-crawled to the door, that while Jed returned to shooting at Watkins's men, Charlie kept his gun aimed at the back door. Then she stood up to remove the bar and flung it open. She was at first painfully disappointed, for there was only the rock staring back at her. Then O'Malley stepped in, followed by his son Brandon. She laughed as O'Malley swept her up in a big hug while Brandon hastily relocked the door.

Grant was shockingly aware of the roundness of his daughter's belly but subdued his reaction, covertly signaling Brandon to hide his shock as well. For the moment, the important thing was that she was alive and apparently unhurt. He relinquished her so that Brandon could give her a brief hug. Then he helped cover her and push her to the floor when several bullets hit the walls around them.

"You could say there's more lead in the air than might be healthy," Charlie drawled.

Leanne hastily introduced the four men to each other. "It's so good to see you two, but you've stepped into a lot of trouble."

"We know all about it." When she opened her mouth to speak, Grant shook his head. "We can talk later. There's some work to do now." He helped her into a sitting position, keeping his body between hers and the windows. "You got a safe corner to tuck yourself into?"

"Yes." She pointed to her shelter. "Charlie and Jed have made me stay in that."

"Damn good idea." He nudged her towards it. "Get back in there. Things'll probably get real hot for a little while." As soon as she obeyed, he and Brandon scrambled over to Jed and Charlie. "Been at this long?"

"Started soon after daybreak," Charlie answered.

"He's playing a waiting game," Jed said. "Figures he's got time to set and nip at us 'til we can't nip back." He met Grant's gaze and his eyes slowly widened. "Lookit his eyes," he hissed, nudging Charlie, who slowly had the same reaction.

Before either man could blurt out anything, Grant turned their attention back to the fight with Watkins. "There's four men on our side out there. One's on that lump of rock over there."

Charlie looked where Grant pointed. "Hot damn, it's Sebastian."

"You can recognize him from here?" Brandon asked in surprise.

"Charlie's got good eyes," Jed replied. "That must mean Hunter's here. Circling behind the bastards, is he?"

"Yes," Grant answered. "Him, his brother Owen, and my other son. Things should happen soon."

When Charlie mentioned Sebastian, Leanne had needed a minute or two to strangle the urge to race over to the window to look. Only she would have been looking for Hunter, not the others, and she felt like kicking herself. After what he had done to her, she had to be a complete fool to even want to look at him. It annoyed her beyond words that she did want to—badly.

While it was good to have help, any help, she knew this particular help was going to bring its own trouble. She knew it would be foolish to hope she could avoid seeing Hunter. After riding all this way to help, to risk his life to save hers, Hunter was not going to saddle up and go home without at least seeing with his own eyes that she had survived.

"What a godawful mess," she muttered. "I haven't got a single route of escape."

Hearing her mumbling, Grant looked towards the bales. "You all right, punkin?"

Sighing, she called out, "Yes, I'm fine."

"Talking to herself again," Charlie said.

Jed nodded. "She does it a lot. Me and Charlie figure the baby, y'know, sometimes makes her a little tetched in the head."

Leanne gasped, outraged. "I am NOT tetched."

The way Charlie and Jed warily eyed the shelter made Grant laugh. "Don't you browbeat these boys, Leanne. And about that cute little tummy of yours . . ."

Looking down at the mound that had once been a taut, flat stomach, Leanne was not sure "cute, little tummy" was the right word for it.

". . . soon as we get this nest of vipers cleaned out, you and me are going to talk about that."

She groaned and slumped against the bales. When he had hugged her, she had felt the shock rip through him, had seen it on his son's handsome face before it had been quickly hidden. It had been silly to think that would be the end of it. Now she could add O'Malley to the difficulties still remaining after Watkins and Martin were sent to rout.

"It's Hunter's, y'know." Jed spoke softly so Leanne would not hear.

"I know. Best we keep that boy alive through this fight," Grant said, "because I'm of a mind to kill him."

He smiled faintly when Jed, Charlie, and Brandon just grinned, fully aware he was bluffing. It was good, he decided, that there would be some time between his discovering her pregnancy and setting eyes on the young rogue who had planted the babe. They would be wed, however, as soon as he could drag a preacher out to the cabin. If the pair had not straightened out the misunderstandings between them before they said "I do," they would just have to do it afterwards.

At that moment, one of the men crouching behind cover they could not penetrate cried out and fell, and Grant smiled. "The boys have gotten behind them. Now it heats up, lads. Don't you stick one toe outta there,

Leanne, 'til I tell you," he bellowed, then turned his full attention to the battle.

Huddled behind her straw walls, Leanne prayed for the men. She prayed that Watkins's need for vengeance did not cause her friends and loved ones to be sacrificed. Suddenly, all her other concerns seemed very small indeed. She was even willing to face Hunter, for it would mean he had come out of the fight unscathed. That was certainly worth suffering some discomfort.

As Hunter fought, he kept his eyes open for Watkins and Martin. He was determined that they would not escape this time. Just as he caught sight of the pair, Martin was shot. As he staggered and fell, he jostled Watkins. The path of retreat they had chosen was steep and rocky enough for that momentary unbalancing to send Watkins tumbling down it. Hunter raced towards the man, reaching him just before he could right himself completely and retrieve the gun that had slipped from his grasp.

"Get up real slow, Watkins. Real slow. One wrong move, and you end up like Martin."

Rising slowly, Watkins glanced towards the sprawled corpse of his half-brother, then sought out his gun before looking back at Hunter. "You think you've won, don't you?"

"I know I have. Your men are running for their lives. Those left alive, that is."

"You won't be seeing me hang, you bastard."

"I will, even if I have to pull the damn lever myself. Now, move."

Watkins moved, but not towards the clearing as Hunter

indicated. He lunged for his pistol, ignoring Hunter's shouted warning. Cursing viciously, Watkins was turning the pistol on Hunter when a bullet through the heart ended his life.

Hunter was still staring at Watkins's sprawled body when Owen stepped up to his side. "Think anyone will believe I had to shoot him?" Hunter said.

"They will because I'll tell them so," Sebastian said as he walked up to them.

"You get around pretty good for a man with no boots on," murmured Owen, and Sebastian briefly smiled.

Sighing, Hunter reholstered his gun. "He didn't want to hang."

"So he made you his executioner," Sebastian concluded. "It's not uncommon, believe me."

"What's important is that it's over, Hunter. It's over."

"You're right, Owen."

Sebastian grimaced as he looked from one body to another. "Well, which one do you want to carry?"

"It's over, honey."

Leanne opened her eyes and took the hand O'Malley held out to her. "All over?"

"All over."

"Everyone's all right?"

"A nick here and there. That's all," he assured her as he helped her stand up. "They're tying up the prisoners and collecting the bodies now." He patted her cheek when a look of distress passed over her face. "Sometimes it has to be that way, darlin'."

"I know," she murmured as he led her outside.

As she stepped out onto the small front porch, she saw Hunter. He was approaching the wagon Charlie had brought out to hold the living and the dead. Watkins's body was slung over his shoulder. When he saw her, his gaze was at first fixed upon her face. She waited tensely for him to notice the rest of her. She watched as his dark gaze slipped down her body, watched his eyes widen even as his mouth gaped open and she had to fight the urge to bolt.

Chapter Eighteen

"You're pregnant." Hunter threw Watkins's body in the wagon and marched over to Leanne.

"Boy's sharp as a tack," Grant murmured and shrugged when both Leanne and Hunter glared at him. "Matthew, you go get our horses and bring them here. Brandon, you're riding in to town with that wagonload of human manure and bringing me back a preacher."

"A preacher?" Leanne squawked, staring at O'Malley in horror. "Hunter's already married."

"I am not." Out of sheer perversity, Hunter almost protested Grant's taking over, then decided it would be stupid because a preacher and a quick marriage suited him just fine.

"Well, engaged then. I'm sorry this trouble interrupted your nuptials," she said in her most formal voice. "I thank you for your help. You may go home now."

"I'm not going anywhere, and I'm not getting married."

"Someone's coming, Pa," Brandon called.

Hunter cursed the interruption even as he turned to meet the men riding in. There were nearly a dozen well-armed men, but their stances were relaxed and friendly. He suspected they had thoroughly surveyed the situation before riding in.

"Marshal Tuckman thought you'd be needing help. Seems you don't," said the man at the front of the group. "Deputy Carson from St. Anne," he said, touching the brim of his hat in greeting.

Grant reached up and shook the man's hand. "Thanks for coming. We were just bringing in the prisoners and the dead. Tuckman'll want to see for himself that Watkins and Martin are dead, I reckon."

"He will. He'll probably be waiting in St. Anne by the time we get back."

"But I thought he was wounded," Hunter said. "And in Clayville."

"He is and he was, but the dang fool's headed to St. Anne. Said he means to be there at the end of all this." Deputy Carson nodded toward the wagon. "We'll just water our horses, then take that lot in for you. No point in our lingering here. You can get your wagon later."

"My son can bring it back," Grant said. "I was sending him to town for a preacher. You do have a preacher in St. Anne, don't you?"

Deputy Carson grinned and nodded towards the man at his side. "We do and he's right here. The Reverend Castor Trenton."

The young man nodded in a small bow of greeting. "You have need of a preacher, sir?"

"I do." Grant pointed towards Leanne and Hunter. "I've got me two young people who're getting married."

Castor Trenton stared fixedly at a blushing Leanne for a moment, then dismounted and took a book from his saddlebags. "Looks to me as if they're a little slow to get to the altar, but I'll be most happy to perform that service for you, sir."

"Well, I won't be most happy," snapped Leanne as the preacher and Grant approached. "I'm not going through with this." She looked at Hunter. "Will you do something about this?"

"Certainly." He grasped her by the arm and tugged her closer. "Where would you like us to stand?" he asked the preacher.

"Hunter!" Leanne tried and failed to tug free of his hold. "I refuse to be subjected to this. Look, how do we know he's a preacher? He was riding with a posse and carries a gun. I refuse to be married by a man carrying a gun."

Castor Trenton obligingly removed his holster. "Ready?"

"No, I am not ready! You can't perform a marriage when one of the people does not consent, can you? Isn't that coercion or something?"

"I believe she might be right, sir." He looked at Grant and shrugged. "It would only work if her father gave his approval. Do you, sir?"

"He's not my father. He just acts like it," Leanne grumbled, rubbing the small of her back and thinking absently that it was getting worse. "Now, if you do not mind, I believe I will go and lie down." She tried to leave, but Hunter held her firmly.

Grant scowled, tired of the nonsense. "Maybe I act it because I damn well am."

"Oh, that's telling her softly, Summers," Hunter murmured as Leanne whirled to stare at Grant.

"You're what?" she rasped but even as she stared at him, she knew it was true.

The eyes, she thought, feeling almost dizzy. They were her eyes. She could not believe she had stared into them for so many years and not seen it. Rubbing her forehead, she decided it needed just one more thing, just one more, and she would undoubtedly have a full-blown conniption fit. The way everyone was staring at her, she doubted it would surprise them.

"I'm your father. Now," he said to a wide-eyed Castor Trenton, "marry them."

"I don't suppose it occurred to you some time during all those years to tell me," she hissed at him.

"It did. I just didn't find the right moment. Don't pay any attention to her interruptions," he advised Castor.

"Who the hell are they, then?" She pointed at Brandon and Matthew, where they stood with Owen, Sebastian, Charlie, and Jed.

"Brandon and Matthew? They're your brothers. Remember Kane?" She nodded and Grant continued, "Well, he's your eldest brother. He's the one in Denver, by the by."

"How nice." She was torn between fury over his not telling her and delight that her old friend was the father she had thought cared nothing for her. "You still haven't explained why you've kept it such a big secret."

"I'll tell you as soon as you get married."

"That's bribery."

"Yup."

"You seem to be forgetting that Hunter is engaged to another woman."

"I am not," Hunter snapped.

"And may I ask why not?"

"I never was."

"I saw it written down in your own nearly illegible scrawl."

"Nearly illegible?"

"Worst handwriting I've ever seen."

"Well, I'll explain all that after we get married."

"More bribery."

Hunter nodded, then looked at the preacher. "You can start now." After a brief hesitation, Trenton began.

Leanne was not sure why she was tolerating it, letting them shoo her along into something she had not really agreed to yet. She decided it was because she could not think straight and could hardly put up an adequate defense. No one could think clearly with so much whirling in her mind. Hunter was there claiming he was neither married nor engaged. Dear O'Malley was standing there claiming he was her father, but for some reason he had hidden that fact until now. She glared at her father when he suddenly nudged her.

"What is it now?" she grumbled.

"Say 'I do'."

"I do."

"Good girl."

"I now pronounce you man and wife," Castor Trenton intoned and closed his book.

Leanne blinked as Hunter kissed her cheek while eyeing her warily. "I'm married?" Trenton nodded. "That was quick. Sure it's legal?"

"Quite legal," he assured her. "It really only needs you both saying 'I do' and me saying 'It's done'."

"Wonderful. I pause for a moment's thought and miss my own wedding."

"Are you going to be difficult about this, Leanne?" Hunter asked.

"I'm giving it some serious consideration." She winced and rubbed at her back, wondering what she had done to make it ache so.

"You all right?" Hunter frowned, thinking she looked tired and pale.

Suddenly the pain in her back encircled her and squeezed. She gasped, clutching her middle as she bent over. What little conversation there had been among the men milling about in the clearing stopped abruptly. She glanced up to see them all staring at her in varying degrees of horror. It annoyed her. They were not the ones about to have a baby.

"Leanne," Hunter gasped, feeling increasingly alarmed, "is something wrong?"

"Wrong?" she nearly screamed as she straightened up. "What could possibly be wrong? I've just spent a whole day with a lunatic trying to kill me. A man who's supposed to be in Texas getting married has just married me. A man I've known for years decides to announce that he's my father. Now I'm going to have a baby, and it's too damned soon. Oh, no, nothing's wrong. Everything is just perfect."

Grant swore and looked at the deputy. "Don't suppose you've got a doctor in that group?"

The deputy shook his head, then pointed to a rather dapper-looking middle-aged man. "Jack Tuttle's got ten kids."

"There is a sterling recommendation," Leanne panted as she felt another contraction sweep over her.

Jack Tuttle strolled over to her and smiled shyly. "I have helped my Mabel birth near half of them."

"So you should have, since you keep putting them there," she nearly snarled, but Mr. Tuttle just kept smiling.

"Now, Leanne," Grant decided she needed to be calmed down, "there's no need to get hysterical."

"Isn't there? Isn't there? I'm having a baby and it's not supposed to be coming now. I've just been dragged into marriage and introduced to my father. Most women have other women fluttering around them at such a time. Do you see any women here? No. Men. All men. A preacher who wears a gun, a posse, outlaws dead and alive, Charlie, Jed, a man who can't leave his poor wife alone, and six men I am never going to speak to again for as long as I live." She bit back a scream as she bent to another contraction.

"My Mabel always gets a bit testy at this time too," Jack Tuttle told Grant.

"I'm not surprised, you lecher," Leanne snapped.

Sebastian stepped forward to take Leanne from a ghost-white Hunter's unsteady hold and pick her up in his arms. "I believe she ought to get to her bed. Owen, come take your brother in hand. Maybe someone can find him some whiskey."

Even as Owen hurried to Hunter's side, Hunter stepped dazedly towards Leanne. "But I should . . ."

"Go quietly to a corner and have a few drinks, maybe more than a few." Sebastian grinned and shook his head. "You look worse than she does, and she's having the kid." He started into the house.

"But . . ." Hunter began again.

Owen tugged him aside. "Hunter, you look scared to death and she doesn't need that."

"She said the baby's too early."

Jack Tuttle clapped him on the shoulder. "Babies come when they want. Don't have to be a bad thing."

"You want us to wait around for you, Jack?" called the deputy.

"Reckon I do if you don't mind. Looks to me like this won't take long." He strode into the house, Grant hurrying after him.

By the time Owen got Hunter seated at the far end of the porch, they were joined by Leanne's brothers and Charlie and Jed. Brandon and Jed held out bottles of whiskey. In silent accord, they opened Brandon's first and passed it around.

"She sounded just fine to me," ventured Charlie. "Mad as a hornet and snapping at anyone fool enough to get near her. That's how she always gets when she's hurt or scared. Must be a good sign."

"You might be right," Hunter agreed, a few deep drinks from the whiskey bottle bringing his fear under some control. "I thank you two for taking such good care of her. You put your lives on the line for her. I won't forget that." He smiled faintly when Charlie and Jed looked embarrassed.

"You said you ain't marrying anybody in Texas?" Jed asked.

"No, I'm not and never was." He hesitated, then decided telling the whole story might help keep his mind off what was happening inside the cabin.

*   *   *

Leanne clutched her bodice together and glared at the three men standing around her bed. "You are not, I repeat, not taking my clothes off."

"Now, girl, you can't have the baby through all of this," Grant said and held up her nightgown. "We'll just slip this on you."

She was about to tell him where he could put that nightgown when another contraction took all her attention. The three men mercilessly took full advantage of her defenselessness. By the time she was able to do any more than curse, she was undressed to the point where protesting was now senseless. Once in her nightgown, she lay panting on the bed while Sebastian lightly bathed her sweat-dampened face with a cool, damp cloth.

"My backache. It wasn't just a backache, was it?"

"Probably not," Sebastian agreed. "Now, stop being so ungrateful to Mr. Tuttle."

For a brief moment she felt ashamed of herself. "I'm sorry, Mr. Tuttle."

"Don't need to apologize, ma'am. Fact is, it made me more at ease, it did. You sounded just like my Mabel."

She looked at Grant. "You said you'd tell me all about why you played at being O'Malley and maybe one or two other small details."

"Honey, I think you're going to be too busy in a moment to hear me out."

It annoyed her when he proved right, but she was soon too caught up in having her baby to care. What embarrassment she felt over the intimacies required was also brief. The rigors of childbirth took her over completely. She did, however, find the strength to impugn Mr. Tuttle's intelligence whenever he said things were going well or that it would not be long now.

When her child was born, she clung to Sebastian's hand waiting for the cry, then sagged weakly in his hold when a good strong wail broke the silence. The baby certainly sounded healthy, but it was a few more moments before she knew for sure as the final stages of childbirth were completed and she and the baby were cleaned up.

"The baby's healthy?" she asked as Mr. Tuttle put the swaddled infant in her arms.

"A little small, but those arms and legs were waving about good as any I've seen. He's got all he's supposed to have and a good strong voice. Maybe he wasn't quite as early as you thought, miss."

"That is quite possible." She suddenly realized that Mr. Tuttle had said 'he'. "I had a boy?" Even as all three men nodded, she opened the baby's covering to see for herself. "A boy. Doesn't that just figure?" She yawned and, despite her efforts to keep her eyes open, she finally had to let them close. "As if there aren't enough of them clumping around."

Grant frowned when Leanne said nothing else. "Leanne?"

"Gone to sleep," Sebastian pronounced. "My mother used to do that. Stayed awake just long enough to hear the baby cry, then"—he snapped his fingers—"off to sleep."

"We'll let her sleep, then. I'll wager she didn't get much last night, not after hearing about Watkins and Martin."

After setting the baby in a bed hastily made out of a bureau drawer, Grant heartily thanked Jack Tuttle. The three of them went outside, and Grant found himself accosted immediately by Hunter. After assuring his new son-in-law that everything was fine, he shooed the younger man into the cabin and turned to say his thanks and farewells to the men from St. Anne.

Hunter slipped into the room Grant had directed him to. He stood by the bed watching Leanne sleep for several minutes, then crouched by his sleeping son. It was all a little hard to take in. Only that morning he had been scared to death of losing her to Watkins's twisted hatred. Now, not only was she alive, but they were married and he was a father. Quietly sitting in the chair Sebastian had set by the bed earlier, Hunter waited for Leanne to wake up and hoped by then he would feel less at sea.

Slowly Leanne shook off the grip of sleep. For a moment she felt confused, then her hands went to her stomach. Even as she sat up and looked around for her child, Hunter handed her the squirming infant and plumped up the pillows for her to lean against. The way the baby sucked on his fist told her what he wanted. A glance at Hunter told her he was not going to leave her alone to feed their child. Blushing slightly, she opened the bodice of her nightgown and put her new son to her breast. For a brief moment, she completely forgot Hunter. It was not until his long-fingered, dark hand gently touched the ebony down on the baby's head that she looked at him again.

"He seems quite healthy." Hunter wanted to tell her how deeply touched he was by the sight of her with their child at her breast, but the words were not easy to find.

"Yes, Mr. Tuttle is probably right. He was ready to be born."

"Leanne, I was not planning to marry Patricia Spotford. My mother and Patricia wanted you to think that so you would leave."

"Which I obligingly did," Leanne said, beginning to realize she had been tricked. "I'm sorry about your mother."

"Yes, she didn't deserve what Watkins did to her. We all had to fight a bad sense of guilt, partly because we didn't feel the grief we felt we ought to and partly because we'd all told her to leave. Leave as soon as it was safe, of course, but she insisted on going immediately."

The baby finished with what little she was able to provide and she held him up to her shoulder, rubbing his tiny back as she stared at Hunter. "Your mother was leaving?"

He nodded. "It won't be known now, except amongst family, but Pa had demanded a divorce. He'd been thinking on it and got all the preliminaries done before my trouble began. As he said, how she acted then showed him she didn't care a jot about any of us." He shrugged. "So why stay together?"

"But divorce?" She was shocked, for divorce was something only whispered about, something so scandalous people lived in misery with despised partners for life rather than contemplate it.

Hunter laughed softly. "It still makes me wince. Leanne, it was the snobbery, the deceit she showed in driving you away that finally did it. Darlin', that letter she gave you was six years old." Seeing that the child was asleep, he helped her settle him on her lap. "She and Patricia carefully trimmed the top off where I had written a date." He told her the story behind the letter.

It was hard to believe, yet she knew he was telling the truth. She told herself it was foolish to feel jealous, even hurt, over a six-year-old love letter, but those feelings lurked within her. There was, however, pleasure to be found in the knowledge that he had never broken his promise to her.

"So you didn't just marry me because this little devil was on his way," she murmured, watching their child sleep.

"No. I was coming after you anyway. Watkins and Martin getting free just made me a little more frantic."

"They're dead now, aren't they?"

"Very dead. We don't need to worry about them any more." He smiled at her. "What we might worry about a little is a name for this boy."

She grimaced. "I was never able to make up my mind. I liked one name one day, another the next. It's not an easy thing to decide."

"My grandfather's name was Michael David." He shrugged. "I'm afraid, not knowing I was to be a father, that I haven't given any thought to it at all."

"Michael David," she repeated. "Michael David Walsh. It has a nice sound. I believe it'll do."

"That'll please my father."

"Speaking of fathers, did you know about mine?"

"Nope. Not until I found him. Well, Pa found out where he was. I went there hoping you'd found him too. Don't ask me to tell you about all that. It's his place to explain." He took her hand in his and kissed her palm. "Just listen to him, darlin'."

There was a rap on the door, and Leanne smiled crookedly. "Maybe that's the explanation on its way."

"You're not too tired?"

"Not for that, no."

When Hunter opened the door, Grant stepped in, balancing a tray with a hot meal and coffee on it. "Thought you might be hungry, punkin. Charlie said you didn't eat much at all today. Hell, it's nearly yesterday we're talking about."

Hunter gently moved his son back into his bed, then quietly left the room. There was a lot that needed talking about between him and Leanne, but he decided it could wait. Now it was time for her to get to know her father, to settle all that was between the two of them. When he finally opened his heart and tried to probe the secrets of hers, he wanted her attention to be solely his.

Leanne ate her stew but tasted little of it. All of her attention was fixed upon her father, the man she had always thought of as her friend O'Malley. She listened closely to all he had to say but could make no immediate decision about how she felt. Her emotions were badly confused. After he took her tray and set it on the floor, she met his expectant gaze with a half-smile.

"It's not easy," she said.

"I didn't think it would be, pet."

"My feelings seem to be one great mass of contradictary emotions. I'm furious and I'm pleased. I understand, yet I don't. There's also part of me that remembers life with Charity and asks whether running and scraping by could have been any worse."

"I'm not sure I can answer that. I think it would have been. Binnie believes it. As a father, could I chance it? The answer's no, Leanne. No matter how often I ask it of myself, it's no. I honestly feared for you in such a hard life. You were so small, so breakable."

"I know. If it's any help, I do understand how hard it must have been to decide what to do. It's just that, since Charity tossed me out, it seems as if everything I thought

I knew about myself is wrong. So much has been thrown at me. I need time to sort it all out."

Grant stood up, then bent to kiss her on the forehead. "Don't look so upset. You've heard me out and that's probably more than I deserve. You're also tired. A lot's happened to you in just one short day, not the least of which was having a baby. You just rest. We'll be setting here for a while. You and I can get to know each other all over again."

Returning to the main room, he found Hunter impatiently waiting at the table, everyone else having gone to bed. "I suppose you think you're going to just slip right into her bed."

"I don't suppose it. I know it. Is she upset?"

"Confused. As she says, she's had a lot thrown at her lately."

Standing up, Hunter paused by Grant to clasp his shoulder in sympathy before heading towards Leanne's room and advised, "Just give her time."

Stepping into the room, Hunter was not really surprised to find Leanne awake. "You should be trying to get some rest."

"I am trying, just not succeeding too well. What are you doing?" She frowned at him when he sat down to yank off his boots.

"Getting ready for bed."

"You're sleeping in here? With me?" Since he was still shedding his clothes, she decided that was a stupid question.

"I think Michael David's bed is a little small, don't you?"

"Very amusing." She thought it slightly shocking that, while her body still ached from having their child, she could find watching him disrobe enough to stir a flicker of carnal interest within her.

"Leanne, we're married." He doused the light and slid into bed beside her.

"I know, but I just had a baby." She made no effort to resist, however, as he tucked her body up against his.

"I'm not sleeping alone anymore. Comfortable?" He pressed a kiss against her hair.

She sighed and nodded. Sleeping alone had been hell. It was somewhat comforting to know he had not liked it either.

"How did it go with your father?"

"Not too badly. I don't hate him, if that's what worries you."

"It did, a little. He's a good man."

"I know. Remember, I've known him for years. I just didn't know he was my father."

"And why do you think he showed up as O'Malley?" He felt her shrug. "He couldn't put you from him completely, darlin'. He had to be part of your life, so he played that game. The man loves you, Leanne."

"I know, just like I knew it when he was O'Malley. It's just that—" She shook her head, not sure how to explain what she felt.

"It's just what?"

"Oh, it's just that I was so lonely when I was growing up. Those times with him and his sons were the only times I didn't feel so alone. I just keep thinking that I— well, I had a right to have that all the time."

He held her a little closer. "You did, but Fate decided to take it away. Grant didn't. He gave you all he could while keeping you safe. Just try to remember that as you sort the rest out."

* * *

She did and it helped. As the days slipped by and she spent time with her newfound family, her feelings grew less confused. Through talking with them, she got a very good picture of the hard times they had struggled through. That too helped for it made her see what her father had had to deal with. He had been beset with some very hard decisions.

Hunter watched her overcome her confused feelings about Grant and grow closer to her family. It caused him the occasional bout of jealousy. There was a lot he wished to share with Leanne, but he had to sit back and wait a while. Sebastian was the only one who saw that clearly and, while Hunter would miss his friend, he was glad when Sebastian left to go to his posting. He was not all that comfortable about his feelings being read so clearly when he was trying so hard to conceal them.

Grant watched Leanne as she finished her pie. "It's been nearly a month since the baby came."

"Yes, and I'm feeling as good as new. The baby's growing fast too, isn't he?"

"He's a good, strong boy."

Frowning slightly as she sensed something behind his words, she asked, "Are you leading up to something?"

"Leaving."

"Leaving? For where?"

"The weather's holding mild. I thought we'd get ourselves down to my ranch. It's not that long a trip. Since we won't be riding hell-bent for leather, it'll mean one night on the trail. I'd be sure to stop at one of those farms on the way, so at least you and the baby could be inside."

"Inside would be better," she murmured, wondering if taking such a young baby on a journey was a good idea.

"Honey, I really don't think such a short journey would hurt him." Grant looked to a frowning Hunter. "What do you think?"

Grimacing slightly when Leanne also turned to him, Hunter had to shrug. "I can't see how it'd hurt if he's kept warm. But asking me's no good. You've had more experience with children and all that goes with them."

"All right, I'll tell you what I'd do. The babe came a little early and winter's coming a little late. I'd take advantage of that to get him out of these hills. When winter does set into these rocks, it sets in hard and cold. Even as near as my place is, it's warmer. If the weather holds, you could even keep on going straight to Texas where you don't seem to get much winter at all."

It was the talk of the cold that pushed Leanne to a decision. She might not know much about babies, but she did know what an enemy the cold was to them. She had seen it back East as well as at home. The cold always took the very old and the very young.

"All right, I suppose it would be a good idea." She looked to Hunter for confirmation.

"I will admit to wanting to get home to Texas."

"Fine. We'll start out first thing in the morning."

"So fast?" Leanne gasped.

Grant shrugged. "If we want to get out before winter sets in . . ."

"Then we'd better get out," she finished for him and pushed away from the table. "And I'd better not sit here just thinking about all I need to do to get ready, but do it."

The preparations took less time than she had anticipated. She did not have all that much to pack, nor did

Hunter. While she had simply not wanted to take much when she had left because everything she had had at the Walshes' he had bought for her, Hunter had not anticipated a long stay. What took most of her time was packing away the food. She had time to leisurely nurse Michael David and bed him down before Hunter came to bed.

Lying in bed, she watched Hunter undress and hastily wash up, thinking idly that it was an enjoyable and oddly comforting ritual. When he scrambled into bed at her side, she laughed, then squeaked as he curled his chilled body around her. There, she mused, was the proof of what her father had said. Snug as the cabin was, the cold seeped in even here.

His good-night kiss left them both breathless and aching for more. She laughed softly at his groan of frustration, even though she felt the same. Such proof that he still wanted her, however, compensated a great deal for the discomfort of denial.

Hunter nuzzled her hair and closed his eyes. As she grew more healthy, her recovery from the birth of their son almost complete, he grew more hungry for her. Sleep became more elusive with each passing night. The fact that they had been apart for so long before she had had the child only added to his need for her. So did the obvious signs that she returned that need in full measure.

He was pleased to be leaving for several reasons. Cold was not his favorite temperature. With eight of them in the cabin, it was a little too crowded for comfort at times, and the winter weather that held one indoors would certainly aggravate that. He also simply wanted to get home to assure himself that things were fine there and, he admitted with an inner smile, to show off his son.

Although he felt a little guilty about it, he admitted that he also wanted to get Leanne away from her father and family. They had had a lot of time together, time to overcome their difficulties. He could see that that had been accomplished. Now he wanted his turn. Now, he thought as he felt sleep stroke his mind, he wanted her all to himself for a while so he could let her know how he felt and get her to believe it and to return those feelings.

Leanne felt his body grow heavy with sleep, hoping she could soon join him. Sleep was too often elusive. Lying in bed at night gave her too much time for thought.

Sometimes it was almost painful not to tell Hunter how she felt, but she was afraid. She feared how she would feel if he did not respond in kind. Telling herself how much she did have did not really soothe the need to openly show her love and have it fully returned. The thought of marking off the years holding all she felt close and secret made her shiver. Somehow she was going to have to find the courage to be honest with him, to push aside pride and take that first step. If she was very lucky, she thought with a half-smile, it might just be enough to pull at least a little of what she needed from his heart.

Chapter Nineteen

SMILING FAINTLY, LEANNE WALKED AWAY FROM LAURIE and Molly cooing somewhat inanely at a gurgling Michael David. Although there was always someone willing to watch the boy for a while, compliance had seemed astoundingly quick today. In fact, she had the distinct feeling that Laurie and Molly had been about to offer even as she asked. She decided not to worry about it and to find her husband just as she had planned to.

Yesterday she had been officially declared healed from the birth and 'capable of resuming marital relations,' as the doctor had put it. Unfortunately, after the long trip into town, then back again she had not felt very 'capable' at all. Since it had looked like rain, they had decided not to take the baby. She had fed him before leaving but after a full, exceptionally long day away from him, she had been uncomfortable to the point of pain. When the rain they had worried about descended upon them when they were still an hour from home, she had also gotten soaked. She had fed Michael David, had a hot bath, and gone to bed to fall immediately and deeply asleep.

Now, she thought, her eyes narrowing as she stepped out onto the veranda, she was well rested. It might be more ladylike, more refined, to wait for the night when they retired to their bed. However, she was not feeling ladylike or refined. There were four hours before she had to feed the baby again. She intended to find Hunter, drag him off somewhere private, and be very unrefined for every minute of those four hours. If he was really good, she thought with an inner chuckle, it might be even longer, for she could easily feed the baby and then return.

Entering the neat little cabin where Molly said she thought Hunter had gone, she scowled when she did not immediately see him. If she had to search the ranch for him, she would end up wasting a great deal of her precious four hours. Then she heard the door shut firmly behind her. She turned in time to see Hunter slip the bolt, locking her in. For a moment, she considered telling him that was totally unnecessary, then decided she would allow him his fun.

All her grand ideas about seduction fled her mind. She met his dark gaze, read the hunger there, and felt her knees weaken. He took a step toward her. She took a step toward him. Then she was in his arms without fully knowing how she got there. When he lifted her up as he greedily kissed her she wrapped her legs around his lean hips. The last thing she was aware of, besides a blinding need demanding immediate gratification, was him roughly tugging the pins from her hair and letting them scatter to the floor as he walked somewhat unsteadily to the bed.

* * *

Leanne lifted her head from the pillow slightly to look down at their entwined bodies. "You didn't take your boots off."

Softly laughing as he eased out of her arms, Hunter drawled, "Didn't take much else off either."

"That's true." Her eyes narrowing as she tugged her skirts down, she suddenly realized something that should have been very obvious from the beginning. "You were waiting for me."

"Yup." He sat down on the edge of the bed and tugged his boots off.

"And here I thought I was being so clever by getting Molly and Laurie to watch Michael David so I could hunt you down. Molly even said she only thought you would be here. She knew very well all along that you would be."

"You were hunting me, were you?" He started to smile.

"Yes. I had some thoughts concerning a few leisurely hours of unrefined activity. Can you have leisurely activity?"

He didn't bother to answer that. "Sounds interesting. When do we start?"

"I think perhaps we already started."

Standing up, he finished removing his shirt and tossed it towards a chair in the corner. "How much time do we have?"

"Well, I started out with four hours." She crossed her arms behind her head and watched him undress. "I think we may still have a great deal of that left."

"Then we better not waste any time."

"I didn't think we had." Smiling faintly as he shed the

last of his clothes, she wondered if he had any idea of how good he looked.

"That was just an appetizer." He sat on the bed and began to remove her shoes. "I plan to indulge in a banquet."

"A banquet, huh?" When one foot was bared she began to slowly move it over his chest. "Sounds a little too refined."

"You'd prefer pigs at a trough?"

"Well, I am feeling a little hoggish."

"Are you now." Tossing aside her stocking, he nibbled at the toes of her small feet, smiling when she giggled.

She purred with delight when he slowly ran his hands up her legs, then squeaked with surprise when he abruptly yanked off her pantaloons and flung them across the room. "How very untidy of you. You'll ruin them."

"They're already ruined. I ripped them, remember?" He did the same with her petticoats.

Watching as her petticoats settled on the bureau, she murmured, "So you did. Impatient man."

"If I recall correctly, I wasn't the only impatient one." He finished undoing her bodice, removed it, and tossed it on top of the petticoats.

"Perhaps I was feeling a little inclined towards haste." She smiled faintly as her lacy chemise floated down onto the back of the chair.

Slowly, savoring the gradual full exposure of her lithe body, he eased her skirt off then hurled it over his shoulder. Desperation had made her bold. He intended to enjoy that to its fullest. He eased his body down onto hers, murmuring his pleasure when their flesh met.

"I hope you're feeling inclined to indulge in a little less haste now."

"I could be persuaded," she murmured as she rubbed her feet along his calves. Looking at the clothes scattered around the room, she laughed softly. "That looks very decadent."

His gaze fixed upon the hard tip of her breast, he whispered, "And this looks very tempting." He flicked his tongue over it. "These are all mine for four hours."

She laughed, then held him close as he almost idly lathed and suckled her sensitive breasts. Although she had just fed their greedy child, Hunter's attentions brought forth a trickle of milk. Embarrassed, she tried to pull back, but he did not allow her to retreat.

"Tastes good," he mumbled as he slowly kissed his way to her throat. "Now I'm even more jealous of the little devil."

Smiling slightly, she kept her eyes open, watching him as he teased her mouth with quick, soft kisses. "He's going to be dark like you," she said. "Dark and dangerous."

He gave a startled laugh and looked at her. She was beautiful. He suspected he would think so when she was eighty. Elusive too, he thought with an inner sigh. At times he caught a certain look in her eyes that raised his hopes, but then it was gone. Sometimes, when they lay in each other's arms still trembling from the ecstasy they had shared, he felt like a thief, as if he had broken into her heart as he had that bank in Clayville and taken something she had not really wanted to give him. He told himself that love was making him a fanciful idiot.

"Dangerous, am I?"

"Mmmm, especially when you take your clothes off. I have developed a perfectly scandalous liking for watching you take your clothes off."

She saw his eyes grow nearly black. He clearly liked to hear her say such things. She recalled the way she always felt when he spoke to her in such a bold manner. The things he said made her blush. They also made her ache. She wondered idly if she could do the same to him. Slipping her hands down his back, she felt his taut backside.

"I especially like this. I think you have the finest-looking backside I have ever seen on a man."

She was going to drive him right out of his mind, he decided. "Just how many have you seen?"

"Quite a lot actually. They do seem to be everywhere one looks. Not naked, of course."

"I should damn well hope not." Even as her soft, husky flattery was stirring his desire, he frowned at the thought of her eyeing the backsides of other men, disliking it as intensely as he liked to hear her claim his as the best.

Although that touch of jealousy was worth pursuing, Leanne decided she would have to ignore it this time. She had made the decision to drive him into a frenzy and she would not allow herself to be diverted. When she got him into that state, she was going to say those three little words she so ached to say. It was cowardly, because there was a good chance he would not hear her. However, it would serve as good practice. Perhaps if she said it aloud enough times she would gain the courage to look him straight in the eye, say it and suffer the consequences.

"Do you know what I think about sometimes when I'm just watching you move around, even doing the most ordinary things?"

"No. What do you think about?" His voice was husky with desire.

"I think about all the things I should like to do to you if I was bold enough. Shall I tell you?"

"I can be a little slow to understand sometimes. Maybe you'd better show me too."

Laughing softly she nudged him, and he rolled onto his back. She straddled his hips and looked at him.

"Having you in this supplicant position did figure large in my idle musings."

"Consider me your slave." He was not sure he wanted her to know just how close to the truth that was.

"Oh my, that does offer up some very interesting possibilities. Now, first of course, I would kiss you."

She slowly lowered her mouth to his, kissing him deeply. Then she began making idle patterns with her tongue and brushing gentle kisses over his taut warm skin.

Gritting his teeth, he fought to lie still as her soft warm mouth moved over his lower abdomen, then groaned when she abruptly turned her attention to his thighs. "You thought about torturing me, did you?"

Nipping the inside of his thighs, then soothing that light sting with prolonged strokes of her tongue, she chuckled. "This is torture, is it?"

"Sweet torture."

"And what is this then?" she murmured.

He groaned with pleasure as she turned her full attention to his aching groin. "Heaven. Pure heaven." He burrowed his fingers in her thick, silken hair. "Not sure how long I can savor it."

"Shall we make this a test of your endurance, then?"

"What an intriguing idea."

She did her best to make it last, to hold off that final crescendo for as long as she could. It was not easy, for she found that being the leader in this intimate dance was one of the most exciting things she had ever indulged in. The moment the finale could be delayed no longer, she slowly, tantalizingly, united their bodies. It was the last purposefully languid movement she made. When they were mutually flung over passion's precipice, she clung to Hunter and spoke her heart.

Hunter stared up at the ceiling as he held a somnolent Leanne. He could hear those husky words in his head, but was suffering a crippling attack of doubt. There was always the chance that he had imagined it. When a person wanted something as bad as he wanted to hear those words from Leanne, imagining them was a real possibility.

"I heard you." He wondered if she would know what he referred to, if he was right in thinking that she had not really intended him to hear her avowal.

Drowsy from their lovemaking, Leanne was not sure at first what he said. "Hmmm?"

"I heard you." He felt her tense.

Suddenly Leanne felt wide awake. She was not sure if she should consider this a catastrophe or not. She briefly considered denying she had said anything. But that was not only cowardly, it was perhaps just a little childish as well. What was done was done. Perhaps it was even for the best. Hiding what she felt took some of the joy out of it. She just hoped being honest would not end up hurting her too much.

"You weren't supposed to, you know," she murmured, not brave enough to look at him as they talked. "I tried to plan it so you wouldn't."

Hunter felt his heart skip. That remark was nearly as good as an admission. It was an effort not to demand she say it again, make his own declaration, then end it by making fierce love to her. Instinct told him he could lose a lot if he moved too quickly, that if he probed just a little, his elusive Leanne might reveal a great deal. It was, he decided, far past time for them to have a talk that would ease any doubts they held, clear up any continuing misconceptions and, on the whole, strengthen their relationship and their marriage. He would be a fool, he told himself, not to try for that.

"I wasn't supposed to hear?" He slowly combed the fingers of one hand through her thick golden hair.

"Nope. I thought I'd planned it perfectly. You were supposed to be in a—er, frenzy."

"Oh I was that. Yup, I reckon you could call it a frenzy."

"Then how did you hear me?"

"I'm supposed to be deaf when I'm in a frenzy, is that it?"

"Well, I certainly seem to be. Deaf and blind. A marching band could probably go through the room and I wouldn't notice." She smiled crookedly when she felt his chest move with silent laughter.

She began to feel a little less uneasy. There was no sound of discomfort in his voice, as if her words were not really welcome. Indeed, he sounded positively jovial. While she might not get the full return of her feelings she so craved, she began to feel certain she would not face the rejection of them. Tentatively she looked at him and received a gentle kiss on the mouth.

He brushed his knuckles over her cheek. "You look almost scared."

"You really weren't supposed to hear me."

"Why say it then?"

"This may sound silly." She grimaced. "No, this will sound very silly. I was sort of practicing. I thought that if I said it a few times when you didn't hear me, I could eventually look you straight in the eye and say it knowing you could hear every word."

Cupping her face in his hands, he urged, "So, look me straight in the eyes and say it."

She stared at his mouth. "I haven't practiced enough yet." She heard his soft laughter and winced. "Please, Hunter. Please don't laugh at me. I can't bear it."

"Leanne, my purple-eyed beauty, I'm not laughing at you. I would never laugh at you. It's our godawful cowardice I'm laughing at."

"Our cowardice? You're no coward, Hunter." She frowned at him, not sure she understood what he was talking about.

"Oh, yes I am. I couldn't even bring myself to whisper when I thought you might not hear me." He almost laughed again at how huge her eyes grew. "You can give me a lot of courage, pet."

"I can?" She wondered a little wildly if the swift pace of her heart was particularly healthy.

After briefly kissing her, he urged in a soft hoarse voice, "Look me straight in the eyes and say it."

Swallowing hard, she took a deep breath and said, in what seemed to her a rather weak, unsteady little voice, "I love you."

Hunter pulled her tightly into his arms. He could not believe the wealth of emotion those three little words produced. Although he had not found out all that much about the various twists and turns of her feelings, he knew that would come easier now—for both of them.

"When did you figure that out?"

That he had not immediately responded in kind stung, but the sting was greatly eased by his obvious delight. She decided she must have misunderstood what he had meant about cowardice. He could not be without some deep feeling for her if knowing she loved him could please him so. For the first time she could see what she so desired within her grasp.

"Oh, by—well, the first time we made love."

"Yes, I should have seen it. A girl like you would have to be sure."

"I hope you mean that in a flattering way."

"Only in the most flattering way. It should have told me how you felt. In all, I have been somewhat insensitive."

"No. No, you haven't."

"Young lady, if I'm going to humble myself, you could have the courtesy not to disagree with me."

"I beg your pardon. Do continue." She had to bite back a smile, noticing he did as well.

"Well, if I hadn't been so complaisant, you might not have fallen victim to my mother's tricks. I never really said more to you than how I wanted you to stay with me so I'd marry you. That wasn't too damn much to hold onto when given evidence to the contrary."

"It was pretty strong evidence, Hunter. I'm not sure there's much that would've fought that except, perhaps, you there in person proclaiming it to be a lie. Even then I might well have given you a bad time or two. That letter was in your handwriting and it spoke of your love for Patricia and how you'd marry her when—"

"I know what it said. I don't know why the fool woman kept such nonsense."

"Women like to save love letters."

"That particular love letter was old news by the time she married Spotford. After looking closely at how I felt about that, I realized that what I felt was infatuation with a pretty face. I soon viewed it all as a very lucky escape. I was only twenty-two."

"A mere babe."

She had to restrain the urge to hug him for his obvious lack of feeling for Patricia Spotford. His opinion of how he had felt upon her marriage to someone else might not be the whole truth, but she did not care. Her fear had been that the love he had written of in that letter might still lurk in his heart. In his voice was the proof that it did not.

"Perhaps a bit naive."

"Hunter, I don't think you can blame yourself for my believing your mother. It seemed worse than it was, perhaps, because of the trouble with Watkins. He made a life-and-death situation out of a simple misunderstanding. I was—well, weak then. I still thought my father had cast me aside the way Charity did. I think I was prepared to believe you'd reject me too, no matter what you'd said to me before leaving. I was scared and that letter seemed the justification of my fears."

He held her close for a while, saying nothing. Her fears were easy to understand. He had suffered similar ones and with far less justification than she had. Despite being reunited with her father and learning the reasons for his actions, he suspected that fear of rejection still lingered, would remain a part of her for a long while. He swore to himself that he would do his best never to feed those fears.

"There are a lot of other things I should have seen,

should have taken a minute to really look at." He grimaced. "For a while, though, I made a real effort not to see."

"Why would you do that?"

"I was neck-deep in trouble, wasn't I? I looked at you and saw even more."

"Trouble, was I?"

"More trouble than you know."

She began to get the feeling that he was working his way around to saying some things she was very eager to hear. Propping herself up on one elbow and cupping her chin in her hand, she studied his face, wondering if there was any way to make him get to the crux of the matter just a little faster.

"All things considered, I thought I behaved very well. Can't see where I was much trouble."

"No? I was supposed to be after Watkins. That required my full attention and every ounce of guile and wit I could muster. The minute you burst into that bank, I started getting diverted. I spent far too much time thinking about making love to you, then doing so. Then I worried—worried about keeping you safe from the law and bounty hunters, safe from all the unseen dangers of the places we traveled through, safe from Watkins or safe from Luke."

Shaking his head, he marveled at his own obtuseness. "The way you tied me up in knots should've told me I loved you."

Blinking rapidly, she stared at him. Never had she imagined he would say something so important in such an offhand way. Even after saying the words she had been praying so long to hear he lay there frowning, mulling over the past. She gave some serious thought to hitting him.

"You love me?"

Hunter looked at her in surprise. "Of course. I said that. That's what all this is about."

"No, you didn't say it. You said I had to give you courage by saying it, so I did. Then you went on to ask when did I know and go into a general conversation about feelings." She frowned. "Mostly mine." When he started to laugh, she swore.

Pulling her into his arms he held her tightly as he laughed. "I'm an idiot."

"The possibility was considered."

"Ah, Leanne, my sharp-tongued pixie, I love you."

She clung to him as she let the words soak through her mind and heart. Hearing him say that was not the cure-all for her every doubt and fear, but she knew a lot of them would vanish because they had come from the fear that he could not love her. It made what they had seem so much more secure, gave it some underpinnings.

"That's what I was rambling on about, how I should have seen it. The few times I sort of considered what I was feeling, it was to think about how much trouble that would bring and decide I would put a stop to it."

"And when did you realize you hadn't—er, put a stop to it?"

"The first night after I left to go to Watkins's trial. I got to thinking about you, then realized how often I did that. One thing led to another and it was suddenly all very clear to me. That's when I started suffering that lack of courage I mentioned. Suddenly I had a whole new set of worries."

"No need to list them." She grimaced. "I am painfully aware of what those are."

"Then, when I thought I might not reach you in time to

keep Watkins from getting you . . ." he faltered and briefly tightened his hold on her. "I'm not good at this, darlin'. The words don't come easy for me."

"If there even are words for such feelings," she murmured. "You've said the ones I need, Hunter."

"I was hoping for a little eloquence," he said and smiled wryly when she gave him a look full of amused understanding, then grew serious as he studied her. "You're the other half of me, Leanne. I knew when I was riding hell-bent for leather to keep you from Watkins that I was riding to save the only future that held any meaning for me."

"I know that feeling very well," she whispered. "When I thought you had chosen Patricia, I knew I'd lost the chance to be really happy. The only thing that kept me from true despair was the child I carried—our child. He gave me a reason to be strong. While it would never be all I needed, I knew I could find at least some contentment in being the mother of your child. I do so need you, Hunter." She ran a finger slowly over his lips. "I do so love you."

He kissed her deeply, then held her close. Emotion held them silent for a moment. It was going to be all right now, he thought. While he was not fool enough to think the future would be all smiles and happiness, he knew they would overcome the inevitable bad times. No matter what they lost or gained, they would have each other.

His emotions settling a little, he looked at her and smiled, thinking of what had spurred on this mutual out-pouring of feeling. "I suppose you won't need to practice saying it anymore." He put what he felt was the appropriate tone of regret in his voice. "Of course," he mused aloud when she looked at him, a slow smile curving her mouth, "I might still find myself tongue-tied on occasion."

"Blackmail."

"Quite possibly. You never know what heights of eloquence one can achieve while in a frenzy."

"Frenzies can be very inspiring," she agreed.

Rolling over so that she was beneath him, he gave her a grin that held both love and anticipation. "I believe this is a matter that should be thoroughly looked into."

"I concur, husband. We must have an hour or so left."

"No," he murmured, growing serious again for a moment, "a lifetime."

"Yes," she agreed softly as she tugged on his hair, pulling his mouth down to hers, "a long and beautiful lifetime."

New York Times *bestseller Hannah Howell's extra-ordinary Wherlocke family returns with the story of a passion that will heed no resistance, no matter how deadly* . . .

When Lorelei Sundun first finds Sir Argus Wherlocke in her garden, she's never heard of the mysterious Wherlocke clan—or their otherworldly abilities. That changes the moment she watches Argus—the most tantalizing man she's ever seen—disappear before her very eyes. What she's witnessed should be impossible. But so should falling in love with a man she's only just met . . .

Pursued by a madman intent on harnessing the Wherlockes' talents as weapons, Argus meant to seek help from his family, not to involve a duke's lovely daughter in the struggle. But now, the enchanting Lorelei is his only hope for salvation—and the greatest temptation he's ever faced . . .

Please read on for an exciting sneak peek of Hannah Howell's
IF HE'S DANGEROUS,
now available!

England—summer, 1790

THERE WAS A NAKED MAN IN HER FATHER'S ROSE GARDEN.
Lorelei Sundun blinked her eyes several times but the
man was still there. She wondered why he was staring at
her in astonishment. She was not the one standing naked
in a garden, a fat white rose the only thing protecting her
modesty. Lorelei was certain she should be the one doing
the gaping. In fact, she mused as she allowed her gaze to
travel the long length of his lean body, she should be on
her feet and racing toward the manor, perhaps even
screaming for help. Loudly. Instead, she was utterly fascinated.

For a moment she wondered if she had been sitting in
the sun contemplating her lack of a husband for too long.
She was not wearing a hat. Could one get a brain fever
from sitting hatless in the sun? Lorelei was not sure that

even a brain fever would cause her to see a naked man. Certainly not one with a big, fat white rose hiding his manly parts, the part of a man she was most curious about. Lorelei was certain that the drawings in a book she had found hidden in her father's massive library could not be accurate concerning those parts of a man. A man could never hide something that large in his breeches. She doubted a man could even walk properly with such an appendage and suspected the looks on the faces of the women in those drawings were not ones of ecstasy but excruciating pain.

He was, she decided, a very handsome man. It might be why she found it impossible to look away as any woman of sense would do. His hair was thick, hanging far past his broad shoulders and a black so deep and true the sunlight caused it to glint with faintly blue highlights. His features were harsh, almost predatory, but there was no fear in her heart. His eyes were dark and she was tempted to move closer to see what color they really were. He was tall and lean but she could see the firm muscles beneath his smooth, swarthy skin. There appeared to be the remnants of bruises marring his fine body. Lorelei clasped her hands together in her lap to quell the sudden, and startling, urge to touch that sun-kissed skin, to soothe those hurts. He had good teeth, straight and white, she mused even as he shut his mouth and revealed lips that had a seductive hint of fullness to them. Those lips and his enviably long lashes were the only soft features on his hard face.

"Who are you?" he asked, his deep voice holding such a strong note of command she could feel it tug at her mind, and had to quell the instinctive urge to immediately refuse to answer him.

"Lady Lorelei Sundun, seventh child of the duke of Sundunmoor," she replied, thinking that she ought to be the one making demands. "And you are?"

"Sir Argus Wherlocke." He scowled at her. "This is not where I wished to be."

"I suppose it is somewhat awkward to find oneself standing unclothed in a duke's garden."

"And you should not be able to see me."

"Why not?"

"You have no Wherlocke or Vaughn blood, do you?"

That was no answer to her question, she thought, but swallowed a flare of annoyance. "Neither name appears in the family lineage."

Lorelei decided she could not leave the man unclothed any longer. His state of undress was stirring an unwelcome curiosity within her. She stood up, walked over to him, and handed him her fine shawl made of Italian lace. His eyes widened as he took it in his hand and she could see that those eyes were the dark blue of the night sky. When she realized how close she stood to him, how her palm itched to touch his skin, she took a step back. She briefly averted her eyes as he tied her shawl around his waist for he had to step back from the shelter of the rose. Before looking away, however, she had noticed that the look of utter astonishment on his face had begun to lessen.

"This is most strange," he muttered and frowned at her. "You should not be seeing me. You most assuredly should not be able to hand me this shawl nor should I be able to hold it."

"And you should not be standing unclothed in my father's rose garden," she said. "Yet here you are. Where did you wish to find yourself?"

"I sought out one of my family." He cursed softly. "I am being pulled back."

"Pulled back where?" Lorelei knew her eyes were widening as the man appeared to be slowly losing all substance, the roses behind him beginning to show through his body. "You appear to be fading away, sir. Are you a ghost then?"

"No, not a ghost. Heed me now for I have little time left. You must find someone in my family, a Wherlocke or a Vaughn. Tell them that I am in need of help. A man who calls himself Charles Cornick is holding me captive. He seeks knowledge of our gifts."

"Your gifts?" The man was so faded now that she could see right through him and had to clench her hands tightly against the urge to grab hold of him and try to hold him in place.